THE FALCON

Cover Image – General George B. McClellan on the Battlefield of Antietam, by Christian Schussele, 1863.

THE FALCON

BOOK TWO: WILLIAM HANLIN'S CIVIL WAR

A NOVEL IN SEVEN PARTS

RR HICKS

For more information on the author, the Hanlin Series, essays, and future writing projects please go to:

RRHICKS.com

To Contact the author:

rolandrhicks@gmail.com

Also:

Look for RR HICKS on Facebook

This is work of fiction, some characters are real, some are not, none are alive today. Historical characters often speak in their own words, when they do not every effort has been taken – while juggling the needs of creativity and fictional flow – to keep them within the realm of the speakers' beliefs and attitudes.

Unless otherwise noted, all images are courtesy of the Library of Congress

FORLORN HOPE PUBLISHING

TO CDH
Strive, Seek, Find, Never Yield

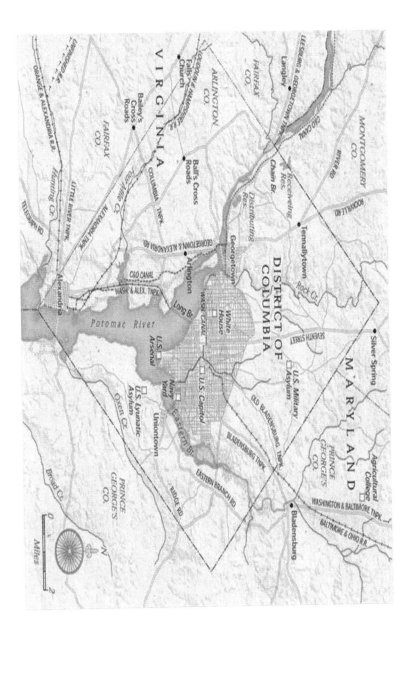

Therefore the flight shall perish from the swift,
and the strong shall not strengthen his force,
neither shall the mighty deliver himself.
Amos 2:14

BOOK III: The Young Napoleon

Why may not that be the skull of a lawyer?
Where be his quiddities now, his quillets, his cases,
his tenures, and his tricks?

~ *Hamlet*, Act V, Scene 1

1. Denton

Miles from the city I had early olfactory warning of the approach of our nation's capital that was in no way figurative. It was palpable, a there – gone – there again whiff of something awful that slid under wisps of engine smoke that filtered through our car. A dull, growing, insidious presence, like

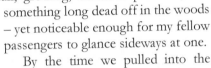

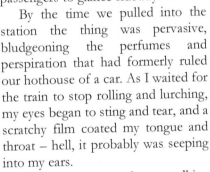

something long dead off in the woods – yet noticeable enough for my fellow passengers to glance sideways at one.

By the time we pulled into the station the thing was pervasive, bludgeoning the perfumes and perspiration that had formerly ruled our hothouse of a car. As I waited for the train to stop rolling and lurching, my eyes began to sting and tear, and a scratchy film coated my tongue and throat – hell, it probably was seeping into my ears.

Instinctively we knew talking would be a precious waste of oxygen – what little remained in the stagnant air – and we moved soundlessly into the, relative, cool of the station. The smell hovered there, not quite holding its own with wax, cleaners, tobacco, and ancient smells of a public place always crowded, always open.

Smells, like pain and orgasm, are easily (always?) forgotten once they pass. That fact, and that fact alone, accounted for us making the mistake of stepping through thick oak doors and out onto the streets of the District of Columbia. We walked headfirst into a wall woven from the reek of rotting garbage, shit, piss, sweating horses, leprous bodies, week's old offal, sulfur, and the evil, vaguely alive, mud-slime

1

of the streets.

It punched me in the balls, grabbed and pulled down.

I gasped, grabbed a brass railing to steady my reeling self, yelped when it seared my palm. I looked out toward the mall and I will swear to my dying day the Smithsonian hovered unattached over burnt lawns.

Five, ten, fifteen steps into my Washington experience I fought as a man underwater for breath, finally achieved some measure of equilibrium whereby short, pant-like gasps got enough into my wrecked–for–life lungs to sustain me for another few seconds. That struggle required an intensity of purpose that allowed me to overlook the heat and humidity and the fact I was sweating like a racehorse. The sun – the only object in the washed out sky – burned through my jacket, seared my back, sugar loaf hat, and scalded my unprotected neck.

"This place reeks," Osgood gasped beside me.

"To think Congress is out of town," I wheezed.

"Funny," his mirthless reply.

"Probably my dying words."

"Can only hope," he spat, "you do know where you're going?"

"Be hard to miss the War Department, it's right behind the President's House."

"Far?"

"Yes."

"Good God."

"I'm thinking this isn't exactly your kind of town," I said taking note of the third and fourth dead horses bloating in the street, each doing their part to bottleneck the already jammed road, "you can wait with Seth and the rest, the Mall's two blocks down the street."

"Can...not...do...it," he staccatoed in oxygen deprivation, "not here, not now."

"Suit yourself."

"If I suited myself I would be back at Olga's."

"The nation appreciates your sacrifice."

"Damn well better," he muttered.

We pushed through streets teeming with blue clad, inebriated, unrestrained by discipline or convention, soldiers spilling out of taverns on the way to the next barroom, brothel, both. Not a civilian to be glimpsed – for that matter I did not see a female of any species. Anywhere.

I was alert, made so by the stench, heat, and soldiers bashing off each other like besotted billiard balls, happy to have a sidearm and surprised to my core. My last trip to Washington was on my belated way to Mexico. It was a town then – a town with large Greco-Roman classical buildings scattered about, but a town nevertheless. A quiet town at that. What Osgood and I staggered through that August day was a crowded, stinking, steaming, screaming about to explode its seams town infested with blue clad slugs.

It took me a few blocks to realize the street signs had been switched. Perhaps by drunken soldiers, as a ridiculously misguided security measure (would an invading force really be stopped cold by the illogic of 9th Street following 6th?) or, my bet, a new form of Congressional logic.

My sole defense for contributing two wrong turns in five blocks.

"This bodes well for the field," Osgood snapped when I reversed course for the third time.

"I made the mistake of reading the street signs instead of—"

"Studying the sun, charting the stars?"

"Using common sense."

"Why start now?"

"Serve you right if I abandon you out here."

"I will take a stool in one of these bars and wait for Charlie to show up – at least he has the capacity to find his way home."

I nodded to the multiple truths of that, "Come on, it's a straight shot up the street," I announced.

"Sure it is," he moaned, moved to match my slightly more enthusiastic pace.

We were there in twenty-five brutish minutes, mounted the stairs, walked by two comatose sentries and stepped into an interior that made the surrounding streets seem serene and orderly. Bedlam would be an understatement of epic proportion: profusely sweating men darted – sometimes in packs – in pattern-less, random directions leaving a moderate rainstorm's worth of perspiration on the floor behind. Their routes made all the more difficult as every square inch not occupied by desks, chairs, filing cabinets, coat racks and tables were jammed with officers of every shape, size, and description who stood, leaned, slouched, crouched, knelt, and… waited.

There were no signs; none of the bustling staff would as much as glance at those waiting, they rushed by pretending to study the sheets in their hands; not a single desk-bound clerk would look up from the equally fascinating papers piled before them; nary a fellow favor seeker would look another in the eye and risk being asked to impart information – had they any to impart (though it is embarrassing, at least, to admit one has been standing in a packed oven all day and has learnt nothing) – for fear their own ambitions be usurped.

Osgood took it all in for a few teeth grinding minutes before he passed judgment, "This is insane," said with such ferocity he got an aggrieved smile from an ursine major jammed between two filing cabinets that dwarfed him by at least a foot.

"Welcome to the Army," I said by way of simple explanation.

"Jesus Christ."

"Exactly."

"Now what – we grow old, die here?"

"The heat and dehydration will kill us long before we get a chance to get old," I, reasonably, pointed out.

"Comforting – is there anything we can do?"

"We don't have to do anything, they'll find us."

"No, really."

"I mean it," I motioned to the room, "understand that none these gentlemen are expected – none. They're here to beg for a favor, appointment, command or, worse, have a grievance or complaint. They are part of the never ending circle of horseshit and –"

"But –"

"And," I interrupted him with a confident smile, "they're to be shunned at all costs. Even the lowliest staffer, hell, even the janitors are expected to ignore them. We might be the only ones in here who are supposed to be here – they'll find us."

He scanned the room slowly, "You really fucked Huntingdon," he said with reverence.

"*We*," I stressed the pronoun, "did indeed."

"You knew all along it would be like this?"

"Fairly sure," I agreed absently. I was fully engrossed in a captain sweating a puddle in the corner. As wide as he was tall – he was a good four inches taller than me – snow white hair, beard, heavily waxed mustache, he slouched, took a monocle from one eye, cleaned it strenuously with a bright red plaid silk handkerchief, put it in the other eye, twisted each frozen end of his mustache in turn, repeated the monocle cleansing and returned it to the opposite eye. He did this without expression, eyes fixed solidly ahead on a wall clock that was not working.

"You are evil," Osgood reminded me, breaking my concentration.

"Am I?"

"You knowingly sent that man to this fate."

"He was an odious pr—"

"Agreed, but to do . . . this," Osgood gestured the room.

"I thought you thought I was too lenient?"

"You were, once –"

"Didn't you tell me to be harsh... unfeeling... cold?"

"I did, and more – but I never ..." He trailed off in wonder.

"Do I sense respect in there someplace?"

"Perhaps."

"I'm touched." I stopped, a small, fussy looking lieutenant was actively scanning the crowd, the first official recognition of the existence of the waiting masses. I nudged Osgood – probably harder than I had to – nodded in his direction.

Right on cue the lieutenant yelled, "Twenty-first Connecticut" in a high pitched, nasal-impaired voice that pierced through the room and my spinal cord on its way to annoying every dog in a ten block radius.

"Here!" A relieved Osgood yelled and stepped right through a milquetoast captain wearing the gray tunic with emerald trim then sported by Vermont. The unfortunate Vermonter had valiantly tried to take the opportunity of almost eye contact with the searching lieutenant to sneak in with a question that was doomed to be ignored.

The captain bounced off Osgood and became just another anonymous spectator. He knew it, sagged in that acceptance, mouth hanging low. We followed our Virgil as he deftly dodged through a maze of desks, scores of moribund bodies, into a narrow, unlit, filing cabinet lined hallway, up a shoulder wide, sauna-like staircase to, finally, a small, impossibly hot corner office windowed on two sides – to no effect. The curtains hung impossibly still, no doubt attempting suicide. The desk in the room's center – if anything so small could have a center – was piled high with files, papers, ledgers.

Behind which, papers mid-chest on his 5'7" frame, stood my friend, Albert Denton, Captain, regular Army. A red faced, unshaven, fatigue all over his handsome, unadorned face captain currently studying, with obvious disgust, a drooping sheet of paper.

"Captain," I said lowly and waited for acknowledgement that came slowly. With silent but noticeable effort he stopped reading, stroked his chin stubble, peered up with something approaching malice ready to cut loose with regular Army invective at yet another volunteer officer's sheer insolence in just showing up.

His eyes reached mine, he blinked twice, sighed, could not stop a crooked grin from creeping out, "Colonel? You're a stinking Colonel?"

"Just lieutenant colonel... Captain, there is a slight difference . . . slight."

"Colonel," he repeated, "Christ, this is troubling."

"Don't worry, Captain," I said expensively, "you don't have to call me sir," I reached across the paper files and took a limp wet hand, "in private."

"What?" He snarled.

"What, Colonel?" I corrected, "Seeing as we're in a public place and there are impressionable young officers about."

"Why you son of a —"

"You know I don't care, Captain, but, well, it's the uniform not the man, you know. Captain"

He regarded me for a long, hot moment, "Let me say something now that I've been dying to say since I was a plebe... fuck you, Colonel"

"I noticed you glanced out the door before committing such a grotesque act of insubordination."

"I was looking to your Captain there," he nodded to Osgood, who beamed back, "being one of yours I'm sure he fully supports the sentiment."

"I do that," Osgood gushed, and introduced himself.

"I knew him back when, you know," Al explained, "talk about lacking the moral authority to command."

"Jealousy does not agree with you, Captain," I observed with sadness, "not at all... Captain."

"How many times are you going to work my rank into your sentences?" His head shook in dismay.

"As many as I can, Captain," I answered in perfect honesty.

"Unbelievable."

"Captain?"

"That you're still an insufferable prick."

"I strive for consistency, Captain."

"You have achieved it in that regard... General WeeWee," he grinned wickedly. I shook my head in panic, put up a hand as if to ward off a saber...

... too late, "General WeeWee?" Osgood snorted, "General WeeWee?"

A look of triumph, absolute and final, flashed across Al's face, "Oh, I'm sorry... Colonel... was your friend unaware of your West Point moniker?"

"He was," Osgood chortled.

"He never liked it," Denton went on, "sent him into a rage his first two years. We picked it up from —"

"His brother, Christian," Osgood answered for him.

"Yup, little guy was running all over campus telling every animate object about his General WeeWee. It stuck. Hard."

"Could see where it would," Osgood agreed.

"Got changed to Willie our third year, was no fun so easily pissing him off anymore."

"Stopped being fun after I beat the snot out of George Pickett," I corrected.

"Might have had some influence, sure," Al laughed, "where's the little guy now, anyway?"

"The little guy's the size of a factory and a Captain in the Twenty-first."

"Really, serving under General WeeWee is he?"

"All right, Al, all right," I laughed, "good to see you too."

"Been too long, Willie."

I nodded, "You have our orders?"

"Right here," he motioned the pile, noticed my dubious look, "don't judge it by its looks, this is a well-oiled machine."

"I'm sure," I agreed, waited while he stared at me. Hard.

"Hell, you haven't heard, have you?"

"Heard what?"

"Mac was just given commanded of the Eastern armies, relieved

McDowell yesterday."

"Mac?" I uttered in confusion.

"Mac," he reiterated with an edge, "don't you read the papers or do you have people that do that for you now?"

"McClellan?" I regrouped.

"George B, yes," a smug Denton answered, "our next-door neighbor at the Point, you may have run across him once or twice... an hour," he rolled his eyes.

"My God, that's... that's . . ."

"Incredible?"

"Miraculous," I mumbled – as it truly was. George B McClellan... Mac... One of us... Class of '46. Young, dashing, dynamic... No relic from the War of 1812 or the Seminole Wars ... army friend of Andrew Jackson... a friend.

I could tell by the look on Al's face he had already calculated all that and had taken it to the next, logical permutation – in the grand tradition of the regular Army.

"Amazing," I said, "I'd say you won't be stuck at a desk much longer... Nor at Captain"

"I believe so, too," he smirked, "see, I know it doesn't mean as much to you, Willie, but I stayed in while you went gallivanting off to God knows where after Mexico," he shook his head, "no lawyer like you, or railroad president like Mac. I came out of Mexico a brevet Captain, for Christ's sakes, reverted to lieutenant the minute I was back on U.S. soil. Took ten years to get the goddamn bar back. The rate I was going I was looking at Colonel in 30 years. But now..."

No need to finish, the opportunities inherent in a war were incrementally enhanced when one's classmate became commanding officer of the largest Army ever formed by the United States. It spoke for itself.

"He here yet?" I asked, involuntarily glancing around the office.

"In front of the Senate, taking a bow."

"And when he is free to see old friends?"

"I will request a combat command immediately."

"As the fastest way to permanent grade?"

"You know anything faster?" He asked with real interest.

"Staff job – quick and a lot safer, too."

He started shaking his head halfway through, "Can't take the chance if this only lasts a few months, combat's the only way I can see making Colonel before it's all over."

"How about general, why think small?"

"God willing it goes on long enough."

"I'll say prayer for an extended conflict and a boon to your self-interest."

"That would be most kind," he answered with a straight face, "mind you, I'm not asking for dozens of battles and the deaths of thousands, just a decent period of conflict to get me to a colonel's half pay – then I'll be happy to see it settled with a handshake and we all go home."

"You're a hell of a good sport."

"Thank you, Willie, it's important have limits on the number of bodies one is willing to climb over in quest of a pair of eagles I think."

"Your humanitarianism is both startling and refreshing."

"Isn't it?" He agreed, pulled a sheaf of papers out of a pile, spilling papers everywhere, "your orders, Sir."

"Thank you."

"Picked out your campsite myself – good spot, nice breezes."

"Important."

"Especially when it gets hot."

"Gets?"

"What, you think this is hot?"

I sighed, wiped a sheen of sweat off my brow, "By the way, any word on my wayward company commander?"

"He was here for three days," he grinned, "and they were hot. Three days of annoying everyone with constant complaints and wild claims of invitations to meet Scott and McDowell, among others.

"He was escorted from the building by two large sergeants who may or may not have introduced him to the muck of our streets – that matter is in contention, or would be, had he not fled the city. Or so I heard, I would never have had him followed or anything like that."

"Course not," I agreed, "so, they didn't shoot him?"

"Alas no, that would have been a mercy."

"Well, thanks for your help with this, Al."

"My pleasure, tell me the full story over a few beers after you get your men settled."

Al was frantically summoned down the rickety hallway, we left to trudge to the Mall and the 21st. Down the hill, past the White House, we were there in ten minutes. Osgood glared, I shrugged.

2. McClellan

The summons came two weeks to the day later. It was delivered by an immaculately attired regular army captain who was all stiff-backed propriety until he made obvious note of the 'V's between my maple leafs. He instantly dropped the twin veneer of formality and rigidity, practically flipped a calling card in my general direction, tossed a salute that would have had to improve a hundred fold to be half-assed, pivoted raggedly and stomped away.

Despite the passage of time the handwriting across the back of the card was reassuringly familiar, the strong cursive ordered '6 pm, Tomorrow' and gave an unexpectedly tony address a few blocks from the War Department. Even with abundant foreknowledge the ornately printed reverse was still a jolt, visceral proof of an old acquaintance's sudden ascension:

'George B. McClellan, Major General, USA.'

A major general at thirty-four, highest previous rank captain. A thing of great, almost baffling, wonderment to anyone raised in the moribund, strictly stratified system of the old army. A miracle really, as the example of one Bull Sumner aptly proved: a lieutenant in 1819 he received his colonelcy in 1859.

I kept the card as a talisman of sorts for just over a year.

I received the call outside my well positioned tent atop a gentle rise overlooking the Potomac, a pleasant outcropping above the flats where so many others – poor devils they were too – camped and dealt with floods, pestilence, and fetid, dead air. Our spot a favor from Denton and final repayment for many a late night tutoring session.

I left that bucolic campsite with great reluctance as we were experiencing a cool spell; high winds brought refreshing, welcome relief that I was loath to leave for the putrid hell of the capital…

… which was not all that bad this time, and that was not solely attributable to the weather. The streets had been watered, refuse and dead animals removed, the blue mobs were gone, the sidewalks sparsely occupied, provost guards on every corner. I knew intuitively that only my rank kept me from being stopped and questioned. It was crystal clear someone had taken control.

No need to check house numbers on Jackson Square, McClellan's

Jackson Square

was the only one with guards in full dress uniform flanking the front door. They snapped to arms with frightening precision, fast and sharp enough for Clio, unhappy as always to be tethered to a hitching post, to snort and nod. They were perfect symbols that I opened the door to cross the threshold back to the Regular Army.

The hallway was lined with expectant officers standing against the walls pretending to pick lint off their uniforms. I was scrupulously ignored as I pushed through, past a former sitting room were stood a dozen men in shirt sleeves around a clattering telegraph, papers strewn across the floor; past a plush parlor and men with eagles and stars on their shoulders lounging indolently, some hiding behind newspapers, all shrouded in heavy cigar smoke; before reaching a foyer.

That was occupied by a prim, proper lieutenant suffused with the arrogance a junior officer could only display when directly employed by the general in command. Detachment joined arrogance when he spied my 'V's. I knew nothing I could say would interest him in any way, instead I simply handed him the calling card without comment, an act that mystically removed the scarlet letters from my shoulder straps.

"Colonel Hanlin, sir," he said without the irony he knew I knew he used when citing a volunteer's rank, "if you wait here, I'm sure the general will see you now."

He handed the card back, rose, turned sharply and marched down the hallway leaving me alone to endure stares of utter hatred thrown like poisoned-tipped javelins by those shuttled aside to wait for that indefinable 'when the general has a moment' moment.

A few minutes later I was beckoned down the hallway, moved without a glance backward though I could feel their stares right up to the moment I stepped through the doorway into the study of Major General George B. McClellan.

He was up from behind a mammoth desk before I realized he was in the room and advanced on me with pace. Before I could snap to attention, never mind salute, McClellan had my hand in an iron clasp.

"Willie," he boomed, "it's been too long," he stepped back, retained my hand in a firm shake, "you know, the circumstances of your leaving –"

"Were unavoidable, General," I pulled my hand out of the vice and managed a quick salute, "congratulations, Sir."

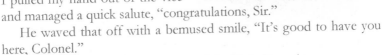

He waved that off with a bemused smile, "It's good to have you here, Colonel."

"Thank you, General," I answered the lilt in his voice.

He caught it, "Listen to us, colonel, general… doesn't seem real does it?"

"Like a game we didn't dare play at the Point."

He nodded, pointed to a high backed chair and strode back to his desk. I watched as he sat, struck as always by the fact he had the upper body – massive chest, thick sinewy neck – of a giant and the legs of a dwarf. On horseback, behind a desk, he was an imposing physical specimen who appeared to be at least 3 to 4 inches taller than most. Standing, he stood five foot eight and his most distinguishing feature was a jet black mustache that straddled low over his mouth and hid his expressions

He looked every bit the general, though, his gray eyes radiated intelligence, he projected – always had – unbounding energy, as if the big man trapped in that body was about to burst out any moment. In short, he made one believe, to me the essential quality of command.

"You catching up with our classmates?" I asked as we sat.

"You're the first from our class, actually," he chuckled, sat back, stared. I had only been back in the world of the real army for a matter of days so that simple declaration did not set off the alarms it should have . . . would . . . in the not so distant future.

But then, there, I was oblivious and simply said, "No one?" Instead of fleeing the room and thereby changing my history.

"Not our class," he reiterated as though hinting, "of course I've seen Fitz John Porter, Stone and Burnsy – they all have brigades."

"Burnside has a star? Ambrose Burnside?" I could not hide my surprise. Burnside, a year older than us but a year behind due to illness, was one of the warmest, kindest man I had ever known. He was also unlucky, pathologically ineffective, and failed consistently at almost everything he tried. None of that a secret to anyone who knew him.

"Rhode Island moved quickly, Willie," Mac took my shock for pique, "and Burnsy was in longer, wounded by the Apaches no less and, well, right place, right time."

"I'm sure he'll do a fine job," I managed sincerity.

"He will," McClellan happily agreed, "you know, he worked for me at the railroad, did very well."

"Glad to hear that," I did indeed know, as I also knew he had gone bankrupt trying to produce breach loading rifles of his own design for the Army and would have been homeless if not for George.

"He has never forgotten your kindness, Willie," George went on, "he speaks of it often."

"Was my pleasure," I replied with a shrug. Burnside was late joining us in Mexico, typically he had a series of misadventures on the way down, then promptly joined a serious card game. Cards were Burnside's passion and he was astonishingly bad at them. He lost quickly, efficiently and big, losing six months' pay in hours. He was facing resignation and humiliation when he poured out his woes to us over drinks in an ancient cantina well into the early morning hours. We bought. Just before dawn I went by his tent and gave him the funds to repay the debt

"Your subsequent disappearance from the Army most upset him – he has been caring that sum around for you for some time."

"It's of no matter, I considered it a gift," I answered with sincerity – Burnside made one want to help . . . he was usually in such obvious need of it.

"Not sure Burnside feels that way, but that's for the two of you to discuss."

"I'll make a point to ride out to his command."

"I hope that's not needed, Willie," He glanced at some papers, looked up with a crooked smile, "I was rather hoping you see him on a regular basis, I would like to detach you and have you join my staff . . . in a fashion."

"I'm honored, Mac," I answered through my shock, "but I have a regiment."

"You are second in command to an amateur."

"A talented amateur, once he has combat experience he'll be the equal of most."

"Worse for you, then, in the long and short run," sharply said, a warning to a wayward friend, "no credit, no advancement, luckily," he unleashed a winning smile, "I need you."

"How?"

"Well, Colonel," he gestured expansively, always magnanimous with friends, he seemed to revel in the fact he could now do so with the capriciousness of a god, "you disappeared an infantry officer and reemerge a lawyer – I find myself in great need of a friend, a lawyer, and a professional soldier. That would be you."

"I detect an offer to join the JAG," my sudden hopes fell quickly and dismally, "I didn't rejoin to be a prosecutor, General, I could have stayed in Hartford and pursued that to my heart's content."

"No, no, Hanlin," McClellan protested immediately, "you misunderstand. I need a trusted liaison with the JAG, and I need that someone by my side as we move south. If you're ever called upon to prosecute anyone it would only be because it is of vital importance.

"I don't need you for discipline, I need your advice. Once we are south of the Potomac there will be . . . very many legal issues. Messy, complicated legal issues."

"Contrabands," I surmised without brilliance. Contrabands, the issue of the day – what to do with slaves that fall into Union hands.

"Contrabands, southern property of all types, tobacco, cotton, parole, peace initiatives, and a host of issues we have yet to encounter," he named them as if rehearsed.

"But mainly slaves that come into our lines," I shortened the list.

"No, but I am concerned with the power the damnable

abolitionists in Congress will try to utilize when we are in control of wide sections of Virginia. After all, we're not fighting for the nigger, though some would have us think we are."

"You want my legal advice on Congressional decrees or do you want my best efforts at disrupting them?"

"Both."

"General – "

"Willie," he waved a hand, "you'll create legal precedence in the territories we bring back to the union. Think of it, we'll be the only federal authority on hand for God's knows how long, and you'll be the man guiding me," he levelled me with a warm, direct, gaze.

"I need you, Colonel," he smiled winningly, "take the position, else I'll be tempted to order you."

"My friends and family are with the Twenty-first," I started, the kernel of an idea opening while I spoke, "I trained them, my baby brother is a captain —"

"Christian's a captain!" He roared, "Now I feel old."

"As do I," I agreed, "I cannot leave them to fight without me . . . so, what if I accept with the proviso I do not do so."

"Willie?"

"I am temporarily assigned to your staff, I am with the Twenty-first when in harm's way."

"Capital idea!" He thumped the desk, "the very essence of what I propose to do with the army. Mobility and utility! Outstanding! You, sir, have a deal."

We shook on it, long, hard. McClellan cut it off, reached into a desk drawer, took out a small box, and threw it at me with an easy, graceful flick of the wrist.

"I thought you'd agree," he beamed, "those are yours."

I snatched the box cleanly, fumbled it open. Inside was the shoulder strap of a regular army lieutenant colonel.

"Mac?"

"It's official, Willie. Congratulations."

"Thank you," all I could manage at the moment.

"Well I can't have valued counsel snubbed as a volunteer mustang, can I?" He chuckled at his derisive term for our Texas volunteers in Mexico,

"I suppose not," I happily replied, "when do I start?"

"Now," he laughed, "and, by the way, please bring your friend Osgood aboard with you."

I was caught short, stared back.

"I think he and my head of intelligence will get along quite well," he smirked.

"Probably," I confirmed.

3. Holt

Colonel Joseph Holt was angry, a state I would have found disconcerting sitting as I was three feet from his dark red face, had I for a moment thought his ire was directed at me.

That it was not was an immense relief for Colonel Holt was very, very good at anger – an expertise he had acquired over years of public service until finally honing it during his few months as Buchanan's last Secretary of War.

He was so angry he turned his back to me, swiveled his chair and stared at the unfinished Capitol dome. He was, after all, a Kentuckian and, as such, politeness effused his every pore. I was not the reason for his anger, he would not risk offending by taking it out on a relative innocent. For now.

I sat quietly and rued my decision to take the position while, not coincidentally, reflecting on the weekend I had just spent with the 21st in camp. And my decision to leave for the time being – the distance of my new offices from our bucolic camp precluded staying in the field. I was forced to take a room in a house on Lafayette Square recently vacated by a dismissed McDowell aide. An immediate lesson I vowed to heed once I figured out exactly what it meant.

My friends, indeed the Regiment in general, were thrilled to see me attached to headquarters, counting it a coup for the unit. Mac had been in charge for a matter of weeks and was already revered – a natural occurrence when a previously defeated mob found itself organized, disciplined, and fed in short order and then kept that way. The fact that the 21st had nothing to do with the rout at Bull Run did nothing to lessen those feelings in the Yankees from Connecticut. They had heard enough from the veterans camped around them to take it as gospel. Hence joy at my entry to Olympus.

"I hope you understand," Holt said with remarkable restraint as he twirled to face me, "your presence would be most welcome."

"But?"

"But it reeks of oversight, Sir, and this office must be an independent one."

"I understand, Colonel," I replied, carefully. I knew my audience: a Kentuckian, yes, but a staunch, hawkish Unionist who had seen his recommendations for dealing with Sumter ignored by a weak willed president. I would not toy with that man's frustration, "no oversight is intended, I assure you. General McClellan will need legal advice in the field and he does not want it occurring in a vacuum."

Holt weighed my words, the red in his cheeks did not rise further. Nor did it recede.

"I can appreciate that," he said in an almost friendly voice, a friendliness that did not reach eyes that continued to bore into me. The man was a good lawyer, freshly appointed to the JAG immediately after a good portion of the army had fled in the face of the enemy. All critical factors, just in what combination to what final sum I had not a clue, "I realize we're all new at this, but I don't see why he shouldn't follow normal channels."

"I think he feels your office too important to leave to normal channels," I replied quickly and earnestly, sensing an opening, understanding that at least part of his mood was attributable to the late news that his native, heretofore neutral state had been invaded by Confederate forces, "it's more a matter of staying out of your hair while keeping the general informed. It should – will – make less work for you."

"You will be in the field with him?" He sat forward, demeanor changing.

"I will."

"You went to West Point with McClellan?"

"I did."

That earned a steady stare, silence. He managed to ready and light a cigar without moving his eyes. I affected relaxation, vowed not to break the silence.

"You a Mexican veteran, Hanlin?" He asked at long last, handed me a cigar and match. I took both, delayed my answer while I prepared and lighted it.

"I am," I answered, received what may have been a smile.

"But you prefer a staff position now?"

"No I do not," I answered promptly, "I came here with the Twenty-first Connecticut. My agreement with General McClellan is that I rejoin them for any fight. That, sir, was not negotiable."

"Yes," he said without inflection, "you in much action in Mexico?"

"All of Scott's, General."

"Excellent," he leaned back, relaxing for the first time since me and my mission were sprung on him earlier that day, "and you have prosecuted capital cases?"

"Many," my turn to employ no inflection, I did not like where the conversation was headed.

"Then I have a proposition for you, Colonel," he flashed a rare but winning smile, "you do as your friend, our General suggests – hell, no need to tell me anything, just keep Mac happy, leave me right out of it." He took a long, casual puff, and eyed me for signs of intelligence.

"I detect an impending quid pro quo," I observed to his enthusiastic nod.

"When – notice I did not say if," he pointed at me, "we start prosecuting for actions under fire or in the presence of the enemy, I need an officer with combat experience to do it."

"Better to win by," I said dryly.

"I'm not planning on trying heroes, Hanlin, only the drunks, cowards, and shirkers."

"I told the general I did not rejoin the Army to prosecute men who volunteered to fight for their country.

"You'd prefer to see the enlisted men entrusted to wastrels?"

"Of course not."

"Good, then help me," his was an almost conspiratorial tone, "I have many lawyers, William – all ardent, most probably too so. What I do not have are JAG officers who are combat experienced and I'll not try a man for an offense under fire by one who has never been there."

"That's admirable, Sir."

"Isn't it?" He asked to our laughs, "Since you're all I have at the present – at least until some prominent lawyer has a limb blown off, I need you."

I found myself, as I was meant to, wanting to do a favor for the general. A man worth a hundred Nelsons, it went without saying. I could not go too easily, however, least I end up granting many favors. And, as well, there was the implicit New England – Mid-south rivalry to consider- I would skewer it agreeing too quickly.

I counted to ten, "My alternative?"

"Ah, your alternative," a slightly raised eyebrow his only reaction as he respected my respecting the rules of inter-regional negotiation, "as a liaison for the commanding officer of an army – not the Army – is not a recognized position I feel it only fitting that I clear it with the War Department. They, of course, are busy with —"

"More important things", I completed, meekly.

"Exactly. I fear they may decide that what you and McClellan propose may very well be a staff position best left to Congress to authorize."

"That would be another delay."

"Interminable I should think," he puffed heavily in commiseration.

"And in the meantime, while I await word?"

"God forbid I do something not authorized," he croaked.

"Like surreptitiously ordering supplies to Sumter?" I warily asked. Rumors of his attempts to act in lieu of Buchanan's lack of backbone had been rife in the news for months.

"Vicious, unfounded slander, Sir!" He retorted, not at all in the manner of the aggrieved.

"Or," I offered with wiry amusement, "treating Charleston's demand to abandon Sumter as an offer to purchase the fort?"

He waved that off, "They lacked sufficient consideration in any case."

"That was evident," I chuckled, "I see a long wait while I explain to McClellan why I can't perform my duties."

"I think I can safely predict, if everything goes right, your grandchildren may get a response," he puffed contentedly.

"Well then," I said in good cheer, "honor has been satisfied, I accept your kind offer."

"Excellent," he grunted, put a hand out that I quickly took in a hard grasp, "and now we will studiously avoid one another until one of us need something. That work for you?"

"I could ask for no more," I agreed. Holt rose and escorted me out of his office, one hand on my shoulder, the other stuffing a handful of his excellent cigars into my pocket.

On my way down the street from his offices, still smoking my cigar, it occurred to me that I had been in the District of Columbia for a fortnight and had already cut deals with power-brokers. I yearned for the field.

4 Pinkerton

I was three steps into headquarters when he strode up to me as if in challenge. He was short, stocky, heavily bearded with expressionless eyes, and he was blocking the hallway.

"You Hanlin?" He demanded in a voice as devoid of expression as his eyes.

"Who are you?" I, logically, inquired. I did not use an honorific for he was not in uniform and I was damned if I was going to call him sir.

"I asked you a question," he demanded yet again, in a manner I had only previously heard used by police officials addressing the disenfranchised.

"Excuse me, I'm late for a meeting with General McClellan," I explained only because his broad shoulders barred the hallway and I felt it was too early in our relationship – whatever that may be – to pound him into the wall and move on. Though it was close.

"You are Hanlin," he surmised with an edge I did not like.

"I'm Colonel Hanlin," I snapped, "who the hell are you?"

He put his hands on hips, stuck his chest out, "No need for profanity," he replied with self-righteousness.

Self-righteousness was to me what lame elk were to wolves, "There is and there will be if you continue to refuse to introduce yourself and your business with me, whoever the fuck you are."

That caused a blink. A single, begrudging blink. Then he made me wait while he calculated something and I contemplated some form of mayhem.

He decided first, "I am Major E. J. Allen."

"You're out of uniform, Major," all I could think to say.

"Perhaps," he nodded, "though I think you will find I have rather more authority than a uniform can convey, Hanlin."

"That's . . . exceptional, Allen, now, really, I'm late for my meeting," I made a move as if to pass by, he twitched not a muscle. I scanned hallway for help the way a houseguest confronted with a large, unruly pet would the owner – to no avail, for once the hall was empty.

"You may see him when I am finished with you, Colonel," he smiled as if first learning how.

"Finished with me . . . ," I trailed off, tried to engage his eyes, he did not cooperate – nor did he move. He was certainly close enough to see the red rising up my neck, filtering into my cheeks, "we *are*, whatever you are, finished, now get out of my way."

I stepped quickly to my right, he anticipated, slid to his left and deftly blocked me.

"You . . . Colonel . . . must speak to me before you see the General . . . it really is that simple . . . sir," great strain with each honorific, as if their use stabbed him in the neck.

"Why?" I asked. Carefully.

"Simple, really," he seemed to take my question as some kind of acquiescence, "the General appointed you while I was out of town. I vet candidates, all candidates . . . since I missed you, I need to ask you a few questions . . ."

"What sort of questions?" Heat filtered up my cheeks.

He almost smiled, "Associations, memberships, affiliations, that sort of thing," he answered as if it was not only self-explanatory but the normal course of business.

I was nonplussed, hoped I did not show it, knew my cheeks had to be glowing, was suddenly ridiculously worried that he would take it as admission of vague guilt at some vaguer charge.

"No," I said, almost involuntarily.

"No?" He rocked back as if struck – clearly not a man who heard no often.

"I find it insulting – for myself . . . and for General McClellan, for you insult his judgment as well."

"Listen, Hanlin —"

"No, you listen, you —"

"Willie," McClellan's voice stopped me, he had just stepped out of his office. He moved down the hall, clasped my shoulder, "I see you've met Alan."

"Major Allen, yes," I answered, voice neutral.

Mac started laughing, "No, Willie, meet Alan Pinkerton, Pinkerton, William Hanlin."

"Come on, Colonel, we have a lot to talk about," he was oblivious to the fact Pinkerton and I did not shake hands. Pinkerton smiled

24

nastily at the precise moment I realized I had just clashed with America's most famous detective.

I had no time to dwell on the potential implications, McClellan all but shoved me toward his office, slamming the door behind us.

"That's a winning personality," I motioned toward the hallway.

"He's rough," Mac agreed readily, "but he gets the job done. He was invaluable at the railroad, is fast becoming so here as well."

"You need a detective?"

"I need spies," he smiled, "Pinkerton runs my secret service."

He must have noticed my look, for he hastened to add, "He is really outstanding, William – he's gone out into the field himself, when he was with me in the West he went undercover in Kentucky and Tennessee. Man even had dinner with General Pillow."

"Gideon Pillow?"

"The same."

"I'd say I hope he shot the bastard," I spat – thirteen years later and I still felt instant, palpable distain for the United States' answer to Santa Anna. An incompetent, dangerous fool, "except I find great comfort in the fact the South has given him a command."

"Amen to that,"

We walked into his office, sat while I offered a recitation of the meeting with Holt.

"Well done, Willie," he started when I finished, "I did not anticipate that he would perceive this as some sort of threat – I should have, you never know with these political officers."

"It's of no matter, I liked him well enough," I said absently, trying to work in the question I had been rehearsing all morning in my head, "I heard a rumor this morning . . ."

He laughed, "You'll have to narrow it down if you want me to comment."

"You declared a state of emergency, citing an imminent attack on the Capitol?"

He nodded, "I did, earlier in the week. Beauregard is a fool not to attack us as scattered and disorganized as we are – outnumbered too. I would have, then the war would be over."

"Should I head for the Twenty-first?" I asked with hope.

"No, the threat has passed – though we are outnumbered still."

"Well, I —"

"You know what that . . . General Scott said when I asked Cameron for the state of emergency?" Mac snapped suddenly.

I shrugged.

"He claimed I outnumber then! That because they only had fifty thousand men at Bull Run it would be impossible for them to have over one hundred thousand now."

"Scott?" I momentarily lost my point of reference. Winfield Scott was, simply, a god to the men who followed him to Mexico City. McClellan very much included.

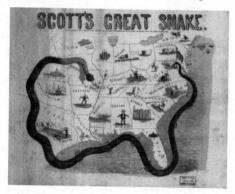

That obviously registered on my face for Mac went on, "Yes, Scott – he's changed, Willie. He's far from the Scott of Cerro Gordo. Warfare has passed him by – I don't think he understands railroads and steam ships can transport men almost instantaneously . . . worse, I don't think he intends to learn."

I was rocked, remained mute.

McClellan did not, "His ridiculous Anaconda Plan – well, the very fact he proposed it shows he's not the Scott of Mexico. Imagine that man wanting to wait, and wait, and wait to choke the Confederacy to death rather than fight.

"I tell you, Willie, it would break my heart to see him this way if it wasn't for the fact his obstinacy wasn't so frustrating . . . and dangerous."

"I am heartily saddened to hear this," I replied, quietly.

"As I am to report it," he said without delay, "just another obstacle to overcome, though I believe I have the President's ear at present. Neophyte that he is, he understands that I need to be left to my own devices with my army."

He said that last with such a dose of innuendo, a thought – probably the thought he wanted me to have – hit me hard, "He's going to remove Scott?"

He smiled a thin smile, "He's due to retire shortly, it's been intimated I am to replace him."

"Good God, Mac, that's—"

Thankfully, he cut me off, as I had no idea what I was about to say next, "We'll see," he held a hand up, "we'll see."

Stunned, I was about to excuse myself when there was a loud knocking on the door. Without waiting for an answer, the door swung open and three men, two in magnificently tailored uniforms, the other dressed like a private, strode into the room.

McClellan was on his feet in an instant, moved to them with hand extended. He shook hands with them in turn while uttering a string of French greetings.

The result of all that was a taxing of my rusty French and my introduction to three surprising additions to McClellan's staff – the Prince de Joinville and his nephews, the Duc de Chartes, and the Comte de Paris. Three princes of the House of Orleans.

They left us in heightened moods, a standing invitation to a night at The Willard, sore shoulders from their back slaps, and a sudden desire for foie gras.

"You know, of course, that the Comte de Paris is pretender to the throne?" McClellan said as their powerful boot steps receded down the hallway.

"Sure," I lied, "and unless you loan him your army when we're done here, he'll be the pretender for life."

"We'll have to see about that," he laughed.

"They'd make you a peer," I observed.

"Well, then, perhaps . . . imagine, Willie, a Prince, a Duke, and a Count on my staff, who would have ever thought it?"

"I don't know Mac, I think our forefather's fought a war to rid us of titles."

"You believe that, Willie?" He answered, no longer laughing, "Before you answer, I remind you that you are a Boston Brahmin addressing a Philadelphia Main-liner."

"We don't have titles designating that, do we?"

"Think we need them, Colonel?"

5. Porter

For the first time in our long relationship Clio had no interest in my presence, wishes, needs, commands, comfort. Nor was she on the prowl for snacks. Clio was responsive to nothing save Major General George B. McClellan's mount, Dan Webster.

She followed his every move while too shy – an adjective heretofore never employed to describe her – to stray near him even though they were loosely tethered less than ten feet apart. If I put myself in her place for a moment I could completely understand, Dan Webster stood a full two hands taller than Clio and was the very embodiment of the term warhorse.

It was a remarkably mild August morning and a dozen of us stood on a knoll overlooking the Potomac juggling coffee and light banter while waiting to review a division or so of the newly designated 'Army of the Potomac'. The Army of the Potomac – it sounded . . . eloquent and it differentiated itself nicely from the rather less ineloquently named army McDowell had commanded a little over one month ago.

McClellan fittingly stood at the apex of our little hill, surrounded by staff, politely turning down repeated offers of champagne from the Princes – who imbibed freely to no discernible effect. The aides rushed about like hyenas surrounded by raw meat – three members of French royalty, McClellan, Fitz John Porter commander of the division being reviewed, four brigadier generals, seven full colonels created a time management nightmare for the professionally obsequious.

I had seen Fitz-John Porter once since West Point, that a memorable meeting outside Mexico City, but he had changed not a whit. Slightly shorter than me, close-cropped thinning hair, full lush beard, darkly handsome – a favorite with the senoritas – he looked and carried himself as the professional soldier he most certainly was.

He was one of the first to arrive that morning, riding up as I tethered an as yet undistracted Clio. I turned to see Porter sitting imperiously on his mount, staring. I stared back and struggled to find an appropriate greeting. It was an unique, strange but common event of those early days: running into an old friend previously of the same rank or social standing or where stood a comfortable informality- or all three – to find that in the haphazardness of throwing an army together on the fly there now existed a wide gulf in rank.

The safest action, I supposed, was to salute, an action I endeavored to execute after additional hesitation. I gave him a familiar salute, the kind one gave a superior one is related to in case subordinates are watching.

"General Porter," I intoned without irony or awe, grinned slightly.

In return – stony silence. Long enough for me to begin to think I had sinned in some way. I stood there, offending right hand hanging by my side, useless, for a full twenty seconds.

Without warning the martial figure on horseback jumped to the ground, grabbed my hands in a full clasp. "William, my God, it is you."

"Fitz," I said automatically, overwhelmed by the ferocity of his greeting, "good to see you."

"Mac said you were joining us," he released my hands, "but I wouldn't believe – not after the way you disappeared."

I shrugged in return, flashed the smile I had now reserved for that particular topic, one I was sure to be tired of shortly. With a moment's reflection, however, I had to admit it would have been disconcerting to discover no one had noticed my sudden absence.

Had we remained alone a 'catching up' session I was not ready for would have followed, such had been our relationship – despite our beginnings as upper-lower classmates and his student-instructor status we found much in common somewhere along the way. That unwieldy reunion, however, would have to wait as the three princes chose that moment to appear.

They reigned up as one, stopped dead at the unexpected sight of a lieutenant colonel and a general, aide-less, at ease and looking expectantly at them.

A most interesting moment as Porter and I outranked our royal interlopers – the Comte and Duc were both captains and the Prince de Joinville was . . . well, the Prince de Joinville was unique and a problem in diplomacy and etiquette unto himself.

Joinville wore no insignia but carried himself with the royal reserve one expected of the pretender to the pretender to the-this-moment-defunct French throne. He was, as well, a Vice-Admiral of some repute in the French Navy, albeit on a hiatus that would be at least as long as Napoleon III's reign.

Then again, the Comte was not so easy a nut to crack either as he was in fact, heir to the throne. To most Americans – those who waited for the Comte to be out of earshot before exclaiming, "He could be King, you know" – that was as good as being de facto king . . . despite the fact the odds of that occurring were roughly the same as Clio winning Ascot.

Indeed, the only thing the Comte had going for him was France's governmental history since the storming of the Bastille. Then, should the hundred or so events – in exact order – necessary to install le Comte to the throne occur, he could look forward to a reign about as long as the lifespan of a fruit fly.

Of course – and I was sure I shared the thought with Napoleon III -all such ruminations would be terminated should the young prince get close to a Southern minie ball unconcerned with royal pedigree.

The moment of unease passed quickly – the princes saluted as one. We returned them, Fitz-John added a curious looking bow from the shoulders that seemed to please them while mindlessly irritating me even while I automatically began to nod, felt idiotic, pretended to scratch the back of my neck.

McClellan and three aides arrived as I finished scratching thereby truncating the opportunity to interact further with royalty. After a brief handshake and a hurried greeting I was surgically removed from Mac's presence by a stolid mutton-chopped captain who stepped in front of me and not so subtly pushed Mac toward the Prince de Joinville. He was oblivious to my joy at being liberated from the hive of sycophantic activity to wander the fringe and enjoy an alfresco breakfast. From a shallow swale I sipped a perfect cup of coffee and watched the outnumbered aides in their ultimately futile attempt to lavish equal devotion on generals and royalty.

Lest one think me too harsh on the aides, most of whom had no individual identities I ever noted, it should be said that from that first day my opinion of them as a class never changed. That is not true, actually, my opinion never improved.

Unimpeded by social responsibilities I wandered over to Clio assured of reaffirming affection. I stroked her neck, she snapped her head around in surprise, saw it was me, sent a hot, irritated snort across my face, and went back to dewy-eyed admiration of Dan Webster. She may or may not have rolled her eyes, I noted with shock she did not investigate the food in my hand.

Alone I enjoyed a beautiful sight: the Potomac in the early morning light empty of all shipping – lying as it did between two sides with plentiful artillery – thousands of brilliant white tents stretched to the horizons interspersed with trim farms on gently rolling hills . . . Maryland beyond the city limits of Washington was beautiful country.

"Excuse me, Colonel," the unfortunate sound that broke my bucolic reverie.

"What?" I answered lowly, reluctantly flicked my eyes off the vista below and into the pasty face of the mutton-chopped aide.

"We're almost ready to leave, sir," he continued as if I had been staring at the river in the fervent hope a pasty faced, mutton-chopped junior officer would interrupt me, "so, I'd like –"

"Who are you?" I very reasonably inquired.

"Lieutenant Jacob Webb," he answered, unfazed in the way someone who through long practice was quite inured to the annoyance of the people he inconvenienced, "as this is the first review you've come on I would like to explain a few things."

"I've been on reviews before, Lieutenant," I replied through teeth well on their way to a hard clench.

"I'm sure," he smiled a smile that clinched my teeth's decision and sealed his Hanlin fate forever – the smile of the uninterested yet patronizing, "but, well, we try to choreograph these things somewhat to, you know, impress the men. This is a new army, after all."

"You mention that to him?" I threw a nod at a lone figure removed from the group at the top of the hill by more than distance – General McDowell, a very lonely second in command of the Army of the Potomac.

"In any regard," he sighed, searched the high clouds over Virginia for assistance, must have found some for he went on, "General McClellan says you are an excellent rider, and – "

"Thank Mac for me," I smiled, he gasped at the blasphemy of employing Major General George B. McClellan's nickname.

"I shall," hissed slowly from his pursed lips, "in any event, the *General* . . . we, ah, prefer the he be the first to arrive at each regiment while we keep a respectful distance – not that we have much choice, as none of us have his skill or his horse," he smiled at his wit.

I snorted, "You think I'd race Mac unit to unit? Best seven of nine regiments takes it?"

He stood hands on hips, mouth agape, with not a clue how to deal with my hearty laughter. When I finally calmed down I said, kindly, "Look, Lieutenant," I almost called him 'Alex' but I was afraid the act of familiarity might send him into convulsions, "does Mac know we are having this conversation?"

"No, sir, I'm just—"

"Then I'll tell you what," I said with all the kindness I could muster, "I won't mention it to him and you'll get to keep your job."

"But –"

"But nothing, Lieutenant. I've been to more reviews than you have had days in the Army, of course I am not going to upstage the commanding general – and it's pretty insulting that you think I would.

"McClellan's the best rider I know and with him on that horse," I pointed at Dan Webster, Clio snorted and looked with a hopeful air, "no one's out riding him and therefore, you insult him as well."

The blasphemy of not employing McClellan's title, combined with my very real passion left the poor captain mute and immobile. He gaped and did nothing else, including, I am almost positive, blink.

"Have a good ride, Lieutenant," I said with warmth and cheer and began to untether Clio, pretty much doing exactly to her what Webb had just done to me. Clio proved to be much more eloquent than me, she snorted long and hard in my face as I pulled her away.

Within minutes everyone had mounted and we left our idyllic hill at a walk. I fell in beside Fitz and we chatted amiably. As it turned out we were directly behind Webb who continuously turned to look at us suspiciously, as if he knew we were plotting the ruin of his parade.

The road was narrow, dusty for a mile or so until it finally opened into a wide plain, white tents in rows few hundred yards ahead, solid blue lines formed against them. A solitary rider left our van and galloped to the first camp, the rest of us formed around our general. We waited, I assume for the out rider to warn of our approach.

After a five-minute delay, during which time Clio, emboldened by the ride thus far, endeavored to take herself, and me, closer to Dan. Dan Webster may or may not have noticed Clio, but Mac noticed us.

"Hey, Willie!" He yelled with great humor, "Want to race?"

"No General, no need to embarrass you in front of your men," I chuckled, out of the corner my eye I saw Webb almost come out of his saddle.

"I don't recall you winning all that often at the Point, Willie."

"Funny, I don't recall losing all that often," I answered to the laughs of everyone save the stricken Webb.

"I should think," the Prince the Joinville said in British tinged English, "a rematch is in order."

"Perhaps," I yelled over the ensuing seconding, "but at West Point we rode horses... I brought a horse today, but the general has brought something out of Greek mythology."

"He has a point, general," Joinville went on, fast making me a convert to his charm, "but still a sporting man..." he trailed off with a smile.

"Would say," I smiled back, "first one to the regimental colors wins, One... Two... Three... Go!" I yelled spurred Clio, she took a quick look at Dan and instantly accelerated toward the distant tents.

"Damn it, Hanlin!" I heard over Clio's hooves.

Dan overtook us about fifty yards from the looming regiment. Clio managed to stay close to Dan for twenty of those yards – lust can work wonders but not miracles – and she flagged to finish a good fifteen yards behind.

We arrived heads down as McClellan and Dan sat waiting, one with a triumphant grin on his face, the other nodding to Clio. The regiment, a New York Regiment, was yelling itself hoarse.

"Well run, you cheat," McClellan yelled over the noise. I grinned, Mac turned away to face to screaming New Yorkers. He waved his black sugar loaf hat, bowed, spoke a few words, and sped off. The rest of the riders joined Clio and I watching Mac and Dan recede toward the next blue group.

"Will you ride with me, sir?" Joinville asked. Without waiting for my response he turned his big bay and left at a canter. Clio, her lather up and pride dented, did not need to be told to follow, she pulled me around and we caught up to Joinville in short order.

Joinville acknowledge our presence on his left flank with a nod. Up ahead, Mac was addressing another regiment. We pulled back to keep a respectful distance.

"You were with the general at West Point, Colonel?" Joinville asked.

"I was," I answered carefully to cover for the fact that I had no idea how to address him. He had no rank, and from long indoctrination I was loath – actually I did not know if I was even capable – to address him as Prince, or God forbid Your Highness.

"Mexico as well?"

"Not actually with him there," I said amiably, "he was with the engineers. I was infantry."

"That is interesting, I think," he matched my amiability.

"Is it?"

"You know, George speaks very highly of you," he quite clearly had not noticed the tone of my voice or had chosen to ignore it, "he says you finished high in your class, but could have been higher."

"He's too kind," I said flatly.

"He is often, but I think not this time," he smiled conspiratorially, "you turned down the engineers for the infantry?"

"The Fourth Infantry to be precise," I replied absently.

"Curious, if you do not mind my saying," he went on with a slight, courteous nod, "the engineers are the elite, are they not?"

"You are an attorney when not a Prince, I take it?" I remarked in rusty but passable French, with a smile to convey humor I was not really employing.

"Well done, Colonel," he laughed deeply, pleasantly, "and thank you."

"For being rude?" I returned to what was arguably my native tongue.

"For treating me like another, equally rude officer, instead of the way your fellow countrymen do," he replied.

"Which is how?" I was genuinely interested.

"As if my shit does not stink like theirs," he reverted to French – which is the only reason for the delay between his statement and my shattering laugh.

"That actually sounds polite in French," I gasped out.

"Naturally!" He yelled McClellan galloped away from the regiment toward the next, just visible half a mile away.

We rode in silence for a quarter-mile, companionably.

"I chose the infantry," I broke the silence, "because my mother had such long reach I would have been assigned to building forts in Georgia rather than accompanying my classmates to Mexico had I chosen the engineers," I surprised myself unveiling it to anyone, never mind a new acquaintance. But then again he was not an American, "I refused the artillery because it's too damn impersonal."

"I understand perfectly," he said with great ease, "George also says you had quite distinguished service in Mexico."

"The general always exaggerates the accomplishments of his friends," I said in complete honesty.

"I have noticed," He answered, looked up the road to where Mac regaled another crisp blue line, "but, again, I think not in this instance," he looked at me questioningly or challengingly, our acquaintance was too short for me to tell.

"What brings you to the Army of the Potomac?" I changed the subject, a fact that he registered.

"To observe," he smiled.

"Americans, the Army, the war?"

"Everything, of course."

"Plenty of fighting out West, why here?"

"This is it, is it not?" He answered quickly, "one major campaign, moving on Richmond in one, grand movement."

"One could say Napoleonic in scale," I smiled.

"You are an evil man," he laughed, "we will get along well."

I nodded, we spurred forward, trailed Mac to another unit. We went on like that, trot, cantor, gallop, walk, for hours through dozens of units riding a wide circle around the Army the Potomac. An enjoyable circumnavigation of the army bolstering goodwill and cheer – quite unlike another general's ride around the same army nine months later.

The sun began to set behind the hills of Western Maryland, McClellan finished saluting an Ohio regiment, left them on a slow trot, stopped and beckoned me to join him.

I pulled beside him, Clio studiously avoiding Webster's eyes, "General?"

"Ride with me to the last Regiment, Willie," he said with remarkable enthusiasm and good cheer considering his evident exhaustion, "they're up and around the bend," he nodded toward a wide curve around the dense copse of trees, "let's race it."

"You must be tired," I replied.

"Then it will be a fair race!" He yelled and spurred forward.

Clio needed no encouragement. We caught them as they rounded the curve, passed as we pulled through it, the blue lines a few yards ahead. Clio and I flew into the center of the camp, I reined her up hard and stopped in a flurry of stones and dust, realized Mac had brought up Dan some yards behind us.

Momentarily, amid the men's shining faces, I feared an injury to Dan. Gradually, it became clear that the cheering faces were familiar . . . we had just made a spectacular entrance in front of the 21st Connecticut.

I dismounted as Mac pulled up. To a man the regiment snapped to attention.

McClellan would have none of it, "At ease, men, at ease," he yelled, his voice still deep and strong, "I've come today to return your wayward son, Colonel Hanlin."

That raised a cheer, Christian and Shay pounded my back.

"You have him for tonight," McClellan went on, "be kind to him, though, I need him back in one piece, good night boys!"

Hence George B McClellan.

In the long months to come, when the politicians wondered about the hold McClellan had on his Army, hell, when I wondered on the hold he had had on me, I would have held out that incident as Exhibit A. Then, I would have rested.

6. A Favor

A few days later I walked into the normally bustling house in Jackson Square to make my weekly report. Which is going to be astonishingly easy as I had nothing. A heat wave had descended over Washington, a heat wave of such ferociousness as to render my previous observations of the city in August stupendously inadequate.

As far as I could tell the only people still working in Washington were in the War Department, McClellan's house and taverns. Even the brothels were shuttered.

I let myself in – the color guards were long gone – and stepped into a cauldron, the shirt sleeved officers within in danger of melting like so many lead soldiers in a blast furnace.

By the time I got to McClellan's office, jacket slung over my shoulder, I was winded and leaving a widening creek in my wake.

A pale, slightly disheveled, red eyed McClellan was shoulder deep in papers, Captain Perry (the inevitable name hung on the Compte de Paris) on his left, the unctuous Webb on his right. He barely looked up as I entered.

"Willie, is it six already?" He asked. The ever obsequious Webb confirmed that it was indeed.

"I'm sorry, Mac," I apologize for the time, someone had to, "I'll wait outside – not that I have a thing to report."

"Have supper with me Willie," McClellan said without looking up, Webb shot a malice laced glare my way, "Darcy's at nine – if you have no engagements."

"I'll be there," I answered quickly, extending Webb's glare.

Darcy's was a small restaurant in Georgetown with an outdoor terrace where I took up residence at 8:30. I sat in an open spot where the faint wind could have some affect, even a seemingly insignificant zephyr brought brief, immeasurable relief. Infrequent but worth it.

I knew McClellan had arrived when I heard the heavy murmur of voices from the main restaurant, followed by a round of applause. A moment later McClellan entered the terrace, the outdoor diners rose, clapped, continued until he acknowledged them with a tiff of his hat.

He plopped down opposite me smiling weakly looking better than he had in the cauldron of his office.

"I would've risen," I chuckled, "but then I thought, hell, I'm already a lieutenant colonel, I don't have to pretend any longer."

"You always were obstinate," he smiled faintly.

"Just trying to ground you in reality . . . think of me as the slave who rode in the chariot behind victorious Roman generals —"

"Whispering all glory is fleeting," he interrupted with a rueful shake of the head, "your perfect job, Willie."

"I could be convinced to give up my JAG duties," I said hopefully.

"No, Colonel, you're capable of both duties," he grinned, nodded, readied himself to deal with the maître d' purposely winding his way through the other tables, his aim so fixed on Mac's stars he was oblivious to the other diners. Had one of them caught fire he would not have paused to toss a pitcher of water in his pursuit of celebrity.

"General," he hissed upon reaching us, "we are honored to have you amongst us this evening."

"Thank you," McClellan threw it out with complete insincerity, "but as I am the Colonel's guest this evening, you must deal with him."

"You invited me, General," I responded at once.

"You can afford it, Colonel, you owe me."

"You are in error, Sir," I replied enjoying the maître d's utter bafflement while I argued with the idol of our age.

"If I am, and I seriously doubt that, Sir, then you should buy supper as recompense for the way you disappeared after Mexico."

"That somehow translates into my buying dinner from a Georgetown bistro whose prices approach war profiteering," I pursued the menu as the maître d's face reddened.

"I could order you to buy."

"That is a violation of the Articles of War, Sir, an abuse of power, and as your liaison to the JAG I would be remiss in not reporting it at once."

"You know for a fact?" He said with snide insinuation.

"Pretty damn sure."

"Enough that you want to go in that direction? I understand the Dry Tortugas are lovely this time of year," he challenged. The maître d's eyes swung to me. I pretended to think it over.

"Well, general, in that case, will you be my guest?"

"Delighted, Colonel"

"I'll send the waiter over," the maître d' announced, walked away, shaking his head, lamenting his brush with greatness.

"Made me work for that, Willie," Mac observed.

"It's fun putting a general through his paces. A rarity for me while an everyday occurrence for you, so you'll just have to forgive me."

"Forgiven," he nodded, smile fading as he looked around the terrace.

"I take it there's a reason we're out here in Georgetown instead of comfortably ensconced at Wormley's?" I asked. Run by a free Mulatto named, of course, Wormley, that restaurant was around the corner from headquarters. McClellan and his staff ate virtually every meal there.

"Aside the fact I'm going to soak you for it an expensive meal?"

"Aside that, and the fact we're not surrounded by staff, visiting officers, politicians . . ."

"I note you were astute enough to choose a table away from the others," he gestured the terrace.

"I did it for the breeze."

"I can see that, it's a wonder anything can stay on the table," he said dryly. A timid, tired, little waiter approached and took our order, scurried away.

"Want to tell me about it," I finally asked, exactly as I had hundreds of potential witnesses over the years.

"Oh, I will," he chuckled, "for if I don't unburden myself I may have to use part of my Army against several departments of our government."

"Well," I matched his tone, "I can see why you didn't want to say that out loud in Wormley's."

"Not for fear of being heard," he grinned, "but for fear one of my generals would do it."

"Will no one here rid me of this priest?" I quipped.

"What?"

"What Henry II supposedly said to his knights concerning one Thomas a Becket."

"And they murdered him," he nodded.

"Exactly."

He met my eyes, "I suppose were I holding court at Wormley's I might have said, 'will no one here rid me of this meddlesome, old, decrepit general'."

"That would be problematic," I sympathized, "Scott –"

"Is either a dotard or a traitor, Willie," he said lowly, "I can't be expected to save the country when he thwarts everything I do."

"Traitor?" I rasped in surprise.

"He is from Virginia."

"Still, Mac –"

"Still nothing, Hanlin, I am leaving nothing undone to increase our forces, ready us, and that confounded old man continuously gets in the way. He understands nothing, appreciates nothing, is a perfect imbecile. The only thing he's successful at is stopping me.

"I tell you, Willie, if I can't get him taken out of the way I won't continue. I'll resign and let the administration take care of itself – I don't think it will survive after that."

I sat, speechless while he stared awaiting a response. "That sounds," I said on the way to one of the grossest understatements of my life, "irreconcilable."

"It is," he eagerly went on, "we're on a precipice and he cannot see it. All he says is 'impossible!' 'Impossible!' To every request. Nothing's possible that's noy in his interest. Nothing!

"Scott's the most dangerous antagonist I have right now – and I include Beauregard. The enemy has at least three times our numbers and Scott and I," he sighed, something he was not good at, ". . . we cannot work together."

"You have the President's ear, General," as far as I got before his face clouded to the consistency of a ripe plum.

"Lincoln's an idiot," he stated flatly – which did nothing to take away from the intensity of the sentiment, "Scott has as much of his ear as I have. There's a disaster looming and I'm precluded from doing my duty . . . a duty I never asked for."

"We're in danger of imminent attack?" I asked the vision of rejoining the 21st flicking through my head. A quick, hopeful vision.

The answer was put off by the approach of our tray laden waiter. The tiny man precariously placed plates made enormous by his tiny hands on our table. That gave me time to run through the permutations of the last few minutes. We were outnumbered, in danger of attack, and the general of the union's largest – and most important – army was at total odds with the Commander-in-Chief. That that Commander-in-Chief was the first soldier of the nation, a man we grew up awed by, a man we had followed through the deserts and high country of Mexico from victory to victory, was as unexpected as it was disconcerting.

The little man teetered away and Mac answered, "No, it's fine for now, I have spies out there, we'll know long before they move. You won't miss anything, trust me at that."

"Thank you," I stuttered, "what are you going to do?"

"I've already started," he replied brightly, dived into his food, "I've reached out to several prominent Republicans," he began to chew with gusto.

"Republicans?" I may have yelped, I know my blood ran cold at the thought of McClellan among the pit vipers, "you're a resolved Democrat."

"I know my politics, thank you," he shook his head, resumed chewing.

"Then –"

"I spoke with them because they put Lincoln in power and promised to prosecute the war to its fullest, that's what I want. My urgency is retarded by men who do not share nor even see the need for alacrity. It's their mandate that's being ignored," he made a modicum of sense.

Had I taken a moment to think, I would not have asked the question that formed instantly on my lips, "Who did you approach?"

"Sumner," he confirmed with a wan smile.

"Sumner? Have you taken leave of your senses?" I hissed. If we had not been in such a public place I probably would have yelled, grabbed and shaken him. Quite possibly never stopping.

"It's not as bad as that, Colonel," he replied sternly but without reproach.

I had to hand it to my old friend, he was undeniably charismatic, he cared deeply about his mission, he had a tremendous memory, and he did not flinch when he realized that I now realized the real reason we are having supper miles from our usual haunts.

He went through with the charade anyway, "Ah, that's right," finished swallowing, he flashed a brilliant smile, "you're of long acquaintance with the senator, aren't you?"

"I introduced you to him at our graduation, as you may recall," I said slowly, which only served to widen his smile, "he was a guest of my mother's, not mine."

"Didn't the senator assist in your appointment to West Point?"

"He was not a senator then," I corrected his history, picked up my fork, stuck something in my mouth and began to chew. He watched. He was going to watch me a very long time before I spoke, and longer if he expected me to offer to do what he sought.

It may have been as long as five minutes that the general watched me eat before he yielded to my aforementioned obstinacy.

"Would you speak to him for us?"

"Us?"

"Us," he said in a manner wherein we could both understand that he meant the army and country.

I sat back and leveled a stare at him that was accepted without discomfort. I did not immediately reply for number of reasons. First, I was not sure it was asked as a question. Second, there was still the implication of the term us. Last, in personal terms, he asked a favor of the highest magnitude.

"What did you ask of him?" I ignored his question, opted to filibuster instead.

"Ostensibly to request Andrew to rush more troops to Washington as soon as possible".

"An act he is capable of doing on his own. What did you relate to Sumner with the request?"

"I may have," he snickered lightly, "mentioned that we are in a state of emergency and Scott lacks any sense of urgency, that his thinking has become as ponderous as his weight."

"And then you promised what?" I asked quietly, concern for my friend rising in my chest.

"Only that I would do what I came here to do, put together an army and use it quickly, vigorously . . . win. I can only do that with Scott gone or at least removed from my path."

"That's all?" I said with an irony that was promptly ignored.

"It is," he was pleased with his answer, "a hard quick war."

"I note that destroying slavery is conspicuously absent from your goals," I said as concern became dread.

"Of course," he replied as if insulted, "I told him – I made him understand – that I fight to the death – if God wills it – for my country and the union and not," his face flushed with passion, "for abolition or the Republican Party."

"You are joking," I said with hope.

"No, I told him exactly that, he accepted it and wished me Godspeed."

"In accepting that he did not bring up slavery at all?"

"He did," he shrugged it off, "I assured him that, as you well know, I abhor slavery, but is still the law of the land and I am not fighting to change that. After I triumph, though, I'll do what I can to improve the lot of those poor black souls."

"That sounds I like a campaign promise," I said snidely.

He let that hang in the air and I let him. Throughout our conversation I had been listening with feelings not unlike a man on a floundering ship in a tempest, hopeful and despairing through successive swells and troughs until he at last espies the killer wave.

"For fuck's sake, Mac, what are you thinking? I said through clenched teeth. He visibly recoiled, lost his smug look, "they're called abolitionists for a reason. They want to obliterate the damn institution, not improve anything. They'll crucify anyone or anything that stands in their way. Hence the additional moniker of Radical."

"We are on the same page, I –"

"You're not even in the same damn book," I spit out a trace too loud, drawing looks from the distant diners, "God dammit, Mac," I tried to regulate my words, tone, succeeded only in having them come out in a hiss, "you just told the scion of Radical Republicanism that you're fighting this war on the Democratic platform. You have excluded their cause – their one overriding, all prevailing obsession, an obsession by which Ahab's pales in comparison. My God, you've painted a bull's-eye on your back."

"I don't see it that way," he turned on his smile, his hands moved in support, he leaned forward, engaging. The full sale was on, "we want the same thing – one overwhelming victory to seal it – and I need their help to get at it."

"You're missing my point," I managed to regulate to a more or less normal voice, "probably because I have stated it poorly. So let me just say this: you told him that you disagree with their policies – that's fine, a lot of people do – but you need to know that they can get along with those who disagree but help them but they will destroy those who disagree and don't help.

"So, yes," I nodded and smiled at him, "they'll help and abide you in your position because you can bring them victory, but abide is the operative verb."

He started to speak, I put up a hand, "If they think you aren't doing all you could be, they will make your life a living hell, in every regard. They will savage you at every turn and on every front. So, you damn well had better win this war and win it quickly, you've left no margin for error, my friend."

"I must say, though," McClellan jumped in as if I had not spoken, "Sumner impressed me, he –"

"Is an impressive man, who will back you as long as you are useful and lead him to the promise land," I assured him.

He looked at me with owlish eyes, blinked slowly, "I don't recall you being so cynical, Willie."

"It's not cynicism, general, it's realism."

"He was most reasonable," he said with finality, as if that settled it all.

"He is not," I said emphatically, "a reasonable man, nor would one expect him to be. Not after being beaten half to death in the Senate by a gentleman from South Carolina – a slave owning gentlemen."

"That was a despicable act and –"

"Of course it was," I cut off my commanding officer once again, that part of me not outraged by his seemingly intentional naïveté wondered how many more interruptions I had remaining, "Did you ever read the speech that preceded the attack?"

"I may have perused it, I seem to remember it being quite strong," he replied warily, "but that doesn't excuse the attack."

"It does not," I said wanly, "but remember, the man you found reasonable gave a speech that was such a vitriolic personal attack on Southern leadership they forgot their all-important chivalry and ambushed him. He has the power to inspire that level of hate, and you can easily – now – find yourself the object of his professional invective. And he travels in a pack."

He consider my words for an interminable time during which neither of us ate, drank, or blinked for that matter.

At long last McClellan spoke, "I will consider that, Willie, and act accordingly," he sighed and smiled, "I'll guess I'll just have to destroy Beauregard and get back to private life as quickly as I can, eh?"

"That fits perfectly with my plans, Mac," I smiled back.

"I still need you to meet with Sumner, though," he pretended to look off into the night while he surreptitiously gauged my reaction, "it would help greatly."

"How so?"

"Sit down and outline my plans."

"It will be difficult as I have no idea what those plans may be," I responded with caution.

"Well, glad you asked," he brightened considerably, took my comment as agreement. Understandable, as he knew from experience I was going to cave in eventually in any event, "let me endeavor to enlighten you."

7. Sumner

I had probably known Charles Sumner since birth. His was certainly a constant presence at each and every important event of my early years. Always Mr. Sumner, no honorary uncle or cute, humanizing childhood nickname – not that any would have suited him in any event. Even as a young man the only title befitting him was Senator – in the Cicero, Pompeii, Crassus, paternal, born – leader sense of the word.

Mr. Sumner was a part of Christmas, Easter, graduation, funerals, marriages, countless Sunday dinners. His presence was as constant as it was consistent, he was the formidable specter usually in the corner of the room, inviting little contact until he wished to opine on the subject at hand.

Charles Sumner

The room then fell silent – even the small children – as Mr. Sumner would expound, in the manner that a papal bull is issued, on the subject at hand. Done, he would, on occasion, invite discussion. I recall no dissents – but, then again, my mother's home was seldom, if ever, open to opposing viewpoints.

I had seen him but once since I left Harvard for West Point. That was at my graduation. He was a national figure by then, the mention of his name measured up to his formidable appearance. I was polite, but cold, as his presence through my mother's invitation was unnecessarily provocative; her statement to me and my Southern classmates. For their part, the Southerners recognize Sumner and, within the then Southern probity, found a myriad of subtle ways to let him know of their displeasure. My mother was delighted with the results.

When I unwittingly found myself alone with Mother – a prospect neither of us relished at that point in our relationship – I asked, "I assume Thoreau was unavailable this weekend?"

She laughed heartily, "He was busy, dear, otherwise they'd both be here."

Her sparkling eyes let me in on the fact that she was not only not joking, she would have loved to have seen it: the nation's foremost opponents of the war with Mexico attending the graduation of a class almost unanimously going straight there. Between Charles Sumner and Henry David Thoreau she would have provoked everyone at the Point.

Mother in a nutshell.

Fifteen years later, I sat in his office while he eyed me with a mixture of the amusement, suspicion, and paternal familiarity. I recognized him by a slim margin for he had aged more than those fifteen years. His still wavy black hair was streaked with white perhaps marking were his wounds had been, his puffy sideburns were purest white. The still intense eyes were set back deeper, now accompanied by dark bags. None of that, though, diminished his intimidating presence.

When I had endured his pitiless gaze for the requisite time without looking away or, horror of horrors, talking first, he deigned to speak.

"Your general is transparent, William," he grinned without humor, "did he really think sending an old acquaintance would somehow cause me to overlook his platform statement?"

I did not answer immediately, if indeed he required or expected one. I was engrossed in the nuances of the statement – as any rational individual would have been. I started with 'your general', the use of the possessive certainly intentional; moved to 'William' although I was, of course, in uniform; considered 'acquaintance' over more intimate familiars, finished with 'platform' a term that could only refer to the political.

"As I understand it, Senator," I answered evenly, "General McClellan's platform is to win the war as quickly as possible, nothing more."

"And this he would be ready to go about today," Sumner studied something on his desk with idle curiosity, "except he is stymied by the venerable General Scott . . . the Virginian."

I had no reply, let it stand on its own merit. I was not in the position of, nor had the inclination to, criticize my former commanding general, the man who had pinned decorations on my chest. If Mac had to criticize Scott for the sake of his Army, then so be it, there was no need for me to contribute.

"He sent you to tell me how he proposes to end this thing, while not fighting for the Republican Party," sneer would have been too kind for his facial expression, perhaps royal petulance was more accurate.

"An unfortunate turn of phrase," I understated, "I think he meant that he's fighting for no party, is fighting only to win,"

"Slavery?" He demanded.

"It is the law of the land, however regrettable, his duty is to fight for the Constitution and reunification of the states – as Mr. Lincoln has stated so eloquently himself."

"This war is about slavery," he glowered, "and it will decide the issue, if he does not see this, how can I and the many others relying on him trust him?"

"His only concern is to defeat Beauregard and Johnston. I know he would agree that the government is to decide the rest."

"What a curious turn of phrase, 'is to decide', rather as if he were given us permission to settle the peace."

"I misspoke, what –", I was lucky to get that in before his forceful interruption.

"William, I have known you since before you could talk and I've never known you to misspeak on anything important," he nodded at me carefully, "your general is intelligent, eager, confident, everything one could wish, but he has one trait that I find troubling and I'm sure you have seen it too, do you know of what I speak?"

"Senator," I was careful to keep the glib out of my voice, "in the Army one never volunteers to list a superior's shortcomings, particularly to that superior's superior."

"Well at last," he almost smiled, "a West Point officer who recognizes that the Army answers to civilian authority."

"As Scott does," I took a stab.

"As indeed he does, and I seriously wonder if the Young Napoleon understands it as well as Old Fuss and Feathers does."

"That is McClellan's failing?" I asked, falling into his trap.

"Only a symptom, the disease," he shot me an accusatory look, "is that he is an ambitious man who is blind to his ambition. That is troubling."

"You afraid he would negotiate his own peace treaty like Taylor?" I asked with a degree of incredulity. Tyler, of course, negotiated the first treaty with Mexico without congressional authority. That led to Scott's ascendancy in the Army while Taylor settled for the White House.

I stared at Sumner while he pretended to mull that over. I could not see that scenario occurring, had not even considered it. To reply too quickly, however, would indicate I had thought it out, thereby lending it credence.

"Senator," I said at length, "Taylor was thousands of miles from Washington with a small army unsupported for some time. He did what he thought he needed to do. General McClellan will be fighting miles from here. He'll be in close proximity to Congress."

"Literally or metaphorically, William?" Sumner asked with an edge

"Senator, I —"

"Why you are his staff, William?"

"I'm not a staff officer, I'm his liaison with —"

"Semantics," he waved me off, "question stands."

"When we are not in the presence of the enemy," his eyebrows, bushy black things, raised precipitously, "I will assist him in the field with legal questions that will undoubtedly arise in occupied territory."

"And when in the presence of the enemy?" He inquired politely.

"My agreement with General McClellan is that I rejoin my regiment."

"Admirable," he may have meant it, "those legal questions would revolve around the question of property?"

"Secessionist property, of course," I replied unnecessarily.

"That include slaves?"

"According to our Supreme Court."

"That," he stared icily, "should not apply to slaves in rebellious states."

"Then, Senator," I shelved my first thought of 'but it's fine in the non-rebellious states' and went with my second, "change the law, it will make things simpler."

"If it were only that easy," he surprised me, "until that occurs – and it will – it is a matter of interpretation in the field," he smiled grimly, "I believe that that interpretation should be slave ownership is terminated upon occupation."

"That could be construed as a violation of the law."

"Spoils of war is a more ancient law."

"Not covered by the Constitution," I pointed out.

"And outside the control of this body, at the present time," he motioned the building, "hence my concerns."

"Concerns a general obeys the current laws of the United States?"

He puffed up his cheeks slowly exhaled, "You were always difficult, I fear law school has merely exacerbated it," as he neither laughed or smiled I chose, perhaps in self-delusion, to accept it as a compliment, "why did your 'Mac'," the nickname was invoked with some distaste, "send you?"

"He wanted me to tell you his plans for ending this thing."

"Really," he said without surprise, "why does he wish to confide in me so?"

"Lest you question his ability or ardor," my simple reply.

"I do not question his ability," he said without inflection, "what does he plan to do and, more importantly, when will he do it?"

"He will turn Washington into an impregnable citadel, amass and train and concentrate the nation's power here, for one campaign to Richmond. The fortifications are almost complete, he is frustrated on other fronts."

"One such front being General Scott."

"I think it is more of a disagreement on strategy. General Scott's Anaconda plan is not compatible with McClellan's charge as commander of the Army of the Potomac. McClellan believes it stretches us too thin for no discernible advantage while he wishes to concentrate for the main campaign.

"He further believes that Johnson and Beauregard are similarly concentrating and that the thing will be settled in Virginia in one campaign," I sat back, relaxed, my duty to McClellan complete. I waited only for an opening to make my escape.

Sumner nodded very slowly before he intoned, "I am not enamored of the Anaconda plan, it seems… leisurely, almost relaxed. It will take years."

Point made, I endeavored no response. Sumner and I locked eyes.

"McClellan's plan is direct," he said without inflection, "but will it be quick – let me rephrase that – when will he be ready?"

"When he has the men and they are trained."

"That does not answer the question."

"It is as much of an answer I can provide while right now. I can say, however, that fortress Washington is complete."

"I'll sleep better tonight," he quipped, "so we are clear, William, McClellan asserts that Scott is the sole obstacle keeping the army near Washington?"

"Yes."

"Once removed, he is free to do as you have outlined."

"Yes."

"You understand what your friend faces should he fail to act?"

"Of course."

"Have you explained to him what he faces should he fail to act?"

"Graphically.

"Well, then, William, we shall see about unshackling your eager general," he made a show studying the clock on the mantle behind me, "my next appointment is here," he rose and tottered toward me, I rose as well, "no, no, William, sit. You may want a few moments with my next guest. Wait here," he headed for the door, I imagined several scenarios, hoped against the most likely. My imaginings were interrupted when he reached the door and said over his shoulder, "you did well for your general, William."

He shuffled out into his outer chamber, closed the door. It was several minutes before it swung open again and my mother sailed into the room.

"William, dear," she said without surprise.

"Mother," I managed without a sigh, a significant achievement. She tacked toward me. We pretended to brush each other's cheeks with a quick kiss.

She stood back and surveyed me from a safe distance. I resisted the urge to cross my arms.

"You look well, William," she sing-songed.

"You look the same, Mother," I replied absently but truthfully. I not seen her in over six years and she had change not at all. She was just tall, lithe, graceful, her still pretty (once famously so) face was dominated by incisive blue eyes. Her auburn hair barely touched with gray, she resembled the young woman she had never been.

"Thank you," she acknowledged with a tilt of the head, "you are quite handsome in that uniform, I'm very proud of you."

To my credit I did not dissolve into laughter. I barely even smiled, "Never heard you say that before, though you certainly had the opportunity as I wore nothing but uniforms for a good eight years or so."

"This is different," she replied without artifice and as if the words were explanation enough.

"Right war this time?" I inquired.

"Of course," she answered with conviction – naturally – and finality – naturally.

"Yet I wear the same uniform," I said to no one.

"What is your rank, dear?" She asked as if it were the foremost item on her mind.

"Lieutenant Colonel," I answered wearily.

"That's good?" I nodded, she smiled, "I understand you have accepted an important position with McClellan," had he been a Republican it would have been General McClellan, hell, she would have called him the Young Napoleon.

"I have, but I'll be with the Twenty-first and Christian when the time comes."

"Of course you will," she smiled tilted her head slightly.

"Doesn't it worry you to have two sons in the infantry?" I asked.

"My goodness, no, William!" She laughed heartily, "No, not with you there – you, my dear, are a survivor and have been since you were an infant. You just stay near Christian, he doesn't have it as strong."

I was about to tell her about the more capricious aspects of modern warfare when Sumner strode in to reclaim his office.

"I hate to break up a family reunion," Sumner boomed in a failed attempt at good humor, "but Senator Wade will be here in a moment."

"I must get back in any event," I said by way of excuse, "thank you for your time, Senator." He nodded.

My mother remained seated. I bent down to give her another near-miss kiss. As quick as a snake strike she grabbed my forearm, pulled me close, and whispered, "If anything happens to Christian, don't bother returning to Boston."

Before I could respond, she clicked off me, unleashed a brilliant smile on the bachelor Sumner and started a conversation as if I were now some unseen sprite.

I was halfway down the capitol steps before it occurred to me to wonder why Mother was in a meeting with Senators Wade and Sumner.

8. Politics

"I am always amazed," Osgood was sitting feet on my desk, joyfully blowing cigar smoke in my direction, "how quickly you make friends."

"It's a skill," I answered modestly, "I presume you're referring to Pinkerton?"

"How did you manage to narrow it down so quickly?"

"Actually, I guessed."

"Good guess, you made quite an impression on him."

"Nowhere near the impression I would've liked to have made," I understated.

"And him, you," Osgood replied without expression, "he is not accustomed to people speaking like that."

"Acting is he does you'd think he'd be used to it."

"Every sane person he runs across has the sense to back off – as one would a wild boar."

"That sentence is full of insights on both of us," I pointed out without rancor.

"It is."

"You've obviously been speaking with him."

"One of us had to," he may have sneered, "he was on the verge of calling you out."

"That would've been a mistake," I said with assurance.

"So I explained to him, to his satisfaction," he glared, I smiled widely, "which, normally, would have made the situation even worse – he would've turned it over to any number of his operatives. I do not think your background could stand that type of scrutiny – do you?"

I shrugged uselessly, "But he's not going to do anything."

"Of course not," he answered with some heat at my lack of faith, "but it was close."

"It's over?"

"Yes."

"Thank you," I mumbled, hoped the conversation was over. I pretended to go back to the pile of reports in front of me, minor infractions from newly appointed martinets attempting to turn each and every one into the trial Major Andre.

Osgood made no effort to acknowledge my thanks. Nor did he move. An inch. He just continued to stare unwaveringly. I made him wait while I pursued a court-martial request against a private from Iowa charged with shooting at squirrels and upsetting his colonel's horse. I denied it while I suggested that, unless the private was employing a cannon, the colonel might want to get a new horse before the move south.

Finished, I pretended to notice Osgood's continued presence with insincere surprise, "What?"

He honored me by not faking spontaneity, "You have any idea what you're surrounded by here?"

"Here?"

"Yes, here," he replied.

"I would guess," I exhaled slowly, "I'm surrounded by men organizing and training the largest army this country has ever raised, although by your look you have a different interpretation," I finished with as much self-righteousness as I could muster.

"You are deliberately trying to annoy me."

"Is it working?"

He ignored the question, blew a perfect smoke ring over my desk, "Let's start with an easy one, did you know that Pinkerton has two jobs here?"

"Aside being an ass."

"Yes, Willie," he sneered, "first he runs the Secret Service and controls intelligence resources throughout the countryside – at that he is slightly more than adequate."

"High praise from you."

"Yes," he agreed, "the second is to watch your friend's back as this may be the campaign headquarters of the next President of the United States – and at that, he is superb."

"That's ridiculous," I said automatically. Osgood, however, did not make inane remarks for affect. I pushed back in my chair, waved away the hovering smoke, waited for further exposition.

"Have you noticed," he started in a way that indicated I of course, had not, "the political associations of your fellow staffers?"

"You know the answer to that."

"Guess then."

"Whigs, Tories, Federalists, Free Soilers?"

"Funny."

"Thank you."

"Try to pretend you're as intelligent as everyone says."

"People say that?" I asked with enthusiastic hope.

"No longer I think."

"I'll venture," I began with a sigh, "that most are Democrats."

"Not most."

"All?"

"All," he confirmed with smug satisfaction.

"Well," I tried to appear unimpressed, "McClellan's a Democrat and like attracts like," then something hit me, "wait a minute, I'm no Democrat."

"Probably not too late to join," he smiled without warmth.

"I'll stay unattached, thank you," I answered absently, "is it a requirement that one be a Democrat to be on staff?"

"Apparently."

"Then —"

"But," he interrupted with an unseemly degree of glee, "your own affiliation combined with your moment as the darling of the movement, short as it may have been, has caused some consternation."

"With whom?" I asked icily.

"No matter," he flicked a long ash on a rejected request, "and it's Pinkerton's duty —"

"His self-appointed job," I corrected.

"His self-appointed task," he agreed weakly, "is to ensure there are no dissenting viewpoints in this headquarters. No embarrassments coming down the road."

"Military or political?"

"Think there's a difference right now?"

"Not really," I muttered, "so staff is comprised mostly —"

"All."

"Virtually all, of men who agree with Mac's politics. How unusual," my turn to turn the screw.

Well —"

"Unlike, say, Washington, famous for employing Tories."

"Oh, for Christ's –"

"Or Jackson's propensity for allowing opposing views in his tents," I managed to keep a straight face.

"You done with the history lesson?"

"For the moment," I nodded, studied my pen, "tell me, how does Mac doing what every commanding general has always done translate into running a political campaign from headquarters?"

He blew an exceptionally voluminous white cloud in my direction and attempted to level me with a glare, "God knows," he started, not bothering to hide his pique, "you are quick to spout history to back your arguments, and you are very good at it," I acknowledged with a nod that elicited a stare, "as good, apparently, as you are ignoring history that supports the opposite."

I closed my eyes, let out a deep breath, "You refer to Jackson. And Taylor. And Scott. Generals and presidential aspirants," he began to speak, I put up a finger up to stop him, "none of whom were planning their military campaigns along with their political ones."

"Probably not," Osgood smiled in mock agreement, "but none of them were camped in Washington while they planned their wars. None of them was surrounded day and night by the nation's powerbrokers."

"Granted, but –"

"No buts, William," his eyes glowered, "this situation is unique in your history, more like something out of Rome."

"Senators whispering in generals ears?" I asked archly, "That's not the United –"

"While your naïveté," he truncated my thought with chopping block efficiency, "may be somewhat attractive to the fair sex, it's just plain fucking annoying here."

"Now wait –"

"Listen!" He snapped, humor gone, "none of this," he waved a cigar in the general direction of either my office, the house, city of Washington and/or the North, "can be found in any American history book," he noted my move to interrupt, ended it with a look, "this is unique. And unique is dangerous."

"Opportunity, too," I offered offhandedly, just to show I was paying attention.

"Hah!" He erupted, "opportunity for a political animal with long-term goals," he brushed me away with a wave, "that most certainly does not describe you."

"Does that relegate me to the dangerous category?"

"No one knows who you're behind, no one knows what motivates you... 'The man thinks too much' – sound familiar?"

"'Such men are dangerous'," I finished quietly, "you know, Osgood, I'm not about to start declaring anything."

"You have already declared," he staccatoed, voice softening like a teacher about to tell a favorite student he is failing, "you went to see Sumner. That was a form of declaration, William."

"Declared what?" I replied with some heat, "You're telling me that carrying out a favor for my commanding general was a political act?"

"That one was."

"Then I'm fine."

"No."

"No?"

"In this building you're perceived as an unaffiliated officer who did a favor for a friend just as a friend on one side of the Potomac may do a favor for a friend on the other."

"That's ridiculous."

"It most certainly is not, that is how they think here."

I peered through the cigar smoke out the window, flicked back to Osgood's unblinking black eyes, "What's your point in all this, Osgood?"

"Probably what you can figure out for yourself."

"At this stage of my life," I said sharply, "I am not all that enamored with the Socratic method."

"This is really getting to you isn't it?"

"No," I replied with petulance, "what's your fucking point?"

"Be careful," he finally acknowledged we had reached the point where continued wordplay would be counterproductive, "this place," this time his wave was obviously intended to encompass the house, "is a cauldron of intrigue – get rid of Scott, despise McDowell, freeze out the Abolitionists and Radicals, ignore Cameron until he goes away, end the war on our terms, make our friend the next president – oh, yes, and win the war in the process. In that order."

I pondered his words while he turned his attention to his slowly burning cigar.

"He didn't tell me he was going to Sumner," I started in a contemplative tone, "I upbraided him when he told me what he had done," I took a deep breath, "I was hoping I could fix it . . . that was the extent of it."

"You have noticed the shit flying around here, though?" He asked.

"Not so much that," I mused aloud, "I'm more struck by the obsequiousness of the staff. There are times I think Mac could cede Ohio to Confederacy and the staff would not only applaud the action, they would quite patiently explain how it not only made sense but was the greatest military maneuver since Austerlitz."

Osgood nodded, I looked up at the ceiling, "I can say, however, that McClellan is above it – he doesn't encourage it . . . fuck, Osgood," I grunted, "I'm here to help an old friend anyway I can and I'm surrounded by asses."

"Entirely self-inflicted," Osgood said matter-of-factly.

"Look, we'll be in the field soon and I'll be back with the Twenty-first before I kill someone."

"Any likely candidates?"

"Webb. Someday soon Mac is going to stop suddenly and it'll take the Corps of Engineers to haul him out of his ass."

"Stay away, he's connected —"

"So is everyone on staff," I pointed out.

"Exactly!" He shouted, holding the cigar like a triumphal torch.

"That," I observed sadly, "makes this posting rather less enjoyable."

"Just think," he smiled ruefully, "any one of these men could end up outranking you . . . here or in the cabinet."

"I've said this a thousand," I said with force and conviction, "you are astonishingly unfunny."

"Be aware, William," he rolled his eyes, "just bide your time until you get to the field."

"Soon, I'm told."

"It had better be soon once Scott is retired," he snapped quickly.

"I didn't think that was public information yet."

He shrugged, "Nothing is private in this cesspool of a town," he took his feet off my desk, sat forward, launched a jet of smoke at me, "that's why I love it so."

He stood and headed for the door, "Where are you off to?" I inquired with a chuckle.

"Information is the currency of this city," he said over her shoulder, "I'm off to get rich."

"Good luck," I called out.

"With luck," he paused for a moment, "I will find out if McDowell prefers the missionary position – I'm sure that's worth something to someone around here."

He let himself out, I shook my head, though I agreed with his assessment.

9. Camp

The 21st was arranged in crisp lines with greater military bearing than ever as they stood by company for my inspection. In the two weeks that had passed since I last saw them, they were incrementally closer to regulars.

Lest I worried that my clerks, farmers, factory hands were becoming hardened, disciplined veterans, their taunts, jibes, and just plain insults assured me that they, thankfully, had not changed.

Early morning, sunny, warm but nowhere near hot, breezy, I was home with my people in our bucolic, shady campsite. They were expecting yet another review by McClellan midmorning and had turned out to rehearse for their once and future Lieutenant Colonel

The men were dismissed with the admonition not to disarray themselves. I joined the headquarters staff for a light breakfast. Canvas chairs on a slight rise overlooking the camp, we sat comfortably and ate well while Phelps buzzed about.

"They look fantastic, Seth," I said as we settled, coffee mug burning my hands, "I'll take them for regulars next time I see them."

"Thank you, William," Seth replied with pleasure, "perhaps you can say a few words for me when I go before the review board." McClellan had instituted a fitness review board for all regimental commanders. That had already had the happy effect of forcing a flurry of resignations from the old, obese, befuddled, or the so clearly overmatched it was obvious even to themselves. It had also led to a shortage of fit colonels.

"You're all set on that score," I answered with a broad smile.

"That's kind of you, William, but –"

"You misunderstand, Seth," I cut him off, "no review board for you, you've been passed."

"God, I'm, well, thank you, I –"

"Thank General McClellan when you see him," I muttered while blowing on my much needed coffee, "it was his doing."

"Was it?" He asked dubiously.

"Certainly," I affirmed, "not that you wouldn't have sailed through in any event."

"Congratulations, Seth," Shay gave him a thunderous thump on the back, "you'll –"

"But," I cut him off gravely, "there is the upcoming matter the sergeant major's examination. It's in English, so that may prove to be a problem, Mr. Shay."

"Well you headquarters lackey shit," Shay started before he was drowned out by.

"I'd tell you to appeal to Mac," I resumed with glee, "but staff officers get somewhat upset at being referred to as lackey shits."

"Well I didn't mean him, I –"

"Insult one, insult us all."

"For Christ's sakes," Shay appealed to the others, "he's worse than ever."

Agreement swept around our small circle, including a suddenly ungrateful, vociferous Arnold.

I waved a dismissive hand in their general direction, "It's foolish of me to expect raw volunteers to understand the sophistications of Washington."

With that I was pelted with objects. Happy to be back, I took it, settled back, stuffed myself with startling fresh bread, and waited for someone to ask the question tangibly hanging everywhere.

"When are we moving south, oh connected one?" Arnold threw it out between bites

"Not for a while," I answered, all the exactitude I had.

"Remarkably concise as usual," Arnold sighed.

"Great, brother, thank you," Christian, with a grin, "I'll pass the word that we definitely could be moving out someday."

"I can't narrow it down to anything more specific than I'm sure we'll head south before you reach maturity."

"Your posting in Washington has neither sharpened your wit nor lightened your moods," Christian replied, to Wycroft's very enthusiastic nod.

"What's this, Captain," I inquired of him, "has my brother charmed you into some sort of alliance?"

"I must say, William," Wycroft cracked without changing expression, "I had not previously paired charming and Hanlin together prior to meeting your brother. Perhaps," an eyebrow may have edged up, "it is a generational difference."

"You know, Wycroft," I yelled through ensuing shouts of encouragement and agreement, "I liked you so very much more when you were afraid to speak."

"I was never afraid to speak, Sir," he replied with honor- affronted indignation, "I was merely biding time."

"My God, Seth," I turned to Arnold, "what have you brought down upon us?"

"Not I," he smiled with pomposity, "you."

"Your brutal reign of sarcasm and irony is at an end, brother," Christian bellowed from the corner.

I looked around the happy faces, "I'm gone for a few weeks and you orchestrate a coup?"

"To be fair," Arnold stepped into the breach, "it started almost instantaneous with your exit."

"It was fully formed before you disappeared over the horizon," Shay added with entirely too much satisfaction.

"If that's how it's going to be," I announced as Phelps ladled something onto my plate, "I'll have to tell Mac I may have found the perfect regiment to send to Utah."

While the others laughed, Phelps leaned into my ear, "I was against it from the start and you'll be needing help in the city anyways, right? Boss?"

"I never doubted you for a moment, Charles, don't worry, you'll be comfortable in Washington while the rest of them are adapting to the snows of the mountains and the heat of the desert."

"Thanks, boss."

"That's all right, Charles," I waved away his abject thanks, "just reward for loyalty such as yours."

Christian hit me square between the eyes with a fresh piece of wondrous bread. "By the way," I said over their joint mirth, "where did this amazing bread come from?"

"Our neighbors," Seth bloomed, "First Minnesota, over there," he pointed to the left, downriver, "great neighbors, mostly transplanted Maine lumberjacks. They built brick ovens, permanent huts. They offered to cut wood for our own, but everyone says it's a waste of effort if we're going to move soon."

"Build the huts, Seth," I replied without hesitation.

"Aha, so, we're not moving soon, are we?" He asked, "I knew I'd get it out of you."

"Hate to disappoint you," I answered in a tone of voice that indicated the opposite, "I don't know, but –"

"You just think it'll take a while to replace Scott, that it brother?" Christian asked.

"What?" I ingeniously asked.

"Everyone knows nothing's happening until Scott's removed, or resigns, or retires –"

"Jus' gets out of the way," Phelps completed the line of thought.

"And L'il Mac takes, over runs the whole shebang," Seth finished

"L'il Mac," I chuckled, "you really call him that?"

"Everybody," Arnold affirmed matter-of-factly, "calls him that. Everyone knows him, he's always around, talks to anyone regardless of rank – the men love your friend."

"Well," I laughed lightly, "you can take it any way you like, but I said build the huts because in the army you take every chance you can to be comfortable. You just do."

"We'll have them get to work then," Arnold nodded back.

"Excellent," I confirmed, "what other rumors are floating around?"

"Everything you could think of and then some," Christian grinned impishly, "McClellan should become dictator, McDowell's a traitor –"

"Southern operative, actually," Arnold corrected.

Christian nodded, "Something about that ridiculous hat he wears," Christian went on unimpeded, "it's a signal to the rebels . . . the British are going the land and join the rebels . . . Beauregard's getting ready to attack us with five times our number . . . Seward's running the country, Lincoln's just a figurehead . . . more where those came from . . ." He took a long, much needed breath.

"That all?" I laughed. Christian took a swig of coffee, shoved a fist sized chunk of jam-dripping bread into his maw.

"Tha' mo' credib' uns," he munched back. I put my hands up in surrender

"He said," Wycroft interpreted, "those are most credible rumors, the rest are just crazy."

"Those are credible?" I asked, incredulously.

"No," Wycroft snorted, "just fun to relate."

"Of course not," agreed the jam filled Christian.

"They're scandalous," Ashford echoed.

"Fookin' irresponsible drivel," Shay spit out.

We all looked to Arnold, he remained quiet, studying the Potomac.

"Your silence," I started, "indicates some disagreement. Is that correct, Seth?"

"Well," he replied with evident embarrassment, "sort of," he looked sheepishly around the clearing, "I like the McDowell theory. I know it's stupid, but, well, it has a certain… panache."

"You've gone and done it, Colonel," I said gravely.

"Done what, William?"

"Bought into the rumor mill, especially were concerns a general . . . good God, Seth, you're just like a West Pointer now!"

"Thank you… I think," he muttered into his buttered bread.

"You don't really think McDowell's a traitor?" I had asked.

"No, no, no," Arnold waved bread at me, "but it's so inventive, and makes everyone feel better about Bull Run."

"Fair enough," I laughed with the rest, "tell me," I asked no one in particular, "when do you form up for McClellan? Must be a long day standing in ranks, waiting."

"We get plenty of warning," Shay dismissed my concern, "the first out-rider gets here a good half hour before he comes, then they come regular about every ten minutes until he shows – no way we wouldn't be ready."

"Efficient."

"What we expect now," Christian neatly summed up McClellan's contribution to the war thus far.

"No surprises with McClellan in charge," Wycroft seconded

"How's your soul coming?" Ashford, with a tremendous non sequitur. To great merriment around the circle.

"It's a soulless city, Reverend," I gathered myself enough to answer.

"Which is why," Ashford smiled indulgently, "I'd like to invite you to services on Sunday mornings – if you can disentangle yourself from whatever vice you embrace the previous evening."

Expectant faces turned toward me and I was leveled by a stabbing thought "Have I have neglected you?"

"Oh, no, of course not, you're busy." Wycroft.

"Nah, headquarters needs ya' more, we know that." Shay.

"L'il Mac needs you, that simple." Christian.

"Christian's right, you must stay where needed. We're getting along, though your presence is missed." Arnold.

"Of course ya' have, ya' self-centered ass — we've seen ya' what, twice since your coronation?" Phelps.

Uncomfortable glances confirmed Phelps' assessment.

"I apologize," I said with sincerity, "I'll be there."

"Excellent, this Sunday I will talk about the prodigal son." Ashford.

"The men will be pleased." Arnold

"Tis' a grand idea, William." Shay.

"I look forward to Sunday's now. Oh, sorry, Reverend" Christian.

"That's fine, Christian." Ashford.

"I'll believe it when I fuckin' see it, boss, Colonel, William," Phelps seemed ready to go on but was interrupted by sudden arrival of a dust caked rider who flew in the camp, stopped in a flurry of cinders, stones, dust, and announced, "General McClellan is just a few regiments away!" Before vanishing in a cloud of debris like something out of Washington Irving.

Arnold was instantly on his feet, yelling for Biggs. The others followed, Christian ran for his company. In seconds I was alone.

I made myself comfortable watched Biggs call assembly — which the 21st did quickly, efficiently, professionally. But not quietly — slurs filled the air, Shay and Arnold strolled along the lines correcting imaginary defects. After a time, I meandered down from the rise and approached the immaculate lines, feeling a most definable pride. Further reflection was interrupted as I neared the men and they serenaded me with a deafening chorus of insults, jibes, and scurrilous comments.

I reached Shay Seth just as a second rider appeared at an easy trot.

"General McClellan'll be here in a few moments!" He shouted to grins, smiles, and nudges all around, "be sure to give him three cheers!"

He rode off, I turned to Seth, "Isn't it somewhat superfluous to tell them to be sure to cheer McClellan."

"Probably," he smiled, "but they always ask."

"Always?"

"Every time."

I processed that as McClellan appeared, tall and erect on Dan Webster, coasting to a stop dead center of the Regiment where he sat, soaking in three rousing huzzahs.

It would have gone on for hours had not McClellan called for silence. His cavalry guard caught up, a dusty officer dismounted and approached the general.

"Sean Shay," McClellan called out, "front and center."

A visibly surprised Shay stomped to that center with British army precision while McClellan handed the officer something.

"Major Shay," McClellan addressed the regiment, "I've heard a great many great things about you. I can only hope you help our army as well as you have others," the regiment laughed with him.

Shay looked bewildered, unsure, "Sir," he interrupted the laughter in a shaky voice, "Beggin' your pardon, General, but it'd be Sergeant Major . . . sir."

"Major Shay," McClellan bellowed, "do you think I don't know the rank of one of my most experienced men?"

"Well. Sir, I —"

"I can assure you, sir, you are most assuredly a major," McClellan smiled, saluted, and rode off.

The cavalry officer handed Shay a small box, shook his hand, backed away and saluted.

They were gone in a flash, leaving Shay surrounded by friends, examining his sparkling new maple leaves

Again, hence George B. McClellan.

10. Joinville

I despised my dress uniform. As style dictated it was restrictive, heavy, and the accessories felt ridiculous even though I categorically refused to wear an overgrown feather in my hat.

I stood unhappily before the Chase house – mansion – with the Prince de Joinville in a slow moving line awaiting entry to the dinner party of the week. The Prince, resplendent in a French Vice Admiral's uniform, was openly enjoying the fact he was dragging me back into society. I made it a point to make my unwillingness as unadorned and obvious as possible. He noticed, it served only to brighten his mood.

We climbed the stairs one riser at a time assaulted by insipid chatter above and below us, the utterers sick with anticipation to advance to the receiving line within – a line moving at the rate of a half crushed, salted snail.

"Isn't there some kind of royal protocol that allows a prince only thirty steps removed from the crown to cut in line?" I asked at length.

"It is nowhere near thirty steps, William," he replied with patience, unsuccessfully trying to hide a grin, "and you may have noticed we are not in France."

"If my reading of the current world situation is correct," I responded at once, "while you are presently unwelcome in France, you have all your princely powers fully intact here in Washington. I merely ask that you exercise one of them now."

"I cannot."

"Why?"

"It would be rude," he said as if self-explanatory.

"Rude to use the royal prerogative here and now?"

"Of course."

"Pardon me," he looked at me with eyes narrowed – as he always did when I employed courtesy, "are you implying that French royalty is renowned for politeness in dealing with the commoner?"

"Yes, and I am surprised you have to ask that," he responded with no surprise whatever.

"I do note that Louis XIV was exceedingly polite to the Huguenots."

"He was ill advised."

"You know," I began earnestly, the evening suddenly filled with the possibility of entertainment, "I've traveled the Palatine – they still remember your . . . what, great, great uncle forty-two times removed – seems he razed most of their castles."

"They rudely refused him entry after many courteous requests."

"Ah, perfectly understandable."

"Yes," he agreed, "beside, the Germans do a reasonable job of razing their own castles."

"Granted," I begrudged.

He pretended to become engrossed in the starred shoulder straps of the gold-sleeved adorned man in front of us but looked at me out of the corner of his eye, "You know, my friend, I am from the House of Orleans, Louis was a rather more direct ancestor than your statement would indicate – through a favored mistress I am told."

"Narrowed it all the way down to a tenth of the female population of Europe then, have you?"

A very Gallic sigh and shrug, "Your discourse on my country's history is becoming somewhat tedious."

"That your polite way of telling me to shut the hell up."

"Good God, yes."

"I'm sorry," I gestured with magnanimity, "far be it for me to continue to discourse on your deposed family."

"Most kind, thank you for your consideration."

"I do have one question, though."

"Of course you do."

"Don't you think it ironic that you, of the House of Orleans, find yourself an aide to a man nicknamed 'the Young Napoleon'?"

"You are insufferable," he began, then descended, degenerated really, into a string of French oaths that belied the concept of the innate politeness of the peerage, if not the very idea of noblesse oblige.

"You do remember that I speak French, don't you?" I cut him off mid-oath.

"Is that what you call that ghastly, guttural assault on my senses you resort to at the most inopportune times?"

"You told me I speak fine French," I answered with all the hurt I could summon.

"Ah. Politeness!" A flourish of smug, self-satisfaction. The men in front of us stepped into the house, "Try to be less difficult once we are through the threshold. Please. Remember, we represent General McClellan this evening."

'Not by choice' therefore remained unsaid. Instead, I substituted, "Well, then, I won't offer my condolences to Chase for not winning the Republican nomination."

"You are deliberately attempting to perturb me I think."

"Would I do that?"

"Yes, certainly,"

"Well, I deserve some entertainment his evening."

"Seek it elsewhere."

"Fantastic," I answered, "see you tomorrow,"

"I think not," he said without inflection, "perhaps you will find something feminine enough inside to keep you occupied and, God can only hope, quiet for a time."

"I understand our hostess is stunning," I replied with a lilt of hope.

"Devastatingly, and spoken for."

"Really?"

"Yes," he was pleased to inform me, "to the Governor of Rhode Island."

"Couldn't she get a bigger state?"

"William," he elbowed my ribs, "he is a guest this evening, mind your wit – please note that I infer quote marks around that term as it applies to you."

"That's hurtful, I expect better from royalty."

I received a perfect Gallic shrug and we stepped up and into a wide foyer. I had a chance to glance about – long enough to be almost awestruck by the eloquence of the carpets and furnishings. It reeked of wealth, studied wealth, as if earned Tuesday and spent Thursday

The moment passed swiftly and I found myself eye to eye with Salmon B. Chase. Governor, Senator, Secretary of Treasury, eternal-President-to-be Chase. Tall, thick-chested, clean-shaven, steely-eyed.

"Secretary Chase, Lieutenant Colonel William Hanlin," Joinville managed to introduce me without rancor. Chase took my hand in a professional politician's handshake.

"Good to meet you, Colonel," he said in a strong, indefinably careful voice, "I am an admirer of your mother," I made a conscious effort to pull my eyes off his curiously drooping right eye while he prattled on with the inevitable Radical Republican epithets for my mother, ending with the equally inevitable, "I admired your stance on the railroad assault several years ago, sir, well done."

"Thank you, Mr. Secretary," I lied, "Honor to meet you."

I took a step to my left to once again be almost eye to eye with a Chase, those eyes, though, steady, deep, lovely brown that sparkled intelligence.

"Miss Kate," Joinville's voice, mellowed considerably, announced, "William Hanlin."

"A pleasure, Colonel," her voice was crisp, clear, almost musical, it worked through the initial paralysis caused by taking her hand. Eloquent, tall, slim, blond, I saw why she was reputed to be the most beautiful woman in the country. Her signature asset, a stop-dead-in-one's-tracks-and-ogle-in-admiration-and-lust asset – a long, perfect, alabaster neck that allowed her to gracefully, imperiously, survey all about her.

"The pleasure's mine, Miss Chase," I managed to reply without stuttering. She nodded and I was swept out of her aura into the reality of a house full of important people, self and otherwise.

The clock in the foyer relayed the sad truth – I had just under an hour to endure meandering, idle chit-chat before we were seated to dinner and my universe would shrink to that of my immediate, pre-ordained companions.

My first thought (to be honest, my second, my first, already dismissed, was to throw Kate Chase over my shoulder and make a dash out of town) was to get a stiff drink, nurse it in a corner of the room and amuse myself watching the crowd. With luck, I would met another anti-socialite. In that event, of course, some do-gooder would inevitably take it upon him or herself to include me in something.

Any possibility of testing that theory was quickly dissipated when Joinville began to introduce me to . . . everyone. It was Joinville's self-appointed obligation to do so and no amount of animus on my part was going to deter him. I plastered an inane smile on my face, bobbed my head up and down at the appropriate moments and followed him about mentally gauging the countdown to the dinner call.

Together we went through a litany of congressmen, obliquely important personages, newly minted volunteer officers and their star struck wives. The men were brusque in their rush to get to the more important, the women managed to tear their eyes off Kate Chase barely long enough to be polite. The Queen of Washington clearly outranked a French prince and unknown lieutenant colonel.

Names, titles, and faces flashed by as we cut our way through the immense room – I was told repeatedly that it had housed several dozen wounded after Bull Run. I counted twenty-six people in there beside Joinville and me. The table we were bound for – I had also been told innumerable times – sat thirty. Two guests were beyond fashionably late, who they were was the object of much speculation.

Almost finished with our tour around the room, we approached an odd couple in the far corner almost hidden behind some sort of pre-historic fern. Two men deep in conversation, the rotund, red-checkered one with square glasses was animatedly using his hands to make a point while the short, wiry, wavy-haired colonel in an over the top uniform nodded like a steam piston.

"Ah, Your Highness," the rotund one cut off his conversation with the braid-encrusted colonel and hastened out a quick, curt bow that strained his vest, "always a delight to see you," his voice was affected clipped British that did little to nothing to hide the underlying lilt of Irish.

"As it is to see you, Mr. Russell," Joinville replied with warmth, "may I present my friend William Hanlin . . . William, meet William Howard Russell."

"My pleasure," I shook a plumb, limp hand as his muddy brown eyes captured mine, "like everyone else, I admired your dispatches from Crimea, sir," I said to the foreign correspondent of the *London Times*.

"Thank you, Colonel," he responded slowly, puzzled by something he saw in my face, "may I present Colonel William Sprague. Colonel Sprague, His Highness the Prince de Joinville and Lieutenant Colonel William Hanlin."

Sprague clicked his heels and bowed deeply to Joinville, a bow fit for an emperor, at least. He glanced out of the corner of his eye in my general direction and made a nod so shallow no air was disturbed. He then launched into a long, obsequious monologue in bad French lauding Joinville's family while disparaging the current government of France.

Done with his decidedly one-sided conversation, he clicked his heels once again – far more annoyingly – bowed deeply, started a flourish, decided against it at the last possible second and almost teetered over. In backing away from the Prince he brushed into and past me.

I did nothing more than raise an eyebrow, Joinville started a warning look that was not needed. Silence in our corner for a three count before Russell asked, in a voice that now made no attempt to hide the Irish, "Have we met before, Colonel Hanlin?"

I froze momentarily, held his eyes, realized there was a keen intelligence behind the mud, answered slowly, with force, "No, Mr. Russell, I would certainly recall that."

The man whose persistence had led to the end of the siege of Sevastopol and had inspired Florence Nightingale to action was not easily distracted by oblique flattery, "You are very familiar, sir . . . London? Dublin, perhaps?"

"When last in London, Mr. Russell," I replied easily with a tightly enforced smile, "I was sixteen and a few months removed from West Point," he nodded in agreement, though his eyes never left mine, "I was in Dublin, however, briefly, in the winter of 'Fifty-one, but – "

"Did not meet me as I was in Russia, sir," he laughed lightly, blinked, went on, "in any event, unless you do not age, you cannot be whoever it is I am reminded of, please excuse me."

I nodded, he made his excuses and departed, I waited until he was a good five steps away and was sure he was not going to turn around before I exhaled deeply.

"Do you know him?" Joinville asked.

"No."

"You seem rather pleased he has left us, hence my question, William?"

"The man I remind him of," I addressed the fern, "is a former . . . acquaintance about whom I am not enamored of speaking."

"Of course," he amicably agreed.

We stood quietly, observing the room. I tried but failed to stop staring at the eloquent Kate Chase basking in well-deserved limelight. I was entranced up until the moment Sprague sidled beside her and put a claiming hand on her shoulder. I was pleased to find she was taller than he.

"I don't see the attraction," I muttered.

"You would if you saw his bank account," the Prince replied at once.

"It's got a lot to compensate for."

"It does, and a great deal more – he is reputed to be the wealthiest man in New England," Joinville smiled with malice, "he can certainly afford to finance the Secretary's run for the presidency."

"A daughter for the presidency," I mused aloud, "that must appeal to your dynastic instincts."

"Indeed," he sighed, seemed ready to expound further, stopped as there was a sudden stirring in front of the room and the Chases dashed out.

"Our late guests, I presume," I ventured.

"Important guests at that," Joinville added, "to be so late and to make the Chases rush to them."

"Self-centered enough to need to make a grand entrance," I sneered, stopped dead my head filled with the images of two such important personages, "oh, no . . ."

"William?" Joinville asked.

I simply pointed as an older, attractive couple palpably projecting power strode into the room. A room that quieted as Senator Charles Sumner and my mother set about greeting the common folk.

11. Mother

It took them twenty minutes of curtsies, handshakes, nods, smiles, and implacable facial expressions to reach the fern.

To spare one of us the embarrassment of having to choose between acknowledging her first born or greeting royalty, I spoke when they were still a good five feet away, "Mother, Senator Sumner," I managed lightly, "may I present François-Ferdinand-Philippe-Louis-Marie d'Orléans, Prince de Joinville."

Governor Sprague and Kate Chase

Joinville's bow was delayed a millisecond while he cocked an eyebrow at my recitation of his full name and rank (for the first and only time). To my astonishment, Mother curtsied deeply and Sumner jackknifed in a bow. My mouth hung agape, it was if Robespierre and Madam Lafarge had so greeted Louis XVI.

Joinville surreptitiously caught my eye, I tried to mentally telegraph my fervent plea that the next words out of his mouth be "Arise my children."

He disappointed me by merely saying, "Madam Hanlin, Senator Sumner, I am delighted to meet you at long last. Your works on behalf of the enslaved are much admired in my country.

"William, my friend," Mother's eyes did a funny little dance at the sobriquet, "shame on you for not telling me how beautiful your mother is."

Mother batted her lashes, an act as suited to her as a hooded cobra, and mumbled, "Merci."

Sumner shot me a look of 'how could you not have.'

There being no proper response, I stood mute while Mother and Joinville traded compliments in French. To be fair, she was marvelously fluent and Joinville was obviously enjoying the bantering – right up to our call to dinner.

Joinville took Mother's arm and escorted her to the dining room leaving an obviously put-out Sumner and I to shuffle together in uncomfortable silence behind them.

Mother was not, thankfully, next to me at the river raft of a dining table. She was, however and alas, diagonally across, well within normal conversational distance. Worse, she sat between a Brigadier General, Volunteers (!) from Illinois (!) with no political clout of national import (!) and a congressman (!) from Maine (!), a personal friend of the Vice President (!). The latter sat frozen in abolitionist awe at his proximity to the Queen of the Movement.

I was between two attractive, vivacious, completely inane products of perfect breeding and fine finishing schools. They anesthetized me with discourses on the origins of Kate Chase's dress which served only to remind me of Bridget – who easily eclipsed the pair, even fully clothed.

The tedium and my fervent hope the enormous, crystal chandelier immediately above me would snap off its moorings and end my misery ended when the first course was served. That silenced the girls (I will go as far as to speculate that my lack of response may have contributed though they did fall upon the food like half-starved river otters) and allowed me to pick up snippets of conversation from all around.

It was immediately obvious that Mother was miserable and looking for any escape possible from her neighbors' banality. As conversation with her oldest son was out of the question she was on the prowl for amusement, regardless of expense.

Her eyes darted around the table like a badger's seeking prey. She was bored silly and that made her particularly dangerous – make that a hungry badger with a thorn in its paw. I knew she was already holding it against the Chases for placing her in that disagreeable state and she would have no compunction provoking to amuse herself with some form of verbal pugilism.

Her eyes connected with mine, too late for me to inspect the table cloth, and I knew, she knew I had just been calculating all that. As my mother's child, she knew I would not stop her, I despised boredom as much as she did.

Like a roulette ball slowing and bouncing toward its final destination her eyes settled, perhaps inevitably, on Governor-Colonel William Sprague. He was sitting next to the blond on my right, directly across from my suddenly armed and ready mother.

Mother perked in her seat, smiled most unpleasantly, and said, "Colonel Sprague," the use of his military title a sure sign of the direction she had chosen to go in, "your regiment was at Bull Run, wasn't it?"

Sprague snapped up from his turtle soup, eyed her while suspecting nothing, reacting to her soprano sing-song, interested blue eyes and radiant smile. He clearly bought the façade: an innocent question from an attractive, innocent woman. Had she appeared anything else he may have politely refrained from answering – Northern discussion of Bull Run was currently held in the same regard at the dinner table as sex, religion, and one's bowel movements.

"As was I, Mrs. Hanlin," he said at last with the half-smile of a self-congratulatory quipster. A few nearby diners chuckled.

"My goodness," Mother pretended to sputter. Having never been flustered a day in her life she did a poor job of it, "of course I did not mean to imply you were not with your men, I –"

"Please think nothing of it," Sprague interrupted, a show of magnanimity he would shortly regret, "just a soldier's humor, madam."

Mother tossed a 'hear that he thinks he's a soldier' look my way before turning to the self-satisfied Sprague – the worse possible look he could have sported for Mother reacted to self-satisfaction the way Jesuits did heresy.

"Quite humorous, too," she said without a hint of a smile, "what happened out there, Colonel? One reads such . . . things." She captured the attention of a fair portion of the central table, a fact Sprague noted with edgy little looks.

"Ma'am?" he sputtered.

"I would very much like to hear what happened at Bull Run by someone who was there . . . Colonel," she repeated. I could have warned Sprague what Mother became when required to ask the same thing thrice and would have had I thought for a second I could eventually like him.

He sighed, looked wanly about for alliances that were not in the offering before replying, "We were beaten, Mrs. Hanlin," to his credit he said it straight, without hesitation or anger, "it will not happen again."

"I am well aware, Governor," she smiled as she changed his title, "that we lost the battle – it was in all the papers," she paused to accept light laughter, "I would like to, at last, hear what it was like to be there."

"Well, my dear woman," he sloughed off her hard question with cheer, "it's quite complicated. The military arts are arcane and I'm sure any explanation I could manage would not make much sense, especially to the uninitiated," he said radiantly.

Mother matched his smile perfectly, "Try anyway, Governor."

"Excuse me?" Shock radiated from the man who had been in uniform for less than twenty-four hours before Bull Run. I knew he and my mother had had dealings before the war, it was impossible on many levels that they had not, so I found it hard to believe he was so grossly underestimating her persistency.

"I am very interested, Governor," she maintained a sickeningly sweet smile that had long ago outlived its usefulness, "and I just happen to have my very own military expert with me to explain the big words."

Mother now had the attention of most of the diners – as she intended and Sprague now suspected with something approaching polite panic.

"With all due respect," he started, no respect evident, "a lieutenant colonel is hardly – "

"Regular army, Colonel," Mother's change of honorific caused Sprague to serial blink, "and West Point graduate," she finished, the first time she said that in a complimentary manner.

"Still," he was either unimpressed or had become obstinate at Mother's insistence, "one cannot really grasp what occurs in battle until one experiences it. It's nothing like the books."

"I have never considered that," Mother ruminated, Sprague smiled indulgently, "have you, William?"

My sudden inclusion in the conversation held me back for a moment before I responded, "I've had amble opportunity to do so,"

79

I answered with a short laugh, "and I certainly agree with Governor Sprague."

"That's right," she nodded slowly, "you were in rather a lot of battles in Mexico, weren't you?"

"I was."

"At the end, you commanded a regiment, didn't you dear?"

"At the end," I said through my shock.

"Well then," she announced brightly to all who attended – which by then was the entire table, "we should be able to muddle through, William has a nice way of explaining, making the complex simple . . . so, if you do not mind, Mr. Sprague . . . Manassas? "

He swayed, sagged against the ropes, manfully pushed his way upright and rallied enough to give his response at least the timbre of authority, "I can only speak for the First Rhode Island, of course –"

"Of course," Mother purred.

"Well then," he delayed while scanning the faces around the table, a moments reflection and he had to know his response would be circulated far beyond our room, "as for us, I'm afraid all it comes down to this – we deployed with our division, moved forward for what seemed an age with nothing in front of us, gunfire and cannon fire in the distance until we finally came upon the rebels.

"They were a motley bunch," with that Sprague settled into his tale, Mother feigned rapt attention when she was not glancing to gauge my reaction.

Sprague gave a colorful description of seemingly every rebel he saw; reasonably conveyed the impact of the first volleys and artillery sweeping the field; threw in a few watered down yet still gruesome deaths; had the diners leaning forward as he took us on the chase of the retreating rebels; produced an audible gasp when the chase ended with the appearance of a solid line of rebels marching through the trees; got a tangible jump when he mimicked (poorly, I found out some eight months later) the yell that accompanied the rebel advance on his lines.

There he stopped, picked up a wine glass and theatrically drained it in one swig. The table was quiet, the blond next to me breathed softly, rapidly, pink blotching her neck – in my Bridget-less state I considered leaning in and whispering in her ear, "I've been on the winning side of that," but thought better – a few guests nodded, no one else moved.

Mother sported a fitting Mona Lisa smile and dissected Sprague with her eyes. Mother alone, apparently, had noticed the deficiency in the tale. Although, even if others had noticed it, Sprague need only have worried about one pointing it out.

"That," Mother began ten seconds after Sprague's wineglass softly touched the table cloth, "was remarkable . . . let me see if I can summarize: you moved forward, found the rebels, pushed them south, were attacked by fresh troops, held them . . . and," she paused, the diners' attention riveted on her every word, breathlessly awaiting whatever euphemism she now choose to employ, "by the time the sun set found yourself on the streets of Washington."

While she did not use the grossly profane verb 'run' her choice of words had the same effect – it buzzed around, over, through the table. Sprague was rocked and down for the count, the only question being who would administer it and with what degree of mercy.

I realized, without Mother's subsequent glance, that I was the referee, the only person in the room who could stop this before real blood was spilled – should I choose to accept the position.

It was a split second decision and I made it after a 'fuck it' gulp of wine, "You misunderstand, Mother," I chose, stepped between Sprague and the bullet that was sure to be the death of his social standing in the Northeast, "The Governor's brigade – indeed, his division – were on the advance, but they were not supported by the rest of the army," I began in a light, almost bantering tone and went into a description of what happens to an untrained army that is hit in the flank by fresh, pissed off troops. I made it clear – at least twice – that battle-hardened troops could not have withstood Joseph E. Johnston's onslaught, even pointed out that is was unique in the annals of history – the first time troops were transported by train to fight the same day. Russell took note of the latter, Sprague gave me a look of naked gratitude, Mother clicked off – whatever it was she wanted when she had engaged she had evidently achieved.

I finished with assurances that of course Sprague's men had retired in good order, of course they were not in Washington by nightfall, of course they must have formed the rear-guard (as if McDowell had had one). Note that I had no knowledge whatever if Sprague's men had held for an hour or ran at the first volley, never mind retreated in an orderly fashion and thereby becoming the outliers of the Army of the East. It did not matter, Sprague certainly was not going to correct me and, in any event, I held no particular malice for any unit in that late, unlamented, army – they were untrained and had no business within fifty miles of an opposing force. They were no better than militia and George Washington and Daniel Morgan would have observed their behavior at Manassas with rueful shakes of their heads and knowing shrugs. Who was I to cast aspersions?

I finished with all that left unsaid, of course, but must have conveyed the sentiment for I received a litany of 'well dones' and an obviously relieved Sprague tipped a refilled wine glass toward me and boomed, "Well spoken, Colonel, well-spoken indeed."

Later, interminably later, when the sexes separated and the men shared brandy and cigars, Sprague sought me out. He joined Joinville and I for an amiable chat, in the end I was forced to admit he may have had some charm.

13. Burnside

I was handed the file before I stepped into the foyer, such was the frenzy of the ursine lieutenant waiting by the door jamb for my appearance. I was at least ten minutes early, such was his urgency. I took it, had little choice in the matter as he stuck it in my abdomen by way of emphasis, stepped away, told me McClellan wanted to see me almost as an afterthought.

I thought it prudent to read through the file first, did so, immediately regretted showing up: Private William Scott fell asleep on picket duty, was arrested for dereliction of duty in the face of the enemy, a court martial was to be convened within the week. I failed to grasp the urgency of a matter that should be handled at the regimental level.

I was ushered into McClellan's office, file tucked under my arm, stopped short well before his desk for a general was seated with his back to me, therefore presenting a problem in military etiquette.

"Here he is now!" Mac yelled as if he had not seen me in weeks. The anonymous general leapt to his feet, pivoted with dexterity and hurled himself at me. Bald pate, thick, bushy ropes of hair dipped to his jawline, curved up to form an equally thick mustache, burly, surprisingly fast. Ambrose Burnside was on me in a flash.

"Willie!" He shouted in my now deafened left ear, "My God, am I happy to see you"

I then did something rare for me when confronted with an anaconda not a woman or my brother, I hugged back. Hard. I had missed him as well.

"I am very glad to see you as well, General."

"General?" He bellowed, "Don't you dare call me that, Willie."

"Sorry, Ambrose," I smiled abashedly, he beamed in return, "I must have had stars in my eyes."

He laughed, disengaged, slapped me on the back, "Well said, excellent," he guffawed and sat down while I pondered a military system that allowed generals to pound the backs of inferiors with impunity.

"I'm glad to see you two reunited," a pleased McClellan said from behind his paper strewn desk, "we can catch up this evening – I presume you are both free to dine with me?

We nodded vigorously, "Good," he continued, "now, about the file under your arm, Willie, have you looked at it yet?"

"Briefly, I'm trying to understand why this is here and not being handled by the regiment or brigade."

"A death penalty case?" McClellan asked, eyebrows arched.

"Death penalty?" I was genuinely rocked by his response. Capital case never occurred to me – nor should it have, it was that far outside the facts in the file.

"His brigadier decided this was a capital case," Burnside stepped in, "and asked me to convene a divisional court martial. I had concerns and brought it to Mac."

"Well . . . good," I stuttered, still not seeing it, "send it back, reprimand him and get rid of this, it's not worth the time."

Burnside looked at McClellan with an easily readable expression – 'I told you so'.

"We cannot," Mac said simply, without emotion.

"May I ask why?"

"It is . . . complicated," he answered quickly.

"I'll try to keep up," I smiled with insincerity.

McClellan matched my expression, but with a tiredness I did not share, "Let me ask you this – how would you defend Private Scott?"

"In my sleep and I'd still win," I said honestly, suddenly feeling queasy holding the file.

"Great, tell me how . . . Colonel," he sighed and commanded.

"Alright, we'll start with the facts – exemplary soldier, he drilled all day, volunteered to cover night duty for a sick comrade, drilled all day the next, end of the day his company commander drew lots to decide who would be on sentry duty – rather than, God forbid, issue an order. Scott drew the short straw, I'm starting to think he's one very unlucky soldier, fell asleep in the wee morning hours . . ."

I trailed off, my recitation of the facts had not captured the room.

"That the extent of it?" Mac asked with an edge.

"Just getting started," I answered quickly, "I would then point out that for this to be anything more than a company offense, a so-called dereliction it had to occur in the face of the enemy, then —" I stopped dead, a faint glimmering of understanding whacked me upside the temple.

"Then what, Willie?" Burnside asked quietly, McClellan stared with intent and nodded.

"I would then," I replied slowly, "point out that the nearest Confederate soldier was miles away behind a very wide river."

Mac expressionlessly eyed me for several heartbeats before saying, equally slowly, "Your point being that as there was no immediate threat this is really a . . . misdemeanor?"

"Exactly."

"Would it surprise you," Mac went on, slight smile playing over his lips, an ironic one, it turned out, "to discover that the brigade commander is from Massachusetts, personally appointed by Andrew?"

"Not at all," I saw it at last

"He is perfectly capable of using a successful defense as a platform to attack me," he locked eyes with Burnside, "and this is a very poor time for that."

"Refusing to go ahead with this farce – "

"Would reek of cover up," Mac cut me off with an angrily raised hand, "and make their point for them."

"A tough spot for everyone," I surmised, "especially Private Scott."

"You are right about his luck," Burnside cracked, started to laugh, stopped abruptly when he realized he was alone in that regard.

"How would you prosecute it, William," a somber McClellan asked

"I would not," I said flatly.

"Pretend I ordered you to."

"Am I being so ordered?"

"Just a hypothetical, so, please," he motioned compliance.

"I would, if I could, submit evidence of peril to the unit and the explicit instructions outlining such perils to the pickets. Really, Mac, anything I could hold onto to make it look like the future of the Republic was hanging on Scott staying awake."

"Just what I was expecting," he attempted a smile, failed.

"What's Holt have to say about this?" It finally occurred to me to ask.

"He's in Kentucky," Burnside answered, "Lincoln sent him, it's looking dire out there."

"So in his absence you are convening a court martial?" I asked with an edge probably inappropriate in a room with two generals.

"Actually," he managed to fully engage a smile, grim as it was, "you are convening a court martial."

"What?"

"What, General," he corrected with a chuckle.

"What, General?" I amended.

"Since you'll be president of the court, technically, you will be the one convening it."

"I have many . . . issues with that," I muttered with measure.

"I do not," the Commanding General of the Army of the Potomac replied forthwith and directly, "would you feel better knowing Lincoln has issued a fiat that he review all death sentences?"

"You assume much with that statement."

"All I am saying," he hastened to add, "is that should such sentence be pronounced I am certain it will be commuted, in which case —"

"It will go back to me as President of the Court and I will be able to _"

"Impose any or no punishment."

I mulled that over for an unimpeded minute, "What if you don't get the verdict you seek . . . need."

"It's wartime. He fell asleep on picket. His misfortune to be in a company, regiment, brigade commanded by martinets, and brought to our intention."

"There is the matter of you two improperly communicating with the Court," I tossed out there, lest I acquiesce too easily.

"Willie," Burnside laughed, "are you saying you can be swayed? Had we suspected that at West Point we might have tried persuasion occasionally!"

Mac smiled deeply, sincerely, "Knowing you as well as we do, I'd say we just insured that the defense will get every opportunity – and then some – to make their case."

I sighed in agreement, "Who will be on the panel with me?"

No snicker of victory, just a brief triumphant gleam of an eye, "Two majors, both division staff officers, both volunteers, albeit with strict views of military propriety."

"Let me guess, they're from New York and Ohio, and they're both Democrats," I ventured.

"Perhaps," he had the decency not to smile.

"Have you discussed this with them yet?" I asked the one man in the room constitutionally unable to utter a falsehood.

"Charges only," Burnside replied without batting an eye, "along with a very accurate description of you." He and McClellan chuckled evilly.

"I'm uncomfortable," I shook my head, "but – as you probably guessed I would in the first place – I'll preside if only to insure some element of fairness creeps in, at least give Scott a chance."

They did not rise to the bait, just sat and watched me. Carefully. Waiting.

Then it occurred to me to ask, "Who's prosecuting?"

"Officer from a New York regiment," McClellan responded with alacrity.

"That is illuminating," I observed, "he have a name?"

"Francis Barlow, Colonel Francis Barlow," Mac, in a whisper, as if hoping I did not hear.

"Francis Barlow," I drawled long and hard, "Jesus Christ, why didn't you skip straight to the firing squad?"

"You've heard of him?" Burnside – I assumed rhetorically.

"Looks like a twelve year old, is the *New York Tribune*'s pit viper lawyer – yes, I have heard of him," I answered anyway, then asked, "Scott will not die?"

"If he is found guilty," McClellan said in the manner of one wondering if the sun would set, "you may pocket the death warrant until Lincoln reviews it. I've no doubt that the combination of the facts, your usual persuasiveness and the President's squeamishness, Private Scott will be back in the ranks somewhat wiser before we move south."

"Will you pardon him if all else fails?" I asked, though I knew the answer, just wanted to hear it for myself.

"You know I can't, but I'm sure it won't come to that."

"You sure too, Ambrose," I asked again as insurance.

"I am, William."

"Alright," I said reluctantly, "though I'd much rather defend."

"We could not have that," McClellan sternly replied, "it would be a cause celebre with the Republicans . . . and a referendum on my generalship."

"Understood," I said with petulance, "when's the trial?"

"Tuesday."

I nodded, it gave me three days to brush up on military procedure, enough for a trial that now promised to be short and direct.

I went to dinner with my two old classmates, managed to cleanse my palate of the taste left over from the Scott conversation with strong drink while I picked at my plate.

At the end of the evening, an inebriated Ambrose – to be truthful, he was only a tad more lit than me, hence my superiority – forced an ancient, battered envelop on me. Payment for 'my kindness' in Mexico.

I lurched home, dumped the envelop in a faceless church's poor box on the way. My original gift, though, had already done its damage.

14. Welles

Five days later I had a death warrant for Private William Scott in my pocket. Though expected it was nevertheless uncomfortable.

The trial was anticlimactic, Colonel Francis Barlow submitted a brief that postulated that falling asleep at one's post in wartime was in essence a strict liability offense that entertained no mitigating circumstances. It was brilliant, compelling, and would have taken a legal giant to refute it.

Francis Barlow

Poor Private Scott had no such weapon in his arsenal. His attorney was tall, fat, flushed, verbose, and so far out of his depth as to be asea. Barlow, short, frail, ashen faced, was as cold, efficient, deadly as his opponent was obese. We had no choice but to accept his argument, hell, we would have been hard-pressed to refute any of his steeped in common law points.

The only issue left at trial, then, was to prove Scott was indeed asleep out on the picket line. Barlow produced the requisite witnesses – it seemed that Scott was, in fact and to his ultimate detriment, a rough snorer. I might have argued – after hearing him compared to a freight train, fog horn, rutting wild boar – that he was doing us all a favor of national import scaring away potential rebel raiders but that would have been grasping at straws.

Scott was not helped when, the day before the trial began, Confederate cavalry detachments under J.E.B. Stuart raided supply depots throughout Maryland. The papers and McClellan were irate, it was just as well the warrant resided in my pocket.

Where it comfortably nestled when I entered the Navy Department on an overcast afternoon that promised afternoon thunderstorms and a turn of the weather. A half block from the War Department geographically, it was another planet in reality – quiet, civil, business like. Model ships in beautiful cases lined the halls – things of beauty that would have been so many matchsticks in seconds in the havoc of the War Department.

I had no wait, an impeccable ensign escorted me through an impeccable hallway to the office of the Secretary of the Navy. I walked in to find my old friend standing behind his desk arm-pit deep in papers and charts, carefully perusing a sheaf that dangled from his smallish hands. The ensign cleared his throat, Gideon Welles put up a tiny digit, either to ask for a minute or gauge the wind.

I took that moment to inspect my old friend – it was obvious at first glance that although a member of Lincoln's cabinet for a few months it had aged him. The bags under his eyes attested to that in and of themselves. His portliness, however, had not been similarly affected, nor had his long, starkly white, St. Nicholas beard.

Completely unchanged, of course, was his defining feature, noticed by all, commented by few: the single most ridiculous wig in the history of wigs. White, but nowhere near as white as his very real beard, wavy in exactly the wrong places, made, I assumed, from the droppings of some hopefully long extinct silk worms it was as physically disturbing as it was obvious. It sat on his head like an obese Persian cat on an ostrich egg.

The ensign took his leave, softly closed the door. That sound broke Welles' attention, a sudden storm clouded his usually open face. He recovered quickly, dropped the papers on the pile on the desk.

"William," a smile emerged, "how nice to see you."

I approached, took his hand in a warm clasp, "Great to see you Mr. Secretary."

"Oh for Christ sakes, Hanlin, the navy is stifling with formality. Hell, they think these damn hallways are ships, all mind-numbing formality all the time. They're going to polite me to death."

"Well, hell, Gideon," I took a chair without asking leave, "if I had known, I would have been over here insulting you from the get go – you should have sent for me earlier."

"Believe me, I thought you'd come on your own accord until I realized someone needed to pry you off the Young Napoleon's arse."

"I would have pried myself off to visit," I replied without blinking, "but I assumed the navy was busy contributing to the war effort – I should have realized you were sitting around waiting for the army to win it first."

"Good to see that despite the uniform you remain a bastard."

"I see your hair travelled well."

At that we relaxed in our chairs and laughed at each other. Or ourselves. Or both. So it had been between us since the day I left the Goodwin and wandered into the Brown & Gross bookstore. He practiced his acid wit on my choice of books, I complimented his barber. We were friends ever since.

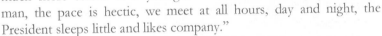

"You look tired, Gideon," I said when our laughter faded.

"I am," he answered without hesitation, "a cabinet position under present circumstances is much more suited to a younger man, the pace is hectic, we meet at all hours, day and night, the President sleeps little and likes company."

"What's he like?" I asked the predictable question.

"You'd like him, he has a wicked wit and he tells great stories."

"Great, what's he like?"

He sighed, "I don't know yet," he said simply, "I can't get a gauge on him – he's so damn calm, accepting of things, but I can see the machinery moving behind those eyes . . . I'm waiting, I'm hopeful, I like him, who knows?" He pointedly looked out the window to the White House.

"Promising, if a misanthrope like you has hope," I said, he shrugged, "How's the Navy Department? Any fears about taking on the vast Confederate fleet?"

"Don't be an ass," he snapped without successfully hiding a smile, "we've plenty to do and have a host of plans and contingencies that would benefit both of us."

"Us?"

"Army and Navy," he spit in annoyance.

"Sorry," I may have meant it, "I've been trained to disparage the navy."

"One would have thought the War of 1812 would have disabused the Army from that activity."

"Would have – if we had seen a single sailor on the way to Mexico City."

"See any at Bull Run?"

"I wasn't there," I laughed, "Osgood was right, you do learn fast."

"Christ," he sighed, "what did that prick have to say?"

"He merely inquired if you ever dipped a toe – a crusty, old toe, in fact – in the ocean, never mind knew what a navy was."

"He in town?" He asked with a crusty, old edge, I nodded. "In uniform?"

"Captain of volunteers."

"Tell the bastard to stay away from the docks or he'll be on a sloop heading to the Orient before he knows what hit him – I'll cut the orders to Shanghai him tonight."

"Why would I warn him?"

"Now you're talking," he smiled absently, stared out the window as if expecting a wave from Abe, "how is the Young Napoleon?" Asked with neutrality so studied it could only have come one who had already made up his mind.

"Confident, organized, smart, frustrated," I replied. It sounded rehearsed even to me.

"He know you're here?" It obviously sounded rehearsed to Gideon as well.

"No, I'm allowed out all by myself these days."

"Sorry for questioning your independence," he said grimly, we've had a few unfortunate episodes with his . . . acolytes recently."

"How so?"

"Solid, clean-cut young men from the best families, all dye-in-the-wool Democrats, all speaking of McClellan's confidence, impending actions, grand plans, and . . . "he spread his arms wide, "Nothing. We make requests, suggestions, recommendations, are glad handed to death . . . and nothing."

I considered that for a long moment, he let me, I noted, "I know you well enough to know you did not invite me here to pump for information about my boss or fill my head with problems you're going to solve on your own in any event."

One vigorous nod before, "I needed someone to insult without fear of recrimination or creating a major political or diplomatic incident."

"And I missed visiting with your hair."

"Stick around long enough and you may just inspire me to reinstate flogging."

"I'm outside your jurisdiction."

"Willing to bet your backside on that?"

"No, actually."

"Good," he leaned forward, elbows on desk, "I, of course, wanted to see you and, please, consider this office open to you. I can use the break from this damn all-prevailing civility. I also remember," he found my eyes, "a long discussion with you concerning the siege of Quebec. Perhaps you recall the substance of that discussion?"

'The coordination between the British Navy and Army before the Plains of Abraham?"

"That would be it."

"You did a nice job emulating it down at Pamlico Sound, you —"

He had no interest in platitudes, "That was nothing, child's play," he said with irritation, "compared to what we can, should, be doing," with that he stared at me with malice.

"What's stopping you?" I asked, suspecting the answer.

"Your boss," he said without hesitation, "and the shit going on with Scott."

"Let me guess," I started, "Scott and McClellan hold differing opinions on something you have in mind and that thing is completely blocked," I guessed this in the manner of a man guessing the tide would recede in a few hours.

"Of course – what it comes down to is just this, your general blocks every one of our proposed ventures, at every turn, before the proposals have been fully conveyed."

"I'm sorry to – "

"Do you know," he wanted nothing of my apology for things I did not control, "we have a naval board of senior officers who meet and plan operations?"

"No, I – "

"And then we take them to Scott – who last I checked was the supreme commander of all our armies. He endorses them, we move to implement and McClellan does all he can to interfere or abort."

"It would probably be easier to ask Scott to distain an expedition, then Mac might back it," I offered.

"It is disturbing you should say that, even in jest."

"Not in jest, Gideon."

"I appreciate your honesty, then. Will his attitude towards us change when he takes Scott's place?"

"Is that question coming from a member of the cabinet or my friend?"

'How about both?" He asked with hope.

"You know I am not involved in strategy, right?"

"I also know you are not a deaf-mute oblivious to your surroundings. And while not a fanatic, I think you will endeavor to protect and aid your friend where you can . . . and he needs that help here."

"That include the Cabinet?"

"Not yet," he answered slowly, emphasis on 'yet'.

"I understand."

"See if you can get him to too as well," he smiled grimly, "please."

I was about to warily agree when the door exploded open and a lean, bronzed, brown-haired man with drooping mustache slouched with insolence into the room and made toward Welles' desk.

I did not see his four stripes until he was almost past, which accounted for my delay in rising and saluting.

Which he would have none of, he was not to be delayed getting to Welles.

"Captain John Dahlgren," Welles smiled widely, "Lieutenant Colonel William Hanlin."

The captain spun, caught my hand in a bony grasp, "Pleasure, Hanlin," he said with what can only be described as efficiency.

"Honor to meet you, Sir," I answered. Dahlgren was the world's foremost ordinance authority, the inventor of the standard navy gun.

He nodded, "Same here, Sir, it's not every day I meet another man brave enough to comment on the hideous apparition on Neptune's head," he smiled at a head shaking Welles.

"Neptune?" I had to ask.

"Lincoln's name for our friend here."

"I see the resemblance," I stared hard at a reddening Welles.

"I knew it was a bad idea to introduce the two of you," the Secretary remarked.

Dahlgren waved a dismissive hand at him, dropped into the chair next to mine, threw a bony leg over the arm, looked me in the eye and said, "So, when's your friend McClellan going to help us retake Norfolk?"

15. Mac

"No," McClellan said for the third time in fifteen minutes, finally looking up from the papers spread over his desk to emphasize the last no with eye contact, "I cannot spare the men to take Norfolk. Not now, not soon."

He pushed back in his chair, unleashed a 'you're going to agree with me' smile, "When we execute the plan I have in mind the rebels will have to evacuate it anyway and it won't cost us a man."

"Mac —"

"No, Willie, listen," he held a hand up, "it's enough they've asked for the Seventy-Ninth New York for some harebrained scheme to take Port Royal and I'm probably going to have to give them up."

He was gathering steam and I had no choice but to settle back and wait. At West Point I had once tried in vain to talk him out of his conviction that not only did he not deserve his second place in chemistry and natural philosophy but that a great injustice had occurred.

His subsequent soliloquy was impassioned, well-reasoned, persuasive, and delivered in total disregard for the fact I was the cadet who finished first.

"I am not sending another four thousand or so men to Norfolk. Where they'll have to stay. Pinkerton says Beauregard and Johnston have a hundred and fifty thousand men," he waved toward Virginia, "I have almost one hundred thousand, I cannot afford to send men away on pie-in-the-sky outings.

"No sir, the Army of the Potomac will decide this war. Not outside expeditions, not taking Norfolk, Port Royal, New Orleans for God's sake, can effect the final result. It's up to us, Willie, everything else is a sideshow."

The only sound in the room was the clock on the mantle. McClellan glared at me for a long, long minute. The man had no viable way to get at his tormentors, I was their surrogate. Which was fine with me, I had been through it before. But, I was not about to be a lamb about it.

"The navy ..." I started.

"Welles is a silly old goat," he snapped back.

"Gideon Welles is my friend," I said with measure, "a good friend. He's smart as hell and in case you haven't bothered to notice, he's a moderate. That puts him in a small minority of people who are on your side despite politics."

"My side?"

"Your side."

"How does stripping troops away from me support my side?"

I sighed. Arguing with George B. McClellan was draining for one party only as he was remarkably obdurate, "He's giving you the chance to use a small part of the army to win a few victories – not the Waterloo you seek, but victory nevertheless. Let the papers crow for a while instead of chiding you for non-action."

"It's hardly all the papers," he shrugged it off, as if he did not take them as personal attacks.

"Take Norfolk and the papers will be yours for weeks, help the navy reopen the Potomac and the results'll probably be just as great."

"It will open itself when the army moves and the batteries are outflanked," he said with confidence.

"We have plans?" I asked.

"No," he smirked, "I have plans."

"To cross the Potomac?"

"Indeed."

"Dare I ask when?"

"When we are ready," the smirk returned.

"Alright," I raised my hands in surrender, "just understand that Welles is being proactive and he's not against you."

"I can accept that," he said in the spirit of reconciliation, "as long as he knows – feel free to tell him – that that has no influence with me. I move when I am ready . . . did you see what Greeley wrote yesterday?"

"No," I sighed again.

"He wrote that only the commanding general knows when his army is ready for battle, decried my critics 'palpable inadequacy'," he smiled widely, "I rather liked that phrase."

"Don't you find it somewhat telling Greeley felt compelled to write that?"

"No," he replied quickly, "I appreciate his insights – let me remind you, Colonel, that soon –very soon, I hear – I will be named commander in chief, Scott will be gone and I'll be directing actions in other theaters. They'll be plenty of actions to write about then."

"That's disingenuous, General," I said wearily, to his look of annoyance, "you just said that it all rests on the Army of the Potomac."

"You just said that any victory, regardless of scope, would ease the pressure on us."

"Any victory by any element of your army – you organized it, you trained it, you named it for Christ's sake," I took a breath, "a victory by the Army of Tennessee is not going to obscure another 'All's Quiet on the Potomac' bulletin. And that's entirely your fault —"

"Fault? How dare —"

"I hurried to cut him off, "It's your fault because the Army of the Potomac looks so damn good. The training, the reviews, people look at it as the best army in the world – shit, Mac, you've got foreign observers crawling over themselves to see it in action. That's because of you. You've set expectations high... people sour at having expectations raised and then – nothing."

"Would it be preferable," he responded as I finished, "to build their expectations so high and deliver another Bull Run?"

"Think this army is capable of another Bull Run?"

"No, but would you bet the life of the country on that? Because those are the stakes I play with every day.

"Then wait as long as you must," I gave it my last shot, "but let a small piece of it make some news – it'll buy time."

"Now we're back where we started," McClellan smiled, somewhat wanly, "do we need to do this again or can we call it a draw?"

"You're the general," I snapped, "you call it."

"Thank you," he may have grinned, "apparently that's about the only thing these stars are good for at times – winning arguments with old friends."

"Just be careful when arguing with the insignia-less, "I quipped."

"Hard to tell who outranks who with them, that it?" He smiled.

I did not, "Not at all, General . . . they all outrank us, it's as easy as that."

He started to reply, must have thought better as he simply grinned half a grin and shrugged.

16. The Willard

Two hours later I walked into The Willard with Osgood and Joinville. Joinville was in the lead spearheading our advance through a densely packed dark-blue sea of officers. Osgood was nonplussed at the usurpation of his crowd-clearing duties, particularly as the Prince's non-violent approach was clearly more efficient. Those few not completely engrossed in discussing the proper conduct of the war recognized our royal companion, nodded or half-bowed and tried to get out of his path. That, created a cascade of blue dominoes falling

away and leaving us a path to our table.

We reached it untouched. Ours was the sole table not pressed in on by the crowd. It struck me that the President would have been jolted and pestered by that mob, a mob that would have stood around his table making no attempt to conceal their eavesdropping whereas a prince from a nation that no longer employed princes was afforded privacy.

"You are displeased," Joinville said in French, the irregular circle around us widened. We were an island of cultivation in an ocean of gossip, rumor, and speculation.

"Osgood was looking forward to bulling through the crowd, your royal aura stripped him of that," I answered.

"He was not speaking to me," Osgood growled.

"Wasn't he?" I asked absently, scanning the room for service that was nowhere to be found, "Perhaps," I observed, "if the Prince had worn his crown we would have some service."

"Do the constant allusions to my ancestry amuse you or are they simply some sort of nervous tic?" The Prince de Joinville inquired.

"Funny, you sure you're not a descendant of Voltaire instead of a long line of despots?"

"I consider him royalty of a sort in any event."

"That will flip him over in his grave."

"It would secretly delight him,' the Prince replied without pause, "you know the one thing I would happily embrace from the days of my forefathers?"

"I couldn't begin to guess."

"The opportunity," he sighed deeply, "to have you thrown on the bayonets of the Musketeers."

"You're a very bitter man," I pointed out, "was there a pea under your mattress last night?'

Joinville laughed, I endured a nasty look from Osgood, "A little respect, William, don't you think?" He hissed.

"I forgot I'm with such a well-known defendant of crowns," I snapped – it was beginning to occur to me I might not be in the best mood.

"Nice spot you picked, by the way," I called above the low roar of the crowd to the Prince, " Unobtrusive, private," that last spit at an obese major three feet behind Joinville, He may have taken it for a threat for he immediately began an intense study of the head of his beer.

"Sometimes it's best to hide in plain sight," Joinville, with a direct gaze into my eyes, "but please, go on, vent your spleen . . . then shed whatever vile mood you are in," he scanned the crowd behind me, as did Osgood.

"Somebody joining us?" I asked.

"Perhaps," Osgood answered.

"So much for an off the cuff dinner gathering," I observed.

A Gallic sigh followed by, in French, "Sometimes, William, my friend, you can be a cynical fuck."

"Cynical fuck?" I repeated, jolted to the soles of my feet, "I suppose . . . sounds like a court position, actually."

"Yes," his sigh deepened, "it is, just below Exchequer, slightly above jester – another position would fit you well, would that you were humorous."

Osgood laughed deeply, the Prince did not. "Is this where I apologize?" I asked.

"One would hope you do not really need to ask," Joinville smirked, unbecoming in a prince.

'I am concerned for Mac," I started, " I tried to discuss it with him, got nowhere – exactly where I thought I'd get – and I suppose it's bothering me more than I care to admit." I finished with a flourish.

"That's an explanation," Osgood jumped in, "not —"

"An apology," Joinville finished for him."

"It was both," I said defensively.

Joinville turned to Osgood, "Perhaps in America . . . only."

"No, Prince, even here that would be considered rude," Osgood helpfully added.

"As I am the only one at this table born in America, I think I am the one best qualified to rule on this point."

"And?" Joinville demanded.

"I'm sorry," I said with feeling.

Joinville nodded, was about to say something when he spotted someone pushing through the crowd, "Ah, here he is."

A short, skinny man wearing a red checkered suit was disgorged from the blue clad crowd like red tide onto a beach.

"Zacharias," Joinville called out, "how good to see you. You know Captain Osgood . . . this is William Hanlin, William – Zacharias Griffin, New York Times.

We shook hand, I made a quick look in Osgood's direction, he gave an almost imperceptible shake of his shoulders to say 'of course I know the correspondent from the *Times*.'

"Zacharias is assigned to the Army of the Potomac," Joinville resumed, "he has already met with most of your important officers, now I thought he should meet you."

I pretended to laugh with the others while I assessed the reporter, He had thin, oval, wire-rimmed glasses that sat high up a nose that began narrow and ended in a bulbous tip that hung over a carefully trimmed, deep brown mustache. His equally narrow face was framed by deep sideburns. Behind the lenses intelligent, amused, brown eyes appraised me as openly as I did him.

I broke the silence, "We were thinking of shooting up a flare to attract a waiter."

"Oh, I think he'll find us shortly," Griffin said with confidence.

"I seriously —" I stopped, a white jacketed waiter had materialized out of the blue.

"My friends, Paco, don't make them wait again," Griffin said good-naturedly.

"No, sir, Mr. Griffin," he said quickly, efficiently, and not at all in the manner of a waiter. We gave our orders and Paco faded away.

"You, sir," I was moved to say, "are truly powerful to be able to conjure up service in this place."

"I'm here a lot," he answered with a self-conscious grin.

"Of course," I agreed, "and when you're not, Paco is your eyes and ears," I guessed. Correctly, judging by the reappraising look he threw my way.

"I'm sorry if I'm late, I was meeting with McClellan and lost track of time," Griffin, with looks around the table.

"He fill you in on when the army's moving?" I asked, laughing.

"He did," he averred.

"What?" Joinville and I asked almost simultaneously. Osgood, however, stared at us with an indefinable look of knowing something we did not.

Griffin did not smile, smirk, or grin, he just answered, directly, firmly, "He's sending a division toward Leesburg, couple of regiments across to the bluffs over the Potomac – hoping to open up part of the river."

"When?" Joinville asked for us, I was too flabbergasted to speak.

"Around the Nineteenth."

"He told you this today?" I finally blurted out.

"Not for publication of course," he answered hastily, "in case I want to go along – write about it."

"That's great, but—" the rest of my no-doubt pithy comment remained unsaid when Paco returned.

As he arranged food and drink around us, I asked, "Paco, anybody around he talking about the army moving out soon?"

Our suddenly suspicious waiter looked to Griffin, who nodded, "No, sir."

"Not even a couple of officers talking about taking a quick stroll on the Virginia side of the river?" I persisted.

"No . . . of course not."

"Why 'of course not'?"

"Cause they got more important things to gossip about today . . . sir," he said with the attitude of a rich man in a city where information was currency.

"Like what?" I ignored the attitude and asked with real curiosity.

"General Stone's spat with Governor Andrew," Paco, snippy, put out, like one forced to explain to the children's table what the grownups were talking about.

I turned to Osgood for clarification. He leaned in and whispered, "Thought you knew, sorry."

I thought I saw Paco roll his eyes to Griffin. In any event, Griffin said, "I'll fill them in, thank you, Paco," thus allowing an obviously relieved waiter to flee the dangerously uninformed.

"Some slaves from Maryland farms escaped," Griffin began, "took refuge with the Twentieth Massachusetts. Stone found out and —"

"Ordered them returned", I interjected, "that I know, it's the general orders of the army, Stone informed the JAG he was enforcing it."

"Unfortunate orders," Griffin observed.

"In place," I answered with resignation, "because the Twenty-first Massachusetts took in a fugitive slave, gave him supplies, a row boat, and set him out north. That slave was owned by the Governor of Maryland . . . that was a problem, what with trying to keep them in the Union and all."

"Well," Griffin considered, "this is a bigger problem as the men of the Twentieth wrote home about returning the slaves and their families went straight to Andrew. – who reprimanded their colonel. A Colonel Lee."

"William Lee?" I asked.

He nodded, "Know him?"

"West Point, graduated with Jefferson Davis," I answered matter-of-factly, "friend of my mother's," Griffin did not blink at her mention, "abolitionist, so the rebuke would doubly sting."

"But as an old Regular—" Griffin started.

"He wouldn't dream of ignoring orders – no matter how ill considered."

"Ah, you find them ill considered?" Griffin, with thin eyebrows arched.

"Going to quote me?"

"Of course not."

"I do."

"Thought so," he absently grinned, "anyway, Lee took it to General Stone – you know him as well, don't you?"

"He was in my class at west Point, I like him."

"Pity," he said, "because he wrote a letter to Andrew telling him to stay away from his officers as they are in federal service and no longer subject to a governor's control or influence."

"He did not," I said reflexively.

"He did, "Griffin answered with a deep nod, "was General Stone terribly tone deaf at West Point or did he develop that skill after graduation?"

I had to smile, however briefly, "Charles Stone would never ignore an attack on his authority . . . and Andrew is the last man on earth to be told to mind his own business where his men and his war are concerned . . . I suppose this has gotten worse?"

"Oh yes," Griffin almost laughed, "much – Sumter denounced Stone on the floor of the Senate."

"I suppose he was his usual gentle self," I sighed.

"Sure," Griffin chuckled, "and your friend wrote him a note that one could easily interpret as an invitation to a duel."

"If the weapons are anything besides verbal invective or common sense, put me down for Stone," I observed.

"Indeed, Griffin nodded.

"This is what comes of Democratic generals and Republican Senators," Joinville commented.

"This is what comes of an army of one hundred thousand men sitting on top of the Capitol," Griffin corrected.

"You think it unhealthy?" I asked.

"You're a student of history, what do you think?" His quick reply.

"I can't think of a single positive to come from so many newly minted generals hanging around members of congress, the cabinet, or – shit," I shook my head, "I've just described my own miserable experiences in this damn city so far."

Joinville and Griffin laughed, Osgood studied the contents of his plate. He did not have to tell me that Griffin laughed because he knew of my political adventures. Or that I was at least a little too visible,

"So, Mr. Griffin —" I began.

"Zack, please."

"Zach, William," I resumed, "while it's nice to meet you, it's pretty apparent you don't need us for information."

"Of course I do," he smiled indulgently, "especially as I get the impression that Mac —"

"Mac?" I asked, archly.

"Yes . . ." he stuttered, "anything wrong with that, he did ask me to . . . should I not do so out of his presence?"

"No, no, no," Joinville and I overlapped before Joinville went on, "it's just that he is extremely circumspect about rank, manners, and the like outside his West Point friends . . . it's rare for him to allow such informalities, never mind request them."

Griffin looked around the table, "I know at least four other reporters who call him Mac."

"He seems to be adopting different rules for the press," Osgood observed with an edge.

"My opinion exactly," Griffin beamed, "he's a smart man cultivating us, but I don't know that he understands that all the cultivation in the world is not going to appease in place of action."

"Honestly said," Joinville agreed.

"My original question still stands," I resumed, "why do you want or need us?"

He was good enough not to hand me some line about cultivating friendships and sources or other equally specious reporter horseshit. Instead, he earned my trust, a trust never betrayed, by saying without hesitation, "Because your general comes across as quite confident, if not cocksure with us, and I know by talking to those that know him he is more than another crowing commanding officer. I think he deserves a chance and to give him one fairly – at least in my paper – I want to know as much about him as possible. . . without breaking confidences."

A long, companionable silence descended over the table. Griffin seemed exhausted by his little speech, slowly sipped his beer looking neither left nor right.

I broke the silence, "Let me tell you about the time I beat George out in chemistry."

17. Ball's Bluff

It was a disaster. Not in the thousands-dead-army-on-the-run-Washington-in-peril Bull Run near catastrophe sense. Certainly nothing near the Armageddon-sized defeats to come, but most assuredly a disaster.

Ball's Bluff had no value, no military significance, no last-stand like heroism, no hero. It offered only a nearly annihilated brigade – some shot, many drowned, most captured. Nine hundred and twenty-one casualties out of seventeen hundred engaged.

And one very dead colonel. Center shot, forehead. Colonel Edward Baker. Senator Edward Baker, Oregon, late of Springfield, Illinois. The same Senator-Colonel Edward Baker who called the Lincolns his second family. The man whose last act before joining his men was cavorting with Willie Lincoln on the White House lawn.

I was in the JAG office when the first news made the rounds, ran outside to snare as many 'Extra Edition' broadsheets as I could. Disturbing, nauseating, the losses – for once the papers had an early, accurate count – from what was supposed to be a 'demonstration' so out of proportion as t be appalling.

Half the broadsheets proclaimed 'DISASTER AT BALL'S BLUFF!' the other half, 'SENATOR BAKER DEAD!' By the time the evening editions came out the banners universally shouted the death of the valiant Baker.

Any fool could guess the effect that was going to have on Baker's forty-three remaining colleagues.

I could feel a backlash coming even there in my small office. Where I was sitting, feet on desk, pencil in mouth, staring out my window contemplating the unfinished Washington Monument when Osgood tumbled in.

"This is going to get ugly, quickly," he said without preamble.

"Good afternoon, good to see you, have a seat," I replied without humor.

"Seriously, this —"

"I know," I cut him off, "I've been thinking about it, as a matter of fact, though I don't see what this will have to do with the JAG and —"

"Horseshit, have you looked at this?" He slapped a broadsheet.

'Come on, Osgood, Baker was important, sure, but —"

"Fuck Baker, he was an amateur and now he's dead. Haven't you heard the punchline yet?"

"Punchline?" I had not a clue.

"Baker's brigade was under Stone's command — your General Stone," he delighted in my surprise and sudden consternation, "to boot, one of the butchered regiments was the Twentieth Mass."

"The same regiment," I began, automatically, "that —"

"Got him in dutch with Andrew and Sumner, yes, that regiment."

"Shit" I summed nicely.

"Shit indeed."

"This is bad —"

"Rumors that it's no accident are already circulating."

"Of course there are," I agreed, "it just looks . . . ugly."

"Could get a lot uglier," he added with a glint that indicated whatever he was about to add he was going to take perverse delight doing.

But first, I had to ask, "How?"

"About two people know this and they both like McClellan, so . . ."

"I'll run right to Sumner with it," I snapped with considerable acidity.

"You know I did not mean that," he shrugged, "anyway, McClellan received the telegram with the news of Ball's Bluff while walking the White House gardens with Lincoln."

I waited for interminable seconds before irritably asking the obvious, "So?"

"McClellan read it, pocketed it, never said a word to the president."

"Well, that's —"

"The telegram also had the news of Baker's death."

I stared, numb.

Osgood nodded slowly, "Lincoln found out hours later . . . what kind of man does that, William? Not tell a man his best friend is dead? It's not like he can plead ignorance, everyone knows Baker and the Lincoln's are family.

"I find it hard to believe . . ."

"Please," he shook his head.

"Sorry, of course . . . I'm just . . ." I could not articulate further as I could not fathom it.

I stared at Osgood while I tried to think of something to say, he stared back. The more we remained in that position the more I wondered, the more I wondered, the more I became aware of something.

"You don't like him," I blurted out.

"Like who?" He startled.

"Mac."

"Why do you say that?" He asked with measure.

"You would never have relayed that story to me if you did."

"Sure I would have," he grinned, "I just would have enjoyed doing so a little less . . . but no, I do not like your friend"

"Fine," I considered, "good to know."

"For a lot of reasons."

"Alright."

His mustache twitched, he looked out the window, "You know why he didn't give the telegram to Lincoln?"

"No idea."

"Because he thinks he's superior and he despises reporting to him," his black eyes took on a more than usual ominousness, "I may not have been born here, but even I know it's not right for a general to think himself so far above your elected leader."

As that passed for a speech for the normally taciturn Osgood, I gave it solemn contemplation.

"McClellan does tend to do that, doesn't he?" I admitted.

"And more, but that's not the point today."

"No," I agreed, "it's the fact that the Stone matter is going to blow up."

"No," he corrected me, "the Ball's Bluff fucking disaster has already blown up, Stone's involvement just makes it worse."

"No one will think it a coincidence, especially if the story you just told me gets out."

"Not the way this town embraces speculation."

I looked out my window toward the Hill, "Shit, I can hear Sumner now."

"I don't envy you that."

"He and his friends won't bother looking for the truth, Democratic general, dead Republican senator, a chopped up regiment of Abolitionists, Christ, he'll have a field day."

"Stone will be eviscerated, it will mean his career."

"I don't know about that," I replied like a man who was unaware of where he had been living these past three months, "He has friends and I doubt he did anything wrong."

"It won't help," he let the naiveté slide, "the real question is how far up the ladder can they take this?"

"Depends on who they want," I redeemed myself, somewhat.

"Precisely."

18. The Investigation

Early the next morning I was summoned to attend McClellan 'at all speed'. I was ushered directly to him by a suddenly friendly and diffident Webb, thus I was sufficiently warned I was about to be put upon by the twin banes of duty and friendship.

McClellan was standing, waiting when I walked through the door. He rushed to me, shook my hand fervently and led me to a chair. My heart sank with each gesture. Had he personally offered to fix me a cup of coffee I believe I would have fled the scene.

Webb returned with two steaming mugs, sealing my fate. McClellan waited for Webb to shut the door before, "I suppose it obvious I need your services . . . immediately," he said the obvious with a wan smile, "you can probably guess why."

I shrugged with affected indifference, my regular army training pulling to the forefront. The only thing I could accomplish answering would give him an idea he did not already have.

"This Ball's Bluff matter promises to . . . persist. I've been informed a Congressional committee will be formed to look into the matter."

"Not surprising with one of their own dead and nothing to show for it," I pointed out the obvious.

He waved that off, "Of course, normally I would not care," he blatantly lied, "but the timing could not be worse . . ." an incongruous smile broke out, "I've just been informed that Scott's resignation has been accepted and I am his successor – it'll be announced in a few days."

If he had told me he had resigned, been fired, transferred to the Navy, I could not have been more poleaxed by the news. Not that the news was not expected, but the timing.

"Congratulations, Mac," I said automatically, without all that much enthusiasm. At that point I was too worried about me. And, I had to admit Osgood's story was still bothering me.

"Thank you," he may have said it somewhat warily, "now we can get down to it, move ahead unimpeded," he made a stern-full-of-purpose look, "I cannot afford distractions."

"They'll be many with your new title, General," I agreed.

"Exactly – which is why I need this Ball's Bluff matter handled for me . . . and disposed of as quickly as possible."

I nodded, it was evident he expected more. He was not going to get it without asking.

So, he did, "Investigate it for me, Willie. Drop everything, talk to whoever you want or need to, go wherever you need to go – I'll give you a letter authorizing you to act in my stead. Just get everything you can and be ready before Congress is."

"How long do I have,

?" I thereby acquiesced.

"They'll bumble in their usual way, you know that . . . I'd guess six weeks, maybe more. But don't wait . . . and keep it quiet."

"Word will get out that we're conducting a competing investigation," I said with great good sense.

"Try not to let it," he answered, apparently seriously.

"How do I do that in this town, Mac, have their tongues cut out after I interview them?"

"If only you could," he chuckled, "well, try to keep it circumspect."

I nodded, hoped we both realized the hopelessness of it, "I'll need help."

"I assumed so, take whoever else you need."

"Joinville and Osgood would be fine."

"Of course," he waved his hand and made it so.

"I'll start today," I said, stood, "I'll go give the good news to Joinville."

"Excellent," he did not look up, "Willie," he said in a low, serious voice just as I grabbed the doorknob, "don't spare my feelings, do this without regard to me. Get the truth, that's all."

"I will, General," I answered, surprised both of us by saluting.

I stepped into the hall, closed the door gently behind me and walked right into Joinville.

"Just the man I'm looking for," I said as we disengaged, "you've just been assigned to me for the foreseeable future."

He looked as if he was waiting for a punchline, realized I was serious when I motioned him to follow me and headed for my hole in the wall in the attic office . . .

. . . where Osgood already resided, chair on two legs, leaning against the wall. He nodded greetings to Joinville before starting, "You agree to conduct the investigation into the Ball's Bluff fuckup?"

"Anybody else in this house know about it?" I asked directly.

"No more than six or eight. This minute. Check back in the morning, should be at least double by then."

"How long before it's the topic of conversation at the Willard?" I asked the man who would know.

"McClellan asked that this be kept to headquarters staff", Osgood, with a sardonic grin, "so I would guess a week at most – sooner if you actually interview anyone."

I sighed, noticed Joinville looked lost, "I asked McClellan if I could have you assigned to help with the investigation – you game?"

"Most definitely . . . honored," Joinville said without any apparent irony.

"Alright then, we're a team," I smiled for the first time that day, "we need to start now – I'll need the rosters of the regiments involved, brigade and division headquarters and where the wounded are."

"I'll have that this afternoon," Osgood avowed.

"Mac is giving me a letter authorizing us to act for him, I suggest you use it with impunity—"

"Great," he cut me off.

"Sorry, hate to make it easy for you."

He grunted, made it clear he thought it unsporting to employ such an instrument.

"There is a wounded officer at the Chases" Joinville broke in, "we can start as soon as we walk over there."

"He wouldn't be just any officer to be recovering there," Osgood observed.

"Captain in the Twentieth Massachusetts . . . an Oliver Wendell Holmes."

"The poet?" I asked without thinking.

"No, sorry, Oliver Wendell Holmes the junior. Quite intelligent, I met him at a party a few weeks ago."

"He in any shape to talk to us?" I asked.

"He will have to be, William," the Prince pointed out, gently, "the worse off he is, the more vital we hear his tale, don't you think?" The last said in French, so it had a far less harsh sound to it.

"The good Prince," Osgood observed, "is very nicely telling you that you cannot afford to waste time in gentility."

"Alright," I nodded, "Osgood get the rosters, see if you can track down the orders cut for the brigade and – just so you can enjoy yourself – you don't have to use the letter."

I turned to the Prince, "Let's go, see if Dr. Holmes' son can tell us anything – if not, I think I'll have a long talk with Kate, just in case she knows something.

Groans from my colleagues, then we were off on what should have been a glorious late October walk.

19. Captain Holmes

Oliver Wendell Holmes, Jr. was a big man. One currently propped up on a small bed, shoulder swathed in bandages, a slight beading of blood leaking through by his collarbone.

He was ashen and still, eyed us warily through his all too evident pain. I did not begrudge him his wariness, it was not every day one was woken by a French Prince and a JAG officer from Army of the Potomac headquarters.

Joinville did the honors, having hit it off with the captain at several social functions, including a gala downstairs.

"I know your father," I said in lieu of the handshake he was incapable of making.

"Oh . . . shit," he smiled weakly, "you a Calvinist?"

"Hardly," I laughed at the absurdity of that, "I loved *Elsie Veneer.*"

Oliver Wendell Holmes, Jr.

"One of the few that I've met in the army . . . thus far."

"At least they read it," I pointed out.

"He does sell books, doesn't he?" He brightened.

"That's all that counts, I —"

"How's Christian?" He interrupted with a knowing grin.

I was stunned for a moment, then chagrinned – the imposing even while wounded captain in the bed was one of the tow-head children tearing through the house on Beacon Hill on my infrequent trips home after Mexico.

"I'm sorry, Captain —"

"Oliver, please, sir."

"William, Oliver, I –

"Not Willie?" He laughed until he realized it was hurting him, "we all idolized General Willie," he finished with a grimace.

I smiled, felt a chill for his obvious pain, "Christian's fine, "he's a captain in the Twenty-first Connecticut."

"Tell him to come see me, and to leave Kate alone when he does."

"I will," I answered absently, "I will . . . you know why we're here, Oliver?"

"I'll go out on a limb and guess it's got something to do with the colossal fuck up that did this," he patted his bandage.

"Good guess."

"Who you asking for?"

"General McClellan, he's asked us to reconstruct what happened."

"He had to send a prosecutor?"

"And a prince," I smiled, though I saw his point.

"It wouldn't have anything to do with the Senate being unhappy about one of their own getting killed, would it?"

"You planning a career in the law, Oliver?" I asked gently.

He smirked, "Perhaps."

"Well," I nodded, "it's precisely because of that – congress is making noise about investigating it themselves and McClellan wants the facts first, confidentially."

He either experienced a stab of pain or was editorializing in the term 'confidentiality' in association with the District of Columbia. In any event, he shook his head, "I can't give you anything about strategy if there was any," he said with an understandable edge, "I led my company, that's all . . . heard no discussions, wasn't privy to any of the conferences."

"I think," Joinville said with care, "we are first interested in what it was like – we will look to tactics later."

"Where do you want to start?"

"Wherever you like," Joinville, in perfect timbre.

Oliver nodded once and began without inflection, just a straight monotone – as if he had been thinking of little else since his return to the city, "We took the Twentieth on night march to Harrison's Island – that was quite a lark . . . a camping adventure, really . . ." he looked up furtively.

"I understand, perfectly," I smiled, "Mexico started the same way," I reassured him.

"Good," his return smile ended abruptly, "there were three boats waiting to take us across to Virginia – three, they could hold about twenty-five each . . ." he glared as if defying us to do the math, "it took all night to cross.

"As the sun came up, we started to hear pop-pop-pop from up above – nothing constant, but not fading or going away either. We landed at the foot of a steep hill, the firing was directly above, a couple of pickets pointed the way up a narrow cow path.

"That was a tough little climb, we had these greatcoats on —"

"Greatcoats?" Joinville asked.

He nodded with a strange smile, "Gifts from the Colonel's mother and her friends on Beacon Hill – blue-gray, think, lined in yellow, warm as hell but —"

"A total pain in the ass on a march," I finished for him."

"Sure were," he agreed, "damn things kept snagging on brambles, branches . . . by the time we got up top we were exhausted and pissed enough to strip them off and toss them into the trees.

"We formed up – the Fifteenth Mass was already there, pretty much just standing around, we formed with them. We were in a wide . . . clearing, the far end was all brush and timber, puffs of smoke drifting out, we had a skirmish line out near it, they were firing away into the woods. . there were a few casualties lying about, untended because it was pretty evident that you didn't want to get too close to that end of the clearing."

He took a deep, certainly painful breath, agonizingly rearranged himself in the bed, made himself comfortable while declining our help, though he did accept a glass of water from Joinville.

Resettled, he went on, "We settled in, made some coffee, took a look behind us – straight, nasty drop down to the Potomac – all rocks, trees, scrub.

"We kept sending out skirmish lines, they'd fire for a while, take some hits, come back . . . every time it seemed like the rebel fire was picking up . . . our colonel, Devens, conferred with their colonel – imagine they were discussing the pretty clear fact we didn't have the men to go into the woods and we couldn't stay exposed where we were while some hick Confederate Paul Revere rallied the countryside."

The captain, at war for a few months now, how just completed a perfect tactical summation.

"I think Lee was about to end it and order us down – I hope Lee was thinking that – but we'll never know because that's when Baker came riding up out of nowhere. Rode in like we were all on parade – he waved at us, believe it or not . . . his men were right behind him, pulling two cannon – no idea how they got them up the trail but we damn well knew they weren't going back down.

"Baker conferenced with Lee and Devens, the guns were wheeled to the front and we began to fire into the forest."

"They just started firing into the trees?" I blurted out.

"Yeah," he took a long sip from a glass offered by a rapt Joinville.

"Any idea what they thought they'd accomplish firing into the woods?"

"Can't answer that," he sighed, Joinville wiped a sheen of sweat of his forehead, "but I sure as hell can tell you what it did."

"What?"

"It pissed the rebels off, that's what it did – like bashing a bee hive with a baseball bat . . . their fire picked up, they just pelted the artillerymen – in no time infantry had to fill in on the guns, after a while it was all infantry and they were being dropped too."

"All this time," Joinville asked, befuddled, "your regiment just stood there?"

"No place to go, Prince," Oliver replied wearily, "except the few that went out in skirmish lines or serviced the guns . . . no one to shoot at, no place to maneuver ."

"What were the rebels waiting for then?" Joinville asked at length.

"More men to pack into the clearing," I answered with resignation, "why waste bullets?"

"Well, that's what they got," a look of disgust overtook Oliver's face, "the Tammany Regiment came up, filed in right next to us . . .you must be right, Colonel, 'cause that's when the rebels really starting firing … two or three full volleys . . . scared the piss out of us. When it ended there was dead silence while we looked around for casualties.

"Then everybody started to laugh, falling down laughter – not a man had been hit but our greatcoats were fucking riddled! Just shredded in the trees."

He smiled, looked around the room, blinked, the smile faded, "That's it for me," he threw up his hands, albeit gingerly, "the cannon fired, I took a step forward, next thing I know I'm on my back looking at the sky feeling like a sledgehammer had swung down on my collarbone."

"And so . . ." Joinville began.

"Prince," Holmes sagged, suddenly looked sick and smaller, "I'm alive because I got hit early – they dragged me down the cow path, put me and a few others on the bottom of a sheet metal boat in rancid water mixed with blood that made me heave my guts out . . . and they got me across the Potomac, tossed us on the bank and went back."

Joinville shook his head in empathy, asked, "Were you still on the bank when the retreat began, did you witness any of it?"

Holmes laughed, short, bitter, painfully, "Retreat? Is that what they're calling it?"

"Can read it to you from the *Intelligencer* if you like," I answered.

"No need," he rolled his eyes.

"What did you see?" Joinville, quietly.

"Nothing for a long while – though I heard plenty . . . the firing got steadier and steadier . . . no more cannon fire . . . then more boats with wounded . . . then boats without wounded . . . then sustained, rolling volleys and that fucking battle screech of theirs . . then our men flying over the escarpment, bouncing down off the rocks and trees, more spilling out of the cow path . . . your average pure, fucking pandemonium.

"Last thing I saw before they bundled me up into an ambulance was a bunch of white-eyed men running into the river, swamping the boats, trying to swim . . . just as well I didn't see the rest, I'm told."

He was sweating profusely, his eyes had been shut all through the last of it, he opened them and looked at us almost apologetically.

I recognized the look, the guilt of the survivor, I patted him on the good shoulder, thanked him, promised to send Christian, and went straight to the neatest tavern, Joinville close behind.

20. Devens

With a week's retrospective it was clear October 21st had been a bad day for Harvard Alumni, Boston Society, and Tammany Hall. The casualty lists were a who's who: Colonels Cogswell and Lee, Major Paul Revere and a host of slightly lower ranked scions of Boston and New York now resided in a Richmond jail.

For the most part, the regiments that had rowed over to Ball's Bluff and destruction could be described as blue blooded. Unhappy news for those whose future employment and/or place in history was linked to the fiasco. Ball's Bluff's casualties were very much missed, very much lamented by the kind of people who were used to being heard when they were unhappy. By other important people.

Joinville and I were running out of leaders to interview.

We had gone through close to a dozen NCOs, junior officers, and enlisted men, all with stories similar to Holmes, none with much insight beyond simply trying to survive the day.

Our pool of interviewees would have deepened, vastly, had we been able to get passes to Richmond. The the men held there were not going to be exchanged anytime soon – if ever.

All due to the Navy.

The South, lacking anything close to a real navy, issued Letters of Marque with impunity. Scores of privateers took up the challenge and raided our merchant fleet mercilessly. They were as successful as American privateers were in every war: very.

Just after Ball's Bluff a privateer was taken by the Navy. The unfortunate vessel was further stigmatized by sporting the name The Jeff Davis. Lincoln threatened to hang the crew – or at least the officers – as pirates in a dubious attempt to discourage others from pursuing vast riches.

Jefferson Davis, never known for either a sense of humor or irony, promptly announced he would hang one Union officer for each privateer so dealt. An excellent threat from his viewpoint, Ball's Bluff had provided enough prisoners to back that up for an Armada's worth of captured privateers.

At that point anyone following the Ball's Bluff story would have guessed it would get worse – as it did. The Philadelphia District Court sentenced The Jeff Davis' officers to death; in the darkness of a Richmond prison lots were drawn. Colonel William Lee, West Point classmate of Jefferson Davis and second oldest officer in the Union army, and Major Paul Reeve, grandson of the midnight riding silversmith, drew the short straws, clemency was denied, execution scheduled, the press had a field day.

Ball's Bluff, then, was the military disaster that kept on giving. Lincoln commuted the death sentences to derision from the Radicals for being soft; from everyone else for being indecisive. One would and could not blame him a whit for blaming whatever instrument of fate that had so generously provided the Confederacy with hostage fodder.

The news of our nosing about spread through the tavern mobs to the point where we were approached with information, rumor, and pure speculation at every opportunity.

We set up shop, finally, in Joinville's palatial apartments off the Mall, thereby avoiding the overload of information proffered by those who could not find Ball's Bluff on a map.

We spent two weeks compiling reports, waiting for Osgood to resurface, sojourned out only to interview survivors and to join McClellan and the rest of the staff in a pre-dawn farewell to General Scott. The old, ailing, general said his brief goodbyes in a torrential rain and departed into the gloom. I was depressed until I discovered he had ensconced himself at Delmonico's where he was more than able to imbibe his beloved terrapin at his leisure. Perhaps the one happy officer left in the Union Army.

Eventually, Joinville and I escaped the city and rode west to the campsite of the revamped 15th Massachusetts. After many attempts, we had finally managed to wrangle an appointment with Colonel Charles Devens.

I had never met Charles Devens. I was not predisposed to him in any way, really; I knew of him, of course, but had never given him much consideration.

He, however, had not been similarly ignored by Mother. She had very vocally, very publicly – in words quoted with some admiration in much of the north and with despair, fury, and righteous indignation by most of the mid-east and all of the south – eviscerated the man for his decision in the Thomas Sims affair some ten years ago.

At the time Devens was the U.S. Marshal for Massachusetts. He had the temerity to follow direct orders from Washington and remand an escaped slave, Thomas Sims, back from whence he came and into slavery. That Devens objected to the odious task, that he attempted to purchase Sims' freedom from his own purse, did nothing to call off Mother or her minions. Hence the term 'Abolitionist'.

The moment we met it was obvious the sins of the mother were to be taken out on the son. The only living soul north of the Potomac who had wielded authority at Ball's Bluff made it clear he wanted nothing to do with me and was being only as forbearing as military decorum demanded.

He was short, brusque even to Joinville, had dull reflectionless eyes, was straight backed, straight laced, rigid. I had no problem believing the three sergeants we had just interviewed who claimed he was a martinet of the first order.

He led us to chairs under a copse of elms, our asses had barely touched canvas before he demanded, "What do you need to know?" with a delightful combination of icy authority and arrogance, face frozen, tawny mustache twitching.

"Simply," Joinville started, with a look to me to indicate he had already picked up on the colonel's mood as regarded the Hanlins, "what happened, in your words, your way, at your pace."

He considered that for a long moment – or pretended to just to annoy us. Then he launched into it without preamble, "The Fifteenth was in the van of the brigade . . ."

I knew at once he had rehearsed his account. A good lawyer, he was ready. He had thought it all out with his edits and asides. What he was telling us was all we were going to get, questions were a waste of time.

This was a careful man, we could have saved ourselves the ride and taken a letter. A look passed between Joinville and me, he knew it as well.

Devens repeated everything we had been told by everyone we had interviewed thus far. He was a colonel, but he affected to know no more than his NCOs and privates. Certainly less than Holmes.

I despaired of learning anything until he mentioned the appearance of Colonel Baker.

Joinville caught his tone immediately, cut into his narrative with, "You do not seem much enamored of Senator Baker."

There was a noticeable spasm-like flutter of Baker's eyelids before, "He was a fine politician." He rearranged himself in his chair, had the look of a cross examiner interrupted by a specious objection.

"Baker showed up just as Lee said he considered our position untenable, at best. Here was an old professional telling me we were in essence fucked if we stayed, fucked if we left and here comes Baker with his Pennsylvanians and two cannon.

"I thought the guns were our salvation, said so to Lee – he just rolled his eyes, said 'useless up here.' Then Baker came up to us and, I shit you not, said 'I congratulate you on the prospect of battle.'

"Lee mumbled something about already being in one, Baker rode through our lines yelling 'you want to fight, don't you boys'.

He took a long breath, I was fairly sure it was rehearsed as well, "I thought Lee would have apoplexy – we were standing naked on a hill, woods filling up with rebels and we've got a pedagogue in command over a life-long professional solely by virtue of being elected to the senate by a bunch of Oregon hicks . . . and he's yelling platitudes while the rebels kept massing."

By then, Devens was grasping the armrests of his chair hard enough to turn his knuckles white, the effort to control his temper showed in red splotches that sprouted on his face and neck.

He went on, still rehearsed I guessed, but now struggling to stay calmly on script, "The cannons were like magnets drawing rebel fire, the only thing I saw them accomplish was knock down a bunch of branches while the men who served them were dropped.

"But Baker kept replacing the gunners, like he didn't notice, went on doing so until the Tammany Regiment came up. Their colonel came to us on the jog – I think you know him, Hanlin, Cogswell —"

"Milton Cogswell," I nodded, "yes, he's —"

"A damn fine soldier," Devens spit, "total professional, took him seconds to figure out we were in a bad spot, started to suggest a fall back when Baker rode back, want to guess how he greeted Cogswell?"

He glared as if daring us respond. When we did not he told us, "Baker greets the man with 'One blast upon your bugle horn, is worth a thousand men.'"

He looked to us for reaction, I simply said, "Not the place for Walter Scott."

"No, and not the place for us, but Baker wouldn't hear of it . . . though Cogswell tried . . . kept trying while the rebel fire picked up . . . he finally told Baker flat out that the ability to quote poetry under fire was no substitute for military sense."

"How'd Baker take that?" Joinville asked.

"We'll never know, Joinville, because he pitched off his horse and was dead before he hit the ground."

"Really, gentlemen, the rest is a blur," he stared out toward the Potomac, "we tried to withdraw, the rebels flooded in, it became a rout."

He crossed his arms, dared us to throw a question at him.

"How did you get back to Maryland, Colonel?" Joinville asked.

Devens smiled for the first time, uncrossed his arms, "My father believed swimming built character. I hated him for it, but I swam back. Current was a bit strong, but being shot at was a motivation. Lost a good pair of boots and a fine sword, but I'm here …"

He refolded his arms, glared defiantly. We rose, thanked him and made to leave.

I had my back to him when he spoke, a hard edge to his words, "You don't know, do you?"

"How's that?" I turned back.

"McClellan," he rose, moved slowly to us, "issued a circular to his generals, a short treatise on Ball's Bluff . . . it was all Baker's fault."

Any attempt on my part to speak would have been unintelligible, so I stood mute. Joinville somehow found his voice, "No, we were not aware," somehow he said it without anger, hurt, or surprise.

"Here," Devens said with disgust, reached in to his back pocket and pulled out a folded paper, "take it."

He thrust it in Joinville's hand, "Tell me, Prince, anybody at your headquarters have a fucking clue what they're doing?"

He did not wait for the answer I did not have, spun on his heels and strode away.

21. Committees

October 30, 1861

My Fellow Officers:

As we prepare for the move southward and the glorious victory that awaits, we must remain ever confident and focused on our ultimate goal for it is in our power alone to end this war and reunite the nation. The events in front of Leesburg on Monday are being held up by our enemies as proof we are not up to the task. That incident, while regrettable, is not indicative of the strength, readiness or leadership of the Army of the Potomac.

Ball's Bluff, tragic as it was, was an aberration. While a serious loss, it was a most gallant fight on the part of our men, who displayed coolness and courage. We continue to have the utmost confidence in them.

The setback was caused by the immediate commander. While a gifted orator and politician, he was an amateur and an impulsive one at that. His actions exceeded his orders, his actions, while undoubtedly inspired by patriotism and a sense of duty not yet disciplined by military seasoning, were unauthorized and beyond the accepted scope of his responsibilities. .

◊

It went on in that vein for two pages, small print, devolving into a polemic on duty, responsibility, organization, the glorious cause and the future deification of the Army of the Potomac.

I read a third of it before its overwrought prose got to me and I not so courteously tossed it back to Joinville. Having already read it thoroughly, he rolled his eyes and threw it behind his chair.

We were in Joinville's spacious apartments waiting for Osgood, neither of us particularly pleased with the existence, never mind distribution thereof, of the flyer.

"If a regimental colonel, even one involved, has seen that," I addressed the wall, "then —"

"It has been seen by everyone," Joinville finished.

"How long before the men in the Richmond prisons are reading it?" I asked, only half in jest.

"A week at most," he answered anyway, probably with a fair degree of accuracy, "I think we must also assume this is in wide circulation in Congress."

"A little primer," I opined, "before they start their investigation – or a not so subtle suggestion that they drop the matter before they sully their colleague's reputation."

"You think," he asked with a not so perplexed expression, "George is capable of such Machiavellian ploys?"

"I didn't a month ago," I answered quickly, "but this town is infectious."

"Unhealthy for all concerned."

"Worse for an inactive army."

"They are drilled almost unmercifully," he corrected, "they are hardly inactive."

"That activity has really cut down on the social scene, hasn't it?"

"The point is taken," he grudgingly admitted, "it is hardly an ideal situation, but —"

He stopped when Osgood entered the sitting room, flung himself into an overly plush chair, landed with a 'poof' of compressed down and looked up sheepishly.

"Not quite the entrance you envisioned," I pointed out.

"Somewhat anti-climactic, yes," he smiled disgustedly.

"I'm going to go way out on a limb here and guess that you're not brimming over with good news," I ventured.

"I am not brimming over with anything," he groused, "except the wish to get good, stinking drunk and forget the last weeks."

"Informative," I said, girded for what was sure to come, "you know, we can't commiserate with you unless you fill us in, otherwise you're drinking alone."

"Well," he smiled thinly, "I suppose I cannot have that – but I warn you, to fill you in on everything is to invite a hangover."

Joinville stood, walked to the far corner of the room, returned with a brandy decanter and three snifters. He placed them with a dull thud on the coffee table, poured out three tall measures, "We might as well start now," he said with bravado, "To bad news shared with good friends."

We clicked glasses and each took a pull on what turned out, not surprisingly, to be extraordinary cognac.

"Exiled but not cut off from a supply of good spirits, is that part of the deal?" I asked

"I am French," he replied with a smile, "there are limits to the depravations one is forced to accept even when one is out of favor. The Revolutionaries did not hesitate to remove Louis head, they would not have thought to deprive him of fine food and spirit – that would have been inhumane."

"Viva La France," I muttered, motioned to Osgood to feel free to interrupt with his report.

"Fine," Osgood understated and began, "I will start with this tidbit, just so you know what the atmosphere around here is becoming.

"Congress will be investigating Ball's Bluff, as you have already assumed. They will also be investigating the conduct of the war thus far. Three Republicans have formed the Joint Committee on the Conduct of the War and will start taking testimony in December – Trumbull, Chandler, the chair is Wade."

"A triumvirate of Radicals," I, needlessly, pointed out, "Wade makes Sumner seem tame."

"The three of them met with McClellan a few days after Ball's Bluff at Francis Blair's house. Grilled him until the early morning hours. Said they would not agree to accept Scott's resignation and McClellan's promotion until he satisfied them he would prosecute the war, hard, now," Osgood finished with a prodigious gulp of alcohol.

"Obviously, he convinced them," I muttered, "he was damned sure when he told me Scott was out and he was in."

"He also promised the army would move out at the beginning of December."

"Are we?" Joinville asked, more in surprise than in question.

"See any evidence of that, especially since McClellan just scheduled a grand review of the army for November thirtieth?" Osgood sighed.

"If Mac thinks Wade will let him back off on a promise he's – "

"Much mistaken," Joinville finished.

"Insane," I corrected.

Joinville conceded, "If he does not move us south and the committee sits in December —"

"They will eviscerate him," Osgood finished, "they will start with Ball's Bluff and work down – and, let's face it, there's no other body of work by the Army of the Potomac to present to the Committee, other than one half-assed crushing rout that got a popular senator killed."

"The focus starts solely with that event," Joinville put it concisely, "and even if that can be put aside as handily as the flyer suggests, there is the matter of what he is doing with the army today."

"Better to be in the field," I, again needlessly, added.

"Sparring with the rebels will alleviate the necessity to spar with Congress," Joinville summed up perfectly.

"He'll be sparing with only part of Congress," I offered, "the radical part, the part that already suspects him for his Democratic leanings, his —"

"Democratic leanings?" Osgood sneered, "You make it sound like he dabbles in politics as an aside."

Osgood drained his glass and looked at us with abject world weariness.

"Your naïveté, gentlemen," he refilled his snifter without losing a beat, "is as understandable as it is misplaced. If your general is a tenth the field officer he is politician the South is doomed the moment he takes the field," satisfied, he drank.

"I'm assuming," said I who knew him too well, "you can adequately explain that."

"I am afraid I do not see it myself," Joinville echoed quietly, though I judged by the look in his face he had a clearer idea of where Osgood was going than I did.

'McClellan is in it up to his eyeballs," Osgood made it clear he was only filling us in as a favor, "while professing to abhor politics," he glared at me, "with your help he managed to maneuver Scott out of the picture – that was needed, the army had two commanders, the choice was clear, the thirty year old fresh off a victory over the seventy year old with gout. No problem, had to be done, however distasteful.

"McClellan, though, made promises to the Radicals while courting the Democrats, and that's not only deadly, it's foolish — unless you have ambitions. And as McClellan's latest conquest is Edwin Stanton, he's —"

"Stanton?" Joinville interrupted.

"Great trial lawyer," I answered, "Buchannan's Attorney General, leading democrat..."

"God save us from the lawyers," Osgood sighed.

"Amen," I agreed without irony, "Stanton's the face of the party and no admirer of Lincoln or —"

"Republicans in general and abolitionists in full," Osgood went on, "and therein lies the crux of it. To promise Republicans to prosecute the war to the fullest is to promise destruction of the Confederate armies and the institution of slavery.

"Whereas, to fight for the Democrats is to prosecute the war only to the extent of defeating the rebel army, shaking hands, reuniting the country and going home," Osgood put the political seminar on hold to take a draught of cognac.

"It may sound almost the same – would to me if I had hopped off the boat a few months ago – but, of course, they are not remotely so. Add the simple fact that the longer it takes to defeat the South in the field, the more powerful the Democrats, the weaker the Republicans, a formula well known to both parties. And there is your general's problem, a problem he could not have made worse had he designed a plan to do so."

"Any delay," Joinville made the connections as only a deposed royal could, "by Mac is sure to be seen as an attack on the Republicans, and a betrayal."

"Treason, nothing less," Osgood confirmed.

"George must maintain his professional prerogatives, surely," Joinville replied with some skepticism, "attack only when conditions favor

"He bartered that away in his haste to oust Scott," Osgood quickly answered, cynical smile in play, "he made promises that he will be held to. In reality he has until Congress reconvenes in

December, then the sniping will begin. It will grow louder every day he appears to be sitting."

We sat in silence, sipping slowly but regularly, each lost in thought. Mine came back to the immediate problem at hand and the, in my mind, undoubted cause of Osgood's sudden discourse.

"Ball's Bluff is Mac's Achilles heel?" I asked.

Osgood exhaled sharply, "I do not know yet," said simply but with a certain edge.

"Christ," I probed, "you've got the rest down cold, you must have an opinion."

"One unsupported by evidence," he stared with defiance.

Two questions came to me at once, I chose the first, "You can't find evidence or you haven't looked yet?"

"I've looked," he smiled viciously, "and I can say with certainty that every copy of every order officially issued from the headquarters of the Army of the Potomac concerning the Ball's Bluff operation are currently missing."

That effectively answered my second question, "I would suppose then," I said with a weariness I felt through the warm haze of the best (or most) cognac I had ever had, "I had better talk to General Stone,"

"You think?" Osgood sneered and poured.

THE FALCON

22. Royalty

The Springfield felt good against my shoulder. It felt good even after I fired and it did everything it could to burst through my scapula. As the last weapon I fired in anger was a rifle, the Springfield's accuracy did not surprise me nearly as much as the powerful kick. I assumed that was mostly attributable to the .577 caliber minie ball that blew tightly down the long, grooved barrel. A prodigious chunk of lead.

I had always been a good shot, had always enjoyed good eyesight, and so managed to find the targets with some degree of accuracy – although nowhere near the consistency or precision of Sergeant Robert Hughes.

He stood over my right shoulder making guttural sounds of approval while having the decency not to make any direct comments-they would have sounded patronizingly trite coming from Le Longue Carabine himself.

I fired downhill on a range designed by Shay and built by the 1st Minnesota, the 21st's bosom friends. A series of targets at varying intervals down to the bank of the Potomac. Several thoughts ran through me as I fired, thoughts that not even the pain of the butt trying mightily to rip my shoulder off could dissolve.

The first, foremost, as I fired a rifle for the first time in nine years, was to fire low. The Springfield, as that bruising kick illustrated, could throw a bullet over half a mile and still have enough velocity to kill. With the Potomac as my backdrop, I had an image of firing high, putting a bullet over the river and killing some poor innocent going about his business. A quick flash of self-pity added the particular that the victim would inevitably be carrying Jeff Davis' surrender papers when struck by a Yankee bullet.

Second, I really could not get over the accuracy of the piece even as the distances to the targets lengthened considerably. Once I adjusted to the sights I simply hit what I fired at. No unexpected tumbling, fluttering, wind influenced, sudden gyration of a ball such as

133

one always experienced with a musket – a weapon I had seen miss a man at thirty feet. Deadly precision, reinforced when that chunk of lead whacked into target after target in the same general area as Hughes' perfect bull's-eyes.

That thought, on further reflection (perhaps more of an observation colored by emotion), inevitably led to my third thought: the rebels firing back would also have these things. As sobering as it was frightening – I had led charges against massed Mexicans, endured a musket volley at close range with few hits on any of us before we closed. Now, here I was a dozen years later consistently hitting targets 200 yards away – and more.

Clearly, this war would be different. The men on the other side were no Santa Anna conscripts in pretty uniforms, just men with plenty of practice shooting – game, fowl, runaway slaves, Indians, each other – wielding Springfields, Enfields, and God knew what else.

Whatever satisfaction and comfort the rich-wood stocked, steel-barreled, bucking rifle in my hands gave me were stripped away by the idea of the same aimed in my direction. A horrible truth was creeping under my scalp – anyone who could absorb the instrument's kick while taking a modicum of care to aim the damn thing was probably as lethal as a squad of men armed with smoothbores at, say, seventy-five yards. Anything further, he was probably worth a company. That thought was either sobering or cause to get ripping drunk.

That last thought bouncing around my skull, I pulled the trigger and sent my last shot splashing into the Potomac.

"Didya' get tha' fish, William?" Shay melodiously inquired from my right.

"You know I still outrank you, right?" I shot back, reloaded hastily, I was not about to quit after such an egregious shot.

"It's such a minor difference as ta' be inconsequential . . . at least among secure men."

"Of course, but I still outrank you, Major," I said with authority, employed the ramrod with more force than was necessary or safe.

"Now, well, while tha' might be technically true, I'll point out that we both wear maple leafs an' mine are gold," he smiled while staring bullets at my silver ones, "whereas . . ."

He was rudely cutoff by the retort of the Springfield and my grunt. The shot smacked into the target a fingernail's width away from Hughes' very lonely dead center hit.

"Well done, William," Hughes said with less enthusiasm than I would have expected, "of course, and please do not take this the wrong way, that was the target I felt I misfired on – not that that should take away from your achievement in the least. A fine effort, no matter what."

"Thank you, Robert . . . I think," I replied with caution for First Sergeant Hughes had learned much since leaving his ivory tower at Trinity and hobnobbing with the common folk. Just as his truly amazing sharpshooting abilities would never have been uncovered had he come in as an officer, so too his other supernatural talent, one I was told manifested itself after only a few days among the rank and file – Professor Hughes was a Mozart in the art of the insult.

The fact that he could combine his two talents without any observable decrease in the quality of either endeared him to the men, who vied to be the target of the latter gift.

"Oh, I mean it, William, very nice shot . . . especially for an officer."

"That's very kind Sergeant," I said slowly, "Right now, I am wondering how well you handle a sword."

"Never had the opportunity to wield one . . . Sir."

"How unfortunate. Perhaps I shall endeavor to give you a lesson next time you see fit to comment on my marksmanship."

"That sounds like a threat, Colonel."

"Should sound like a promise, Professor."

"Sir," he chuckled, looked to Shay for support that was not forthcoming.

"I think it obvious to all, as well," the help was not there because Shay had not left the previous subject, "tha' along with my gold leafs I enjoy a significant moral superiority as well."

"Jesus Christ, Shay," I snapped, "leave it alone, I outrank you. Legally. Officially. Morally. Regardless of the colors of the damn leafs."

"I feel I have to speak up here," Christian, happily and uncharacteristically silent through my target practice started as we began the walk up to camp.

"Please don't think it mandatory," I said with a sigh.

"No, I want to," Christian jabbed, "just to point out that Sean looks the part. When you think about it, actually, he carries himself above the maple leafs, that's obvious to everyone."

"My point, 'zactly," Shay beamed.

"You don't need shoulder straps at all, Sean, you've natural authority," my brother gushed.

"Aye, 'tis true," Shay admitted, shaking his head at the truth of it, sorry for me that I could not see it.

"Then you would be perfectly happy in a private's tunic," I observed with malice.

"Of course," no hesitation, "some of us don't need tha' trappings of power to wield it."

"That's Shakespearian, Sean," I replied.

"Well known Irishman."

"Since when?" I asked, not unkindly.

"Well known, little reported fact," he waved off my ignorance.

"Very little reported."

"You 'ave your history, we 'ave ours," he snorted, went silent.

"What?" I said, it was obvious he had self-edited himself. A refreshing change I should have embraced.

"Ah, jus' thinkin' tha' it's never all tha' great for us when your history intersects with ours, tha's all."

"Very philosophical,

"We are well known as a race of philosopher-warriors."

"I thought it was poet-warriors?"

"Like I said," he answered with an implicit 'tsk' at my rigidity of thought.

We, thankfully for my continued sanity, arrived at camp, clomped to our tents spread under trees still half full with-dead leaves. Arnold and Joinville sat in the clearing, chatting amicably, coffee mugs in hand. At home, the first snows would be threatening, on the banks of the Potomac in mid-November we basked in sunlight without jackets. It did not atone for the oppressiveness of the summer, but it came damn close.

"Will you join us, Robert? I asked as we neared the dislocated prince and industrial mogul. The request was genuine and a real comment on how far Hughes had come in six months.

"No thank you, William," he smiled, accepting his inclusion with aplomb, "I need to get back to my men."

"You are more than welcome, you know," Christian added.

"I appreciate that," his face said he did indeed, "but to stay in the company of officers too long is to risk infection," he finished with a laugh and peeled off from our group, double timing it down the hill toward his company's street. Without turning he waved goodbye over his head.

"I hope he realizes that I'm going to ruin his life after our first action," I muttered and watched him disappear.

"How so, brother?"

"He'll be promotin' him to exalted status," Shay answered for me, "'afta the first engagement." Christian remained silent, fully understanding the implications.

Phelps came flying out of nowhere toting chairs, set them down around Seth and Joinville, flashed out of sight. We barely settled in the chairs before Phelps reappeared with mugs for the three of us in one hand, a pot of coffee in the other. With total efficiency he distributed the mugs, filled them, turned his back on us and approached Joinville.

"Kin' I getcha' anythin', Your Highness?" He asked with an obsequiousness I never suspected he possessed. An obsequiousness that was further highlighted by the fact he studiously avoided looking into the Prince's face.

"No, thank you, Sergeant," Joinville replied with warmth. Charles backed away three or four steps before turning and fleeing into the shadows.

"What in God's name. . . ." I began.

"Charles is in awe of royalty," Arnold saw my bafflement and hastened to enlighten.

"You're joking," my only possible reply.

"No," he confirmed, "he's a fan of royalty, can recite who's who in the houses of Europe at the drop of a hat."

"I would never have thought it," I said in wonder.

"I find it refreshing," the object of the idolatry announced, "and quite hospitable makes me feel like I am home."

"They treat you like that in Bath?" I asked with malice.

He did not blink, "Of course, the English are unfailingly polite and —"

"Class fixated," Shay offered with a low snort and a quick look around our little circle, blinking in surprise from having said it aloud.

"Of course, Major," Joinville smiled, and made an expansive motion with his arms, "not being a nation of kings like your Ireland they have had to adapt system of mores to account for the differences among men."

"Almost makes one pity 'em," Shay sadly intoned.

"Indeed," Joinville agreed.

I rolled my eyes as obviously as possible, was studiously ignored by all. Joinville and Shay went on agreeing with one another while I sat back, sipped coffee and watched Christian and Arnold enjoying themselves watching the spectacle of a French Prince and Irish soldier-king bantering, changing from English to French and back effortlessly. It would not have surprised me in the least had they switched to Gaelic at some point.

I behaved myself and did not interrupt to break up the tete a tete by pointing out that Sean Patrick O'Shea sported Legion de Honores won fighting for the glory of the usurper, Napoleon III. Even I thought that rude and poor sportsmanship. Eventually the two would be kings reached a lull of mutual coffee drinking and Christian hurriedly filled the breech.

"Are we going to war with Britain?" He asked, expression unreadable.

"Are you," I answered as Joinville and I exchanged glances, "asking us because you think we know something official or are seeking our opinions?"

"You know anything official?" He asked archly.

"No," Joinville and I answered as one.

"Then your opinions will be fine."

"We'll patch it up with the British, find a way to return Slidell and Mason without admitting wrong and it'll all go away," I offered.

"I have to agree," Joinville added grumpily.

"Don't sound so thrilled about it," I said to the petulant Prince.

"It worries me to agree with you, it makes one doubt one's judgment," he replied, happily, "especially where it concerns an issue of tact, decorum or diplomacy."

"While I may not oft time employ those overrated skills," I explained with sense and good cheer, "I not only recognize but even admire them in others when done well."

"As they are now?"" Christian asked.

"Even with Great Britain's saber rattling anything else would be stupid," I felt every bit the big brother, enjoyed being the big brother, wondered briefly how I could get out of the swamp of headquarters to be the big brother on a permanent basis, "Imagine fighting simultaneous wars against English speaking peoples. Sad."

"Cromwell did it," Shay opined.

"How so?" Joinville asked.

"Fought tha' Crown and tha' Irish, of course."

"We were discussing English speaking peoples, Sean," I pointed out.

"Ah, ya' shit, serve ya' right ta' have ta' deal with Red Coats from the north and tha' rebels from tha' south."

"You'll be standing right next to me," I reminded him.

"Unless I get a better offer from my former employers."

"And go back to Sergeant-Major?" I needled.

"I was referring to the French, ya' daft bastard, they'd surely join tha' bloody British. Be nice to wear a star."

"Glory seeker," I observed at precisely the moment Charles reemerged into the circle laden with a tray piled high with breads and muffins, fresh from the 1st Minnesota ovens.

He approached Joinville as one would a sacred relic of obvious antiquity, eyes down, voice low, making recommendations, lingering in the Prince's aura. Until I could take it no longer.

"Did you taste them first, check for poisons."

"Wha'?" Phelps snapped, eyes agog in horror as Joinville, timing perfect, took a sizeable bite of the muffin he had quickly selected.

"Too late," Shay said mournfully, "now all we can do is sit and wait."

"I feel quite well, actually, good muffin," Joinville offered, taking another healthy bite.

"That's the first symptom," I observed.

"A French Prince, ev'n a dispossessed one – sorry, Prince," Shay started, the good prince waved off the sad description of his current status, "dyin' in a Union camp, that'll bring tha' French in and the British will have to follow."

"Good God," I gasped. Joinville, another generous bite firmly encheeked, nodded, "we can't beat three armies at once."

"We'll be eating escargot with our bangers and grits," Arnold said with resignation.

To that Charles straightened, looked at Joinville with the hurt of the suddenly disillusioned, turned to me and said, "They're as loopy as you, Boss."

He shook his head, handed me the tray, "You can help yerselves, you know where the coffee is, I'll be a groomin' Clio – more refreshin' brand of horseshit with her." He strode off with nobility.

"You have insulted him, I think," Joinville observed as Phelps' faded away.

"He's used to it," I replied, "and usually gives as good as he gets, but to be betrayed by the very royalty he so admires —"

"Betrayed?"

"Betrayed, he thought better of you than to go along with the likes of us."

Joinville looked at me in puzzlement, "He is employed by you, is he not?"

"Alas, yes," I answered, "now supplemented by the United States Army."

"I do not think I will ever understand the American concept of served and server."

'We are a complicated people," Arnold commented.

"So you would like to think," the Prince de Joinville slayed us with a nasty smile followed by the coup de grace on his muffin.

23. Ashford

Late afternoon, the day perfect, temperatures balmy, Joinville set up an easel and endeavored to paint our idyllic slice of the Potomac. He was attaining the relaxation he sought escaping the city with me – a Washington teeming with rumor and men intent on relaying them.

I sat nearby, worked on a draft of the Ball's Bluff report, considerably less restful than my royal companion. I had scores of facts via firsthand accounts, a decent understanding of what had happened, a shuddering appreciation for how poor the choice of ground, pictured the retreat in a memorable nightmare – all that, and more.

What I did not have was any substantial knowledge of why Baker went over the river in the first place.

I did not have a statement from General Charles P. Stone, West Point, '44. It was not from lack of trying, Joinville and I had tried everything short of royal decree to get to him and were diplomatically, systematically, very professionally turned aside. To add insult to injury, Osgood could find no orders, anywhere, and had promptly disappeared on a 'quest' to repair that deficit, among others.

Had I been preparing a criminal case, I would have cut and run, dismissed it, thrown out the file so as not to contaminate other cases lying nearby. It was a screwed-up military boondoggle, preceded only by two or three million others in the history of warfare. Military stupidity and waste, while not rare, were also not crimes. Not, at least, to date.

Neither Joinville nor I had seen Mac since I was charged with the most open sub-rosa inquiry in history. The time we spent interviewing survivors, combined with Mac moving his personal quarters to H Street to house his wife and new born daughter; his added duties as Commander of all the armies; Ellen's immersion, much chronicled, full bore into the social scene; and, the fact that Joinville and I were actively ducking him, kept us apart for over three weeks.

I suspected that our avoidance was mutual and Mac was no more anxious to hear our report than we were to give it. I had known George McClellan since he was sixteen and knew beyond a shadow of a doubt he would do everything he could to avoid the damnable subject, even while knowing that such an approach was sure to exacerbate it and further fuel the political cyclone that was forming.

It was not fear of discovery, the need to cover up a mistake or blemish of character, embarrassment at a defeat (however minor) or any number of other reasons to avoid the issue. It was, instead and solely, arrogance. Arrogance that a West Point educated, decorated Mexican War veteran, War Department attaché to the courts of Europe, official observer in Crimea, President of the Central Illinois Railroad, could and would be second guessed by a group of men who did not know the difference between an Enfield rifle and a trebuchet.

In that opinion the Young Napoleon undoubtedly would have been joined by the original Bonaparte himself. Like McClellan, he had been besieged at various times by the Directory, a group responsible for the Terror and therefore nearly as ferocious as Wade, Sumner and company, if not as subtle.

Napoleon solved his problem by taking over the government and various and sundry continental Ancien Regimes. Options that were not constitutionally available to McClellan.

So, I wrote. What I had so far mostly agreed with McClellan's circular without extrapolating further into a political treatise or general call to arms. Colonel Edward Baker took his brigade piecemeal over the Potomac; deployed in an indefensible clearing; engaged the enemy – an engagement his force was too small and inexperienced to handle – without reconnaissance; quoted some very nice, inspiring poetry; was shot by an unappreciative, prose loving rebel sharpshooter; left his force to swim for it.

It did not take me that long to write, even with frequent pauses to rue that I was blaming it all on a dead man. While true, so far, it felt cowardly. And wrong, for the man was never trained, had no consul, no mentor and had been put in charge simply because of who he had been before the war started. One of Mac's major peeves, the thought that success in civilian life made one a candidate to be a successful officer. I thought long and hard about that when I finished, leaned back, watched Joinville paint, and simply enjoyed the non-political sounds of the camp.

Ten, twenty minutes of thought, there, then, and I returned to the pages on my lap and wrote, in large letters, underlined, 'Preliminary Report' across the top of each page.

My deep feeling of unease and my conscience thus at least temporarily assuaged, I closed the bulging file. As if on cue, Reverend Ashford strode over, a canvas chair slung over his broad back. He stopped first to gaze down over an oblivious Joinville, nodded with approval, snapped the chair open and plopped down beside me.

"So, you escaped the Sodom and Gomorrah to the east, eh?"

He started with great good humor, enough to drag me out of the doldrums I had put myself in.

"That's a bit harsh, don't you think? For the capitol of our nation?"

"You like Washington?" To be fair, he managed to ask it without inflection or distaste.

"Hate it," I said out of the corner of my mouth, "I just think the biblical allusion's a bit strong."

"What descriptive would you use?"

"Power, filth, wealth, stink, dignity, squalor, naiveté, cunning, impressive, sad, 'the city of magnificent intentions' – the usual Dickensian contradictions.'"

"I'll note cynicism is not one of your adjectives."

"I reserve that for myself."

"It serves you."

"Thank you," I replied with a wan smile, "look, my opinion of the place when I am in the state of mind I am at present – while trying to avoid returning there for as long as possible – is that it's a cesspool that offers ample opportunity to drink oneself blind while contracting venereal diseases at leisure. With the added bonus of the lip-smacking possibility of discovering some politico en flagrante and stumbling into a lifetime annuity or high office."

"Sounds like Sodom and Gomorrah to me, William."

"Ah, just a bad day to ask my opinion of Washington," I shrugged it away, brightened, "I've a question for you though, a Biblical question –"

"Well, I'm . . . thrilled," he almost gasped in surprise.

"Always bothered me."

"Then, please . . . I hope I have the answer," said in earnestness.

"What was Gomorrah doing that Sodom wasn't? Sodom spawned a verb while I have never heard of anyone being Gomorrahed . . . or going around Gomorrahing. Why is that?"

If he was disappointed, offended, or a hundred other emotions, none showed, indeed he smiled slightly, "Why, you're Gomorrahing me right now, William," he laughed – an instantly contagious laugh.

"Sorry, Reverend, I overstep," I said with a fair degree of sincerity, smiled. Satisfied with myself, I watched Joinville intently dabbling away with his watercolors – there were so many hues of brown, red and orange still clinging to the trees he would be mixing colors for days.

I became aware of the Reverend's close study of my face. I studiously ignored it, began to flip through my paperwork.

"I can't decide, William," he broke the silence, "whether you are truly so damn cynical or you project it to get a reaction from the likes of me, which I have already supplied by swearing." He finished with a smile, solely not to offend for it did not touch his eyes – probably the same smile he gave the irredeemable seeking deathbed absolutions.

"Not offered that way, Thomas, certainly not with you."

That it was not sufficient was obvious to me even before I noticed a certain stoniness settle into his features, "You know, Colonel, sometimes people are not happy to be kept long outside a joke."

"I'm not joking, I prefer to think I offer descriptions of the human condition with astute observation, not cynicism."

"How refreshing for you."

"Sarcasm, my dear Reverend?"

"No, William," he chuckled lowly, "that was genuine, unless you're infectious."

"Now, that was sarcasm."

"Perceptive," he laughed, shifted his bulk carefully in the fragile chair, "you know, I've become close to your brother, no, don't worry," he guffawed when my head snapped at that, "he's in no more imminent danger of my saving his soul than I am at finding yours."

"For a man of the cloth, you're a vicious bastard, must be Yale," I observed without rancor. And sent him into a spasm of mirth.

"Despite the age difference," he eventually recovered and doggedly went on, "there are many similarities. As a matter of fact you would be virtually twins, I think, if not for the darkness you try so valiantly to hide."

I was caught short, almost breathlessly so, rallied, barely, with, "A few bad memories of Mexico, that's all. No valor involved, something to live with, like others do every day."

"Not like others, I think," he replied in an instant.

"You've had the time to think about this?" I asked without acrimony, "I would like to think you have more important issues than your executive officer's dark moods."

"Who said anything about dark moods?" He grinned widely, "See, you've inadvertently stumbled on it – the enigma I now get to observe at least every Sunday —"

"You asked."

"Indeed, happily," he accepted the interruption with grace, "the enigma that you present is one who is never a dark presence, nor evinces dark moods, and yet, I don't know, there's an idealism in you tempered – if not imprisoned – by something . . . dare I say, unholy." No laugh or grin then, just a look of frank, honest curiosity.

"I —"

He held up a hand, "By that, I mean something that happened to you, which, in my humble opinion, it would do well to discuss with . . . . someone."

"You trying to convert me to Catholicism, Thomas?"

"There you go," he almost smiled, "though I understand this may be . . . uncomfortable . . . for both of us."

It took me a minute to respond, "Really, Thomas. I am astounded that you care enough to think of me, in any way." I offered it with almost humble sincerity.

"I think it prudent to know as much as possible about the men I'm following into battle."

"You mean that metaphorically, of course?"

"What?"

"You don't mean *in* the actual battle line."

"Why don't I?"

"Because, Reverend Ashford," I began evenly, "There's nothing more demoralizing to a regiment than seeing its spiritual leader decapitated or eviscerated. It tends to make the men somewhat less sure God is on their side."

"I can appreciate that, but —"

"I will reinforce that sentiment, no matter how simplistic, superstitious or ill-founded you and I feel it may be, and I'll do it at bayonet point or with you in locked in an ambulance."

I held my unhappy regimental chaplain's eyes in a hard stare, "Better the men think me soulless than them staring at your all too mortal remains as they pass by headed for the enemy."

Something in my diatribe struck him as amusing, he stifled a chuckle, coughed out, "Perhaps, then, I meant it metaphorically, but I need to lead my flock by being part of it, experience what they experience and with them knowing I have."

"You'll see enough from the rear to more than get the gist, trust me on that."

"I will," he very clearly choked back 'for now', "though my curiosity about you persists . . . for many of the same reasons."

I shook my head resignedly, "Chalk it up to Mexico, at least for now, Padre."

"Padre?" He yelped into the beginning of a smile at the invocation of the epithet of an accepted, respected army Chaplin, "Why thank you, Colonel," the smile became a beam that extended across his face

"Well earned."

"I appreciate that," the smile settled into a grin, "but I don't accept Mexico as an explanation for anything except your insistence this regiment be well trained."

"That is —"

"Correct?" He was incisive once again, probed my eyes with intensity. I realized in a flash I would employ him to interrogate prisoners if his collar allowed, "the problem, William, isn't Mexico, it's you."

He finished with a look that showed he expected me to not only agree, but to elaborate. . .

. . . which I had no intention of doing at present. Instead, I stood, stretched, smiled and began to move toward Joinville. I had taken perhaps three steps when Ashford loomed over me and touched my arm, "What about your missing years, William?"

I stopped, he almost walked into me. "How's that, Padre?"

"Those missing years, Christian speaks of them often."

"I like to refer to them as my Hawthorne years, half —"

"Half the time and without the artifice," he completed my standard reply with ease.

"My, you have been spending time with Christian."

"It's the formative event of his youth, his idol leaving without word for three years —"

"Just over two," I corrected . . . weakly.

"As if that would make a difference to a ten year old boy," he chided at what he mistakenly took for my indifference.

I shrugged, moved toward Joinville again, was stopped dead by, "It have anything to do with the disappearance of your uncle?"

"What?" All I could say while the hillside swayed a tad.

"Your uncle," his voice acquired a solemnity that invited confidence, "Christian said he disappeared just before you left, he's always wondered if you were searching for him . . . he has conjured many a fanciful adventure for you in those years."

I appreciated his gentleness, tact, caring . . . especially the caring. Still, as I tottered back to my chair and slumped into it I desperately wanted to knock him down.

I sat, let the urge for violence ebb away, sighed more than once, closed my eyes, opened them to find Ashford sitting as well, empathetic eyes hard on mine.

I spoke unaware of having made the decision to do so, "He did not disappear, Thomas," I began, voice raspy, "he was killed . . . February seventeenth, Eighteen-fifty, late night. Shot to death on the front steps of my mother's house in the middle of a blizzard. Mother's brother, our uncle."

Quick look of confusion ripped through his eyes while his face stayed stoic, "Then why —"

"Does Christian think he disappeared?" I muttered, stared out over the Potomac.

"Yes."

"When did your family found Ashford?" I asked with resignation.

"Seventeen-fourteen."

"Got any skeletons buried out there in the woods, beaver ponds, church cemetery?"

"I imagine, a few indiscretions, a few Tories, dubious business dealings during the War of 1812 . . . ." he let that hang, waited.

"Half my family's been in Boston since there was a Boston," I addressed the Virginian shore, "hell, one of my ancestors escorted William Blaxton out of town – "

"I'm sorry, I'm not conversant in – "

"Boston scandals?" I asked.

"Yes."

"Lucky you," I grunted, "Blaxton was the first settler in Boston, invited the Puritans over from Charlestown, got booted out for religious differences – as in he believed in tolerance . . . "

"Of course . . ."

"Well, since then my family has amassed enough skeletons to fill the closets of the Commonwealth . . . and that was before my mother's herculean efforts —"

"Your mother —" he began with reverence.

"Married outside the circle and has since reaped the whirlwind – and has not been shy about sharing it with her offspring."

"I'm not sure I understand, William," Ashford said in a manner that conveyed my last statement had been too heated.

"My uncle's murder would have brought very much unwanted attention to her, us, my family . . . the cause," I looked into the Reverend's widened irises and waited.

"So he disappeared instead," he whispered at length.

"A young, overworked physician with no family of his own working all hours at Mass General . . . I understand it didn't even make the papers for weeks."

"He really did disappear," Ashford nodded solemnly.

"With the blood I cleaned off the steps in the snow."

"Then you left."

"Two days later, I had preparations to make."

"You knew who killed him," it was not a question.

I looked back out over the Potomac before, "That, Thomas, is pure conjecture and a matter for another day, different circumstances."

"Indeed," he agreed without inflection.

With that I slouched, watched the Potomac flow by, and dozed. Ashford sat with me, silent. I was long in his debt for that.

24. The Grand Review

The Grand Review of the Army of the Potomac came off as well as the chosen adjective promised. We rose well before dawn, dressed by firelight, the smells of coffee and bacon wafting about.

Once in our finery, coffee cups in hand, we wandered through camp checking the men, each and every one as alert and nervous as if headed for the altar. Joinville had opted stay with us, a gesture our officers and rank and file took as a singular honor. As did I.

By the time dawn broke the 21st was in column, bayonets affixed and glowing like St. Elmo's fire in the low sun. We tramped happily through the frost to fall in at the tail end of the division, a division we had had no previous contact with, which affected our men not a whit.

We emerged late morning past packed review stands and onto the vast plain McClellan had selected to show off the might of his army. Eyes left, we marched past the President; my friend Gideon – who doffed his cap to his native state's sons; past the cabinet, senators, hundreds of high-hatted politicians and their gaily turned out ladies; past brilliantly colored, braid-encrusted officers from foreign lands; past lower grandstands crammed with- less important but far more vocal everyday citizens, openly and obviously imbibing in liquid refreshment.

As for Mac, he was everywhere at once on a lathered Dan Webster, personally bringing units into battle line, conducting mock advances complete with volleys and charges, artillery batteries flying by, skittering to teeth rattling stops to unlimber and fire in completely unrealistic but highly entertaining fashion.

Done smiting the imaginary foe we settled into a casual line on the fringe of the plain. Like the invited guests and uninvited masses that managed to find their way out of the city, the 21st had front row seats to the cavalry review that followed. Charges shook the earth, rattled the make shift grandstands.

In the end we filed back through the chewed up turf and stood in formation, infantry in the center, cavalry on the flanks, artillery behind, bands amassed front and center. We stood like bit players in an ensemble watching the stars take bows while the bands played, the generals strutted and the throng cheered. A single volley by the massed artillery brought the performance to a close.

Joinville and I sat in companionable silence on the flank of the 21st awaiting our turn to disperse back to camp, our horses carrying on some elaborate equine contest. Clio kept nuzzling, hard, Joinville's bay, Roxanne (of course). Roxanne replied in kind with snorts that Clio was either too lady like or intimidated by to respond to in kind.

We watched regiment after regiment wheel into column and slog off, the stands emptied and the sun dipped behind the hills of Western Maryland – the temperature dropped in direct proportion to its height on the horizon. I was entranced in the movements of the troops, hypnotized by the sounds of clinking metal and the measured tread of thousands of boots in step. Joinville broke the trance with a touch of my sleeve.

"I will wager he is looking for you," he gestured at a lone rider briskly darting through and around formations in search of someone. I had to study him for a moment before recognizing him.

"That's Webb," I muttered with some bitterness Clio and Roxanne stopped their activities and looked up.

"Who?" Joinville said absently, his attention captured by a New York Zouave regiment tromping by in red pantaloons, trim cut, short blue jackets and red fezzes.

"Remind you of France?" I asked.

"Tunisia, I adore Tunis," he replied, "have you been there?"

"Toured Carthage, the Roman ruins."

"Beautiful country."

"Amen."

"Oh, look, it is Major Webb," he announced as if waking.

"Major," I echoed in horror.

"Major," he confirmed, happy in my annoyance, "you would not want a mere lieutenant to act as chief aide to your General-in-Chief, would you?"

"The very thought that one could be promoted for social reasons just confirms to me how much the army has changed."

"Jealous?"

"Of course," I answered as Webb reached us.

"Prince Joinville," he intoned gravely with a half bow, "Colonel Hanlin, how nice to see you, sirs." He smiled, genuinely enough, perhaps major suited him.

"Major," we replied as one.

"General McClellan's compliments – he would like you to join him if you have no other plans," Webb continued, pleasantly, as if inviting us to tea.

"Delighted," Joinville took it as such. I added my nod and the three of us rode off together to resume Webb's earlier weave through static and moving units, the maze of the Army of the Potomac – an animated, pleased with itself army going home for supper and congratulatory draughts of alcohol.

We came to a knot of horsemen sitting casually watching the army fade into the descending evening. McClellan was in their midst, his preternatural height on Dan Webster's bulk left him unmistakably looming over his companions.

Those companions included Fitz John Porter and Ambrose Burnside, both beaming as I rode up.

"Generals," I said tiredly, eyes heavenward, throwing a lame salute as an all too apparent afterthought.

"Willie," Porter, trying not to laugh, almost succeeding, "there are two generals here, I notice only one salute." Burnside smiled widely, the act pushed his bushy cheek hangings apart.

"I've known you for years," I observed with malice, "that precludes me from mistaking your stars for anything more than the miracles they are."

"That's hateful, Willie," Porter boomed.

"Says volumes you thought I was talking to you," I said to Porter, winked at Burnside, passed through to get to McClellan.

"Giving your superiors a hard time?" he yelled over while I edged involuntarily around him, Clio having decided to play coy with Dan Webster.

"Always," I answered truthfully, reined an unhappy Clio into place beside an arrogantly disdainful Dan.

"It is one of your strengths," Mac replied absently, his eyes drawn to a regiment marching by in straw boater hats.

"Congratulations on a great show," I offered, idly wondering how happy the rebels were going to be to use those hats to find the range.

"I'm delighted beyond words," he shouted. His words were genuine, I had no doubt, I did not require the additional evidence of the red blotches on his face and the light of triumph in his face to confirm – but they were there nevertheless, "In my wildest dreams I hoped to emulate a review I saw of the French Imperial Guard; I dare say we have done so."

"The French Imperial Guard," I said archly, timed it perfectly with Joinville's arrival, "well, I —"

I was cut off by Joinville's quick, guttural greeting to Mac. It took me a good ten seconds to realize it was in German. Mac replied in kind, the two them looked at me, laughed.

Hard. Long.

"That was rude," I said with as much petulance as I could muster. I was quickly apologized to by both my friends. In Russian.

I threw my hands up in surrender, the look on my face surely conveyed the rest.

"Sorry, Willie," Mac said without sorrow, "I forgot you don't share our facility with languages," he laughed gaily, exchanged another Russian aside with Joinville that elicited a nasty, flashing smile from the latter.

"You learn Russian in Crimea?" I asked.

"When I returned," McClellan answered without affectation, "I needed to read the Russian accounts of the Sevastopol siege, so I taught myself Russian."

"Who wouldn't?" I wondered.

"Yes," he agreed, "how are your inquiries coming? That damnable committee will be sitting soon."

"Complete," " I answered measuredly, "inasmuch as we can without interviewing Charles Stone."

"You've had no chance to meet with him?" He asked easily, caught and held my eye without artifice.

"None," Joinville answered for me, Mac's eyes never left mine and they did not flinch.

"Then I'll see you get a pass to see him," he said matter-of-factly.

"Why would I need a pass to see a general in the United States Army?" I asked with a sudden hollowness in the pit of my stomach.

"Because he is at Fort Lafayette, under arrest," to his credit he did not break eye contact.

"Arrest for what?" I kept my voice even, I think I managed to wring the shock out of it.

"Suspicion of treason," he looked off, over the heads of the officers around us.

"Arrested for treason, or jailed on suspicion of treason?" I asked carefully.

"There a difference?" He shrugged, "I'm not a lawyer, I wouldn't know."

"Who signed the warrant?" I regulated my voice away from a cross examination staccato.

"I did, had little choice."

"Why didn't I review it first?"

"Bates reviewed it for me."

Stunned. I looked to Joinville, he gaped back. I took a deep breath, "The Attorney General of the United States reviewed a warrant?"

"He is and he did," he averred with good cheer that belied the fact he could not abide Bates.

"Charles is a friend of ours," I, needlessly, pointed out.

"Accused of treason," he could not keep the sanctimony out of his voice.

"He has a lot of friends," I. mused aloud, "they'll —"

"This is not the time or place," he managed a smile, "in the meantime, I'll get you a pass."

"I would like to go as well, General," Joinville chimed in.

"Certainly," Mac, magnanimously, waved his hand in regal dismissal. An audience had coalesced around us, a thick congregation of brass, politicians, and reporters pushing in around us, eager to share the day's success.

McClellan stood in his stirrups and yelled into the gloaming, "We have created a dazzling, dangerous weapon, my friends," he began, the voice as commanding as the stars on his shoulder straps, "One so awful in its potential I feel for our misguided enemies. Be assured, however, once unleashed I will wield this force with a clarity of purpose and without mercy until those it is loosed upon cry for such.

"We shall end this in one great campaign. Each of you, and every man that paraded here today, will be proud to live out his days knowing that once he was a part of the Army of the Potomac!"

McClellan finished to applause, yells of adulation. He doffed his hat with his usual flourish and rode off on his warhorse, the perfect completion of the effect.

The crowd dispersed quickly, Joinville and I brought our horses around, almost colliding with a shay containing two slow to leave spectators.

Mother and Charles Sumner and it was impossible to pretend to not see them – a tactic I, at least, was willing to attempt, a type of social forlorn hope.

Joinville, however, betrayed me.

"Mrs. Hanlin, how delightful!" He sang out and bowed. I would not have been overly surprised had he dipped Roxanne.

"Prince de Joinville," Mother fluttered for a moment in his presence . . . before launching into an eloquent, French, discussion with the suddenly obsequious Prince.

That left Sumner and me with no way to comfortably ignore one another – clearly each our first choice.

We locked eyes, I muzzled myself while my mind toyed with the idea of inquiring as to his intentions with my mother. He remained silent, I was convinced, because, having known me well, he was in mortal fear of me doing just that.

Instead, I asked "Enjoy the review, Senator?"

He visibly relaxed, thus confirming my hunch, "I did, William," he made the attempt to smile, almost made it, but Sumner and happiness were too antithetical, "please call me Charles in social situations, I insist."

I managed to cut off, just barely, the potentially deadly mot: 'Well, it's preferable to Daddy.' I merely nodded and bit a chunk out of my cheek.

"I enjoyed it greatly," he went on, oblivious, "quite magnificent. Now I suppose we just wait and hope the army is employed. Soon."

"One could say it is employed protecting the nation's Capital," I ventured, my heart not really in it but damned if I was going to let a civilian criticize the army on that magical day.

"You know, William," he grew expansive, snuck a peek at the loquaciously Gallic couple to his left, "I'd accept that . . . analysis," he smiled at his choice of a noun, "if the army were daily beating off attacks by the rapacious hordes of the Confederacy – instead of parading so prettily in front of our mostly benign citizenry."

I moved to reply, was stopped by a restraining hand from Charles, "I don't expect a rejoinder, William, not today, anyway. We'll leave it as the grand day it is."

Done with the Prince, Mother turned and unleashed a brilliant smile. Sumner gripped the reins, leaned forward, and, smiling slyly, said, "Tell your general not to waste all the good feeling, Willie."

He snapped the reins and the shay lurched away before I could respond.

25. Lincoln

I arrived at Mac's house twenty minutes early, as behooved a Lieutenant Colonel summoned to attend to a Major General. It was a home appropriate for the Commander-in-Chief of the Union's armies, brick, well-appointed without being opulent the Chases' in miniature with restraint – hardly a bad thing.

I was greeted at the door by a house servant, a welcome relief from self-important, self-appointed keepers of the Keeper of the Keys. I was escorted without comment to a comfortable reading room, lamps on lowly, a fireplace bright and crackling. I could easily have been home in Hartford. I envied, for the first time, Mac his position.

I snatched the latest Harper's off a side table, Mac's likeness, inevitably, on the cover. The Grand Review was covered as breathlessly as they would have the Second Coming. The illustrations, quickly done to meet deadline, were intricate, stirring, handsomely drawn and not the least bit accurate.

I was, however, happily engrossed and did not immediately take note that the time for my meeting had come and gone. I looked at my watch only when I heard a knock on the front door, followed by voices from the front hall. It was nine-twenty. I assumed Mac, known to work late into the night and into early morning, had scheduled someone immediately after me and was running late.

I went back to my weekly and almost did not bother to look up as someone entered the room. I did solely out of measurable pique at being interrupted. I glanced up from a description of the taking of Port Royal to stare full into the face of the President of the United States.

I jumped to my feet, Harper's slid to the floor and landed with a slapping thud that sounded like the retort of a parrot gun in the almost silent room.

"Mr. President," I hoarsed out, my body uncomfortably stuck in a half-at attention, half-about-to salute position while I idiotically wondered if I should pick up the magazine lest the mess on the floor offend Mr. Lincoln.

His big, somewhat sad eyes lit up in amusement as he instantly perceived my predicament, one he endeavored to solve by extending a hand, "No formalities necessary, Colonel. It is I who intrudes on you."

"Not at all, Sir," I stammered, angry at my performance thus far. At that point in my life I had met three presidents (four if one counted Jefferson Davis), several kings, one Pope, and hosts of Sumner-like would be kings and had managed to keep a cool head. And there I was with, in hindsight, the most tragically accessible leader anyone was likely to find acting and act like a rube.

I managed to take the offered hand, surprised when it completely engulfed my hand and wrist. It was enormous and it was powerful.

"Lieutenant Colonel William Hanlin," I managed to say with some authority. I tried to squeeze back before he tore my arm off and used it as a back scratcher. I failed but he must have picked up on my distress for he let go.

He took a chair closer to the fire, slouched back, splayed his long legs across half the room. I had seen him before, when he spoke at Hartford City Hall, and was immediately struck by how much he had aged – it was as clear in his face as the deep fissures and deep bags under the eyes.

"Are you waiting for our Commanding General?" He inquired languidly.

"I am, sir."

"Hanlin, eh?" He smiled and studied the shadows playing across the ceiling, "the name seems familiar, where you from, Colonel?"

"Connecticut, sir, I'm with the Twenty-first Connecticut, but temporarily assigned as General McClellan's Judge Advocate liaison."

"Ah, Hanlin, that's it, JAG," his face took on a serious visage, "the death penalty case. I've been meaning to have you in to discuss it -- I've had a great deal of correspondence concerning the verdict."

"I'm not surprised," I said as evenly as possible.

"That was remarkably carefully stated," he sighed, gave me a frank look of appraisal, "as it appears, our General is indisposed, perhaps we can make use of our time together and discuss this now."

"Certainly, Sir," I replied immediately.

"Do you requite notes?"

"No, Sir, I tend to remember the details of death penalty cases."

"As should we all, Colonel," he nodded slowly, "I take it you have an opinion in this matter?"

"The president of the court is not supposed to have an opinion," I replied with false piety.

"So you do," he chuckled, "and judging by the formality of your quite proper response," intelligent, empathetic eyes bored into me, "your opinion does not coincide with that of your court."

My turn to stare in appraisal. For months I had heard Mac disparage Lincoln as the 'original gorilla', those same months, I read in innumerable papers how Lincoln was 'run' by Seward and Chase, a dolt of a figurehead. I was disabused of all of that after ten minutes exposure to the man.

"It does not," I answered, slowly, "I must confess, Mr. President, I am opposed to the death penalty in all but the most egregious, disturbing cases. These men are not soldiers, they have volunteered.

I did not enlist to kill my neighbors for violations of military protocol that they have subjected themselves to purely out of a sense of loyalty."

"Well said, Colonel," his facile face conveyed his agreement, "I suppose I should be surprised considering your assignment, but of course, you are a volunteer yourself."

"I am, now, but in the interests of full disclosure I must confess I am a West Point graduate."

"What year?"

"Forty-six."

He smiled knowingly, sat back and continued, "You were one of McClellan's classmates?"

"I was."

He nodded, filed that away somewhere, "Why don't you agree with the sentence, Colonel?"

"I don't agree with the verdict, sir," I corrected.

The lawyer in him understood at once, "Enlighten me."

"The circumstances were extenuated. Yes, Private Scott fell asleep on duty, at post, on the picket line. Yes, I suppose it was technically a war zone, certainly it would have been a serious dereliction had we been across the river."

"But?"

"But, he had been on duty for thirty-six hours due to a scheduling error by his commanding officer – a martinet who was running a general store a few months ago . . . the nearest Confederates were ten miles away across the Potomac," on my high-horse now, everything about Lincoln's posture and expression encouraged me to continue, "The man was on picket duty in a war zone only if by some chance Maryland seceded from the Union during the night."

The man who had prevented just that succession smiled briefly and said, "Sounds to me, Colonel that had you defended him instead of presiding over the court, Private Scott would have been acquitted and none of us would be saddled with this . . . mess."

"The prosecutor was persuasive, well grounded in the law and presenting to battle tested officers, who ——"

"You included in that description?"

"I was in Mexico."

"And yet you do not agree with your colleagues."

"Major Andre Coleman and Major Stephen Dixon, and, no, I did not agree. I was outvoted."

"A major disagreement then, eh?" He grinned widely.

"I suppose so," I tried not to shake my head, Lincoln looked pleased with himself, "I did not agree because it was draconian and unwarranted at this stage of the war.

"Not needed at this point, but ——"

"One never knows – but surely not today."

"Hardly a boon to recruiting," he grimaced a knowing smile, "shooting men for falling asleep under these conditions."

"No," I agreed readily, pushing it home, probably unnecessarily, "I thought from the beginning that the only crime here was the regimental commander's failure to handle it at his level – no, that's not quite true, it was his setting it up by failing to bend enough to let an exhausted man walk away from an onerous duty."

I snapped that off quickly, unburdening myself. Unprofessional, but if felt good.

"I would venture to say, Colonel," Lincoln intoned somberly, "you should be leading a regiment rather than 'rasslin' in the corridors of law." It was clear he offered it as a compliment.

"Thank you," I answered with feeling, he nodded, bemused, "I return to my regiment when it matters, it was my sole condition to General McClellan before I took the position."

"Admirable, tho' I think I can sense the sacrifice you've made forsaking the field for this city".

"No sacrifice, sir," I fumbled, "in forsaking a cot for a feather bed."

He eyed me questioningly, half-smile affixed, made a church steeple of his hands, looked up at the shadows it made on the high ceiling.

"You know, I had dinner with Lord Lyons a few days ago," he stared up, speaking as if I were informed of the comings and goings of our president and Queen Victoria's ambassador on a regular basis, "it went well for a time, I think I was able to sound snobbish and condescending enough to be the equal of any Continental leader, thereby earning his approval."

I laughed, drew his attention from the ceiling, his smile broke the half way mark, "Well, after an hour or so of his supercilious prattle, during which time he continuously reminded us all, indirectly of course, of the wealth and power of the British Isles I grew god awfully sick of the man, began to wish I had never let Slidell and Mason go."

He stretched out, daddy long legs reaching across the fireplace, "Of course," he began to chuckle, "once the limeys start to hear Mason talk, they'll beg us to take him back."

"Anyway, that windbag Lyons spouted carefully worded platitudes that were really just thinly disguised slanders – damn, the very in-artfulness of his way about it was insulting, like if we'd been French he would have been more inventive and discreet. Probably decided Americans are so crude there's no need for more than basic, lazy subterfuge when insulting us.

"I finally got sick of it and I very undiplomatically – I have since been told – invited him to our Washington's Birthday Ball. Well by then the man had become so emboldened – or drunk or both – that he made no attempt to hide his utter contempt for the day, the man, and the event. . . . talented diplomat, he managed to convey all that in less than ten seconds and then blank his face out.

"In any event, I caught it and it angered me. Greatly. So I regaled him with the story of Ethan Allen and George's portrait." With that he pushed further back in the chair and stared directly at me, thick, haggard eyebrows arched – the classic storyteller's posture.

I eagerly indulged him, "I don't think I am aware of that story, Mr. President."

"No . . . well then," he with well-practiced nonchalance, "allow me," I motioned him a 'go on' he did not need, "sometime after the War of Independence Ethan Allen toured the British Isles – I understand he was somewhat of an attraction, too."

"At some formal dinner somewhere along the line things got a little rowdy, a little ribald, and the host – another Lord, I'm sure – said to Mr. Allen, 'Did you know, sir, that your George Washington's portrait is the most popular image in the land?"

"Ethan was somewhat startled, but managed to rasp out something along the lines of, 'Really, my Lord, I had no idea.'"

"To which the noble wit – apparently completely ignorant of Mr. Allen's reputation before the late unpleasantness – replied, 'Yes, sir, we keep a steady supply of them in our outhouses.'

"Allen remained completely, utterly calm, and answered almost immediately, 'I am not surprised, for in my experience, every time the British saw General Washington they shat.'"

I laughed deep and hard and he joined me, managing to finish with, "Lord Lyons shortly found himself indisposed and shuffled out. I think he finds me rather uncouth."

"I do not and I'm glad I voted for you," I sputtered out between guffaws.

"I hope you voted often," he slapped his knees, "Colonel, I'll tell you what, send me the death warrant and I'll commute the sentence to time served and return the unfortunate Scott to duty, only one Scott per year should be run out of the army," he finished without an edge, although I am relatively sure I cringed.

"No need to wait, sir," I could not erase my smile, "I have it right here, "I reached into my breast pocket and pulled out the well creased parchment.

"You carry it with you?"

"Yes."

"Why, if you don't mind me asking?"

"Silly precaution, probably rank superstition if truth be told, make sure it remains unexecuted until all reviews have been exhausted."

"And then," he bolted forward, "what then – assume we never had this conversation and you thought me a particularly bloodthirsty fellow?"

"In that case, we are governed by paperwork, Mr. President, as I'm sure you understand, so much paperwork . . . sometimes things get lost."

He stared, smile affixed. When he spoke it was apparent he was doing his best to sound stern, "We have both sworn oaths to uphold the laws of the land, Colonel."

"Luckily, none have been broken," I wondered briefly at my temerity talking to the President in that way. All I can say is he invited casual candor.

"Excellent point," he slapped me across the knee hard enough to make it sting, took the offered warrant and stood, "I will take care of this in the morning. Private Scott will be back on the picket line a wiser man by sundown."

"Thank you, Mr. President," I sighed, pleased to be free of a burden.

He looked at me oddly, I stood as he did, struck by how he loomed over me.

"I must go," he said with warmth, "Mr. Hay will be wondering what has befallen me." He held out his hand again, I took it, prepared for the vise like grip – which did little to mitigate the pain.

"A pleasure, Colonel," he smiled and leaned into me, "go back to your boys as soon as you can, they deserve to have you."

In two bounds he was out of the room. I glowed in the remnants of our conversation . . . until I was overtaken by the stone cold realization that my West Point friend, erstwhile Commandeer of the Armies of the United States, had just ignored a visit by the President.

26. Rosecrans

December 12, 1861
Somerset, Kentucky

W.

I know well the witticisms your mind is constructing – to be appreciated by you alone – on noting from whence this is written. Try to hold them, this is a charming town in a pretty setting. Reminds me of Wexford, the people are exceptionally friendly, pleasant and speak with a lilt not unlike a brogue. Very refreshing after years of the nasal monotones and dull idioms of Connecticut.

I am in Kentucky for two reasons — it is where my inquiries into the Ball's Bluff matter have taken me and I am assisting Pinkerton. You can stop cursing while I assure you he is not as odious as you suspect and is certainly more intelligent than you credit. He has established a first rate organization of spies, messengers and observers everywhere. True, his conclusions seem more molded to what his superiors expect, I do not think that is totally his fault. True, he is a bully – he is used to people getting out of his way. You, obviously, did not. No harm, your evident friendship with McClellan, to whom he is devoted from their railroad days, and my discussions with him have not only cooled his antipathy toward you, but created an aura of good will that could only be harmed by your presence. That bodes well, one never knows when the amity of such as he will be beneficial.

Before I go on, in the event that General Stone has already been arrested, let me here provide the facts that undoubtedly will not be immediately disclosed – even to you in your exulted status as friend to the throne: several reports have been circulating concerning Stone's activities. You know the type, returning runaway slaves to their owners; flags of truce in the early morning mists for undoubtedly nefarious purposes; mysterious comings and goings at all hours from his headquarters.

All these rumors emanate from a low life deserter who claims he heard Confederate officers speak of Stone as 'a brave man and a gentleman' – damning words indeed.

Pinkerton forwarded the above "facts" to McClellan, doing so only to forewarn as the investigators from the soon to convene Committee on the Conduct of the War were sure to uncover the same. Pinkerton stated that he did not find any of it credible, nor those who reported them. Nothing has occurred since that can be laid on Allen's doorstep, he did not endorse the reports, he disparaged them.

Others did not and they reached the War Department in due course. Worse, it reached those politically motivated to believe each and every libelous word uttered against an admittedly Democratic general. Believe it, circulate it, revel in it, and do nothing else. General Stone, under those conditions was incalculably more valuable right where he was under McClellan's command. Indeed, with luck he would be promoted, perhaps to headquarters where his presence could do the most damage when needed.

McClellan's friends, and by friends I mean political operatives, being no less intelligent or Machiavellian (remember this) moved quickly to abort this. Hence the warrant and arrest, despite the fact that Bates wanted nothing to do with it. I think he saw it for what it was, a naked attempt by the Republicans to show the Democrats running the Army in the East. I know, running is certainly the wrong verb to employ describing the Army of the Potomac. Do not cringe, you know it as well and it obviously concerns you, if not least as a student of military history. (As far as I know, my friend, no general ever became famous for his preparations).

I tell you this because you need to know that forces are at work in this mess. Also, as I know you/well, so that you will not go off and try to right an egregious wrong – you cannot, no one can. Forces have conspired to make a sacrifice of General Stone, they cannot be forestalled, diverted or stopped. Remember that as you climb on that high horse of yours. Unlike your intervention with the Union Station assault, an attempt here will not be viewed as admirable.

Sorry to preach.

I have come to the opinion that Ball's Bluff was, in large measure, McClellan's doing – to the extent that he set things in motion, failed to support the action and had the bad fortune to have a fool commanding on the scene.

What I have is this: on October 19 McClellan accompanied McCall's Division across the Potomac to move toward Leesburg. He ordered Stone to make a demonstration, in such a way as to make it seem as if a larger force was coming across the river near Edward's Ferry. All a big feint to see if he could bluff the Confederates into evacuating

Stone knew all this and fully expected that any force he sent over would have an entire division nearby to rely on for help. I have confirmed from several independent sources that not only did McClellan withdraw McCall's Division on the 20th after the rebels refused to bite on the ruse, but failed to notify Stone he had done so. Baker's brigade had no idea they were unsupported, alone on the south bank of the Potomac. I learned part of this from Stone's adjunct, 'unexpectedly' transferred to General Rosecrans's command the first week of November. It turns out to be an unfortunate choice of exile for there are many on Rosecrans's staff for him to commiserate with concerning your Mac – who is despised at this headquarters.

The reasons for that are simple, McClellan did the same thing to Rosecrans that he did to Stone. At Rich Mountain he sent Rosecrans's brigade around the rebel flank while he held their front with the rest of the army. The agreed plan was that at the sound of Rosecrans's guns, McClellan would attack. The flank attack started later than planned – but go ahead it did, despite terrible weather conditions . . .Rosecrans made his attack and McClellan did nothing. He sat and let Rosecrans fight it out alone

Of course it turned out fine and McClellan was able to release one of his aggrandizing pronouncements and the rest is history. Which is the one place you will not find an account of the above, there is no mention of the episode anywhere. Nor was Rosecrans's brigade mentioned in dispatches.

I spoke to 'Old Rosy" on an unrelated matter (another time, if it pans out) and managed to get him to comment (you would like this man; his men love him; he is unpretentious and an excellent whiskey drinker). Old Rosy confirmed the story and added, for attribution, "He hung us out to dry and then accepted the victory laurels and I'll tell that to anyone who asks."

I will presume once more to anticipate your thoughts; I know it was early in the war; the troops untrained; coordination of units and officers new and crude; the action minor and successful nonetheless. An understandable inconsequential military mishap.

Finally, you will undoubtedly dwell on the fact that I do not like your friend.

I tell none of this to you to undermine your friendship, loyalty, what have you. I tell you because you are conducting an investigation into an incident and you are not one to wish, in any way, to have any details held back due to perceived sensibilities, under any circumstances.

I tell you as well to allow you, as I know you will, to prepare yourself for future eventualities, to leave an eye open as events unfold, especially if you are ever required to make a decision regarding permanently hitching your wagon to your friend's stars.

And that day, my friend, will come, for as I have said since we walked into the house on Jackson Square, your General McClellan is after greater laurels than merely winning the war.

Well, do what you need to do, listen to Joinville, he has a good, dispassionate head on his shoulders. I am sure I will be back in Washington while 'All's Quiet on the Potomac' is still the watchword.

Take care of yourself, keep a watch out, tell Phelps 1 expect him to remain sober at least half the time I am out of town.

Best,

0.

27. Ft. Lafayette

Joinville and I stood by the rail of our steamer a stiff, freezing breeze off the Hudson cutting through us.

Neither of us spoke as the ship made her way through the crowded harbor. We barely moved, in fact, except to pull our collars tighter and hats lower. Our breaths rose in heavy clouds, our gloveless hands froze on the rail, but we gave no thought of fleeing topsides and miss a moment of the vista around us.

From the dock in Mid-town Manhattan, past handsome brownstones and teetering, teeming tenements of lower Manhattan,  the Navy Yard in Brooklyn — a strange, low, raft-like boat with what appeared to be a giant tin can on its deck sitting high up in dry dock — round Governor's Island and out into the harbor off the crowded tip of Manhattan, we stood transfixed to the moment we docked at Fort Lafayette.

We descended the gang plank trailed by the indomitable Phelps trying valiantly, yet vainly, to subtly convey that the two light bags he toted were the heaviest burden ever to saddle a man. Studiously ignored, he still threw occasional glances at Joinville while sporting the unique visage of a man recently disavowed of a cherished belief.

At the end of the pier we passed through a check point in the sense our uniforms were noted long enough for a fat corporal to throw an insouciant salute and wave us through. Inside the thick stone walls we were directed to headquarters across a snow covered parade ground to a low lying building dwarfed by looming parapets.

We left Phelps in a warm anteroom and showed ourselves to the commanding officer's office after receiving a helpful point in that direction by the master sergeant on duty – he apparently had been ordered to protect the potbellied stove with his life. We had not gone two steps before the sergeant and Charles fell into a non-commissioned officer only trading of weather related complaints that was sure to devolve into a forum on the uselessness of officers.

I knocked lightly, heard a muted invitation to enter, walked in, Joinville a step behind. The one armed captain behind the great oak desk in the corner jumped to his feet at the sight of my shoulder straps, began to snap to attention, right hand half way to an undoubtedly sharp salute – until he looked from my maple leafs to my face. When he found my eyes the hand dropped, his body eased in an instant to a slouch and a grin of naked, honest distain erupted beneath his long, waxed mustache.

"Good Christ," he drawled slowly in a clear, deep baritone – as fitted his barrel chest, "you're back and you're a goddamn Lieutenant Colonel, he squinted at the offensive straps, "merciful God, you're a regular. A regular goddamn officer," his shoulder and a half shook with frustration, "there is no God, you blaspemin' son of a whore."

I stood stock still, looked at Joinville, who stood agog, mouth open, "Don't make any sudden movements and keep your hands away from his mouth and you should be alright,' I relayed to the Prince.

The captain came around his desk, moved slowly but assuredly, toward us. He was an inch shorter than me, blond, brown eyed, with a slightly pock marked face that was noticeable only when one ignored the rigid yardarm of a mustache.

"You are a son of a bitch," he continued as he came on, "you resign without telling anyone, disappear for ten years and have the goddamn gall to walk into my fort, my first goddamn command, and you outrank me?"

"Does that mean you're not going to salute, Captain?" I inquired solicitously.

"No, you bastard," he moved closer, "I don't salute the likes of you . . . it's not good enough," he put me in a one armed embrace.

"Good to see you alive, Willie," he boomed in my ear.

"Good to be alive," I laughed, hit him on his broad, steely, fully intact shoulder, "let me go, Ben, we've confused my guest long enough."

Captain Benjamin Franklin Hoskins pushed me away, extended a three fingered hand to Joinville, "Ben Hoskins, good to meetcha'".

To the Prince's immense credit, testimony to the fact he was a keen observer and admirer of our culture (I think I can equate tolerance with admiration in his case) took the hand without so much as a blink, or grimace when the paw crushed his royal hand.

"Nice to meet you, Captain," he answered without formality.

"Benjamin, this is Prince de Joinville, of the House of Orleans, late of Paris. He's now a volunteer on General McClellan's staff."

"Oh, damn . . . sorry," a suddenly horrified Hoskins gasped, "good God, I thought you were a reporter or something with no insignia..."

"The Prince has no official rank at present as we have nothing exalted enough to properly fit His Excellency."

Joinville replied with an 'of-course' shrug and a faraway look as he contemplated an appropriate rank.

"He is a Vice-Admiral in the French Navy," I went on conversationally, "although at present he finds himself unwelcome on board a French vessel. You have something in common, actually, Ben, as you have as much authority on a French steam frigate as Joinville."

Joinville shook his head in a now practiced motion, "Despite the fact you are obviously a friend of Hanlin's," he made a show of sighing deeply, "I am glad to meet you, Captain. In the few months I have known the Colonel I have found that while he is an ass he has somehow managed to attract fine friends."

"Well, sir, you make a point," Hoskins beamed, happy to have an audience, "Though my lack of, er, decorum when you entered was, of course, based on the fact that one seldom expects to find Willie in the company of men of quality. My apologies, Prince de Joinville."

"Please do not apologize, Captain, for this one."

"Merci, mon Prince."

"You know," I endeavored to interject some sadly lacking professionalism into the proceedings, "you still haven't saluted a superior officer, Captain."

"Who the hell made you a Lieutenant Colonel – and a real one to boot?" He snapped while occupying his arm with tasks not related to performing a salute.

"Mac did," I answered with my best air of superiority.

"You are joking."

"No, I work for him, I'm his JAG liaison, at least for the interim'.'

"You're a goddamn lawyer as well?"

"Goddamn lawyer, yes."

"Shouldn't surprise me," he grinned, "not with your mouth."

"That's very kind, thank you."

"You're here to see Stone," he smiled weakly.

"And to think you finished second to last in our class," I replied evenly.

"Thank God for George Pickett," he laughed.

I smiled back although we both knew that he had finished exactly where he intended to. Bright, at times brilliantly intuitive, he was committed to enjoying the West Point experience in ways that the administrators would have neither dreamed of nor cordoned. All his inventiveness and energies were channeled almost exclusively to the, as he frequently pointed out, Jeffersonian promise of pursuit of happiness. As a result he graduated 64th of 65 while getting more pleasure than the amount cumulatively amassed by the cadets above him. He was the only man not smiling when we graduated, for he was the only man who was going to miss Highland Falls.

"Charles is well?" I inquired without concern.

"Happy as can be expected," the smile faded a tad.

"I need to talk to him."

"Got a note from your boss?" The smile was gone.

"Need one?"

"Would I ask you, of all people, if I didn't?" He looked and sounded pained.

"No," I sighed, "tell me, Ben, what are your standing orders regarding our mutual friend?"

"Simple, no one sees him unless I get a telegram authorizing a visit or some waif comes in off the Hudson carrying a note. Are you such a waif, Willie?"

"I am," I threw my orders on his desk, "Mac needs me to see him."

Hoskins picked them up, glanced through them quickly, lingered only over McClellan's signature. "I'll take you to him myself," he said with ease, rose and beaconed us follow.

"Have you turned visitors away?" Joinville asked.

"Yeah . . . six, seven newspapermen and one congressman I've never heard of – never heard back neither, so he couldn't have been that important."

We tramped back through the anteroom, neither Phelps nor the Sergeant moved a muscle that did not involve drinking from their mugs.

"Jesus Christ, Miller," Hoskins said in wonderment, "if you can't get to your feet for a Lieutenant Colonel and a Prince, when can you?"

"I'm a projectin' my respects from hearah, Captain, anna the gentlemen surely have it."

"Amen," Phelps intoned thoughtfully, tipped his mug in our direction.

"That coffee better be coffee, Charles," I said with considerable doubt.

"Ah, now, there yer go, Boss, assumin' the worst an' insultin' my host," Miller nodded along with the visibly crushed Charles.

"My apologies for any perceived slander, Sergeant Miller," I offered formally.

"Tink no more of it, Colonel, anna' feel free to join us upon your returns, sirahs." He made a short, solemn bow, Hoskins rolled his eyes and we stepped out of the warmth of the offices and into the cold.

28. Hoskins

We walked to the east wall in silence, past a long row of Dahlgren guns, caught the full force of the wind each time we passed a gun port. We climbed a spiral stone stairway in the northeast corner, up to another long row of guns and wind borne saltwater snowflakes.

The north wall had had the guns removed and brick walls constructed across their casements. A thick, solid door with Roman numerals affixed stood every ten feet or so. All new.

"why the new construction?" Joinville asked in the relative silence that followed our escape from the wind.

"We're to hold rebel officers and the like," Hoskins answered, "should your army actually get close enough to capture any."

"Mac's preparing, we're getting there," I was so well practiced with the response it was out before I realized it. A habit I was hoping to break soon

"So we keep hearing," he grinned to take the edge off the words, "the papers, though, disagree, say McClellan's dragging his heels, readying the army to death, planning on attacking when he has an army of veterans. That and other charming sentiments."

"Well, he's got Greeley behind him," I echoed Mac with a cringe.

"That is from Greeley."

"What?" I stopped walking.

"Yesterday's *Tribune*. Greely ended with 'the time to attack is now."

I shrugged ineffectually, "McClellan won't be pleased."

"Easy enough to rectify, move the goddamn army and the goddamn critics will go away," Hoskins said with common sense fueled frustration, "and people will stop cursing the rest of us West Pointers as theory ridden, lazy sots who don't want to fight our southern brothers."

"That what they're saying up here, Ben?" I stopped again.

"And worse, your friend Mac isn't helping anything by sitting around preparing, makes it hard for an officer to walk the streets up river. Unless you like jokes revolving around 'All Quiet on the

Potomac'. Christ, if Scott had acted like that in Mexico, you and me would still be there, married to a couple of Senoritas with a brood scampering under our feet waiting for Scott to be ready, any day, to attack an elderly Santa Anna."

I nodded without comment and began to move. Ben and Joinville stood still. I had no choice but to stop as well.

"You are not enamored of General McClellan, are you Captain?" Joinville asked in a pleasant, friendly manner that held no threat.

Hoskins subtly stole a look my way while Joinville had the good grace to take that precise moment to look out over the parade ground. Hoskins' eyebrows arched slightly; I smiled and nodded, 'Yes, the Prince is alright.'

"No, Sir, I am not, I think, and always have, that he is a goddamn, overblown, conceited blowhard."

"Shit, Ben, don't hold back," I chuckled, "make sure you get it all out."

"Thank you for your honesty," Joinville glared at me, "I take it you have reasons, do they date to West Point?"

"Goddamn right," he snarled. I recognized Ben was unstoppable, leaned against a wrought iron railing to enjoy the spectacle, "George was and is a snob of the first order," Ben finished, thrilled to have an audience.

"If the papers only knew how McClellan ingratiated himself – attached, really – to the Southerners at the Point. Southerners from the best families only, the goddamn aristocracy. He ate all that damn gentlemanly horseshit up. That particular brand of chivalry where you look down on everyone else with condescending distain. On good men like poor Tom Jackson."

"He treated you poorly?" Joinville persisted.

"Ah, now, that's just the thing," I noticed that when Ben emphasized points with his right hand, gesticulating with controlled animation, he kept twitching the remains of his left shoulder, attempting to move an entirely imaginary appendage, "he was nothing if not unfailingly goddamn pleasant and kind to me. The way one of his Southern gentlemen would a valued servant. And, I'll admit right here, I'm probably the only member of my goddamn class who didn't like him, besides Jackson."

Joinville nodded, cast an unreadable sidelong glance my way, "You got along quite well with him at West Point, did you not, William?" He asked finally with a distinct edge.

"You accusing me of being a gentleman?" I asked with real hope.

"Most certainly not," he jeered politely, "I am merely attempting to complete my picture of your background."

"That's easy," Ben said with a grin, "Willie got along with everyone, even the Southerners who, gentlemen though they were, would not have minded seeing his mother tar, feathered and hung – no offense, Willie."

"None taken, it's true enough."

"Willie was one of the few who just got along, him and Burnside, Hancock before, and the poor bastard we're heading to visit. Everyone liked them."

"Amazing," Joinville directed at me. I shrugged modestly.

"Ben," I said easily, "you might as well finish, tell him when you really started to dislike Mac."

"Ah, come on, Willie, I never —"

"Tell the Prince the rest, Ben, he'd like to hear it."

"Alright, Willie, I guess in the interest of thoroughness," he grimaced slightly, took a deep breath of cold air, "after graduation Mac, of course, went to the engineers. I got infantry – what I wanted from day one. The war was restarting after Tyler's truce and Congress authorized ten new, regular regiments. Captaincy of those units were plums. I got one, brevet captain. My father, his senator and a recommendation from Professor Mahan did it. Turns out Mac wanted one for himself and moved too late. It got back to me, quick, that he heard who got the regiments and said all the captains were deficient of the military academy and barroom blackguards – I memorized that particular quote."

"Well, I certainly can see -," Joinville began to commiserate.

"Oh, God, no, that's not it," only to be cut off by an appalled Hoskins, "I can handle slander – sticks and stones and all that, particularly in the heat of disappointment, Willie can attest to that."

"Certainly," I confirmed, "Ben is inured to insults… comes from much practice," I was happy to help a friend out.

"Thank you, Willie," Ben played his part well, always did, "nah, that wasn't it. My regiment was part of the flank attack at Cerro Gordo,

McClellan was with Pillow's diversionary column, goddamn disaster that it was. Anyways, we routed the Mexicans, my men did well, and we were filthy, sweating, bloody powder monkeys by the time we stopped. I'm just getting my men straightened out when I look up and who do I see but Mac riding by returning, I found out later, from Scott's headquarters where that goddamn moron Pillow had – "

"He's a general for the Confederates in Tennessee now," I cut in.

"Thank the merciful gods, Tennessee is saved for the Union," his face lit up at the thought, "Pillow sent Mac to beg for help while we were winning the real fight.

"So, McClellan rides by on a warhorse that scared the piss out of other horses. I yell out, 'hey, Mac!' He ignores it at first, so I scream, 'Mac! Cadet McClellan, eyes right!' He reins up on the great beast, smiles, sees me moving toward him all smiles, drops his and says, 'it's Lieutenant McClellan, Captain,' cold as ice. When I didn't reply, he finished with, "if you do not require anything of a military nature, I will be on my way, sir.' Rode away leaving me standing there like a goddamn idiot. It took me a good ten minutes before I realized the bastard didn't salute."

The look on Ben's face was such that we could not help laughing. He joined after a moment, lightly, and we resumed our walk.

We had gone five steps, at most, when Hoskins added, without looking at either of us, "I'll tell you one thing, and I goddamn mean this – all our former classmates and colleagues from the South, the way they dazzled George with their gentlemanly ways and chivalry and all that, shit, every one of them, A.P. and D.H. Hill, Joe Johnston, Beauregard, the whole lot, George is afraid to fight them. He's built them up in his mind and they're greater to him than Napoleon and his Marshals. He'll never attack them.

"I'll tell you one more thing, if you don't mind," he looked for objections, found only rapt attention, "he's definitely not afraid of the one he should be. Tom Jackson. No gentlemen he, and given the chance he'll rip McClellan to shreds."

He stopped before a door in the northwest corner, "Sorry to pontificate, guess I'm just a goddamn frustrated son of a bitch with one arm, no combat command, and jailor to a friend. Knock and go in, gentlemen, I'll leave you now, if you've got the time come back to the office and we'll have what the sergeants are having, just to warm up."

He leaned into Joinville, said something in a low whisper that the winds bore away from me, stood, saluted me smartly, winked at the Prince and marched away.

Joinville looked at me strangely, I felt compelled to say, "He exaggerates . . . greatly."

"I rather doubt that," he replied lowly, "a most remarkable man, though."

"You have no idea," I mumbled, picturing the two armed Hoskins at Churubusco. I knocked on the door.

29. Stone

A muffled 'enter' was issued with authority. I pushed open a heavy, thick door, and stepped into the room . . . the very spacious, very warm, well-appointed room. It took up a good sized corner of the fort; the gun ports were windowed allowing a spectacular view of the Hudson, a new brick fireplace was aglow with a well-tended fire.

Sitting in front of it, book on lap, slippers on, shirt sleeved, bright red suspenders hanging loosely, was General Charles P. Stone. He looked up at the intrusion without expression, merely removed a pipe from his mouth and gently closing the book – making sure to mark his page first. The epitome of studied, deliberate nonchalance.

I walked toward him, making a show of taking in the surroundings. He sat unmoving, watched with a half-developed, skeptical smile.

"I expected," I started, "something a little more out of *Man in the Iron Mask*, General, not a sitting room out of Jane Eyre."

"A prison by any other name, is still a prison, Colonel," he replied without inflection. Indeed, without moving.

"I can't dispute that," I answered, threw myself into the sofa facing him, not deigning to ask his leave. I motioned for Joinville to do likewise, he did, with considerable more dignity than me, "you might want to make yourself feel better by thinking of all the great men that have been likewise imprisoned."

"I have, actually, and it indeed comforts one to think of one in the company of Galileo and Voltaire.

"I was thinking more of the Marquis de Sade," I offered, gently.

"I'm sure you think of him often, sir, in any regard."

I conceded the point with a tilt of my head and changed the subject, "What are you reading, General?"

"You mean, what are you interrupting?"

"You that busy?"

"I've plans."

"I'm sure you do. What are you reading?"

He smiled, looking down at the tome in his lap, "*The Count of Monte Cristo* . . . a lovely story of a man persecuted for no reason."

"If I recall," I smiled back, "he did blunder into politics of a sort."

"Well said," he grunted, "I see you're still the ass."

"And you're still an obdurate bastard," I replied in earnest, "who should probably be reading Balzac."

"You casting allusions as concerns my present circumstances?"

"Perhaps?"

"No matter how you slice it, what's happening to me," he said it clinically, as if discussing another man's cancer, "is like something out of a French novel, heh?"

"That's comforting and sad at the same time."

"God what is it with the Frogs and bloody, convoluted, interwoven plots?"

It was, of course, a moment to live for and I took it, "By the way, General, may I present my friend, His Highness, the Prince de Joinville. Prince de Joinville, General Stone."

"Of course he is," Stone spasmed, "I'd heard . . .you two . . . ," he put both feet on the floor, leaned forward, dropped the-Dumas on the stone floor with a thud, "I am sorry, Your – "

"Please, General," Joinville eloquently interrupted, "I share your opinion of the, ah, interwoven plots of the French, having been the subject of one myself. Under the circumstances," he waved at the room, "your frustration is perfectly understandable."

"Thank you, most kind," a relieved Stone sighed, sat back and caught my eye. He blinked a few times as understanding flooded into his muddy brown eyes, "you set me up, you bastard. Damn it, you haven't changed a whit, Willie."

I could not keep it in any longer and began to laugh. After a moment Charles joined – he and I had always had the type of relationship wherein time and distance had no effect. Whenever, wherever we saw each other we wasted no time with greetings we just

. . . began where we left off. As if we had merely retired to separate rooms for a few hours.

When the laughter faded, Stone asked the obvious, "Mac send you?"

"He did."

"The one decent thing he's done so far," he snapped off with a bitterness I had not heard before from that most stoic of men, "you'll be fair."

"I'm already fairly pissed off having to come all the way to New York to see you," I shook my head sadly, "then there was that flight of stairs we had to walk up. I'm not sure I can be fair after all that."

"Then again, you've always been shallow and self-centered," he added pleasantly.

"Well, we're done here, I'm satisfied I have enough," I announced to a disgustedly perplexed Joinville, "you all set or do you need him to insult your heritage a bit longer?"

"I'm beginning to think you're enjoying this situation, Colonel," Stone summed up for all of us.

"I was when I imagined you in a dripping dungeon, choosing between the pit and the pendulum. Now that I see you luxuriating in these surroundings, away from the day to day horseshit of Washington and the army – well, frankly I'm jealous."

"Foods good, too," he offered and met my eyes fully. I could not miss his hurt and embarrassment.

"Seriously, Chas, are you alright?" I asked. With feeling.

"I'm comfortable," he said directly, "and I'm mortified."

Joinville and I sat in tacit commiseration for an appropriate, respectful moment.

He noticed, flashed a look of a victim's anger, "So, why the hell am I here, what are the charges and what are you going to do about it?"

"What have you been told?"

He shrugged and made no effort to respond while his face reddened.

"There are no charges," I replied as lightly as possible, "but there are suspicions."

"What the hell does that mean?" Not an unreasonable question under the circumstances.

"You're here on a detainer, there are no formal charges at present."

"I've not been charged with a crime?"

"No."

"Suspicions?"

"Treason."

A blank stare greeted that news, although anyone who knew the man knew he was calculating rapidly.

I broke the silence, "I suppose telling you that this is ridiculous is —"

"That a legal opinion or personal assessment based on knowing me for twenty years?"

"Both," I confirmed, "but I'm very concerned that high ranking Confederate officers have oft referred to you as a gentleman."

"That's part of it, rebel officers called me a gentleman?"

"Brave, too. You're apparently well thought of south of the Potomac."

"As are you, and Burnside, and Porter, and a hundred other West Pointers with friends serving down there."

"Undoubtedly," I agreed, needlessly. His eyes were still running through the permutations.

"But none of you," he reached the sum with alacrity, "ordered Baker to make that demonstration."

"No, none of us did."

"You are not my attorney, obviously, but I consider you a friend – better yet a friend who would not hesitate to relay an unpleasant truth."

"I'd revel in it, actually," I reinforced the sentiment.

"No doubt," he sighed, "do I have anything to fear from a purely legal standpoint?"

"None, any court or tribunal that prosecuted you would be embarrassed by the most inexperienced counsel. A good one would humiliate the army – you're safe on legal grounds."

"Thank you, Willie, I don't suppose I can expect to be released pending a hearing?"

"I would not plan on that, no," I answered directly.

"A writ of hab—"

"Habeas has been suspended in your case."

"Of course it has," he agreed pleasantly, "that legal?"

"Not really, not in my opinion, but once they start revoking it for one reason, they find it easier to revoke it for others. You're another."

"Lincoln?"

"Still President, yes."

"Ass. Can he help me? We became close before the inauguration."

"Thought you were a Democrat," I laughed.

"Liked the man, he liked me," he replied through gritted teeth.

"He can't help right now and I don't think you'd want it anyway. The Republicans will smell a cover up and, in the long run, they'll take it out on you more directly."

"Worse than this?"

"Ever been to Minnesota?"

"Point taken," he mulled over the idea of confinement in the sand blasted fort with its never diminishing sun, "considering my orders from the War Department, I take it as well, that I cannot have a formal inquiry concerning whatever the hell this is?"

"What orders?" Joinville spoke up, he had been following the conversation like a spectator at a lawn tennis match.

"I have been ordered," he sighed it out, "not to discuss the details of Ball's Bluff with anyone, under any circumstances. In the interest of national security."

That took a few moments to sink in. No one voiced that which I am sure we all thought: it was galling in the extreme to give a man orders like that while you were imprisoning him.

"That would," Joinville considered, "make an appearance before Congress rather superfluous, would it not?"

No one replied, the logic was irrefutable. As were the inevitable conclusions.

Stone broke another uncomfortable silence, "Well, you did not travel here from Washington to fill me in on my options, a simple telegram would have done that – 'Stone, stop, You are fucked, stop."

"I would have been more eloquent," I chuckled grimly, "it being the government's dime."

He nodded, "So, why are you here?"

"We are conducting an inquiry into Ball's Bluff," Joinville stepped in, "we cannot finish without you."

"And yet you will have to," Stone may have smiled, if so it was the definition of fleeting.

"I don't know," I mused aloud, "McClellan sent us, he knows why we're here . . ." I let it trail off answered with conviction.

"Is that your legal opinion?"

"Certainly."

"Am I your client?"

"You are today."

"And you are advising me to disregard a direct order from the commanding general of the United States Army."

"In this instance, under these circumstances, yes."

"You and your compulsion to know things," Stone sighed, not unkindly, "it'll get you killed yet."

"But not here and now," I answered with conviction.

"What have you learned so far?"

"You'll comment if I tell you?"

"It might not hurt me to have someone honest and intelligent to tell it to."

"Thank you," I replied modestly.

"I was speaking of the Prince."

"Merci," Joinville happily bowed.

I broke up their mutual snickering with a 'here's what we have' and began a long briefing of the general that encompassed our notes, Mac's flyer, post-action reports and Osgood's letter. The sun dipped behind the fort, Phelps and Miller arrived with plates of steaming food – neither of them paused long enough to catch our eyes and they moved with the studied, careful precision of men who knew they were drunk.

Joinville finished the interview after dark in the deep shadows of kerosene lamps. Stone confirmed everything we knew. A bottle of forbidden brandy arrived courtesy of Captain Hoskins. We paused as we opened and distributed it evenly. I built a roaring fire and took juvenile satisfaction in having done so.

"I should have gone out with them," Stone said at long length.

"Don't be absurd," I answered quickly and with no small degree of irritation, "Brigadier's don't go out on reconnaissance jaunts – and if you'd have gone, you'd be in a Richmond prison, or dead, not discussing this in a den of inequity with an old friend and a French Prince."

"You may have a point."

"Although, with your excellent Southern connections and reputation, you probably could have gotten us through the lines to visit anyway."

"Ass," said through a smile.

"You know," I continued unabated, the brandy had created a warm glow in my chest and stomach and put a colorful aura to the lights flickering across the stone walls, "I've been wondering for weeks exactly' how Baker was to make a 'demonstration' to attract the rebel's attention without crossing the river."

"Come again," apparently the brandy was working on him as well.

"Mac's flyer," I said almost giddily, "said Baker exceeded his authority crossing the river. If he was ordered to make a demonstration —"

"What was he supposed to do," Joinville finished for me, "if he had to stay on our side of the Potomac?"

"Well, now, that is a poser," Stone smiled deeply and took a long, hard, eye-glazing draw from his hardly empty snifter, "I suppose he could have put on a play, a pageant, or something, on our banks, draw the rebel's attention."

"That would have been nice," an inebriated Joinville slurred with warmth.

"A little Hamlet, a little Cyrano, some Stephen Foster tunes, the rebels would have been putty in your hands, Chas," I agreed.

"Would have loved to have seen it," Stone replied unsteadily, "you know who could have – would have – done just that, in the old army, Willie?"

"Who?"

"Prince John."

"Magruder," I laughed at the mere thought, "good God, a frustrated actor," I explained quickly for Joinville, although I did little justice to the man, "his brilliance as an artillerist is surpassed only by his flamboyance. I remember a fancy dress ball in Washington right after the war when he showed up as the King of Prussia, dressed to perfection, speaking German, attended to by courtiers . . ."

"I was with Prince John," Stone took over, "at Fort Niagara. There were a few ancient British regiments posted on the other side. John begged, borrowed, stole and rented fine china, glass, silverware, the works and invited their officers to dinner. He showed up in the full kit of a Black Watch lieutenant, kilt, the works. An amazing night. When it ended an awed British Colonel asked John how he could afford such a dinner on a lieutenant's pay. John answered, 'damn if I know!'."

"Man could make any posting pleasant . . . I suppose he's down there now?"

"General in Virginia."

"He'll end up President."

"No doubt," I agreed.

"Shame," Joinville slurred, "your army could use some color."

"Wait to you meet Phil Kearny," Stone snorted, "you won't think that any longer.

"That's certain," I agreed with a smile.

30. Typhoid

Dec. 16, 1861; Washington, DC

SPECIAL TO THE COURANT: Gen'l
McClellan appeared before the newly formed Joint
Committee on the Conduct of the War this morning
in a much anticipated, ultimately most
disappointing, appearance. Expectations that the
veil of secrecy surrounding the long hoped for
movement of the Army of the Potomac would be
lifted were dashed with McClellan's adamant refusal
to discuss plans in open session 'out of security
concerns'.

This newspaper joins those readers who are
frustrated and concerned by the long history of
promises of action and interminable 'preparations'
now exacerbated by the Commanding Gen'l's
refusal to divulge even the most basic information.

McClellan did comment on Ball's Bluff, reading
from a prepared statement: *'the whole thing took place
some 40 miles from here without my orders or knowledge. It
was entirely unauthorized by me and I am in no way
responsible for it.'*

He refused to discuss the reported arrest of Gen'l
Charles Stone, currently held at an undisclosed
location, on unknown charges. When pressed by
Senator Wade, he said only that 'I have trusted
members of my staff looking into several aspects of
Gen'l Stone's affairs and I will act accordingly after
they submit their findings'.

This reporter believes that one of the investigators is Hartford's own Lieutenant Colonel W'm Hanlin, late of the State's Attorney's Office.

His current whereabouts are unknown even to the men of the 21st CVI . . .

◊

I was pleased to no end to know my whereabouts were unknown. What pleased me to an even greater degree was dropping the paper to gaze in wonderment and perfect contentment at Bridget's naked buttocks.

I was propped against the headboard of her bed, she lay stretched out in the opposite direction, reading a book. It was mid-morning, snowing outside, a fire fizzled in the grate, the low flames reflecting off her porcelain back were mesmerizing.

Affecting as well. I placed the *Courant* over the afflicted area and picked up a book I had no intention of reading just then, or anytime in the foreseeable future. Certainly for as long as she remained nude.

My continued enjoyment of the view ended with, "What are you doing back there?"

"Not a thing," too defensive, too fast.

"Really," she slammed her book shut, turned carefully on her side. She slid a hand over to peek under the newspaper, "I see it is a particularly exciting news day."

"The classifieds always do that to me."

"Good to know," she, unimpressed, dropped the paper back in place, "save me all that fondling, kissing, licking – I can just read the paper to you."

"I can stop doing the same for you."

She moved, the comforter dropped below her breasts, "As if you could, look at you," she sneered alluringly, "you salivate at the mere sight."

"Well, I . . .," I had no answer, moved to touch her.

"And since you mention it," she pulled the discarded comforter around her, "your attentions to me are not . . . not common for. . . New England men."

"That's a rather sweeping statement that is not only an insult to a broad swath of American manhood but indicates extensive study," I looked at her archly.

"You are a bastard," she growled in a way that revived the newspaper, "Women talk, so my observation is based on rather much more than my own experiences – perhaps you have not noticed, what with the half-naked women walking around but I live in a brothel."

I slapped my head, "It's all coming together now. A brothel, I had suspicions."

"You're going to be sleeping with that newspaper tonight, keep it up," she snapped, cocooning into the comforter, "I'm curious, that's all," she said sleepily, employing the sloe eye, "why aren't you like others of your class and sex. Who taught you?"

I laughed easily and took in the hazel eyes for a heart-stopping moment, "I'd like some of the comforter, it's getting cold out here."

"I can tell, the paper is sagging," she noted, "answer the question and I'll think about it."

"I'll admit to certain . . . fumblings and disastrous frontal assaults, early on," I replied, reddening, "which would account, I'm sure, to the utter defeat my friends and I had at the hands of the senoritas."

"Discriminating women."

"Obviously," I agreed, "Lots of frustration to go with the boredom of the lulls between battles."

"So, we've ruled out New England, New York, and Mexico, my God, what an enthralling, titillating story."

"Just building up to it – I know how you enjoy that," I leered.

"I suppose subtlety is not a skill an infantry officer must necessarily possess to be successful."

"No.

"Lucky," she purred, "go on."

"I need to, it is really getting cold out here."

"You could act the man and stoke up the fire."

"Naked? I don't think I can take that sort of risk."

She made a point of looking hard at the limp *Courant*, "I do not think it a significant risk, especially now."

"That's cruel."

"Honesty is the basis of a solid relationship."

"I don't think the sight of a naked man bent over playing with logs, poking at ashes, is a very attractive sight."

"That is certainly true," she giggled maliciously, "so it would behoove you to get to the point."

"It's simple, really," I said as off-handedly as possible, "I lived in Paris for a year." I made a move to enter the comforter.

"Whoa there!" She yelped, moving and pulling to ingratiate herself further into the now well-sealed nest, "That is no explanation."

"It's adequate, the very invocation of the word Paris is, should be – enough. Details, while sordidly fascinating, would be inappropriate for propriety's sake."

An insincere laugh lashed back, "You are priceless," she snorted in a tone that conveyed precisely the opposite, "You have slobbered all over my nether regions and you cite propriety as an excuse not to discuss sex?"

"Nether regions? And you berate me?"

"No," a withering smile, armed and ready, "I didn't want to use a prurient term and risk offending you. It'd be inappropriate."

"What prurient term?" I asked with interest.

"One, describing an area you are never going to see again, never mind touch in any manner, if you don't begin to reveal something of yourself."

"We talk about me all the time."

"We talk about talking about you all the time, which is not the same, nor is it interesting."

"Do we?"

"You are not going to escape this using mindless rhetoric."

"Mindless?"

"Stop it," she threw a pillow, "and talk."

I hugged the pillow for warmth, "I was in Paris for a year. I was not in a very great state at the time and Paris after the barricades was a good place to . . . restore oneself. So I did. Most of my time there is a haze – I drank, tried hashish, opium and found myself with a woman, Collette, an artist and a bohemian, of course. I had money, she had looks, experience and liked to shop."

All true, and probably less than ten percent of the story. Bridget knew, too, I could tell by the way her sleepy eyes were joined by thinly pursed lips.

"Sounds like a match made in heaven," she said presently.

"It was perfect for me at the time, I kept her in her apartments with plenty of food and drink, she taught me many, things."

"Taught or demanded you learn?"

"There a difference?"

"Only in that you must have wanted to learn."

"I hope you'll agree that it didn't hurt to do so," I tried leering again but it froze on my face when she scowled in return, "What, complaints?"

"Not in that regard, no," she more or less snapped, eyes closing.

"I am wanting in other areas," I surmised.

"You're a smart man, figure it out," her eyes remained closed, "just remember, stoicism may be admirable in the company of warriors, but it grows thin with your particular woman friend."

"Stoicism implies silent suffering, which assumes suffering in some regard to start – none of that applies to me."

"You'd like to think so," she yawned.

"You're falling asleep," I observed the obvious, while ignoring the statement.

"I did not get much sleep last night," she yawned again.

"I did not think I molested you that long," I tried a little humor.

"Heh," the attempt was washed away with contempt, "it wasn't the molestation, my tender mercies on your manhood or our joining thrusts — how's that for euphemisms?"

"Outstanding," I gulped.

"I've been thinking of writing an erotic novel, 'The Terrible Confessions of Miss B'."

"I'm willing to take your dictation."

"Pervert."

"Funny."

"I am not tired, William," she moved around in her thick cocoon, "from the sex," a look of smugness at using the operational noun, "you woke me several times with nightmares."

"Did I?" I think I hid my mortification, "I say anything?"

"Just lots of grunts, lots of thrashing."

"Sorry."

"It's fine, really."

"Uh-huh," I replied without commitment. I did riot know where my experiences with women ranked in comparison to my contemporaries and peers, but I certainly knew enough to recognize her last phrase for the freshly baited trap it was. I, leader of men that I now purported to be, had no intention of venturing into it. For many reasons, all of which seemed valid then and proved not only not so, but specious as well. Later.

I remained silent, watched the comforter's breathing slow until its occupant was soundly asleep. I was exhausted myself and there is nothing like watching another person fall asleep to motivate one to do the same. Having stirred up memories of Paris and everything associated with it, I did not feel I could be assured of not putting Bridget through another ordeal of Morpheus Interruptus. I got up, dressed, re-stoked the fire and headed out in search of as big a breakfast as Cook could whip up. Five steps outside Bridget's door I was struck by the sudden feeling that I did not want to, indeed could not, eat alone. As Joinville was that extraordinary royal anomaly who rose early, I decided that he was probably hungry. For food.

A moment later I knocked on Maria's door – she had appropriated him (he went without protest) moments after we walked through the doors the previous afternoon, straight from the train from New York.

My light touch was immediately answered by a boisterous 'entre, sil vous plait.' I stepped into a pleasant room, was assaulted by several sights at once, each causing me to turn beat red, to my increasing discomfiture.

Le Prince de Joinville sat in a woman's silk robe, loosely tied, behind his easel, watercolors arrayed beside him. A wondrously nude Maria was lying on her side on a settee, head propped up on one hand, smiling devilishly.

Which is all I saw of her facial expressions for long, long seconds as my eyes flicked like a metronome between her full, chocolate-tipped breasts and jet black pubic hair.

"Good morning, William," Joinville rang out with élan.

I mumbled something in return and struggled to look a giggling Maria in the eyes.

"Mornin', Willie," she sang out, laughed outright, jiggling her breasts but not otherwise breaking her pose.

Feeling every bit the village idiot, I checked my chin for drool. Finding none, I regrouped, somewhat, "You got an empty space on a royal apartments that need filling?"

"Alas, no," Joinville replied pleasantly – as suited a man in his current position, "While Maria is worthy of the Louvre, this is for her."

Maria expressed her thanks in strange, pleasantly accented French. Which made her shocking, luridly descriptive sexual suggestion sound preposterously elegant.

"Well," I stammered, "my offer of breakfast cannot stand against ... this ... I'll just be off..." I fumbled for the door while attempting to take in Maria for as long as possible.

"Wait, William, I am famished," Joinville called out, "And Maria needs a respite from that position." Joinville moved to put his brush down, Maria sat up on the settee, breasts jutting, legs slightly ajar, smiling coyly. Joinville traded glances with her.

"I will meet you in fifteen minutes, or so," he smiled, "half an hour at the outside."

I left them to their laughter, shut the door behind me and padded down to the kitchen, prepared to eat alone. Instead, I entered the room to find a large, tweed encased, handle-bar mustached man, reading the morning paper and picking at a plate piled high.

Patrons apparently did not frequent the kitchen for he startled upon seeing me, regarded me with the jaundiced eye of a policeman.

"Sanders, I presume," I said, heading for the coffee.

"And you'd be ... sir?"

"William Hanlin, I —"

"Oh, Good Lord," he leapt from his seat to advance on me, a smile pushing apart the long ends of the mustache, "I should have known, I am sorry, Mr. Hanlin, sir, good to meet you, finally." He grabbed my unsuspecting hand, "I am in your debt, sir."

"Consider it repaid upon allowing me to continue to the coffee," I not so graciously grunted in response.

"Oh, yes, sure," he dropped my hand and stepped toward the pot, "allow me sir, allow me."

I meandered to the table and toppled into a chair while he went on, "Yes, sir, least I can do for the man who gave me this assignment – the very least."

I soon had a steaming mug in front of me. I sipped it and eyed his breakfast.

"Cook will be back in a moment," he laughed at my avarice.

"Great," I did not understate.

"Have you seen this morning's paper yet?" He asked solicitously while eying his plate with yearning.

"Please eat, it's fine," I said magnanimously, "I just read yesterday's *Courant*. Anything new?"

"Yes, actually," he replied through a mouthful of sausage, "guess it's lucky you and your friend came north for a while."

"Why?" I asked with trepidation.

"'Cause there's a typhoid epidemic in Washington," he answered, threw the paper in my direction, "General McClellan's at death's door."

Book IV: The Peninsula

And on the pedestal these words appear:
"My name is Ozymandias, king of kings.
Look upon my works, ye mighty and despair."

Percy Bysshe Shelly

1. A Proposal

No olfactory warning of the closeness of our half-a-nation's capital this time – nor visual for that matter. I could not see a damn thing through hard, gusting snow that slammed into the east side of the train with car rocking regularity. My mood since leaving Hartford encompassed an angry, consuming obstinacy that precluded me from moving across the aisle of my nearly empty car to gaze to the snow covered – and rising – west.

The train slowed, the wind abated and I experienced a strange vertigo at the sudden absence of side-to-side lurching. The few passengers in the first class compartment – obviously unseasoned travelers – stood and began to gather their possessions. The train bucked to a jaw snapping stop knocking them into the closest, unyielding abutments. A stream of loud, less than creative curses echoed around the car while they collected themselves and possessions through clouds of superfluous groans and stomped out in search of a railroad employee to blame.

I was the last to exit, such was my enthusiasm for my premature return to Washington. I stepped out onto an enclosed, cold platform and walked unimpeded through the almost deserted station, the storm faintly howling behind the walls. Without pause I strode out the entrance and right into an all-encompassing white, bone-cracking frigid universe dominated by snowflakes the size and consistency of grains of sand driven by furious winds. Winds that cut through my greatcoat, scarf, gloves, uniform, union suit (Bridget insisted – solely for her secret amusement, I had no doubt) to sting and prick my skin as if I were wearing a shift.

I tripped through mid-shin deep snow that was rising precipitously, banking up against anything standing. No hansoms in sight, I resigned myself to groping deeper into the thick, white curtain until I, inevitably, fell into a snow bank somewhere on the mall where I would be uncovered someday to be displayed at the Smithsonian like the great mastodons found in Siberia.

I shivered and despaired, spied a sliver of movement to my right, took it for a sign of life and plowed toward it in the faint hope it offered sanctuary. With every lung freezing step I cursed, in order: Western Union for their audacity operating flawlessly through such a harsh winter; their temerity in interrupting my New Year's house playing with a vivaciously undomesticated Bridget; my mother for demanding a return receipt and thus eviscerating any possible excuse revolving around a lost telegram.

Mostly, though – I found a curb under the snow, plunged an unexpected six inches, almost breaking my ankle, kept my balance only by abandoning all dignity – I blamed me. For leaving the warmth of my house and the equally warm, lascivious Bridget for my mother's summons, purposely mysterious as it was.

I found a glimmer of civilization in the snow-haloed glow of a street lamp, the white expanse streaked by a blue-veined, thin strand of soldiers fading deep into the obscure horizon silently clearing the street.

Some enterprising general had turned out at least part of the Army of the Potomac to keep the most basic of lines of communications open. Either a sincere effort to save civilization or he had a tryst that evening across town, his reasoning did not matter, I lauded him in any event.

I shuffled down the center of the street, the snow finally below my boot laces, contemplated that McClellan was not my savior – the papers reported him still bedridden with a strain of typhoid they had inflated to an imminent appearance before the choir invisible. A brush, I knew via Osgood that was actually relatively minor, nowhere near the tenacity of the strain that had killed so many and had young Willie Lincoln near death in the White House.

Fortunately, the thin blue line was almost continuous and made my route physically easier. I walked unburdened, the obstacle remaining the nasty looks of soldiers who had assumed ownership over the road they had uncovered. My last remaining fear: that my facial features would be sandblasted away by the horizontal snow.

Careful counting of the barely seen streets I passed – one in every three or so being shoveled by other blue lines – finally brought me to the one I sought. Then it was only a matter of counting the blinkingly obscure houses. I went up two wrong walks before I tripped over the steps to the address in Mother's otherwise information-less summons.

The address was itself mysterious. A tony – extremely so – section of Washington not far from the Chases. I had no idea what relation it had to her. Throughout the trip I had girded myself for every conceivable eventuality including the slim but still bile inducing possibility of a smoking jacket clad Sumner lounging about. (My planned-since-Baltimore response: "Mother, not another politician!")

It occurred to me, utterly guiltlessly, that although I had met her three times in three months in three completely different venues I had not the slightest curiosity as to where and how she was situated.

I shuffled through shin deep snow, almost fell onto the heavily dusted porch, staggered to the door and knocked loudly. Then again for the wind had picked up with a ferociousness that could only mean it was coming in for the kill before I reached sanctuary.

I absorbed a full, spine cracking gust before the door was opened enough for me to slip through sideways before it slammed behind me with frightening accuracy.

I shook, stomped my snow clotted boots, dragged gloves off my suddenly aching hands, tried vainly to unbutton my great coat, fingers unresponsive, sighed, withheld a perfect curse, finally looked at my rescuer. Straight into the violet, gleaming, gently mocking eyes of Cassandra, Mother's secretary-assistant-dresser-friend. As well as the first fantastically adult female I had ever seen nude. A fact we both knew and tacitly acknowledged whenever our eyes met after lengthy absences.

As the last time I had seen her was years past, our eyes held for a long moment before she set about unbuttoning my coat and tsk-tsking over the state of my icy self.

"William, how nice of you to come," she sang in an alluring alto, smiled, peeled the coat off, "you look grand."

"Thank you, Cassie," I broke the ice around my mouth with a halting, painful smile, "so do you."

I did not lie, six years my senior, never married, in Mother's employ since she was seventeen, she was short, vivacious, dimpled, still flawlessly blond, still apparently in possession of a perfect figure.

She caught me looking, smiled the smile she gave my sixteen year old self when I saw her in all her glory. As it did then, it melted my heart and sent tiny little frozen butterflies whirling around my very empty stomach.

I swallowed, endeavored to speak coherently to the shaper of my womanly ideal, "Whose house is this?"

"Your mother's," she answered, smile inherent in her voice.

I was momentarily taken aback, showed it, "Since when?" More or less tumbled out.

"Since 'fifty-six, actually, I can give you a tour later, if you'd like," she said it matter-of-factly and yet managed to infuse the simple sentence with suggestion and rapprochement.

I had no reply, smiled like the addled teenager I had once been.

"Later, then?" A lilting question, she did not wait for an answer, "She's in the sitting room, with food," she read my mind, "and it's nice and warm in there."

I followed her down the hall and into a wonderfully warm, ornately decorated room presided over my mother much like Kublai Khan had Xanadu.

"Mother," I said wearily, ignored the impulse to greet the food first, moved toward her chair, bent slightly and brushed an unyielding cheek, "I see urgent did not refer to a health crisis."

"Relieved, dear?" She asked with a dim glint of humor.

"Certainly," I attempted sincerity, judging by her look I was not entirely successful. I had only briefly entertained the notion that 'Come. Urgent.' had been necessitated by illness. Mother's deathbed tableau most certainly did not include family members beyond Christian, the devoted child.

The question of her health settled, I helped myself to the food. She watched while I picked, poked, and selected, unreadable smirk in place. I found a chair, sat with plate on lap, coffee on the table next to me, took a sip, then a bite, and girded for the onslaught.

Mother choose to torment me instead, "Good trip, dear?"

"Blizzard conditions from Philadelphia down, had to walk here," I shrugged. My mother used small talk the way Lucretia Borgia did poison and I had no wish to partake, "but fine."

She nodded as if I had just divulged the secret of the Sphinx. Those who did not know her would have thought she was endlessly fascinated by every syllable. In that they would have been stupendously mistaken.

It had taken me fifteen years or so to figure that out for myself. Which was why I knew with certainty that had I relayed the news that my train had been stopped and ransacked by Tartars her nod would not have faltered.

To discourage her continuing what we both knew was a fatuous – if not customary – preamble to the matter at hand, I took a large bite of a very, very good apple turnover. I knew at once Mother's cook, Marjorie, old for as long as I had been alive, was in the house and had lost none of her skills. Christian used to claim she left one thin whisker in everything she cooked, which would have denuded her not a whit despite her vast volume of work. I smiled at the memories, Mother did not notice.

Cassie walked in to the room, Mother lit up, "Ah, Cassandra," exclaiming as if they had been apart for years, "what marvelous timing, William was just telling me about the trip down."

Cassie tossed a dubious look my way before handing Mother an envelope, pouring a tea, placed it next to Mother. She shimmied out of the room smile affixed.

I stared at the envelope, knew it was the reason for my summons, knew I was not going to like whatever was inside it. With equal certainty I knew my mother would milk the moment even with an audience of one.

True to form and expectations, she slowly sipped her brew and inspected me over the rim of the cup, taking no pains to hide her assessment, still, somehow, implacable.

"Well, William, if you are comfortable, perhaps we should begin," it was not a request.

"We?" I asked with a short edge – as in 'you called me from a warm house and warmer bosom to tramp through a blizzard, did not have the good grace to be at death's door when I appeared and you start off with 'we' as if we have ever been a 'we'.'

"I will begin," she corrected, "this," She brandished the letter, "was delivered here for you. I was told it was important, so I read it first," no hint of apology, Mother's creed, the family's motto, *Si Necesse Facte* – if necessary, do.

She held the envelope out, I half expected Cassie to swoop in, snatch it and deliver it to me, but not even Mother could choreograph the evening that well.

I combined reluctance and eagerness into a new emotion and rose, stepped over, gently removed the envelope from her still pressing fingers, and returned to my seat, pausing for a heartbeat or two to look longingly at my half-eaten turnover.

No need to slit it open, that had been neatly done three days earlier. The paper inside slid easily into my hand, I unfolded it – thick, expensive stock – and inspected a subpoena from the Congress of the United States, Joint Committee on the Conduct of the War for January 16th, 9:30 am.

I made sure to show no reaction, somewhere deep inside I probably expected it. I was unconcerned, irritated only at the waste of time involved and an early morning spoiled. Mother, of course, would know that, she did not raise her sons to quake at Congressional summons – though she did teach them to despise at least fifty percent of that august body for most of our lives.

I stared at the summons longer than needed before I carefully folded it, placed it back in the envelope and put it on the table next to my coffee cup. Mother watched every motion with a stony expression.

"Urgent?" I asked, flatly, picked up the turnover, took a bite, grabbed the mug, nestled into the chair and sipped.

"Of course it is," she replied, perfectly rational.

"I have eleven days."

"In which to prepare," her eyebrows arched.

"No preparation is necessary," I stated matter-of-factly with eyes only for my turnover.

"Really?" She asked before taking a casual as a glacier sip of tea, "What, exactly, do you think you have been summoned for?"

"Before I answer that," implicit was 'while I try to figure out what you know', "answer me this – why would this be sent to your house?"

"They know you are my son, obviously."

"I haven't lived under your roof for years and one would assume with me in the army and all, they would know where to find me."

"One would," she agreed.

Her response was less than satisfactory and she was little inclined to add anything on the topic, so I endeavored to persist, "I am on

General McClellan's staff, was granted leave by the War Department – a leave that does not expire until next Tuesday, by the way – and that order was relayed to me in Hartford . . ." I took a pull of coffee, "so, you can see, Mother, why I would be confused to find you in possession of my subpoena."

"I suppose," she started in her very best 'while-I-cannot-speak-for-them' voice, "they just wanted to insure you received it – they must think you are very important."

"Actually, Mother, their method of delivery says otherwise," I matched her wooden smile.

"Why would you say that?"

"It's improper, Mother," I explained pleasantly, "I am under no compulsion to appear for I have not been served this summons – I find it hard to believe that knowing I am an attorney Congress would be so sloppy."

I put my mug on the table, interlocked my fingers in my lap – my 'I'm done look' – and waited.

Mother regarded me carefully, which is not to say her expression changed. I had her attention but be I her son, a potted plant or coiled cobra nothing was going to show in her face. Not at this stage of whatever the hell we were doing, something we had not done in years but appeared to still be good at. Mother would not show emotion until it could earn interest – which meant it would not be wasted on me.

Mother's eyes stopped their calculations, then she sighed – either a remarkable concession or an affectation, I had no way of knowing. A last sip of tea, her bloodless hands placed the cup and saucer on the table with studied delicacy, she smoothed her dress and started, "I see I will have to be frank, my dear. If you are willing to hear me out."

Hawthorne had once referred to Mother as a woman who thought with the tenacity of Hamlet, schemed with the facility of Burr, and revealed her feelings with the regularity of Mona Lisa.

Mother was thrilled and considered it a compliment. No one in the room, my young self included, recalled Hawthorne smiling or otherwise indicating warmth.

Somewhere in my musings I must have nodded for Mother smiled and whispered, "Good, William," she fixed her eyes a good six inches over my left shoulder, "I asked that the summons be given to me, if and when it was decided to issue it. I wanted to give it to you so that we could have a chat beforehand."

"Why did you think I might be called to testify?"

"I was at several . . . gatherings that included Senators Wade and Chandler."

"I doubt they were so indiscreet as to talk about this business at a social function," I pointed out, eyebrows extended for additional emphasis of disbelief.

"I did not say it was a social function," she may have frowned, "in any event, the gathering was exclusively one of like-minded individuals."

"Abolitionist meeting?"

"We have little need for meetings right now, dear."

"You meet them in the Senate chamber, sit at one of the empty desks?" I was at least half serious.

She had the good grace to chuckle, "No, of course not. But I did have occasion to be present while members of the committee, and others met."

"And my name naturally came up."

"No," she may have mocked me, "your friend's name 'came up' first. Then the matter of Ball's Bluff. Then, after many permutations, you."

"You are threatening my illusions of grandeur."

"You were mentioned," she ignored my comment, "because you are on his staff, are his friend, and are conducting the army's investigation of Ball's Bluff. You were inevitable."

"That's reassuring."

"You can be as flippant as you wish, I think your time in Hartford has too far removed you from events here. I do not think you realize what has been going on here as concerns your general."

"He's been ill," I summarized concisely.

"Until a few days ago he was thought to be dying. A panic spread because no one knew his plans – no one in power. The Republic was looking at the death of its military commander after months of training and preparations and had no idea what was planned, we were looking at starting from scratch."

"Yes, but –" I started.

"No, buts," Mother was not interested, "the country will be out of money in a few weeks. No money, no general, our largest army still sitting around Washington, no plans. Panic."

I saw it, acknowledged with a tilt of my head.

"Do you know how panic is handled by politicians?"

I took it for rhetorical, made no move to reply.

"They do . . . something. It does not need to alter anything, it does not need to address the real issue, but they have to do and will do something if for no other reason but to show they are aware and active. Anything but remain passive."

"Is that where we are now, in a hive of activity?"

"Yes, William, an angry hive."

"An indiscriminately angry hive?"

"What do you think after McClellan's promises?"

"They need scapegoats," I answered with a sigh.

"They will get them," said with assured matter-of-factness.

"I understand all that," I said without affect. It would have occurred to me as well, as soon as the intoxicant known as Bridget wore off, "it explains the summons, it does not explain why it was delivered to you."

"You are appearing the day after General McClellan," her non-answer.

"Alright," I said carefully, I was beginning to get a not unfamiliar queasy feeling in the deep recesses of my bowels.

"I have it on good authority —"

"Wade or Chandler?"

"Chairman Wade," an infinitesimally quick flash of annoyance crossed her face, it was certainly in her voice as she went on, "he will ask McClellan about his plans, demand an explanation for Ball's Bluff, and request formal charges be brought against General Stone."

"Fascinating," I lied.

"Predictable, I would think," she snapped — she had never appreciated the irony oft times employed by her eldest, "all subjects you have knowledge of, it is believed." She gazed at my hairline in expectation.

"Two out of three."

"Dare I ask?"

'What would stop you' stayed where I thought it and I said, "I am not party to strategy, nor do I wish to be."

She smiled unpleasantly, "You were quite erudite on the subject when met with Senator Sumner."

I laughed despite the tenseness in my shoulders, "That was months ago – it might as well be the last war as far as military planning goes. I don't know anything about what's planned today."

"Well, then, I suppose your knowledge of Ball's Bluff and the Stone matter will have to do . . . have you had a chance to meet with Stone?"

That did it, everything about her indicated she knew the answer, as she had all the others thus far in our 'reunion'. Instead of answering I drained the dregs of my coffee, stood, walked past her to the food, piled several pastries on a plate, refilled my mug, waddled back to my chair, put them on the table, crossed the room to an ottoman by the fire, pushed it back to my chair, took off my jacket, sat, pulled off my boots, plopped my stocking feet up on the ottoman, took a bite of an exquisite scone, took a sip – shit, forgot to add sugar – and waited.

"Please, make yourself comfortable," Mother broke the ensuing silence.

I toasted her with the half-eaten scone, made my decision, "It's obvious, Mother, that you are privy to everything. You know I investigated Ball's Bluff for McClellan, you know I saw Charles Stone in New York, you probably know what I had for fucking dinner last Thursday.

"So, please, let's dispense with the multiple layers of horseshit and simply tell me why we are discussing this in the midst of a blizzard with me five hundred miles from my house and the woman I love."

The last surprised me, too late to withdraw it, Mother moved forward, mouth opening.

"Do not," I held up a hand in warning, "ask me if she is from a proper family."

She did not blink, "I was going to ask you to refrain from cursing,"

"Just wanted to see if I had your attention."

"You always have that," she lied without wavering.

"Why am I here, Mother?"

"Things are getting complicated, William, many forces are at work and I want to help."

"I've no doubt," she started to smile, "I just don't know who you wish to help."

She feigned being taken aback, "Why, you, dear, of course, I do not want to see you caught up in something –"

"That you helped create?" I enjoyed both posing the question and my snide tone.

Her eyes looked heavenward in her famous 'oh, please' look – the one that struck fear in the hearts of prospective artists of all ilk, budding young abolitionists; exiled Franklin Pierce, and had absolutely no effect whatever on her family or house staff, a fact she resolutely refused to acknowledge.

"I did no such thing, Senator Wade is quite capable and —"

"I meant the war Mother, not the committee," I smiled to show I meant it.

She blinked that away with a non sequiter, "Are you happy in your current position, William?" Her voice dropped, she rose, put her back to me while she refreshed a tea that had hardly been touched.

"Yes," I answered quickly and untruthfully.

"Have you made plans beyond it?" She continued working on what was fast becoming an astonishingly intricately made tea.

"Have you forgotten I'll rejoin the Twenty-first eventually?"

"To be second in command?" A spoon hit fine china with an unnerving crack.

"Yes," I muttered.

Rapid stirring, as if trying to make butter in porcelain, I waited for the clattering to recede before adding, God knows why, "I didn't ask for the staff position, it was pure happenstance . . . I was perfectly happy where I was, I'll be thrilled to go back and be 'second in command' . . ."

I stopped while Mother returned to her chair, sat, cocked an eyebrow, sipped slowly.

That long before it hit me and I silently cursed myself for an idiot, "Your friends want McClellan removed."

"They want action, or at least movement and they are rather unconvinced your general will do either."

"So, lacking that – "

"Anybody else will do, preferable someone who understands why this war is being fought."

"Not too many Radical Republicans running about with commissions," I pointed out.

"Oh, we have a nice list, dear," she gave a shallow nod to the naïveté of her son, "any one of them will do, after all a Republican general would not have to be prodded and his motives for waiting would not be questioned."

"Going to try McDowell again?"

"Anyone who will act . . . now."

"Let me just point out – as someone should – that the Army of the Potomac is devoted to McClellan and there is the pesky matter of all those Democrats and moderates – like our President, who support him."

She flicked that away with exquisite grace, "If McClellan is removed so ingloriously – and he will be, William- I think you will find future advancement in the army rather difficult . . . if not impossible."

She held my gaze while she tried to will her thoughts and wishes into my head from across the room. At that precise moment I realized I might very well have some aspirations beyond friend to generals. Advancement was in the air for all West Pointers every bit as much as the typhoid.

The revelation surprised me, I regrouped with, "I'll take my chances with the fortunes of war," realized immediately it sounded sophomoric.

"You do not have to," Mother replied with deliberate measure.

I took a deep breath, exhaled slowly, "Really?"

"Options, dear, consider your options," she said with hope.

"I'm unaware of any current opportunities, Mother, unless I'm willing to consider a better offer from that nice army across the river."

She took a sip of tea, deliberately aligned cup with saucer, "Did you know," she started with exactly the same intonation she would have discussing the weather on a perfectly calm day, "that William Sprague is returning to Rhode Island?"

"No, we haven't run across one another at the club recently," she frowned, shook it off with a look.

"He has government and business concerns he must return to," she took a moment to look in my eyes, "he had to turn down command of a brigade to do so."

"Sprague was offered a brigade?" At that point of the war I had ceased being shocked – so I had to settle for outrageously surprised.

"Offered, unable to accept,'" she nodded stiffly, "You know, he thinks highly of you."

"Does he?"

"He does . . . as a matter of fact, if you were to see him, he would be most happy to steer you in the right direction."

"Right direction?"

"I have it on good authority that his recommendation for the post will be accepted."

"Will it?"

"Almost certainly as long as it is someone competent."

'Unlike him' remained unsaid. I took a bite of a suddenly flavorless pastry. Sure of the answer, I asked anyway, "You wouldn't happen to know where I could find him, would you?"

The smile widened, "I do, actually, Friday night, nine, at the Chases. A very small dinner party. They'll be very pleased to see you."

"Will Wade be there as well?" I asked quietly.

"Perhaps," her happy response.

"Should I bring my notes or will my memory do?"

"It is such an excellent memory, dear," she laughed delightedly.

I stared into her now sparkling with plan-executed-to-perfection eyes. I stared until she looked down into the depths of her tea cup. Then I took my feet off the ottoman, pulled my boots on, stood, slid my jacket on, buttoned slowly, picked the subpoena up and walked to Mother.

With every step I took puzzlement and alarm replaced her look of victorious contentment. By her side, I carefully tore the envelope in two, then repeated, carefully placed the pieces by her saucer.

"Tell your associates," I addressed the side of her reddening face, "if they want me to testify they can serve me properly – I'm staying in town, I'm easy to find."

I leaned over, "And, Mother," she remained fascinated by her cup, "an officer who betrays his commanding officer has no future in the army regardless of connections and favors."

I walked out, the clock the only sound in the room.

2. Salem

George McClellan was the epitome of the 'in-the-pink,' the very embodiment of the phrase. He brimmed with good health, showed not a hint of the effect or ravages of typhoid, nor did he look like a man who had dragged himself off his sick bed to meet with the President, an ad hoc war council, congressional delegates and the cabinet.

I irrationally hated him for it, at least momentarily; he was too damn healthy, too damn happy, too damn cocksure. Whereas I was exhausted, depressed and unsure. My resentment was as natural and inevitable as it was suppressed.

It was Tuesday, January 14th, a nauseatingly buoyant McClellan was to appear before the committee the next day. I had not been served a summons despite having made myself as conspicuous as possible over the past week. I did everything short of standing in front of Wade's house waving.

McClellan had apparently cleared the air during his meeting with Lincoln, issued fiats to the forces in Kentucky to move immediately and, best of all, to hear Mac tell it, found as he was dressing for dinner that Cameron had left the war department. Shortly after that welcome news, McClellan's singular friend Edwin Stanton dropped by to ask if Mac had any objection to his accepting the Secretary of War appointment.

A typical McClellan turn of fortune – on his 'deathbed', carped at by politicians, newspapers, fellow generals; he rises and gets what he wanted and desperately needed: a placated President and a friendly Secretary of War. His impending early morning testimony was no more a threat to him than a sudden earthquake swallowing Washington.

All that tumbled out from Mac almost before I got comfortable in my chair. He was animated, almost joyous, certainly confident. It occurred to me, not for the first time, that Mac was a man, an important man, who needed his friends, at least the few who knew him before the trappings of authority were assumed

Finally, an expansive Mac leaned back, looked at me as if for the first time and launched into the reason for our hastily called meeting, "How is Stone?"

"Holding up well, considering."

"His accommodations are comfortable?"

"Very, considering.'

"Good," he beamed. "I wouldn't want it any other way."

"No matter how comfortable," I endeavored to impose some of my mood on the morning's proceedings, "he's humiliated, and he misses his command."

"Of course, of course," Mac waved them away, "to be expected." And there he stopped. I waited, he made no attempt to add anything.

"While empathetic," I began, "your statement doesn't appear to offer much hope for a change in his circumstances."

"Not just yet, I think," he answered stonily, carefully.

"Then when?" I had to ask.

He did not so much as flinch, he simply chose to ignore the question, "What does he need?"

"It's not what he needs, it's what he wants." I answered evenly.

"Then, Willie," Mac smiled lowly, "what does General Stone want?"

"A court martial or court of inquiry, or both," my voice dripped with great good sense.

"Well, he cannot have them," the smile stayed affixed but faded from his eyes.

"It's his right to demand them," I reminded him.

"Fine. He has exercised the right to demand. It's denied. It will work itself out after we move on."

"Not fine, General", I hesitated only a moment, the adamancy of his response, despite his mood, caught me by surprise, "First, I'm not sure you have the authority to deny his requests, his rights under the Articles of War have been violated already."

"How?" He demanded.

"He cannot be held more than six days without being charged, he is well past that,"

"That rule," he said with an authority and finality that did him little credit, "has been suspended under current circumstances."

"That rule," I began to heat up, "was imposed by George Washington. In 1776."

"So?"

"What do you mean, so?" I asked incredulously.

"Circumstances have changed, so has the rule."

"That's not possible," I snapped, "the rule has not been changed, it's being ignored."

"A lawyer's distinction." He smiled, trying to disarm the situation.

"Look, General," he started at my tone, "Washington established that fundamental right in the midst of losing the war, fleeing New Jersey, surrounded by Tories, and the British. This been standard for eighty-five years – unchanged because they are fair and they work. Who the hell are we to change them?"

To his credit, he did not throw me out, demote me, grimace or give me a nasty look. Instead he did much worse, he smiled rather indulgently. As one would to an overly inquisitive child. Wrong and overly inquisitive.

"These are extraordinary circumstances, Willie –"

"All the more reason to follow our laws", I interrupted.

He stared over my shoulder, "Things are... happening quickly, Colonel. Ball's Bluff was as you put it, a fiasco. It has given a sense of entitlement to the Republicans in Congress to meddle in our affairs despite their lack of military knowledge. Emotions are high, the whispers of treason —"

"Specious, as you well know."

"The unconfined rumors," he acknowledged my point with a quick look at my face before he went back to the spot over my shoulder, "are disturbing and a potential disciplinary threat – a threat to the order of the army – should Stone return to duty at the present time."

His eyes flicked to me for a three count, his expression one of 'you're missing the point.' I, belatedly, saw that I had.

"You're going to sacrifice him," I said flatly.

He nodded slowly, "They," he waved a hand toward Capitol Hill, "need someone or it will never end. I'll never be allowed to do what needs to be done. They'll continue to interfere. I have to give them

Stone – just for now, I'll reinstate him when things quiet – and move on. For the good of the army and the country."

"He did nothing wrong," I persisted.

"And?"

I did not answer at once. I caught his gaze, it was cool and he who would ask thousands to die would not, probably could not blink, never mind grieve, over the bloodless demise of one of a few hundred brigadier generals.

"It's a bad precedent," I considered, aloud, "Actually," my cheeks were hot, "I think it's a fucking awful precedent to set."

"You over-react, Willie," he responded with that most devastating of weapons to a man with a temper, calm discourse, "they want a scapegoat for one small action- anyone will do. This needs to be done with. It'll not happen again, no precedence is set."

"Really?" I was not placated that easily, not when I remembered the look on Chas' face, "then blame it on Baker – it's his fuck-up anyway. And he's dead, won't hurt him a bit."

"That's the problem," he, very properly, pointed out, "his death as the dashing Senator turned Colonel and the inane comments he made as he rode to his glorious death have made him untouchable. You're a romantic Willie, I would have thought you'd see that."

"Let me ask you this," I resolved not to go meekly, "we lost a fight, a stupid, minor skirmish and we are sacrificing an officer – a damn good officer – over it. Does it not strike you, my friend, that this may be the type of thing that never ends?"

"How so?" He smiled disarmingly.

"Lose a battle, be tried," I cut off his impending response, "Stone wasn't even at Ball's Bluff, was nowhere near it —"

"Maybe he should have been," smugly said.

"He had no reason to be there, not on what was in effect a reconnaissance – you know that," I said with a sharp edge, "beside, you planning on personally being at every fight, big or small, you have authority over? Might be a little hard to do if you happen to be fighting in Virginia while responsible for an action in North Carolina."

"You are approaching the absurd, Hanlin"

"Am I? Should you have been blamed if the troops at Port Royal had been defeated ignominiously?"

He shrugged, "I know this is all… inane. All of this – the Radicals should be seeing that I get everything I need to move south, not advancing their agendas by using Baker's death.

"And let's be clear, this is all about Baker. He was, of course, incompetent, but now he's a martyr, so we move on to the living. Stone sent him, probably knew he was incompetent, probably thought it was such an easy task he couldn't mess it up regardless. He gets the blame, disappears for a few months, is reinstated when no one's watching or noticing. That's the way the real world works."

"I know how it works."

"Then let it be."

I pondered that for a ten count. "You surely are aware, George," I said at length, "that Salem started with one witch."

"It's over, Willie." George's look reinforced the words, "we'll have the army moving shortly, we'll engage the rebels. And none of this will matter any longer. We'll rip the guts out of the Committee. And we'll be out of this cursed town."

None of that was said with any measure of hurt, it was almost as if rehearsed. I recognized the intractability of Mac's position. He had not asked for the final draft of the Ball's Bluff inquiry complete with Charles Stone's statement. Had not even glanced at the leather bound copy on my lap. He was beyond it.

I conceded defeat and asked the obvious, "When we moving?"

"Soon enough; he grunted through an unreadable smirk, "soon enough."

I left shortly after, the Ball's Bluff report tucked under my arm. Never delivered, never read.

3. Franklin

Soon enough' was not to be measured in days. It was clear it was not to be measured in weeks. As the days continued to pass and emotions rose, one could only hope it was not going to be measured in months.

I did not speak to Mac for a fortnight, therefore I could only join the nation while it stood transfixed by the passion play performed hourly in Washington wherein party leaders squared off; newspapers poked at the wounds; bit players changed sides with bewildering, if ineffective rapidity; and, the army remained static, fallow and still within sight of Washington.

That every man, woman, child, and private in the nation had an opinion was acknowledged fact; that the army en masse would never find fault with their besieged, intractably beloved general was known with certitude and was a tempering reality to McClellan's more voracious critics.

Nothing was helped by the fact those last days of January and first of February were remarkably free of substantial news from another quarter. The only game in town was to speculate on the well-anchored Army of the Potomac. It would not be budged from the front pages.

For those of us associated with headquarters it was a poor, almost miasmic atmosphere in which to work. Unfortunately, it was worse off duty when we were out and about in a city where Republicans ran free.

I was, therefore, more than somewhat surprised when Joinville informed me I would be attending a dinner party with him at Francis Blair's home. It was not a request, the Postmaster General was throwing a 'get together' for supporters of Mac and McClellan being unavailable, the two of us were to partake of Blair's fine wines and gourmet foods while assuring the other guest how much their support was appreciated. Joinville not so tactfully suggested I could best accomplish my part by remaining mute for the evening.

Knowing I was singularly unfit for the task and suspecting that even a pro-union Missourian would hold my mother against me, I decided to approach Mac directly to beg off. I felt a need to concisely express my trepidation at sitting through a long, formal dinner party with the last, if the papers and rumor had at least that right, member of the Cabinet who still supported McClellan. I was concerned with keeping it that way.

It appeared my timing was exquisite: I came out of my office, strode purposefully down the hallway – idly thinking how much Olga's painting would liven it up, reached to knock on his door (Webb, happily, nowhere to be found) when the front door burst open and a red-faced Mac stomped in from the cold. A puffing Webb close behind.

Mac made a beeline for me, as if expecting me to be in that precise position at that precise moment. "That great…. damned… gorilla!" He stammered uncharacteristically. His eyes sought mine, found them and apparently recognized me for the first time.

"Mac —"as far as I got.

"Lincoln," he snapped with fury, "had the temerity to ask if he could borrow my army."

"I'm not sure I understand." I stated the obvious, unwisely.

"Damn it Hanlin," he turned his back, threw open his office door in a plaster ripping crash, stalked in, mashed his hat over the coat rack and began to furiously unbutton his coat. I stayed rooted, gawking. He noticed, "Don't stand there like an idiot, come in!"

I did so. Almost colliding with Webb as he fell over himself to help Mac, off with the hideous burden of the coat. "I can come back —" I tried an experimental step back.

"Sit!" spat with enough venom and force to give Webb's face a solid misting.

Defeated in my effort to gracefully retire, I sat, growing more bemused by the moment. I would not be able to hide it much longer. Mac shook his coat off into the eagerly obsequious hands of Major Webb, stomped behind his desk and launched himself into his chair.

"Lincoln," he hissed it into three syllables, "remarked at how if I was not presently using the army, he would like to borrow it," he banged his fist on the solid wood of his desk, sending two pens off into the unknown, he looked surprised, like someone unused to the ancillary effects of emotional outbursts, "and he did so in front of that blackguard, McDowell. And Chase."

He stared waiting for a reaction that was not quick in coming. For the simple reason I did not know what to make of it. I was also having a hard time getting past the fact I thought it was a good line.

Clearly expected to comment, I said the first thing that came to mind, "Who told you that?" It was instantly apparent it was the wrong thing to say.

"Franklin was there," he sneered, "he just found the courage to tell me now."

"Why, when did it happen?" You can take the officer out of the lawyer, but you cannot…

"Just before I left my sickbed to meet Lincoln."

"Christ, Mac, that was weeks ago, what's —"

"Can't you see it Willie?" He raged with frustration, "Are you that naïve?" He pushed back his chair and let out a long sigh – a less self-possessed man would have bellowed, I knew better than attempt an answer, "They conspire against me, sir! On my sickbed they question my decisions, my actions, they joke and plot my demise. With McDowell the favorite of the Radicals they cannot wait."

"General Franklin is your friend, surely —"

"I despair of him remaining a friend when he takes part in such …. subversion."

"If, "I kept my voice steady, calm, "he was ordered to meet with the President —"

"He should have informed me first."

"On your sick bed?"

He did not respond at once to what I intended as a cold slap of logic. Nor did his visage alter in any way. The silence was palpable – I knew enough to break it. Just when it threatened to become unbearable, Mac spoke, "Why do you defend the indefensible?" Not a trace of curiosity to be found.

"I'm not defending anything, Mac" I replied, too readily, "I'm merely trying to look fairly at —"

"There is no 'fair' here. This is a dirty business and gets worse daily. I have friends and supporters and, then there are the others. They are the ones who would not only keep me from my business but rejoice to see me fail – regardless of the damage to the nation." Pleased with his speech, he stared at the coat rack.

I took a breath, and plunged in, "I understand the pressures you face, General, I really do, but Franklin is a friend and the President has a way with hyperbole and irony, so I —"

"This," he snipped off my thought with the effortless efficiency of a snapping turtle taking a tadpole, "is no time for nuances, Colonel."

"Nuances?" I asked automatically, "What do you mean nuances? Are you," I felt some heat as I thought his intent was as clear as it was unfair, "implying that it's now with you in everything or against you? No room for —"

"That's what it is and must be, "he glared directly, "for everyone, regardless of how long I've known them – these are harsh times." Now his meaning was crystal clear and resentment flooded me.

I resolved to think of what he had been through and take it as one would the bad mood of a good friend. My mouth, however, was not so inclined, "You need me to join the Democratic Party?" I asked with an edge, "Would that reassure you?"

"Wouldn't hurt," he instantly answered.

"What?" I replied back.

"Wasn't it a Roman orator or some such who said only the wicked don't take sides in a civil war? And they should be exiled when it's over?"

My mouth hung agape, and I let it while I rallied – the result of a tremendous, fully conscious effort to control my passions. Very, very measuredly I murmured, "It was a Greek, General McClellan. Solon the Law Giver, he said if a society split into strife anyone who refused to take sides should be exiled and outlawed when order was restored."

"Ah, yes," neither his gaze nor his expression wavered one whit.

I counted ten before going on, in a voice that sounded more deflated than I felt, "You accusing me of not taking a side?"

I expected fumbled 'of course not's and something akin to apology. Instead, he shrugged,

With great effort, straining to keep a normal tone, I answered for us, "I am wearing blue, General."

"So's McDowell," about as blunt as a hatchet.

I froze, utterly, the famous Hanlin wit trapped as if a vent closed. The thought flashed through my slightly aching head that Mac had been made aware of my mother's machinations. Very briefly – Mother was as discreet and careful as she was unyielding and relentless. Just the thought, however, was enough to temper my quickly rising ire with guilt.

"Are you contending," I managed to keep my voice steady, "that a major general in the United States Army is a traitor because he doesn't agree with your political beliefs?"

"He would do whatever necessary to see me removed," he shirked the question while answering with almost evangelical fervor.

"You're putting me in his company." I said in a low, controlled voice that belied the fact I was digging into the armrests with my fingers, "because I am not a member of a political party?"

"How can one not belong to a party in this day and age?" He mused aloud while studying his desk blotter.

"In this country, one has the choice not to join," I pointed out.

"Now you sound like one of them," he observed without emotion.

Mindful of our friendship, his position, the immense pressures everywhere, I took a deep breath and let it out slowly. Unfortunately my empathy and patience went with it.

"Feel free to send for me," I stood, roughly at attention, "when you decide to stop acting the ass to your friends."

I left, turned my back on the commanding officer of the armies of the United States and unhurriedly walked out, waiting for a yell, threat, shout to the guard to arrest or, at the very least, throw me into the street.

Instead, nothing. I flipped the door closed, thought 'I'm getting good at stalking out of rooms'. I realized I left my great coat in my office and I would have to tramp twice through the length of the house to retrieve it, made a quick, prudent decision and walked out into the cold without it.

4. Griffin

My letter of resignation written and sealed; possessions packed for shipment to the 21st; note to my landlord containing the last rent ready to be handed to her ever present self on the first floor; my mind at ease with the impending anonymity of being a simple lieutenant colonel once again; there was a short, loud knock on the door.

Expecting little, I opened it to find a perfectly turned out regular army sergeant major holding, with curious formality, a letter and a small package.

"Colonel Hanlin, Sir," he snapped with such authority my head – still affected by spirits consumed at The Willard and at least two, probably three, lesser establishments I had been dragged to, despite impotent protests, by the esteemed reporter from the Times – threatened to split open.

My immediate thought was he would not have come to arrest me alone. Purely for appearance sake for judging from his size he would have had no problem carrying me away by the scruff of my neck.

"Yes," I managed.

"With General McClellan's compliments, Sir," he boomed, loud enough to be heard throughout the building. He thrust his twin burdens into my hand, pierced the air with a perfect salute, spun on his heel and marched down the hall having not so much as creased his perfect uniform.

I watched him to the stairs, kicked the door shut and tore the envelope open:

February 2, 1862

> *Willie:*
> *I dearly regret any offense you, rightfully, may have taken from our discussion yesterday. While not excusing my boorishness, I hope it plain I had many things pressing upon my mind. I sought companionship while unfit for it.*

Please accept these fine cigars as a token of my regard and esteem. And, my apologies.

You, quite properly, ended our conversation before I could tell you to take the next ten days leave. The same courtesy has been extended to all staff members not presently involved in actively planning the coming campaign. Take advantage, Willie, there will be precious little chance for rest in the future. Thank you for your good work and friendship. See me upon your return.

Best,

George B McClellan

I dwelled on the note on the way to Union Station, all the while feeling the ass myself, having discussed Mac into the wee hours with a seemingly alcohol impervious Zacharias Griffin.

I went to The Willard directly from McClellan's office, my initial excuse: I needed to warm up for a while before covering the remaining blocks without my coat. Before I knew it, I was leaning on the bar, draining an ale and scanning the ever present blue sea for a familiar face. A familiar face – even though I hated every would-be politician among them.

Perhaps it was fortuitous, then, that the man who eventually approached was a civilian sporting a smile and offering to start a tab.

"Would you rather be alone?" Zacharias Griffin started after a long gulp of ale that left a streak of foam across his mustache.

"You must be a helluva reporter," I observed dryly.

"I can leave," he said, making not the slightest effort to do so.

"Sorry," I responded quickly, meaning it, "I'd be happy to have company – preferably of the nonmilitary sort.

"Then I'm your man, I'm as unmilitary as one can get."

"Very good," I caught the eye of the barkeep, ordered whiskey as well. Zacharias did the same.

He knocked back his shot, "You look as happy as your boss," he observed as the empty glass hit the bar.

"When did you see him?" I asked sharply.

"About two hours ago," he replied with a smile, "you?"

"Ten, twenty minutes," I answered, starring into the bar mirror.

"Ah, that explains it," the smile widened.

"Explains what?"

"Your mood."

I considered for a moment that news of the meeting had spread already. Then the narcissistic ridiculousness of it hit me with force and I asked the obvious, "Why do you say that?"

He regarded me over the lip of his beer, "Well, he was hardly brimming over with good news and cheer, was he?"

"I suppose not," I replied slowly, knowing I was missing something.

"Who could blame him?" He glibly went on.

"Certainly not I," I mumbled.

"Not after what he went through today."

"Of course," I said into the head of my ale.

"Colonel Hanlin," Griffin bristled with good-natured malice, "you have absolutely no idea what I'm talking about, do you?"

"None," I coughed over a laugh, "my God, you are a good reporter, Zach."

"The best," he acknowledged, "would you like a preview of my column tomorrow?"

"Would I?"

"Oh, I believe so, very much."

"Then, please."

"First line – in an hour long interview with newly installed Secretary of War —"

"He gave you an hour?"

"Impressed?"

"Yes."

"Good," he smirked, "Stanton announced that the time has come when the Army of the Potomac must either fight or run away. The Champaign and oysters on the Potomac must end."

I stared, agog, pint suspended half way between the bar and my lips, whispered, "Stanton said that?"

"You doubt my veracity?" He asked in mock reproach.

"Never in life," I answered by rote, "I'm . . . stunned . . . so quick."

"One can see from whence your reputation for courtroom eloquence springs."

I shrugged, tossed back the rest of my pint, signaled the barkeep yet again, "Stanton has been McClellan's friend for years . . ."

"No longer, I think," he said matter-of-factly. We watched as all four of our glasses were filled, grabbed the whiskeys before their surfaces had smoothed and drained them.

"You the one who relayed that to McClellan?" I asked before my glass hit the bar.

"Asked him to comment. I got none, he stammered an excuse and escaped me."

"Coming on top of the Franklin matter —" I muttered as the first pangs of regret washed over me, "he's —"

"That's old news," Griffin took up without pause or inflection, "that's been floating around since McClellan was bed ridden."

"He heard it today for the first time."

Griffin sported an all-knowing smile, "They say the captain's always the last to know . . . that's tough, and not really half of it." He contemplated the dregs of his pint.

At length I asked, "You going to make me buy the damn paper?"

"Sorry, no, of course not," he flustered, "I think I've been done in by the day as well . . . Lincoln ordered McClellan to take the offensive by February twenty-second, no later."

"Washington's birthday," I said, unnecessarily.

"Symbolic, no?" He nodded as if I had uncovered a great mystery, "Move or else, I was told, not for publication . . . to top it off, McClellan's two prima donnas in the West – Buell and Halleck – are fighting each other with an ardor that would be impressive if only directed at the enemy."

I flipped back another shot, addressed the regrettably empty glass, "I'm a shit."

"William?"

I looked in his eyes, "I had words with him this evening . . . he was in the mood for a fight, I —"

"You gave him one," he shook his head, "of all the men to pick in that house, he picked you in that state." He flagged down the barkeep – remarkably easy as, sensing sloppy drunks and a big tip, he was hovering.

"Your meaning?"

"Should be obvious," he threw it out without hesitation, "he's surrounded himself with men who agree with everything he says – except for you."

"You don't know that," I blurted into my brand new ale.

"Please," he waved a newly empty shot glass in my face, "you're the outsider . . . my goal is to find out what made you one."

"That a threat?" I grinned.

"That's a promise, I want to know why you're not like the others, I'm thinking it has something to do with you disappearing after Mexico . . . well, it's something that's made you the lone dissenter in a nest of sycophants."

"To be fair —"

"Don't defend him on this, especially when your heart's not in it," two more whiskeys arrived, "he's got a clique and those not part of it are shunted aside to await the royal edicts. You know enough history to know what happens next."

"Enough Shakespeare, in any event."

"Exactly. It is singularly unwise to exclude men like McDowell and it's just plain poor sportsmanship to then carp about possible intrigue when they are left blind to figure things out on their own."

"Can't argue that," I said, mesmerized as my shot glass was refilled.

"What words did you have?"

"Telling you that could find me escorting vagabonds on Canastota wagons through the Rockies for the duration."

"Off the record, of course, William," he uttered with palpable sincerity.

"I didn't commiserate quick enough to either suit him and I chose not to see his tormentors as devious, premeditated, or conspiratorial."

"You communicate that?"

"Called him an ass."

"Well done, he slapped me on the back.

"Really?"

"Of course," he laughed.

"Could it be you're not entirely enamored of our commanding general?" I asked the question I probably should have led the conversation with.

"No, no, no, no, no, no," Griffin showed the effects of drink as he fell in love with the rhythm of his no's, "I like him fine, want him to do well. Shit, I have two brothers in his army . . . fuck it, I'll vote for him for president in Sixty-four if he wins this thing."

"But?"

"What makes you think there's a but?"

"With General McClellan there's always a but."

He nodded, "For me, it's the fact he's coddled, handled with kid gloves . . . fuck it, let's be honest, he's treated like some Ottoman potentate and you can tell he loves it, eats it up. I'd resent that in any American, I think.

"It's so, I don't know . . . fucking autocratic."

"You were about to say Southern, weren't you?" I half-chuckled.

"Nah," he laughed, "sorry, I'm not one to throw out the treason or sympathizer label to anyone wearing blue. As far as I'm concerned the man can have as many peccadilloes as he wants as long as he delivers on his promises.

"My only real problem with Mac is I see him cut off from some basic realities by his staff and by choice – man sees what he wants to see."

"That's —"

"And," he cut me off by waving his shot glass in front of my face, "absent movement – as in your fucking army getting the fuck away from fucking Capitol Hill – I doubt it'll get any better."

That hanging in the air, we got down to the task of serious drinking.

5. Hartford

I slept alone in Bridget's bed. She had left two days earlier and would be gone a week, I was informed late by a tired Olga. She would not hear of me heading off to my closed-up house.

I slept poorly, aware of the aching vacancy next to me, haunted by a blur of unrelated images, vague, unsettling, none of which I really

remembered when I staggered awake for good shortly before dawn.

Heavily robed, warm slippers masking my tread, I wandered through the quiet house wondering if anything was as silent as a brothel at dawn.

Someone, somewhere was awake, however, for the faint smell of coffee caught and steered me toward the kitchen. Cook was there alone, no need for Sanders with Bridget gone.

Cook smiled, poured a cup, pointed that I should sit. I did, suddenly aware I had never heard her speak. I gratefully accepted the coffee and her silence. Cook further ingratiated herself placing cream, sugar, and the *Courant*'s early edition before me and moving to make breakfast.

The sounds were comforting and reassuring – pans clinking, eggs breaking, butter frying, newspaper crinkling, spoon dinging. So domestic, so . . . not Washington.

I flicked over the front page, the national news was utterly unchanged. At least nothing of import, for I did not consider bickering, aggrandizements, and mindless conjecture from experts that could not spell army if spotted an 'a' and 'y' of import.

I was about to start in on the regional news when Olga sleepily wove her way into the kitchen, a coffee cup materialized in front of her in an instant.

"Morning, Olga," I said without conviction.

"William," she answered, fumbled with the cream.

"A little early, isn't it?" I inquired.

"Yes," she succinctly highlighted the stupidity of my question. She took a sip, I noted she was dishevelingly ravishing in the half-light filtering through the frosted kitchen window.

A sip or two later she noticed me staring, "I do not want you feeling an intruder," she forced a smile, "you are my guest, William. Until you have to return. It would be rude for you to think yourself some sort of burden and slink away."

As she had guessed my plan for the day, I could only reply with a meek, "Thank you." She made no semblance of acknowledgement, sipped away, turned the Courant toward her and scanned the insipid headlines.

"How are you, dear?" She asked without looking up.

"Fine."I answered absently while stirring my coffee.

"Didn't expect to see you so soon."

"Didn't expect to be granted leave so soon.

"Sorry Bridget has gone to see her parents – she will be sorry she missed you."

"Where are they?" I asked.

"I'm sorry?"

"Her parents, where are they?"

"You don't know?" She asked in a tone one never wants to hear from one's special woman's friend.

My then tacit admission brought a stare far frostier than anything outside.

Olga ended it with an audible click of the tongue, "Montreal... William, her parents live in Montreal."

"Bridget's Canadian?" I was tired, hungry, hung over, and it was out before I could stop it.

"I understand they speak English there and everything," Olga finished, I thought I heard a cough of sorts from cook.

Olga looked, if possible, more sharply, side, rolled her lovely eyes, "I would tell you who and, more importantly, what her father is," she smiled with all the warmth of the surgeon, "but it would impact your sex life – negatively." With a well-earned, self-satisfied smirk she went back to the paper.

"Really?"

"Ask Bridget, if you dare," she flipped the pages, became engrossed in an ad and left me to play with my coffee while I wondered if Bridget's father was a peer.

Olga abruptly looked up for the paper, "You didn't tell me how you got leave again so soon – not that I am not thrilled to see you."

"I had a disagreement with my boss, he felt bad and assuaged his guilt with some fine cigars and a leave," I replied with the air that that sort of thing was the norm in the army.

Something she bought for not a moment, "You had words with McClellan?"

"Yes," I said easily before taking a gulp of hot, sweet coffee.

"How bad?" She asked.

"I called him an ass," I muttered. in her presence, it sounded trite, lame.

"And in return for that rather concise sobriquet, he gave you a present of cigars and leave?"

"You had to be there," I tried to grin.

"Would that I were, dear."

"To be perfectly truthful," I could not keep up a front of false bravado with that woman, "I was running scared for a good twelve hours, expecting a transfer to Utah or arrest, something."

"Only to receive a gift, instead," she said to her toast.

"Typical McClellan," I explained, "very good at putting aside hard feelings with friends.

I received a long, appraising look, "Perhaps because he has had much practice, William."

My coffee cup was half-way up, I stopped, dropped it back on the saucer with a clang, "He can be ... somewhat ... frustrating at times."

She nodded, "Was he, by the way?"

"Pardon?"

"Being an ass – or did you call him worse and clean it up for me?"

'I didn't have time to come up with anything more colorful, as it was, and an ass he was acting."

She caught and held my eye, smiled strangely, "God, William, what are you doing to yourself?"

It was so sudden, so out of place, so plainly passionate, it took me totally aback.

She noted my look, "Oh, forgive me dear," her tremendous eyes filled with concern, "that was unfair. But we do worry about you."

"We?" I asked, bemused.

"Everyone who knows you and cares."

"A small subset, I'm sure," I laughed.

"Rather larger than you think," she corrected me, "you do give amble cause for worry."

"How so?"

"We're all dreading the day your wit gets you in an inextricable spot with the McClellan's of the world," she arched her eyebrows, basked in the moral superiority of knowing she knew so much more about me than I did.

"I had years of practice with Nelson."

"I'm not sure that translates well with your army duties."

I shrugged at the truth of that, changed the subject, "What is he doing these days?"

"Nelson?" She sneered, not unbecomingly, "The creature is keeping a low profile these days. Probably because the war news has taken over the front pages and it's not worth his time to stir."

"I pointed to the Courant, "Even no war news is war news, I notice."

"Of course."

"No murders?" I asked the one person who did not rely the newspapers for news.

"No."

"It's been about seven months," I observed.

"Curious, isn't it?"

"Perhaps he grew bored," I observed.

"With that?" She waved in the general direction of the murder room upstairs, "He's not ever going to get bored, until he's dead or stopped," disgusted, she paused for a careful sip of coffee, "I am guessing he has left town – perhaps to join your army. For all you know, he's in your regiment."

I knew she did not mean it as a rebuke, would be upset if she thought I took it as such, yet I felt my neck redden.

"If he's in the Twenty-first, he certainly is bored," I editorialized.

"Are you bored?" She asked lightly as Cook placed a steaming plate of eggs, bacon, potatoes, and more in front of me.

"I'm anything but," I chomped out between bites – no power on earth nor overweening sense of decorum was going to keep me from the food while it was hot, "frustrated, certainly. Unhappy with the day to day grind – it's all too much like peace time army drudgery."

"I wouldn't think drudgery a term you would use for the Stone matter," she replied softly into her toast.

I swallowed, hard, "As usual, Olga, you are remarkably well informed. You're right, that wasn't drudgery, that was bitterly disappointing."

She nodded, "Between the day to day drudgery, investigating friends and arguing with your commanding general I can certainly see the attraction of your present position."

"It's not like that," I answered defensively, "not that it matters right now, it'll be over as soon as the army moves out and I'm back with the Twenty-first and all the bureaucratic horseshit is behind."

Olga threw me a knowing look, shook her head, began to carefully, systematically spread jam on her toast.

"What is it?" She forced me to ask.

"Osgood says the Twenty-first will never be near combat, not with McClellan in charge."

I brushed that aside, "Osgood doesn't think Mac capable of action, but we'll be moving soon —"

"I misspeak," she interrupted, bit her lip, flashed her eyes as she pretended to remember, "Osgood thinks the army will eventually move *somewhere*, he just does not believe the Twenty-first will go with them as long as McClellan needs you to be a professional friend – his term, I like it."

"That my official title?"

"According to Osgood. As are all of the staff and most of the generals, and —"

"I get it, Olga," I threw up my hands in mock surrender, "he's surrounded himself with friends and followers and after he wins they'll all be part of the next administration. Osgood's clear on —"

"No, William," she said gently, 'he no longer thinks that."

"McClellan as president in Sixty-four? He's been bashing me with that for months, you telling me he's changed his mind?"

"I am."

"Why?"

"Because, my dear," she replied with utter clarity, "Osgood no longer thinks General McClellan can win anything."

◊

I may have gained ten pounds in stay with Olga. A combination of reading catching up on sleep I had not realized I missed, large meals, being home bound due to ferocious storms that shut down the city – if not the Northeast – and hunger fueled by sexual frustration.

The latter was almost the sole doing of Maria, who pursued me with the audacity of Diane while similarly attired. Days of accidental run-ins with a Maria in various stages of undress, or less. By run-ins I refer to collisions seldom seen away from the rugby pitch.

The weather broke six days in – if by that euphemism one means the skies cleared while the temperature hovered around zero.

That day a bright, perky, ridiculously persistent Maria met me in a hallway wearing only a silk robe she had thoughtlessly forgotten to button or cinch up and offered to share he abundant bdy heat.

I was on the verge of accepting when the hose echoed with the news I had a telegram. Cook brought it to me, gave the immodest Maria a glare just as she accidently rammed a large, firm breast into my elbow.

Thus orders to convene a court martial in New York saved me from an indiscretion that would only have served to further haunt me.

6. Moving Out

March 10, 1862

The artillery was pounding, pounding, pounding, behind, over, under me, the balls visible overhead arching toward the tall black hats of the Mexicans massed on the ramparts.

Pounding, pounding, pounding even as I kicked the covers off, forced my eyes open then panicked when they would not focus. Uncomfortable seconds passed before I realized I was looking out my bedroom window made blurry by a heavy rain that kept the dawn obscure.

I sat up, rubbed my eyes and froze. I was undeniably awake but the pounding was undeniably not abating. After a few moments of abject terror I finally identified it as a rap, rap, rapping on my apartment door.

I staggered out of bed, pulled on a well-worn flannel robe mid-stumble, flipped the lock, walked away to the kitchen and coffee waiting to be re-heated. I had the good grace to yell "It's open," over my shoulder, followed, once in the kitchen, by "nevermore."

The door crashed open, "William," Joinville's voice echoed in the empty sitting room, "get dressed, pack your kit, we are moving out!" I heard him thud toward my bedroom.

I did not deign to respond, worked on starting a fire even when I heard his truncated, "Get up, Will —". Heavy footsteps headed my way, I remained at my task. A moment later his voice was directly behind me, "No time for that, William, the army is moving out, we have to get moving."

I turned, looked straight into the face of a flushed, crazily grinning Joinville scant inches away, "Whose army is moving?" I inquired with measurable irritability.

"Ours," he replied with unappreciated cheer, "the Army of the Potomac!" He hit me on the back, I, perhaps not so involuntarily, made a fist, "Come on, we are on the chase."

I looked over his shoulder and made note of the horizontal rain tattooing the window, rattling it in its mooring, "Mac chose a monsoon to move out?" The 'finally' was implicit.

"My God, are you always this thick in the morning?"

"It's not morning, Prince, that occurs when the sun breaks the horizon."

He ignored me, "The rebels withdrew from the Manassas works."

"They withdraw or they float away?"

"Get dressed," he yelled and shoved me toward the bedroom. Once propelled I kept going, "I have notified the livery, Clio and Roxanne are being readied while you dither about."

"Dither?" I asked with snide overtones and headed for my closet. I dropped the robe and began to round up a uniform I would not mind having rot off my back in the downpour.

"You always sleep in the nude or do you have company cached somewhere about?" Joinville made himself comfortable against the door jamb.

"Habit I formed in Paris, actually," I mumbled, pulled out a pair of never used long-johns.

"What was her name?"

"Collette."

"How cliché," he laughed, "someone's wife, student, professional mistress, or —"

"Painter," I grunted, pulling on pants.

"Really?" His tone changed, "I may be have to be impressed."

"You would be if you had seen her," I wrestled with a half buttoned shirt.

"She corrupt you?"

"Good God, yes," I pulled on my jacket, buttoned the cloth covered buttons with little coordination.

"Ah, William," Joinville's voice grew tenuous, "that is rather a drab jacket – I cannot tell what rank you are in this gloom."

"That's the idea," I grinned, "should we see rebels – rather, should certain rebels armed with long, nasty, accurate rifles see us."

"I see," he nodded.

"Lucky you have no baubles on your shoulders – unlike your cousins."

"Yes," he answered dubiously, "But I will replace the buttons and I shall share this with my cousins.

"Do," I pulled a new oilskin parka out of the corner of the closet.

Joinville made a show of looking about the room with distaste, "When we return, you may want to invest in a maid, William."

"The truly creative cannot be concerned with the orderliness of their lives," I intoned with gravitas.

"Surely, yes, but they can hire help."

"Phelps is with the Twenty-first right now," I offered by way of explanation.

"Then we shall ride with him this day."

"How's that?" I replied idly, began to toss clothes indiscriminately into a canvas bag.

"They are in the van guard and we have permission to ride with them."

"Great."

"William?"

"Joinville?"

"Stop that, give me your key and I'll have my batman come by, pack you properly and add it to my wagon."

"I thought you'd never offer," I dropped the bag and followed the Prince out.

It took three and a half hard trotting hours through intermittent gales of rain, in temperatures barely nudging the 40's to catch-up with the 21st. Three and a half hours dodging rain, mud swamps, and knots of civilians employing every known means of conveyance to follow the well-worn track to Manassas. The powers that be failed to send out the provost guard, clearly underestimating how rapidly the news would travel and how little the early hour and awful weather would deter spectators. After the first march to the Bull Run one would have thought every wagon, dray, hansom, et. al. would have been overturned on the side of the road and fired.

It was too early, too miserable, and too bone numbingly cold for Joinville and I to talk. I ruminated instead on the last two weeks since leaving Olga's, Maria still in quest of her goal. I left that happy house for New York and a court martial – not Charles Stone's, at least.

Mine was a messy affair concerning two officers, a well-known stage actor, a sexual practice named for a spectacularly destroyed

Biblical city (rumored to be prevalent in the British Navy), and government property 'borrowed' from the Tomkins Market Armory.

I held the hearing, unsurprisingly, ex camera even though it promised to be the subject of many a late night campfire for as long as the war lasted. Thus highly entertained I missed the fiasco of Harpers Ferry: Mac took about half the Army of the Potomac (the 21st, as usual, not among the select) to rebuild long torched railroad trestles and reopen the Ohio railroad, threaten to outflank Joseph E. Johnston, and, hope against hope, open the Shenandoah Valley. Ambitious and bloodless, all went well until it was time to bring up boats for the pontoon bridges. They were 6" too wide for the canal locks. Those six inches scrubbed the mission; the papers proclaimed it had died of lockjaw.

The repercussions of that miscalculation were still swirling when I arrived in Washington early Sunday. The papers I poured through were in obvious competition to select the perfect, insinuating adjective and the longest possible alliteration regarding the matter and Johnston's continued existence in Manassas. The more astute editors pointed with alacrity to the European reaction to the United States of America allowing an enemy army to maintain a stronghold less than a day's ride from its capital.

One, unfortunate, uniformity in the coverage, noted on front pages, were gleeful reports on McClellan's standing in the Corps of Engineers – noted with the coy observation that perhaps West Point was in need of rulers.

Deeper into the papers I was sad to see, if not much surprised, that a measure to increase the size of West Point classes had been roundly defeated in the House. It was clear – though the papers took pains to point out anyway – the nation had had enough of 'professional soldiers'.

And yet, here we were, at long last, chasing out after a Confederate Army. Mile after mile of happy, sometimes singing, steadily tramping men slogged through mud, through puddles, over potholes, steam rising off their sodden backs into the cold, saturated air, all moving . . . South.

The full might of the Army of the Potomac became more and more apparent with every yard Joinville and I rode. Even when spaces between units elongated due to mud washes, wagon breakdowns, and/or reticent horses, it was an incredible, never before seen on this continent, show of strength. So impressive, in fact, that we became so inured at the sight of line after line of anonymous backs made black by rain we almost rode by the 21st.

Would have, in fact, had not some wit called out something about me missing my feather bed to muck about in the dawn rain. I reined up and looked down into a mass of grinning, gleaming faces.

A sergeant pointed forward, "Up there. Colonel, can't hardly miss 'em, they're riding horses, too."

"Thank you, Sergeant, I'll see if I can manage to navigate it," I replied to undeserved laughs.

I brought Clio around, overheard a stage whisper from the ranks, "God-bless 'im, same as always, head off in tha' clouds somewhere."

Followed closely by, "That's our dear Colonel, an' every-time you think he don't notice, he does," I rode out of earshot to various affirmations of that hypothesis.

We rode past rows of upturned, friendly faces, acknowledging them every few yards with a touch of our hats. Finally, we rode up behind the twin bulks of Seth Arnold and Augustus, Seth deep in conversation with Osgood; Augustus no doubt ruing his burden in life.

"Camp life must be good," I yelled, "in all this gloom, from behind, I can't tell the difference between man and beast."

"Ah, Christ," Seth yelled without turning, "they've emptied the whorehouses and flushed out the sewers for this march."

"You insult Prince Joinville, sir," I replied with moderation while Clio slid next to a pleased Augustus, "for he prefers to refer to them as brothels and cisterns."

Seth revealed a toothy grin that shone through the gloaming, "Good to have you here, William . . . Prince."

"Good to be here, Colonel," I returned the grin, threw a quizzical eye in Osgood's direction, "the men look to be in good spirits."

"Certainly are," answered without hesitation, "nice, cool weather, little wet, but it feels great to be moving for real. They're practically floating – were singing until a little while ago."

"Probably sensed your approach, Colonel," Osgood offered to Seth's quick, nasty smirk.

"I know it's onerous duty, Prince Joinville," I turned in my saddle, he was having some problem with Roxanne as she tried to move around the stolid Clio to capture Augustus' impotent eye, "but if you don't mind, could you keep Arnold amused while I review the column?"

"Of course," Joinville responded with disapproval, "though it's hardly onerous and your attitude . . ."

I missed the rest when I pulled Clio around and cantered to the side of the road to watch the 21st pass, Osgood a few feet behind.

Osgood started as soon as we came to rest, "Manage to fight off Maria?"

"How'd you —"

"Olga wrote, although it is a well-known, if little understood, obsession."

"How did Olga find you? I didn't even know what state you were in."

"You had only to ask her."

"Convenient," I acknowledged a salute from a lieutenant by Bryce's side, Bryce pretended to be intrigued by something in the cow pasture across the road. I hoped, with juvenile intensity, that while evading my gaze he would trip and splatter into the mire.

I noticed Clio noticing Osgood's horse – his new, beautiful horse, "Where did you get that magnificent animal?"

"He is something, isn't he?"

"Beautiful."

"Found him on a little farm in Kentucky."

"They know he's missing?"

"It was an amicable parting," he laughed, "you did not answer my question."

"Maria," I sighed, "has not yet feasted on the delight that is my love."

"Shithead."

Christian chose that moment to ride over and throw an arm around my shoulder, scaring the living hell out of me that his overworked horse would take that moment to make good on what was undoubtedly a long standing plan to escape his burden in life. Such a move by the beast would have dropped Clio and me.

His horse showed itself a real stalwart and the four of us survived the heavy ordeal intact. The men from Wesleyan filed by and cheered me, us, our reunion, themselves – it did not matter, everyone was in a cheering frame of mind.

"Please get off of us, Captain," I said weakly, my collarbone groaned like a tree branch under a well-coordinated elephant.

Christian reluctantly sifted his weight back to his mount, a move Clio acknowledged with a grateful snort, "We're off, big brother, finally!" He yelled through a gust of rain, numbing my ear drum and warning Richmond of our approach in one swoop.

"Apparently, Christian," I rolled my eyes in his general direction, "go back to your men, we'll talk later," I finished to his back, he was away that quickly. The rain picked up, heavy drops that exploded on impact and obscured the view – unless one considered heavy, vertical lines of black rain a view.

Clio sidled up to Osgood's uber-equine without instruction. I chose to believe it was an effort to get warm. Regardless, it provided us privacy. "When did you get back?" I asked.

"Week ago, while you were in New York."

"Really, I —"

"How did you enjoy your pederasts?"

"I'm not sure I like how you put that."

"No?" He answered with surprise.

"No," I raised my voice above the ever increasing downpour, "so, the word's out on the New York love triangle."

"All over Washington – as are some of the pithier double ententes uttered by the President of the court."

"I deny them all."

"The transcripts are not accurate?"

"You read the transcripts?" I snapped.

"Shit, William, the transcripts were being circulated while they were being transcribed."

"I ordered them sealed."

"So I read," he sneered with delight.

To enforce my own order I changed the subject, "How was Kentucky?"

"Kentucky. Tennessee. Missouri, you mean."

"You've been busy."

"Did not seem that way, reminded me of home, actually."

"How so?" I tried to peer through the venetian blind rain, saw nothing but vague, bent shapes in the murk.

"Hidden alliances, families on both sides, informers on every street corner, ambushes, rumors, men changing sides daily, suspicions freely bandied about, hangings, murder . . ."

"It's as bad as all that?"

"Oh, yes. Worse than home, though, because every asshole out there is armed to the fucking teeth and they all know how to shoot."

"Sounds like you had fun."

"Sure did," he grinned.

The rain spurted off my hat like an overfilled eave and I discovered my oil parka was not as waterproof as advertised. I was considering searching for a cave when it just stopped. Dead. Completely. In a second the void left by the drowning rain was assumed by every sound hundreds of heavily burdened, boot shod, metal toting, sopping wet men could make wading through roads now the consistency of bisque.

A chest puckering cold wind pounded in, I shivered, cold water ran steadily down my spine, and I was given amble evidence my oil slicker was no better against the wind.

"Apparently," I announced to Osgood and the road, "God thought we weren't uncomfortable enough."

"Thought you were an atheist," Osgood observed.

"Agnostic with deist overtones . . . Or vice versa – not the same thing," Osgood shrugged, "Dare I ask what you were doing in the Border States and rebel territory?"

"You can ask."

"What were you doing out there?"

"Can't tell you," he grinned with malice.

"Bastard... At least tell me what who you were working for."

Grin in place, he took the time to peer at me with obvious suspicion.

"I can vouch for Clio's capacity to keep the confidence," I stated in an effort to loosen his tongue.

"I have no question about Clio, but you, you cannot even enforce a simple gag order in your own court."

"You're insufferable," I expressed the obvious.

"Thank you," instead of dropping the grin he took on a sardonic quality, "I worked for General Henry Halleck – heard of him?"

"Met him once," I sneered back, "had to read his goddamn tactical manual, used it later whenever insomnia reared its ugly head."

"That bad?"

"Worse, to think they call him 'Old Brains' in the regulars."

"There is a misnomer."

"Is it in circulation out there?"

"It is the considered opinion of a great many out there, one I absolutely concur with, that Old Brains is the only general on either side who can defeat Grant."

"Grant is as well thought of as that?"

"Grant gets things done without exposition, hesitation, or extraneous movement – quite a change from the East."

"Good for Sam," I said with timbre.

"Sam?"

"Grant's nickname."

"Unconditional Surrender Grant is Sam?"

"Sure is."

"I like it, suits him well."

"Was a quartermaster in Scott's Army, at Chapultepec he took it on himself to take over a battery, got it to the rooftops and covered us. I owe him."

"I'vr heard the story."

I stared at Osgood, the better to gauge his reaction, "He had problems on post out West after the war, something about drinking."

Osgood shook his head slowly, "I heard the same, never saw any evidence of it though. Of course, Halleck is quick to bring up the rumors every chance he gets – the odious fuck. Grant's a whirlwind, but I can see the possibility, I think he gets bored quickly and clearly does not like it."

"Well –" I started.

"Think Mac abhors being bored?"

"All I can say," I staccatoed, "is look where we're having this conversation."

"A month later than we should have," he relentlessly pointed out.

"And," I ignored him, always a good strategy, "he didn't lie about the Twenty-first, did he?"

I was greeted by long, deep, sincere laugh that boomed out into the cold, humid air, "What the hell," he choked out, "do you think is waiting for is out there?"

"Johnston's moving –"

"Johnson will be behind three rivers, digging in, and laughing his skinny Methodist ass off by the time we get to Manassas."

"How do –"

"Please," hand up, head shaking, looking so… knowing while the now light rain seemed to repel away from him, "there's no one out there to greet the might of the Army of the Potomac. This is, my great, good friend, is a motherfucking training exercise."

I refused to give him the satisfaction, if indeed he sought such, of acknowledging I believed him.

All through our talk I had nodded to, smiled back at and otherwise engaged the men of the 21st who caught my eye, always enormously pleased with their reactions, not being similarly blessed at my desk job. Now that Osgood had plunged the dagger and twisted to my rapt attention, I looked up to see wet blue-backs sloshing away and the road completely empty. We were missing three companies and, of course, our train.

Minutes passed and with them my consternation grew. I was on the verge of heading up the road to find our missing men when the rain picked up again and out of the mists sixty or so yards away, as if emerging from under a waterfall, came an artillery battery – regular Army, moving as fast as equinely possible through the muck, probably in the theory that the faster and more recklessly they drove the better the odds of not bogging down.

Obviously, our missing companies had been forced to step aside, rather than be flattened and buried in the mud by the rushing caissons. Unless, of course, they had been unlucky enough to be on hand when the battery got stuck and had been drafted as human beasts of burden.

In any regard, it was evident it would be some time before the rest of our column came along. I turned Osgood, "you better ride over and tell Seth to take a rest until we're whole again."

"Fine."

"I assume that behemoth you're riding won't have any trouble in the muck?"

"He might just fly over it," he laughed and reared creature. Clio jerked her head up and watched him carefully as he rambled away, cutting his own channel through the mud.

Clio and I meandered slowly, carefully up the side of the road in pleasant solitude, our breathes rising in steaming puffs that rose and intermingled. A perfect moment that lasted longer than I deserved.

A solitude finally broken, as if there could have been any doubt, by Master Sergeant Charles Phelps. I was staring at a picturesque farm across the road when I was jarred by a sudden snap of Clio's head and a quick shuffling of her hooves – her, successful, attempt to capture my attention. She had spied Charles ambling down the road alone and he was always good for a sizable snack.

I gave her her head, she had, after all, not eaten for several hours, a rare and unbearable occurrence. Charles did not disappoint, he had food out before we got within ten feet.

"Good to see you, Charles," I was surprised at how heartfelt I meant that.

"Hey, boss," Cleo snatched the treat and dropped her nose for obligatory stroking, "yer' wet."

"Sharp as always."

"Comin' to find us?"

"Yup."

"We was bogged down back there," he waved to the muck behind him, "ever since those artillery Yahoos pushed us off the road, just started moving again a little while back," he smiled wildly, explanation complete.

"Charles?"

"Boss?"

"If they're out of the muck and moving again, where are they?"

"Huh?" The smile flicked out and his eyebrows worked at confusion.

"The column, how far behind is it?"

"Oh, right," he gave Clio a sheepish grin, "they told me to jog ahead and see if I could overhaul the Regiment, tell them to slow down."

"You call your pace a jog?" I asked with real curiosity.

"Not, not then, that was taking it easy apiece, tired myself out earlier, real blistering pace I had going too."

"I'm sure. No horses available for you, or did they just look around for the man who bore the strongest likeness to Nike to send out?"

He whispered something to Clio, threw a suspicious look my way, "Horses all tired out pullin' the wagons outta' the mud, alas."

"Well you can take it easy, Charles. I've already sent Osgood ahead with the same orders."

"Ah, bless ya'," he stopped stroking Clio, his attention clearly replaced by something new. He crinkled his nose, sniffed the air like a bloodhound picking up the trail, and said, "Hey Boss, I smell bacon."

7. Bacon

Not sharing Sergeant Phelps' olfactory sense – and when it came to food only dogs, sharks, and certain rare species of truffle hunting pigs did – it was at least 10 minutes moving south before I smelled it as well. Bacon it most certainly was. Burnt bacon.

The smell was pervasive by the time I reached the 21st – that part of it, that is, sitting quietly brewing coffee in a cow pasture just off the road, a few completely incurious bovines wandering about. With Clio off to be cared for by strangers who were about to become lifelong comrades by dint of feeding her, I headed for the rail fence Osgood and Joinville were perched on, Seth leaning against the post. I detoured to throw my oil slicker over the bare branches of a large maple – I was tempted to use it for target practice, the additional holes would not impair its effectiveness in any measurable way.

The rains slackened, the sky retreated from Armageddon black to disturbing slate gray that was under no threat from the sun. Far to the south there was an expanding smudge of oil-black smoke billowing through the clouds. That sight held my companions' attention even while I added my weight to the groaning rail.

"Is there fighting down there?" Seth asked in a combination of curiosity and anticipation.

"Can't see where it could be," I shot a look at Osgood, "no sounds, no frantic messengers flying about, cavalry rushing through, nothing – all we have is the smell of bacon."

"Smells good, though," Arnold said with a bashful grin, "you know, we have some good quality bacon in the train . . . maybe if we stay here a little longer –"

"We won't have the time," I answered lowly.

"That's fine, why cook our supply when there's obviously tons of it just down the road?" Seth made a valid point, "Already cooked, too!"

"You planning on digging in as soon as we get there?" Osgood inquired.

"Might look around first, then we'll see."

"It better be a prodigiously large pile of pork," Osgood stated the obvious.

"One can only hope," Seth looked wistfully south.

"It's a trap, Seth," I explained, "those rebel generals are devious. They know the portliness of our average colonel, put out a ton of bacon, are sitting behind it with cannon loaded with canister, and . . ." I put my hands up in a 'poof'.

"I'll chance it," he glared south in defiance.

"They know that," I added. It did little to blunt his enthusiasm. A combination of smoking bacon and the prospect of battle anesthetized him to my wit.

"That is an enormous amount of smoke for a pig roast," Joinville spoke up, "sure there is no fighting?"

"Absolutely," I averred.

Glances tacitly passed between us for the time it took to cover every possible combination while we contemplated a long walk without action at the end.

Seth broke the stare fest, "Well, it's a pity."

"Shame," Joinville sadly agreed.

"Not fair, really," Osgood threw a look my way as if it were somehow my fault.

"I, on the other hand," I smiled around the circle, "am perfectly fine with it and intend to enjoy the ride south."

"Woman," Seth snorted.

"Disturbingly effeminate, yes," Joinville glowered.

"Pederast," Osgood snorted.

"Yet, remarkably happy, nonetheless," I jumped off the rail, the first of our missing men were just coming into view, "being the only one here who has actually assaulted an enemy position."

Three steps toward them, Phelps voice boomed down the road, "Hey, boss, look what I brung ya'." He was sitting high up on the buck board of a still snow white covered wagon, right next to a pile of mud with reddish hair and human eyes. A towering pile that somehow managed a feeble wave. I gawked in incomprehension.

To Phelps quick, obvious, indignation, "What, you don't say hello?" He motioned the pile.

"To whom or to what?"

"It's Reverend Ashford, for Christ's sake – oh, sorry, Reverend," Phelps thundered, the holy pile of muck shrugged off a pound or two of mud from shoulders so broad they could only belong to our regiment's man of God.

"Reverend," I touch my hat.

"Colonel!" He yelled down with glee, white teeth flashing across his brown visage, "you missed all the fun!"

"Fun, Thomas?"

"Marching in the rain, getting down into the mud to pull the great beasts out. Exhilarating, William, working as a team, the camaraderie, the –"

"I get it Reverend," I yelled up, "you have a perverse delight in extreme weather." His laughter shook off great chunks of mud, revealing smudges of blue as if a Golem was suffering a disfiguring disease.

"You happen to know," I shook my head at my afflicted Padre, "how far behind the next regiment is?"

"Captain Wycroft is endeavoring to find out," Ashford waved behind him, pounds of semi-solid mud flew away, "but when they hit the divots we left – where the road flooded after the last deluge – they'll be all day."

"Good," I said and jumped onto a running rail just behind Charles, "the meadow ahead is solid enough, pull in there," I pointed to several men widening a gap in the fence, "the companies behind the wagons?" I asked Phelps' right ear.

"Aye," he expertly flicked the reins, "poor lot, covered with filth, hadda' unrig the wagons and pull with the horses ta' get the cannons out – the horses were the only ones happy with tha' relationship."

"We'll get them all a rest," I assured him absently, watching a lone rider picking his way off the road, gingerly moving toward my friends on the rail. The rider leaned over in conversation with Joinville who pointed in my direction. Joinville jumped down and moved toward our grazing horses. I got the gist immediately, stepped off the running rail and easily outpaced the wagons to the clearing. Halfway there I met the rider – Webb.

"Colonel," he hail-fellow-well-met me, "I hope you're having a good morning, sir."

It was sincere enough to inspire me to false civility, "Morning, major." He grinned as if I had promoted him, evidently pleased it had gone so well, so early.

"General McClellan's compliments, Sir, he invites you and Prince Joinville to attend to the head of the column, he would like you to be present when we cross the entrenchments."

"They will be empty, right?"

"Sir?" Thin eyebrows ascended cautiously in a belated attempt to give him a personality.

"You're not asking us to lead an assault or anything, are you?"

The bastard actually laughed, high and watery – nothing gusty about it, but recognizable just the same, "No sir, we're just riding in, they'll be no opposition … it's historic in any event, though, isn't it?"

I nodded without enthusiasm, "Let me get my horse, Major."

"Very good, sir," he snapped off an efficient salute, "I must report back, follow the road, they'll be provost guards posted to show you the way."

"Oh, I think we'll manage," I groused, off he went, taking pains not to splatter me when he turned his horse.

I picked my way to Seth and Osgood, the care in my walk was noticed, "Don't want to attend Court functions with muddy cuffs, William?" Arnold inquired with an elbow to Osgood's ribs.

"Upset I'll get to the bacon before you, Colonel?" I inquired judiciously.

"You better leave some," he warned, suddenly grave.

"I'll try," I said, together we watched the wagons lurch and totter into the clearing, the mud covered companies right behind, catching every manner of derision known from the relatively clean, coffee infused, lounging men. Seth allowed it to go on just long enough to identify the most vociferous companies, then ordered them to give up their fires to the siciously muddied. New hoots and catcalls rained down on the selected.

Wycroft rode in, he was splattered lightly as only a supervising officer would be, "Next regiment's an hour behind, at least," he said without preamble with a, for him, rogue-ish smile, "probably more."

"Nice work," I returned.

"Thank you," he yelled over his shoulder, "I'll let Colonel Arnold know we've got some time to rest, enjoy your ride with the general."

He left me marveling – not for the first nor last time – at the speed and efficiency of the regimental grapevine. That musing was broken by a strong, petulant nudge from Clio. I threw myself into her saddle, she gave a derisive snort and nodded something to Roxanne.

I was about to pull Clio's reins to follow the Prince when a strong hand caught Clio's bridle. I looked down into Osgood's black eyes. "Want to come visit your favorite general?" I asked with measurable malice.

"For the victory party? I think I can miss that."

"It may not be very glorious, but I can attest to the fact it will be much more enjoyable than the alternative."

"I note you will not be enjoying yourself with your friends."

"No enemy out there," I motioned south, knowing it pompous, "no need for me here right now."

"You really think that matters?" His uncharacteristic look of bitterness diminished in no way when Clio stuck a moist nose in his cheek, he gently stroked her lower jaw while locked on my eyes. Uncomfortably.

"I –"

"Go, record the moment for history for your general, for all we care," acidity dripped from his mustache. He gave Clio a pat, hit my leg, and strode away.

8. Porter

The Confederate entrenchments were indeed impressive, and in all probability would have proven impregnable from frontal assault had we been unlucky enough to have tried. Well sighted for wide, clear killing fields, embankments as thick and high as any stone or masonry fort. Manned by men with rifles and some reasonably modern artillery . . . well, it would have been ugly.

Riding through the deserted lines snapped the hairs on the nape of my neck to attention and sent aquiver various sundry lower abdominal and groin muscles — feelings that intensified when I spied the low, black silhouette of a cannon poking through a parapet, as silently ominous as an unattended but cocked and fully loaded pistol pointed at one's head.

For reasons best left unexplored I was drawn to it, edged Clio — who registered her objections with not very subtle snorts and neighs — toward it. The instrument of death loomed larger, a light, coating mist rose from the ground around it, which is the sole reason it took me so long before exclaimed, "Ah, shit!"

"What is it?" Joinville asked from somewhere behind my left shoulder.

"Merde, merde, merde," I tersely summed up, dismounted without waiting for a response, strode through ankle deep mud to the artillery carriage that supported a perfectly round, very black . . . Log.

Joinville vaulted off Roxanne, brushed by me and put a hand on the definitely nonmetallic surface, as if checking it for legitimacy, "This is not good," he understated with non-Gallic simplicity.

"Only if there's more than this one," I answered, a forlorn hope and I knew it.

As did the Prince, "There are, I am afraid," he sighed and waved at the line receding from us – a line replete with the low humps of faux cannon – now that I knew, it was easy to note the absence of tapering in their too square snouts.

"I assume the press is already here?" I uttered a stupidity.

"Not only are they here," he had the good grace not to roll his eyes, "they are well ahead of us – that wagon over there," he pointed ahead," is a photographer's wagon."

With exquisite timing the back flap burst open and a man in a somber suit that was a little too close in style to an undertaker's jumped down with a tripod on his shoulder.

"I suppose," I mumbled, "it would be unsporting to shoot him."

"Alas, more would spring up to take his place," Joinville stated reasonably.

"We'd better share the good news with Mac," I said with all the enthusiasm of a horse archer elected to give bad news to the Khan.

I slogged to Clio, remounted and headed west toward a dense clump of mounted men gathered on a hilltop a few hundred yards away. The still prevalent bacon odor was overwhelmed by a thick, oily, altogether unpleasant pungency that was utterly unidentifiable. If forced to guess, I would hazard it a mix of whale oil, months old unwashed linen from a leper colony, scum off the Niantic River mixed with a few tons of bat dung marinated in camel urine, then set ablaze. Somewhere over the hill we rode toward was the origin of the stench – the thick smudge we had been following like the Magi the star was a series of fires that weaved together and rose as one. This close, whenever the wind changed – which was often – the smoke came at us head high and coated everything it wafted over and through with a greasy film that, like Greek fire, only got worse with water.

Mac was on the pinnacle of an upwind swale, looming over all on Dan Webster, waving animatedly, pointing at features in the works, holding court, basking in a bloodless victory. Clio pushed her way through the lower ranks, aides and insignia-less men scribbling on damp pads, and made it about half way up before we were intercepted by a smiling Fitz John Porter.

"Why so serious, Willie?" He laughed, stuck out a meaty hand.

I took it, replaced whatever was showing on my face with a wan smile, "Good to see you, General – I'm sorry to report we may have a problem . . . thought Mac should know as soon as possible."

"Problem," he slowly surveyed the vista immediately before us, his face easy in a 'there-can-be-no-possible-problem-on-this-day-of-days' expression, Inspection complete, he queried, "You find out they're hiding around here or something?"

"No," I snorted a laugh solely because he had stars on his shoulders, "but I've found a battery of phony cannon – logs on carriages."

"So you found them!" He seemed delighted, "How real do they look?"

"Pass . . . a . . .ble," I actually may have stretched it out further in an effort to mask my surprise, "from the distance, I guess. You knew about them, obviously."

"For weeks," he looked around the circle, the throng was happy, completely engaged in one of Mac's lectures, one we could not hear. Satisfied, he went on, "Pinkerton reported them in early February,"

"Then – "

"It was never our intention to attack here. Matter of fact, Johnston moving out like this has thrown a large wrench into the works."

"We wanted Johnston to stay here controlling Northern Virginia?" I left out 'to the increasing wrath of the President, Congress, and most of the Northeast'.

"While we move from Annapolis —"

"We?"

"The Army of the Potomac," he gave me an unprepared student about to earn a demerit glare, "we already had hundreds of ships and barges ready – to Urbanna on the Rappahannock, then across to West Point on the York." Ever the teacher, he let that hang in his version of the Socratic Method.

Luckily, I saw it at once, in Porter's presence, with the look he held me with, I would have been mortified otherwise. It was, really, simple: move the army unseen to Urbanna, thirty miles from Richmond, ninety miles behind Johnson – who would have to abandon his works, move by rail and whatever other means possible – in hodge podge manner, no doubt – to engage Mac on the field of his choosing. Or leave Richmond to its fate.

"Nice plan," I said at length, judiciously withheld my second thought: it also left Washington wide open, "now ruined."

"I suppose we failed to copy Joseph E," Porter smirked, "since he's now headed toward Fredericksburg."

"We following?"

"His ground now, his choice of field," he slowly shook his shaggy face, "we'll tarry here awhile, rethink it all. At least Washington will quit whining about rebels in Manassas."

"There's a photographer setting up by one of the fake guns," I finally got to it.

"Dull picture, I should think."

I detected no hint of irony, waited for, got none, so I prodded, "I'm sure the Republicans will find it endlessly fascinating.

"Fuck the Republicans," the sudden venom from his normally placidly ursine face pushed Clio back a step, "we're in the field now, Willie, Mac's alone, in charge, for a change – they can debate all they want, we're not down the street anymore . . . they'd have to inconvenience themselves to get to us – that would require effort, so, no more interfering with us for a while."

"I don't know, Fritz, there's this new invention called the telegraph. I understand it's pretty much everywhere."

He laughed, a great guffawing shaking laugh, "Ah, Willie, you're still doing it."

"It?"

"Using wit to let your superiors know when they're full of shit."

"I don't know what you mean . . . Sir."

"Of course you don't," he agreed amiably, "well, let's just say telegrams reach everywhere, Colonel, and they may send suggestions, complaints, second guesses, requests, and orders, for that matter. But, Willie —"

"General."

He slapped me on the back, "They only work if they're read . . . who knows when the wires are up or down, or how hard it is to find the addressee."

"Like Nelson at Copenhagen," I said to a blank stare that lasted too long, "Jesus Christ, Fitz, you're from a navy family, how can you not know this story?"

"The sea stories I grew up with, Willie," he did not miss a beat, "concerned the good Commodore and were loath to give the British much credit beyond that of deserving victim."

"Leading his squadron into Copenhagen, Nelson was informed by an aide that the flagship was flying the recall signal, to which Nelson put a telescope to his right eye and said, 'I see nothing.'"

"That's the eye he was blind in, right?"

"Right, he went on to a resounding victory and half way to the high column in Trafalgar Square."

"Perfect object lesson, then,"

"Because he won," I intoned, "had he lost, blind eye or not, he would've been another Admiral Byng."

"Ah, Willie. . ."

"British admiral executed for losing a battle . . . we would do well to contemplate the metaphor."

"You worry too much," he reared his horse around, "come on, I want to show you something."

He rode away from the worshiping crowd, I fell in behind, nodded to a hesitant Joinville to join us. Roxanne, at least, was quick to be part of our company, Clio welcomed her with a snort that Roxanne was too haughty to return.

We rode without comment through full brigades laying out camps; provost guards directing traffic; gaily dressed curiosity seekers scavenging souvenirs to bring back to timid friends; troops of reporters and politicians smiling or frowning furiously depending on their predispositions while they generally got in the way; independent sutler wagons that could well have been selling to the rebels yesterday opening for business; a few elderly blacks rooted to whatever geological feature they stood on while they tried to figure out if they were free, to be returned south, re-enslaved by us, prisoners of war, criminals, or best of all worlds, ignored; a troop of cavalry uncomfortable on beautiful, equally uncomfortable horses, flags sadly cased, jangled by at a walk, their unfortunate major clutching a wind ripped map.

Through all that, then up a gentle greening slope where a half a dozen men sat behind easels scribbling furiously – magazine illustrators on deadline- until we reached the crest. There we were hit by a blast of superheated air and the full fury of the stench before we rode down into Dante's Inferno.

At first there was so much smoke, too much stinging stink, too vast a conflagration, to make sense of. In time I got it: the pyre had been a two story, city block long warehouse. It had obviously been packed to the rafters when it went up, it burned still with a funny blue-white fire that peeked out below billowing clouds of fats and syrups.

A river of bubbling molasses ran downhill, joined midstream by other, less muddy, liquids, occasionally flaming for no reason save some unknown alchemy. Closer inspection, as close as we dared and not without Clio's strong protest, I could see great globs of wax in the stream. The fire itself was shapeless save for obscenely broken beams glowing like smithy irons.

We moved away from the choking cloud to a respectable distance where we could still hear the crackling, sizzling, snapping conflagration and ourselves as well. Porter, mesmerized by the glow, pointed to it, "They fired it all, Willie, Prince, probably more supplies than all their other armies combined, but they fired it and they ran. Why do you think they did that?"

It was not so much of a question as an oblique object lesson illustrated by the long burning fire. I had no answer beyond a half smile, raised eyebrows, and turned up palms.

That pleased the expansive Porter, "Fear, Willie – they feared having their main army so far from Richmond, so open to having their lines of communication and supply cut, so susceptible to . . . us."

"One could take that, General —" Joinville started.

"So susceptible," Porter cut off royalty, so pleased with it all, "they moved as quickly as they could – to the point of firing an acre's worth of supplies." He seemed to finally notice the toxicity of the flame and smoke and began to edge away. We followed, our pace increased, we ascended a low, tree covered rise and breathed deep the fresh, scrubbed air.

Porter pointed at the now distant blur of blue around McClellan, "Mac's explaining that to them right now because the truth of it is, the action they so derided outside Harper's Ferry set this chain of events in motion and led to a bloodless taking of otherwise impregnable lines and the rebels fleeing so quickly they destroyed their stores rather than cart them off."

"I see it," Joinville said with a lack of joy that was noted by Porter with a brief flash of a general's pique – very brief, for royalty still trumped rank in our United States, "solid tactics, General, but done, I must say, in an . . . arcane manner, it is . . ." He faltered, searching for the perfect, diplomatic expression.

I skipped the diplomacy and finished for him, "Solid tactics don't make great headlines, the public doesn't go in big for victories that have to be explained. The absence of headstones on either side gives victory all the air of a successful negotiation."

"Exactly," Joinville agreed, "no laurels conferred."

"Ah, Willie," Porter replied without hint of rancor, "you're too cynical . . . what do you say we try and just enjoy the day," he flicked a short, dismissive salute and imperiously rode off.

I turned to a smug faced Joinville, "I merely finished your point for you and I'm the cynical one?"

"It's in the manner of the delivery," he answered, apparently seriously.

"You don't attribute it to your well flouted royalty."

"I attribute it to being French," he coolly looked me over, "one would think a man with a French artist mistress would have absorbed enough . . . culture to understand that."

"Had I once acted like a Frenchman, Prince," I began with a self-satisfied snarl, "had I affected French manners at any time, our affair de coeur would have been truncated with ferocity."

"Really?" His royal eyebrows achieved a perfect arch.

"Oh, yes," I averred with enthusiasm tinged with a long buried ache.

"Such passion," he said absently, "perhaps I can look her up one day?"

"Then you'd better perfect your colloquialisms."

"I speak perfect English," Joinville said in perfect English.

"Perfect English ain't American," I answered and headed out to find the 21st and a hot meal – preferably with bacon.

9. Wilkes

I dreamed of Collette. Her lithe, dusky body and stabbing, mocking eyes were prominent, engaging and alluring even though I was at least dimly aware it was, indeed and alas, a dream. But, as it was infinitely preferable to the reality of my cot and hemp-scented canvas tent, I chose to let it run as further insulation against the pre-dawn cold in the sure knowledge that to move was to submit to assault by an iron maiden of icicles.

And so, a very awake Collette flitted about my mother's Washington drawing room wearing only my unbuttoned uniform jacket. That incongruity I was willing to bear and bear with pleasure – pleasure that ebbed rapidly when she began to call me 'Colonel' and died completely when her provocative, slurry voice metamorphosed into a basso insistence that could only belong to a low level functionary.

I was wrapped like a mummy in several layers of blankets and coats that left one eye uncovered to open to the pitch black interior of my tent. I opened that eye hoping to convey the same level of threat as when a sleepy crocodile moves its opaque eyelid. That thought was overwhelmed by the instant realization that even if I had successfully expressed pique at being woken seconds before Collette disposed of the jacket, the bastard could not see it. Verbal communication was necessary.

"What?" My eloquent opening.

"Colonel Hanlin?" The voice questioned.

"Worried you're in the wrong tent?"

"Not now, Colonel," the voice wavered nary an octave – nothing worse than absolute conviction before dawn, "General McClellan's compliments, sir —"

"What time is it?"

"Sir?"

"The time, whoever you are," I moved not a muscle, exhaled my demand, took in a lungful of Arctic air.

"Two fifty, Colonel, I —"

"And McClellan sends his compliments? For what, sleeping soundly?"

"You do that well, sir," it said without hesitation.

I groaned lightly, "Do I detect a Philadelphia accent?" The better to know my newest tormentor.

"No," the voice intoned, "I speak fine . . . sir. You have an accent, one that would place you among the Boston Puritan set."

I endeavored to begin the process of rising, not unlike a moth from a cocoon, "Lieutenant, Captain —"

"Lieutenant,"

I struggled up, my back assaulted by waves of tiny ice pricks jammed into my bare back like an acupuncturist run amok. I grabbed the long johns next to the cot, wrestled them on under the blankets thus sparing, at least momentarily, sensitive areas of my body still thinking of Collette.

"I take it you're the son of a congressman, senator, general?" I asked largely without venom.

"Way above those, Colonel," he said easily.

I pulled what I assumed was my undershirt over my head, "He's in newspapers, then," I surmised, pleased with myself.

"He is a newspaper . . . sir," to his credit he did not snicker, titter, or outright laugh.

"Would you be so kind as to hand me my pants, lieutenant . . .?"

"Wilkes, Colonel, Jefferson Wilkes," something wool found my hand.

"What newspaper, Lieutenant Wilkes?"

"Philadelphia *Sentinel*," he wielded the banner like the cudgel it was.

"I see," I uttered though that did not begin to cover it – second largest paper in Pennsylvania, staunch supporter of one Major General George B. McClellan, "when did you join the staff?"

"While you were out on leave," he threw my jacket at me.

I donned it, slipped into my boots, stood in the frigid air, "Now McClellan can complement me on my ability to dress in the pitch dark."

"To be fair, sir, you did have help."

"I've done this before on my own," I pointed out with pride.

"Perhaps," his doubtful reply, "follow me sir, the general promises all the hot coffee you can drink."

I stomped in the general direction of the tent flap, Wilkes pushed it open, the darkness merely lightened a fraction. I stepped out into the even colder outdoor air, felt a stinging on my cheek, promptly lost both feet, became parallel with the ground for a heart stopping moment, landed with a resounding thud on rock solid ground coated in cold, wet-glass.

"Sleet and freezing rain," Wilkes carefully explained.

"Yes, I see, thank you," I answered from flat on my back, face tattooed by the aforementioned sleet. I sat up, Wilkes found my right hand, hauled me up.

We skated our way through a camp made deathly silent by the hiss of the sleet. The only other sound, the occasional thump of a large, fast freezing raindrop hitting the marbleized sod.

My coat was cracking and snapping by the time we got to the well-lit headquarters, an otherwise dilapidated farmhouse less than a half mile from my cozy tent.

We walked into a blaze of lights that stung my eyes. McClellan stood over a long, solid table covered with maps, pen in hand, Fitz Porter peering over his right shoulder; a tall, older general with bushy, shocking white beard to his immediate left gawked at Wilkes and me with distain; a turtle-eyed, eyebrows permanently arched, face deeply creased, heavily bearded major general was busily scribbling directly across from Mac; a trim, handsome, general projecting an overwhelming aura of fussiness effected a bored expression he clearly did not believe in.

In order, Generals Sumner, Heintzelman, McDowell. I snapped a decent salute considering the hour, no one in the room gave a damn and their looks let me know it. I tried to drop my hand as nonchalantly as possible, ended up brushing chunks of ice off my shoulders that fell to the hard wood floor with thuds that intensified the generals displeasure.

Wilkes saved me, helped me off with the damn thing, crossed in front of me, rolled his eyes, shook his head.

"Do you need an invitation sir, or would you care to show some initiative and joins us at the table," Edwin V. Sumner bellowed, causing the others to cringe. Sumner was known far and wide and with evident pride as 'Bull' – for obvious reasons.

I did not answer, just walked as purposely as possible to the table to take up station beside Porter. He clapped me on the shoulder, smiled a very tired smile.

"We have a very important task for you, Willie," McClellan tried hard to sound up beat and inviting, instead he sounded like a very tired man trying to sound up beat and inviting, "and for you to carry it out, we must include you in our plans."

It seemed a grudging admission to me, despite his attempt at bon homme, so I did not reply, gazed instead around the table and into the appraising looks of the leaders of the Army of the Potomac.

I looked down at the maps of Virginia's northern coastline spread haphazardly across the table. Maps that had been drawn on, redrawn, scratched out, and abused in a hundred other ways.

For the next hour the group of sleep deprived generals – McClellan faking enthusiasm; Heintzelman snapping with irritability; Sumner blunt, blustery, bellowing; McDowell silent, watchful; Porter occasionally trying to instill amiability into the discussion with mixed results – explained their plans.

I figured it out long before they finished but there is little profit letting a general – never mind a gaggle of them – know their plans are not as wondrously intricate and unfathomable as they would like to think.

It went like this: McClellan would bring the army to Alexandria, down the Potomac, to Chesapeake Bay, then to Fort Monroe on Old Point Comfort. Fortress Monroe. Largest fort in North America, so powerful and easy to supply from the sea the Confederates had no choice but to leave it be.

A piece of Union held land twenty miles from Yorktown, seventy-five from Richmond, McClellan's intelligence service reported there were excellent roads up the peninsula, it was lightly – if at all – defended, and it was a very, very long haul for Joseph E. Johnston's army to move to intercept.

A good plan, maybe great, if all the assumptions accompanying it were correct. Nothing about it, however, was of any concern to a lieutenant colonel/JAG officer.

In that group, then, I could only take it all in with a 'how best may a peon like me assist you captains of strategy' look plastered across my face.

Porter watched me do it in open admiration. Mac was not buying it for a moment and seemed braced for my mouth to betray my rigidly attentive stance at any moment.

They finished the dissertation, one McDowell was to present to Lincoln that night. No one looked or spoke to me.

Finally, I mumbled something like 'great plan' wandered over to the coffee, poured a mug, shoveled in sugar, dropped a splash of what looked like fresh cream, turned and faced the firing squad.

As the mug touched my lips, McClellan spoke, "Have you heard the news of the Merrimac?"

I was momentarily nonplussed, a fact I covered up by taking a long, cautionary sip. Then I remembered Dahlgren.

"The ship?"

"The ironclad ship that sailed out of Norfolk Saturday, sunk the Cumberland and Congress, forced the Minnesota and St. Lawrence aground and stood poised to destroy the rest of the blockading fleet on Sunday," Mac confirmed with all the grimness a shattering, revolutionary event should carry — as in the end of two thousand years of wooden warships.

"Stood to?" I mumbled into my mug.

"While we were marching Sunday our Navy's own ironclad engaged the Merrimac to a draw — the fleet is at least temporarily saved," Porter answered.

"Great," I mused aloud while wrestling with the term 'our ironclad', "why temporary?"

"Who knows how it will come out next time," Sumner snorted, making it as clear as humanly possible without actually spitting what he thought of the Navy.

I nodded, 'If the Merrimac sails into the middle of our transport ships —"

"Exactly, Willie," McClellan interrupted, no need to go further with the thought, "we need to know if the Navy can screen us with that ship out there."

"Then telegraph the Navy Department," I said without thinking.

"It's too important for that," Heintzelman said in a slow, methodical voice, "we need someone reliable to hear it first hand and to gauge the trustworthiness of that reply. General McClellan says you are that someone."

I nodded, substituted in my head the sobriquet 'reliable' with 'only member of staff on first name basis with the Secretary of the Navy.'

I replied to McClellan, "You want me to see Welles."

He lit up as if he had just thought of it himself, "Yes, Willie."

"When do I leave?"

"Now, and take Wilkes with you," he replied, happy that it had turned out so well.

10. The Merrimack

They were waiting for us at the front door, McClellan having wired ahead and throwing something like 'most urgent' into the mix – something dire enough to get our mud splattered, ice covered selves taken directly to the secretary's office.

With typical Navy preparedness and efficiency we were relieved of our coats, given a quick brush, handed boiling cups of hot chocolate and ushered in.

Gideon Welles was right where I left him, behind his whaleboat-sized desk scribbling furiously, a strange model in front of him approximating the unique shape I had glimpsed in the Brooklyn naval yard.

We approached his desk, he wrote; we got closer, he wrote; we stood more or less at attention, he dotted i's and crossed t's. That was when I knew we had walked into the middle of ... something. Welles was acerbic, witty, blunt, sarcastic, and occasionally ruthless, but never rude.

He made us wait, dipped pen twice more before carefully putting it down, sitting back, intertwining his fingers and deigning to speak.

"Did McClellan really think sending you on whatever critical mission you're here for would predispose me to think better of the army today?"

I took a long sip of chocolate, looked my Hartford friend in the eye and replied, "You can at least be courteous before flogging us. I thought that was the Navy's way – courtesy with pain."

"Ah," he waved the air clear, "sit down, welcome, and all that . . . not your fault anyway. Besides," he smiled expansively, "in those uniforms you'll probably get the hell kicked out of you on your way out of the building."

Wilkes gave me a dubious look, took an offered chair, I moved toward the model on Welles' desk, "I think I saw this in Brooklyn Navy Yard."

"You did," Welles answered in a more personable tone, "*that* is the U.S.S. Monitor."

With a nod from Gideon I picked up the foot and a half long, flat decked Monitor and looked at it in wonder, "This round thing on top . . ."

"We call it a turrent."

"It turns?"

"Try it."

It turned with a clicking and clattering of many gears. Surprise must have shown on my face for Welles added, "The model's exact in every detail."

"She can shoot in any direction regardless of her course?" it was so revolutionary that a rhetorical question was not rhetorical.

"Yes, and she's impervious to shot," his pride was evident.

"She seaworthy?" I asked and handed the model to Wilkes.

"Not very, but she got there . . . she'll be deadly in coastal waters."

Wilkes admired her, albeit gingerly in obvious fear of breaking the Secretary of Navy's prized toy.

"By the way," I stared, "Secretary Welles, this is Lieutenant Wilkes, his family sells newspapers. Lieutenant Wilkes, Secretary Welles, he edited newspapers on his way to the top."

"Good to meet you, Lieutenant, I know your father," Gideon endeavored to smile.

"An honor, sir," Wilkes said slowly, trying to do what everyone introduced to Welles for the first time tried to do – ignore the ridiculous wig. Like all before him, he failed and reddened with the realization of that failure.

Gideon was as immune to the stares of others as Michelangelo's David, it bothered him not a whit, so his stare back at Wilkes had nothing to do with Wilke's fascination with the wig and everything to do with the fact that in his embarrassment Wilke's was mishandling the Monitor in ways the Merrimack never could.

I gently removed the vessel from his hands, replaced it on its stand and asked the obvious, "Why are you particularly indisposed to the Army today?"

Gideon hesitated, just long enough for Wilkes to interject, "I am not here in any capacity to do with my father, Mr. Secretary, however, allow me to step out for a —"

"You'll do nothing of the kind," Welles, snapped, "I'm sorry I gave you that impression, it's been a hard few days."

"Sorry to hear that, Gideon," I took the chair next to Wilkes, made a hopefully sympathetic look for losing four of the Navy's best frigates in a few hours to an enemy whose navy heretofore consisted solely of small, fast privateers, "The army has not made it any easier?"

He sighed, deep and long, "Do you recall our conversation last fall?"

"Of course."

"Did I not express, with some heat, I believe, my view and fervent wish that the army take Norfolk?"

"You and Captain Dahlgren, profanely in fact."

"And we laid out a series of well thought out, eminently sensible reasons, did we not?"

"Yes," I nodded to Wilkes.

"And Dahlgren gave you a quite graphic description of what we thought the rebels were doing with the hulk of the Merrimack and the danger it posed, correct?"

"Yes."

"Then, William," my bewhiskered friend began with yet another sigh, "you will understand my ill-temper when due to the Merrimack's onslaught, the Secretary of War promptly blamed the Navy while crying for recriminations."

I dwelled on that – as I was sure I was meant to – for a solid minute while Welles stared at the miniature Monitor, "That's . . ."

"Unconscionable," he finished.

"I was going to go with horseshit,"

"So was I," he chuckled, looked up from the Monitor, spread his hands, had all the airs of a demented St. Nick, "had the army taken Norfolk the rebels would have burned the Merrimack in dry-dock and the C.S.S. Alabama never launches, sails out and sinks four of my best ships and kill scores of fine men.

"With all that, Stanton blames us, helps spread panic through the streets of Washington by claiming we have to sink hulks across the Potomac before the Merrimack sails up and destroys the capitol."

He glanced at the two us with a slightly abashed look, "I tried explaining to that . . . miscreant, that the Merrimack draws too much to get near here, but why argue facts when blind, fucking panic and invective will do."

"The Navy has been magnificent, sir," Wilkes spoke up.

"Thank you," he smiled weakly, absentmindedly patted the bow of the Monitor, "you're not here to hear me prattle on like a politician," he revived to his usual self, "you're here on urgent business."

"We're here for your opinion." I answered before giving him the short version of McClellan's move to Comfort Point.

I finished with, "This doesn't work if the Merrimack gets out, that's why we're here."

"Go," he said in an instant.

"Go?"

"Go. Do it. Make the move. No one will see hide nor hair of that damnable ship."

"You seem rather . . . certain, Gideon," I whispered, I had never seen him with such ardor, "you already have plans to deal with this?"

"We have since Sunday, William, when we realized that the Monitor can't really harm the Merrimack and she can't harm the Monitor, the Merrimack can simply ignore the Monitor and proceed to dispatch our squadron at her leisure."

"That doesn't really sound like a plan." I pointed out to his scowl.

"With that scenario in mind," the scowl lingered, "we have devised a method to stop her and stop her we will."

"How?"

"The Monitor will harass the Merrimack – she's slow, the Monitor can run circles around her. While the Monitor bangs away, we have three frigates ready with steam up at all times. They have orders to ram the Merrimack. She may get one or two of them, she won't get three. She's so low in the water she'll go down like a stone."

I was breathless. Wilkes and I were silent for long seconds while Welles stroked Monitor's bow and looked expectantly at us.

I broke the silence, "You'd sacrifice three major warships to sink the Merrimack?"

"No," he answered slowly, "we'd sacrifice ten, we're just sure that three will do."

"I'm —"

"This is the Navy, William, we know when to sacrifice . . . and how to do it. Tell McClellan he's free to move. If you get the time, perhaps you can explain the lesson to him as well."

11. Mt. Vernon

Osgood stood at the bow trying, with moderate success, to orate from a broadsheet that petulantly insisted on assisting the propulsion of the Quinnebaug by acting as a sail the steam frigate did not need.

I leaned on a rail, basked in all enveloping sunshine, and watched the Virginia coastline slip by. It was glorious but Osgood was singularly unaffected – the grandeur of the moment paled beside the edict he held in his hand.

An edict he insisted on sharing, "I have held you back that you might give the death blow to the rebellion that has distracted our once happy country," he boomed above the wind like an over-emoting King Lear.

"Held us back?" He questioned sarcastically.

I ignored him. Joinville, standing dead center of the bowsprit turned toward us, "How is it that there are copies of that everywhere?"

"Good question, that," Osgood gave me a knowing smile, "say, William, how is it that McClellan's address to the Army of the Potomac is everywhere?"

My sigh was blown away by the wind, "Mac has a printing press on wheels, it's part of our train," I said matter-of-factly, as if all successful generals since Guttenberg had done the same.

"How very far sighted," Joinville opined, squinted into the sun and wind, "of him to provide Osgood with such entertainment."

Osgood's coal eyes sparkled with appreciation, "The moment for action has arrived and I know that I can trust you to save our country," his eyes slithered from the sheet to Joinville and me and back, "the time is right . . . now?"

"Evidently," Joinville answered, motioning to the Armada around us.

"Well," Osgood considered, "I'm glad he trusts me," he sneered, went back to the sheet, "I will bring you now face to face with the rebels, where I know you wish to be – on the decisive battlefield," eye contact around the horn again, "I suppose once has stared down the barrel of a Quaker gun, everything else is easy."

"You're not being —" as far as I got.

"Wait, wait, wait," he held up a hand while a satanic grin usurped his features, "Here's my favorite part – 'I promise to watch over you as a parent over his children, and you know that your general loves you from the depths of his heart.'"

"The enlisted men love that —" I was denied again by an Osgood on a mission.

"That sounds paternalistic," Osgood acknowledged my cut-off comment, "and goes so nicely with 'it shall be my care, as it has ever been, to gain success with the least possible loss.'"

"Comforting," Joinville opined.

"I'm not too sure what McClellan's Republican friends will think about the cautionary tone of that," Osgood pretended to give the matter deep consideration.

"Now wait, I —" but it was useless, Osgood was on a roll and would recognize my voice when he chose to.

"Of course, I will admit the sentiment is somewhat tempered by his following demand of 'great heroic exertions, rapid and long marches, desperate combats, privations,'" he looked up from the sheet, "hey, that is good, maybe the army can use that as a recruiting slogan."

Joinville could not suppress his laughter, I rolled my eyes and bit hard at the inside of my cheek.

"I will give you this, though," Osgood's vicious veneer relaxed, "he knows how to end, 'we will share all these together and when this sad war is over we will all return to our homes and feel that we can ask no higher honor than the proud consciousness that we belonged to the Army of the Potomac!'" Osgood finished with a flourish worthy of Edwin Booth.

Osgood lost the sneer and grunted, "Got to give it to him, that is positively Napoleonic. Although I —"

"It is Napoleon," I muttered to the wind and Joinville's nods.

"That's what I said," he snapped.

"No, Osgood," I interrupted before Joinville could, "it's not Napoleonic, it is Napoleon – it's from his address to the Army of Italy. It's always been one of Mac's favorites."

"Now it makes sense," Osgood brightened considerably, "he plagiarized the last part."

"Listen you —"

"I think," Joinville cut me off with an edge, "it fits well, it certainly has been embraced by the men and that is what really matters, is it not?"

"Works well with the press, too Osgood the badger was not about to let go, "a cynic would argue that that is its intended audience."

At 'cynic' Joinville looked questioningly in my direction. Before he could say a word, Osgood slashed whatever thought he was about to express, "Don't look at him, Prince, he's no cynic when it comes to McClellan – or anyone he thinks is a friend for that matter."

"His cynicism knows bounds?" Joinville seemed dubious.

"A narrow band, but yes."

Joinville eyed me suspiciously, "I am . . . amazed."

"I do see a problem with his stolen ending, however," Osgood rattled the sheet as if trying to shake loose the offending words, "this sad war? That will piss off a lot of radicals, hardly sad for them."

"I can see that," Joinville replied without enthusiasm.

"I bet Napoleon's original didn't have that in it."

"No," Joinville confirmed.

"If you are going to steal from the greats, you might as well get it right, don't you think?" Osgood's smirk was all encompassing.

"For Christ's sake, Osgood," I snapped, waited for an interruption that did not come, "It also sounds like Henry V, and probably a hundred other generals, and it'll probably be used a hundred times during the rest of this war. We're looking for inspiration here, not originality."

"Fine," Osgood accepted that and let the wind take the broadsheet, "I can only hope you do not defend your general to the grave, infamy, or obscurity." That last said almost gently, and was therefore more cutting than his sharpest barbs.

"That was well turned, Osgood," Joinville allowed, linguistically standing between us, "although, perhaps, you are too harsh on General McClellan – not to mention our friend here."

Osgood favored me a glare, the better to spare royalty. His jet black mustache twitched like a pointer waiting for the command to fetch while he obviously held back some cutting remake.

A perfect time for me to ruin the moment, "Just note where we are and where we're going."

"I think you said just that on the way to Manassas." He spit back.

Joinville missed the flash of Osgood's eyes – not being their intended victim, and so innocently added, "This is the most impressive military maneuver I have ever witnessed," he waved at the warships, barges, sloops, yachts, ferries, brigs, schooners, excursion boats and everything else that could float and carry troops, horses, artillery, ambulances, and trains surrounding us.

Osgood nodded with infinite slowness, "It is that," he smiled sincerely, "be truly perfect if only the Twenty-first were here to see it, don't you think William?" That asked without irony or rancor only because he had exhausted them when we first heard the news the 21st had been assigned to McDowell the Washington defenses.

It fazed Osgood not at all that over twenty-thousand troops had been so designated. It was assuredly a random act, a roll of the die that kept twenty-percent of the army married to the outskirts of Washington.

"I wish they were here, too, Osgood," I replied with some heat, "you know —"

"I have to hit the head," flatly said as he strode away.

"He is as unrepentant as he is consistent in his opinion of General McClellan," Joinville observed.

"He is that," I agreed.

"Ever known him to be wrong?"

The question, asked honestly and directly by a man I now considered a friend – a good friend – flummoxed me. I stood rooted, breathed the answer out, "I have never known him to misread a man's – shit, or woman's – character."

We both stared at a baroquely decorated Hudson River steamer to port, remained silent until it was well in our lee.

"You must find yourself in a most uncomfortable position," the Prince observed.

"Yes."

"Unless ..." he left it there.

For me to pick up, "What, Joinville?"

"You know, I have never heard you voice a single doubt, concern, or opposition, for that matter, on ... anything theses past months."

"Should I apologize?" I asked lightly, almost teasingly.

That was met by a Gallic sniff and, "I must ask, William, is the reason I have heard none from you because you are reticent to bring me into your confidence?"

"Oh, good God," I exclaimed in equal measures surprise and embarrassment, "I would never hesitate to share a confidence with you, Joinville – never," I shook my head furiously.

"Why then —"

"Because right now I'm afraid to bring me into my confidences," I laughed.

He smiled but did not laugh, "So, you do have had doubts yourself?"

"Yes," it felt good to say it aloud, "I haven't spoken of it because it does not seem right, it seems . . . disloyal . . . and certainly like piling on.

"I've known George McClellan since he was sixteen, Prince, he has infuriated me as often as I have delighted in his company. And now he is not only my commanding officer, but the second most powerful man in the nation. So, yes, I keep my doubts to myself because they matter not a whit."

"There is nothing wrong with voicing one's doubts to one's friends, William," Joinville was stoic though his eyes flashed, "remember, I saw you with General Stone – you were angry at his condition. You tried to cover it up, but anyone who knows you could see it – and then you encouraged your other friend, Captain Hoskins, to share his feelings about McClellan."

"There a question in there someplace, Prince?"

"Just an observation, but I would —"

He was interrupted by cannon fire from the sloop off our bow, she was raising and lowering her flags, the men on her deck jumped, arms in air, threw their hats. Around us the Quinnebaug crew ran to the guns and began to prime them.

Men ascended to the deck in droves, animated, pushing, elbowing, straining with much back slapping to get to the starboard tarifrail. A joyful mob.

Joinville and I were safe at the bow, my military and his social rank kept the area around us clear.

Joinville touched my sleeve, "What is happening?"

I pointed at the manor house we would be passing shortly, "That's Mount Vernon, my friend, our American Shrine, George Washington's home."

"Ah, of course," Joinville rediscovered his good humor, "if I remember my history, a much maligned, oft plotted against commander subsequently proven a genius of sorts."

"Indeed," I agreed, "now what do you think about my reticence to speak out?"

He slapped me on the back, "I don't believe for a minute you're afraid of looking the fool, William, but I think we can both agree to pretend, for now."

We turned our attention to the spectacle around us and spoke no more.

12. Contrabands

A British military observer, widely quoted in papers across the North, called our move to Old Point Comfort 'the stride of a giant.' For once there were no dissenters – it was unarguably the greatest amphibious movement in American history.

History was being made and those of us along for the ride had a  firm grasp of that fact. There was elation through the fleet as we approached the Virginia coast, elation barely tempered by the sight of the sunken U.S.S. Cumberland's flags still flying from her topgallants out of the watery grave the Merrimack planted her in a few weeks earlier.

Fortress Monroe was fully a third of a mile wide and in a week's time was dominated by a vast city of canvas while the harbor before it was crammed with so many ships they were individually unidentifiable through a forest of masts.

For almost two weeks Osgood, Joinville, and I watched the parade of ships, the debarkation of tens of thousands with accompanying animals, artillery, and supplies. Two weeks as sightseers with no duties. We were never bored, it was unaccountably exhilarating and it ended much too soon.

It was not McClellan's jubilant appearance at Old Point Comfort, nor his stirring ad hoc speech promising 'grass would not grow under his feet' that killed it for us – it was the summons disguised as an invitation to attend a briefing the day after his arrival. A summit meeting and most unwanted contact with the Army's brain thrust.

So it was Joinville and I found ourselves in Ft. Monroe's great dining hall with two dozen or so of the Army of the Potomac's senior officers, each with two or three aides in attendance. The great hall should have been dark, cool, and damp instead of the caldron the generals, aides, excessive candles and lamps, roasted mutton, heavy humidity, wool uniforms, and vigorous activity in abnormally warm spring weather by men hardly paragons of physical fitness.

Joinville and I stood against a wall far from the maddening crowd on top of one of the few windows. Slight relief, but better than none, and, at least temporarily, out of the limelight – unlike Wilkes, sweltering in the center of the fray assisting McClellan as he presented his plans for the movement up the Peninsula.

The generals packed the middle of the hall, hanging on McClellan's every word, staring at the maps, whispering among themselves, aides buzzing around them. The brick walls were covered by the likes of Comte de Paris, Webb and various sundry important scions of Democratic dynasties.

As McClellan finished I stood immobile and tensed for I had been called upon to address the august body. Tense actually too mild by far for the dread I felt at presenting my brief, albeit important, portion of the evening.

It came too quickly, Mac finished describing the push to Yorktown and the fact it was to start the next day. That energized the room – I dearly hoped McClellan had left something inspiring to share after I was done as I was guaranteed to suck the air out of a room of Democratic-leaning generals.

"Gentlemen," McClellan's voice bounced off the low, heavily beamed ceiling, "we have an important issue to discuss concerning a Congressional decree that affects us all," murmuring started with 'congressional' increased with, "I believe you all know Colonel Hanlin, my JAG liaison – he will read it and take questions," he smiled in my direction, the last smile I was likely to see for the duration, "go ahead, Colonel."

I walked to the edge of the long table, pulled a letter out of my breast pocket, opened it carefully, never looked up and began with preamble, "All officers or persons in the military or naval service of the United States are prohibited from employing any of the forces under their respective commands for the purposes of returning fugitives from service or labor who may have escaped from any persons to whom such service or labors claimed to be due.

"Any officer who shall be found guilty by a court martial of violating this article shall be dismissed from the service."

I finished to utter silence. I glanced around the room, I was stared at with the white hot intensity that in previous ages had preceded to execution of the messenger.

The silence continued long enough for me to begin to wonder if some collective, perhaps unconscious, agreement had been communicated through the room not to comment or vent anger in public. Whatever the case, I accepted the silence with gratitude

Then Fitz John Porter broke the spell, "Want to give us that in English, Willie?

"Cause it sounds like the usual Congressional horseshit," Sumner snarled through the snaggle of his snow white nest of a beard.

A rising crescendo of like sentiment rose around the table, flung itself across the room, echoed back to merge with new furies to create a tidal wave of angry babble. I was seconds from completely losing the room.

"It is not horseshit," I started in a normal voice – to the same effect as a wren warbling into a hurricane. I counted to three, then cut loose, "Ask Charles Stone if it's horseshit!"

That stilled the room to the point where I could hear them breathing. Stone's name had not been spoken aloud in weeks, the looks I received carried with them the quiet, but vicious, distain of believers for the blasphemer.

Well, in for a penny, "Ah, that's right, we can't ask him shit because he is in a prison cell."

Their looks turned cold, but questioning, I started to make eye contact, at least no one turned away, "Gentlemen," I restarted in a conversational tone, "order the return of slaves that come through our lines and they won't have to use Byzantine means to casher you. This is much more direct."

That last rang through, around, over the room until the last syllable finally died. This time the generals looked to themselves; after a time an undercurrent of soft whispering took over the room. An Adagio for Democratic Generals.

McClellan stopped it mid coda, "Colonel," silence descended with audible finality, "are there exceptions to this ... fiat," his evident disgust curiously had a calming effect on his officers.

"None, General," I avowed in my best courtroom voice, "it's simple. Do not return escaped slaves – although I wouldn't be too quick on indentured servants, either," I meant it as a feeble joke, it was instead taken as an additional restriction requiring additional dissent. I was not about to correct the perception. So I took a seat.

McClellan nodded to Porter to take over. He took a slow look around the room, "Washington is changing the focus of the war," Porter started with a mixture of venom and solemnity, "it's not enough to defeat the rebels, we must free the nigger as well – and," he glared, color rising above his beard, "how long before they," he waved vaguely toward Richmond, "learn of it – it will strengthen their resolve. We have been dealt no favors here, my friends."

Agreement swept the room, or at least those talking were the ones who agreed with Porter, more than a few officers looked longingly at the door and egress to the Hygeia Hotel, the watering hole that made a posting to Ft. Monroe much sought after.

The murmuring persistent, my neighbor leaned in close – the absence of a left arm made it a close fit – his Van Dyke beard almost nestling into my shoulder, and said, "Anything in that paper in your pocket say anything about us not fighting?"

I looked into the pale blue, ironic eyes of Phil Kearny, "Of course not, General."

"Nothing about us putting down our rifles and becoming nursemaids to a bunch of freed slaves?"

"Not a word."

"Alright now – and please don't stand on ceremony in correcting me if I'm mistaken – the net effect of the fiat you read is this," he scanned the crowd, took note of a gesticulating general, rolled his eyes, "if any of the people who dig the enemy's trenches, cook their food, fix their roads, build their fortifications, and a hundred other duties come over to us, we get to keep them away from that enemy?"

"Exactly . . . general."

"And we still get to shoot the bastards?"

"We do."

"Well then," he sat upright, "I've got to tell you, I have no problem with any of that," he grinned wickedly, "outstanding."

Kearny released me to attend to the room at the exact moment Porter addressed me with, "Is that correct, Willie?"

My stomach jumped, a student caught unprepared. Porter, however, did not catch it, so intent was he with the issue at hand, "That says we are not to return contrabands, but it says nothing about welcoming them, right?"

I answered with uplifted eye brows, I did not much like his tone – and I was surprised at his lack of sportsmanship.

"We are not required to house, feed, or employ them, correct?"

"Yes . . . Sir," I affirmed lowly. His show of democratic bravado was quickly wearing on me, he knew as well as I that humanitarian groups from all over the North were already descending on our small part of the Yorktown Peninsula to tend to the now homeless ex-slaves.

"Excuse me, gentlemen," Kearny bellowed from my side, "do any of you expect a horde of freed slaves to run over us? Perhaps impede our advance?"

"No, General, of course not," Porter replied with a deference that would not have been there for anyone else not McClellan. Addressing, never mind ordering, Phil Kearny was a command problem in and of itself.

A Columbia College educated attorney, he opted for the army after he inherited his family's wealth – the family that founded the New York Stock Exchange. A graduate of the French cavalry school at Saumur, a veteran of European and North African campaigns, the man General Scott described in Mexico as the perfect soldier, the man who had broken the Austrian center at Solferino, the only American to ever be awarded the Légion d'honneur . . . and it went on.

That man added, "Then I put it to you all," Kearny smiled, Porter had no possible response other than to smile in return and beckon him to go on, "this act of Congress means nothing as long as we act and act quickly . . . nothing means a goddamn thing as long as we take out Johnston – he's our one and only present concern."

Murmurs of agreement rippled around the room, kept low only in deference to political sensibilities.

Kearny was a fighter, a legend, McClellan's eyes noted that, he strode to the center of the room and announced, "We move in the morning, Keyes will take the van, we will fall on them where we find them!"

Excitement ruled the room, contrabands were forgotten, the generals rose as one amid backslaps and handshakes and promises of great actions before heading to their commands.

Phil Kearny punched my arm and invited me to drink with him. I did.

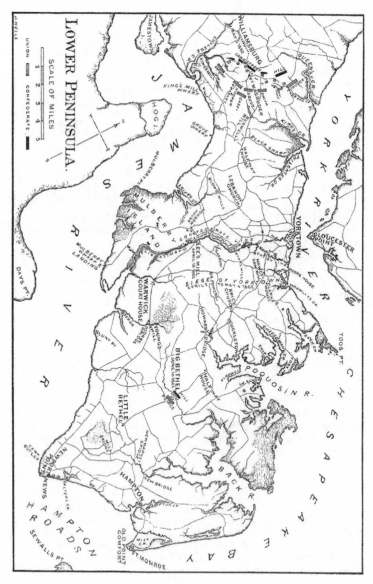

The Lower Yorktown Peninsula -from the Official War Records

13. The Warwick

For twenty-four glorious hours it was a storybook war, a pleasant ride under brilliant skies, through neat farms, around dense woods and moss draped swamps. The trees were covered in white petals, the grass was emerald, roads well packed and dust free, weather warm but not oppressive . . . it was all so, too, perfect.

I rode with Joinville and Osgood in the van with the left wing of the army, having eschewed staying with McClellan at Fort Monroe and walking distance of the Hygeia.

Spirits abounded with the conditions and in expectation of, any moment, brushing up against some or all of the 15,000 Confederates waiting to slow us down. Our skirmish lines were out well ahead, yelling back they would try to leave a few rebels for the columns, scarce heard over the songs the columns sang with élan.

The night in the field was a lark, a marvelous camping adventure. No one slept much, the excitement in the crisp spring air was palpable, the nightingales loud and persistent.

Well before dawn broke we pushed off the dewy ground and moved off through the darkness, our enthusiasm indefatigable . . . even when the first raindrops fell . . . even when it became a monsoon an hour after dawn. Indeed, enthusiasm remained high right up to the moment it became startlingly clear that two of the three pillars of military intelligence we had been operating under were very, very wrong: there were no rebels and the roads were abysmal.

Least one think the latter hyperbole consider – shortly after our initial drenching horses began to sink into the gruel-like substance the road soon became. A yellow substance that could support nothing more substantial than a whippoorwill. Prodding the road with bayonet, ramrod, artillery tampon found no discernable bottom for the simple reason there was none.

We were forced into the fields and a pace it would have been kind to call a crawl. Our standard measurement changed from miles to yards in the course of a few hours. Yorktown seemed a continent away.

By noon the rain, amazingly, picked up. I yearned for the mud of the road to Manassas. The rain slanting, I rode with my head tucked into my jacket collar. Clio stepped carefully, as if plodding through oatmeal, unhappy and not shy about sharing her pique every few steps via snorts, insinuating whinnies, and the occasional dirty look. I could not blame her, I envied her in fact – I had no one to similarly blame for my discomfort and misery.

The immutable laws of military science declared it could only get worse. And it did. The army sunk where it stood. The rain swept down in near horizontal bands of musket ball sized drops like a Biblical plague.

The infantry joined us in the fields as quickly as they could suction themselves off the roads, their curses a murmur under the roar of rain. Soon the meadows became bogs filled with soaked black-blue men with no place to move, no means to do so absent pontoons. We moved carefully through the teeming masses, allowed through with sullen looks.

Eventually we rode near an equally drenched group of generals and staffers huddled around General Keyes under a copse of trees. They were all speaking at once and with the kind of animation that seldom accompanies good news. I edged Clio into the pack of steaming mounts in hopes of gleaning plans. It took a while to cut through the frustration and flying oaths, but the gist finally seeped through: the left flank had literally stumbled onto the third major – and most incomprehensible – intelligence failure in the last day, the unsuspected existence of a river across our front.

Worse, the far bank was piled high with Confederate earthworks. Worser, the river and embankments cut the peninsula in two, leaving us no way to flank the rebels in Yorktown. Worser still, the river was damned in at least five places leaving wide, low lakes, artillery covering the soggy intervals in between.

I left the ad hoc staff conference while a red-faced, mutton chopped, sad-eyed engineering officer finished his hang-dog briefing of a coldly staring Keyes with, "Certainly the most extensive lines known to modern times."

That hysteria ringing in my ears I edged away leaving Keyes immobile in the center, unimpressed and implacable, in the face of engineering science. He was far from calm – on a good day Keyes projected an air of quiet seething – this day he was nearing apoplectic in the gentle manner of Vesuvius before the eruption. In keeping with the metaphor, all about him were oblivious.

I splashed back to my friends, filled them in on my observations. Osgood glanced at the impotent tableau under the trees, "We did not know there is a river here?"

"The maps," Joinville answered with a resigned, proprietary air, "were ancient coastal survey maps and showed only a tiny brook – insubstantial, a few miles long."

"Those the same maps that showed these perfect roads?" Osgood inquired further.

"I believe so," Joinville with a sigh.

"What else is missing from those maps, do you think?" Osgood asked.

Joinville shrugged, I looked out past Keyes, preoccupied with a mathematical computation of vast import: if the rebels had 15,000 men to defend Yorktown and their embankments ran the fourteen or so miles across the peninsula we hardly faced Scipio's legions.

"What are you doing, William," Osgood, with a punch to my arm.

"Thinking," I mumbled, accidentally caught one of Keyes' fuming eyes, looked away, counted three, obliquely glanced back and blew a sigh of relief he was engaged by an annoyingly effervescent lieutenant.

"About what?" Osgood persisted.

"Come on," my curt answer. I pulled Clio's reins, she responded with a blowzy snort, and we edged away from the summit meeting.

Out of the waterlogged pasture and into a sparse wood, our pace slow and measured, we rode past moss-laden, widely spaced trees, rivulets dropping off the leaves the only sound in the desolate wood

"Ah, William," Joinville ventured at length over Roxanne's fretful whinnying, "where are we going?"

"To revise your map," I replied over my shoulder. Shortly we came to the edge of the wood, a broad field open before us, gently sloping to a wide, slow stream. The opposite bank was clear, right up to the new, twelve foot high earthen parapet above which flew the Bars and Stripes and the blue flag of Virginia – sagging but defiant in the steady rain.

We watched in silence. Eventually we began to hear sounds of activity above the rain: distant cries of indistinguishable commands;

the wet thump of boots through mud; a forlorn bugle call; the creak of halyards. All in all, though, rather less than the sounds one would expect from an armed host a quarter mile away.

"Somewhat quiet," Joinville whispered.

"Yes," I whispered in agreement.

"Anyone keeping watch?" Osgood rued aloud – I am sorry to report Joinville and I jumped at the noise. Osgood smirked happily.

"I think so," I replied, my chagrin obvious.

"Really?" Osgood's doubt was palpable, he pretended to minutely inspect the parapets, false expectancy chiseled into his every feature.

"They're watching," I averred without force or effect.

"They are under cover drinking coffee and laughing at us," Osgood corrected.

"I calculate," I ignored him and addressed Joinville, "that if the rebels have fifteen thousand men and their line runs from the James to Yorktown, they have about seven hundred men for each mile they defend. They'll be vigilant because they'll have to move quickly."

"I can see that," Joinville agreed, "but I think –"

I lost the rest when I rode out of the tree line and into the naked field.

I rode a good thirty yards toward the center of the clearing, Clio deftly stepped around fresh hewn trunks. I stopped, rested my hands on Clio's saddle – the saddle of my McClellan saddle, come to think of it – and made a show of casually surveying the battlements. While a single bead of sweat found its way down my spine.

"For God's sake, William," Joinville's yell carried nicely out of the tree line, "you have nothing to —"

The rest stayed in the trees, the only thing I heard was a reverberating rifle shot from the fortifications. I did not hear the minie ball, or see evidence of it hitting, so I stayed where I was despite a slightly nervous prance or two from my far smarter half.

I counted to five before the next 'plotp' banged out, again no evidence of a bullet. A twelve count for the third – that one followed in half a heartbeat by a wet smack ten yards to my left. I turned a relieved Clio and as quickly as honor and probity allowed walked back to the trees.

Instead of a fourth shot a voice rang out behind us, "That's right, Yank, y'all jus' stay behind tha' trees and leave us n' our river alone."

I waved agreement over my head and rode into the comforting trees.

"William," Joinville rasped, "that was —"

"Courageous? Heroic? Inspiring?" I offered, with humility.

"Stupid, insane, suicidal," he corrected.

"Ah, they weren't going to shoot me," I shrugged. "but thank you for worrying."

"I was concerned for Clio," he snapped.

"Oh," I was crestfallen, "notice anything about the shots?"

"There's two of them, the second one has a musket," Osgood answered quickly, "they picked you up the minute you rode out."

"Yup," I grinned – mostly in relief, "thin and vigilant."

"You may have proved your point," the Prince reluctantly admitted, "but to what end?"

"Keyes has more men in the field we just left than the rebels have across the river here," I answered, "I think we should share the news with the good general."

That met with skeptical nods, we turned and headed back. The circle of officers was still there, little changed, same expression on Keyes' face though the gesticulation around him had greatly diminished. I assumed everyone's arms were exhausted.

I edged Clio around the clump of staffers, trying to figure out how to get through Keyes' picket line of sycophants when the problem was solved for me.

"Hanlin!" Keyes bellowed above the rain and drone of his staff, "Come here."

A channel opened to the general, we sidled up to him, "General," my imaginative greeting.

"You rode to see for yourself," no evidence of a question.

"I did . . . sir."

"And?"

"The lines are thinly held, general . . . very thinly."

He stared at me for a very long moment before, "I am under orders not to engage," stated flatly without so much as a blink.

"Might me a good time to disregard orders," I said without thinking.

"That a legal opinion, Hanlin?" Keyes taunted.

"No, just common sense . . . sir," I cringed as I said it.

"Dead on, of course," he relieved me of the burden of insubordination, "but I can't do a goddamn thing," he took a second to stonily survey Clio and me, "Go, tell McClellan what's up there, what I've got ready to go, see if you can get me orders that don't include sitting in the rain with a thumb up my ass."

"If you'll pardon me for asking," I began, "why –"

"Why have I waited?" He snapped, "Well, I haven't, none of my aides can find him. You're his friend, maybe you'll have better luck . . . in every regard."

"I'll do my best, General," I saluted, wheeled, avoided the stares of his staffers, cut back down the channel, collected Osgood and Joinville, and moved off.

We had a nice tour of the lower Yorktown Peninsula before finally finding Mac as darkness fell. Headquarters was a blazing brick farmhouse, packed to the rafters with harried staffers.

We followed the inbound foot traffic to McClellan's office, stood in the doorway for long minutes while he issued a string of verbal and written orders. It was impossible to not overhear, five minutes of getting the gist of the orders and I was certain our quest was in vain.

Osgood spied Pinkerton, touched my arm and was gone, a moment later Joinville and I were invited into Mac's presence. An unexpectedly buoyant McClellan.

"Willie, Prince, good to see you," his smile was brilliant, "I trust you've been keeping busy?"

"Actually," I replied, "we're here on a mission, General Keyes –"

"I just sent out his orders," he glanced down at a map that covered the table end to end. Someone had widened and lengthened the river in heavy blue ink.

"May I ask?" I asked.

"We're going to dig in on this side of the Warwick River and lay siege to Yorktown," he explained with something approaching glee.

My response was automatic and unthinking, "Like Rochambeau and Washington?" Uttered while my head reeled with the incongruities of the past forty-eight hours: the élan of an easy advance; the mud; an army of 80,000 stopped cold by a gentle albeit unsuspected stream; an army of 15,000 holding a key town and 14 miles of said river; the decision to lay siege.

"More like Sevastopol," McClellan grinned. Our army's expert on siege warfare was in his glory. Sieges were exact; sieges were scientific. When conducted properly utilizing mathematics, organization, logistics, success was inevitable. For those uneducated in the art of the siege – such as 99% of the American public and all of its reporters – it was slow, methodical, dull.

I smiled indulgently, "You know, General, Joinville and I were close enough to the river to be shot at," McClellan showed no outward signs of concern for his friends' safety, "the fortifications are very thinly held. You can —"

"I'm sure it looked that way, Willie," Mac shook his head good naturedly at a stoic Joinville, "it's meant to," acknowledging my skeptical look he hastened to add, "all theater, they want us to attack."

"Are you saying," Joinville said slowly, "General McGruder is purposely trying to make his lines look thin?"

"Of course," McClellan responded in the 'I'm glad you are catching up' tone I despised at West Point and despised now, "think of it this way, why would any educated officer man a line that long and defend Yorktown if he only had fifteen thousand men with him?"

"Well, I —" I started.

"It's rhetorical, Colonel," McClellan truncated me, "he wouldn't, it's against every military precept known. Even if McGruder was insane enough to try, Johnston would never allow such folly." That last said with certitude reinforced by his longstanding friendship with Joseph E. Johnston.

"No, my friends," the annoyingly expansive McClellan was not done with the lesson, "the only logical inference is that our intelligence is wrong and Johnston has either reinforced McGruder or has joined him in full."

Joinville nodded while eyeing me. Normally, I would have been reticent to express myself yet again to the commanding officer, but McClellan had so irked me with his smug dissertation I went ahead.

"What if it's the other way around, what if McGruder has fifteen thousand men and pretends to have a host? As a —"

"Rue de guerre?" McClellan laughed.

Joinville came to my aid, "There is much precedence for such deception . . . and General McGruder's reputation . . ."

"Worth considering," I hurried to complete the thought, "maybe he's delaying us until Johnston comes down with the army."

"Ah, Willie," McClellan Laughed deeply, "and perhaps he's feeding his men with a loaf and a fish."

"Well," I affected no hurt, "he is talented."

14. Yorktown

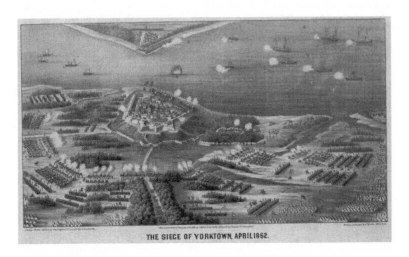

THE SIEGE OF YORKTOWN, APRIL1862.

We sat before the redoubts of Yorktown, a modern army occupying the same ground our grandfathers and great grandfathers had eighty-one years before. A modern army armed with rifles and artillery that while recognizable to our forefathers on the banks of the York would have astounded them with their range, accuracy, and lethality.

For all that, though, we were just another of history's great hosts camped before the walls of our enemy, not all that different from the Greeks before Troy.

One constant of siege warfare had never changed, particularly in the early stages: absent forays by the besieged, or an advancing relief column (highly unlikely in present circumstances) it was deathly boring. Oh, the engineers, sappers, map makers, a few mathematically inclined officers and men, senior staff and messengers were kept busy – that was a given and they were not loathe to let the rest of us know the intensity and importance of their involvement.

For the rest of us, we could either find a comfortable spot to watch the inch by mind numbing inch progress of the traverses and parallels or we could seek entertainment and diversion wherever we could. In rural Virginia and in light of the fact we were currently besieging the only decent town anywhere near us, the options were limited.

◊

Late supper with McClellan, Porter, half a dozen aides, and old friend Baldy Smith. The first hour spent with McClellan and Porter discoursing at length on the advances and remaining challenges in the investiture of Yorktown,

During that less than scintillating – to Joinville, Baldy, and myself, the aides were rapt – discussion, the three of us took full advantage of the others' fascination in the subject and laid waste to the oysters and roasted pig piled high on the table.

The army had discovered, virtually simultaneously with the order to dig in, that the oysters in the area were simply exquisite and wild pigs abounded.

Harvesting the oysters was easy, the pigs another matter indeed. There was a no firearm discharge order away from the front lines, those inclined to hunt boar had to do so with bayonet mounted on a decidedly non-industrial age sharpened stick. Nevertheless, units feasted on pork, the surgeons got to practice their wound care with regularity.

As commander of a division on the line, Baldy had to occasionally look up from his plate to make eye contact and nod sagely at some obscure point. Joinville and I had no such burden and attacked the steaming, aromatic food with abandon. Every time Baldy went back to his plate, he gave the two of us a furious glare, his glittering grey eyes noting the descending levels of available repast. He thought he could cower us as he could those under his command, at that he was spectacularly wrong. Joinville politely ignored him, as only royalty could. I could shrug him off as well due to various and sundry arcane knowledge of him I had acquired during the time our tenures had overlapped at West Point.

In any event, the technical portion of the evening drew to an end, the pork and oysters were withdrawn, the aides dismissed, brandy and cigars distributed, and the real business of the night was broached.

His cigar burning, McClellan reached into his jacket and pulled out a wrinkled telegram, waved it in the flickering light as if it were alive and dangerous.

"Lincoln . . . of course," his voice one of distain tinged resignation, "in response to news of the siege and my request for more troops, I get —"

"His Excellency's advice," Porter sneered with ill-disguised derision, "from his vast storehouse of military knowledge?"

"Exactly," McClellan answered, "imagine, up in Washington, no military experience – I don't believe the Black Hawk story for a minute – supposedly running the country and yet he has time to telegraph a tome to me."

Baldy studied his cigar, jaw set; Joinville stirred uncomfortably, Porter and McClellan did not notice, they were as two actors well into a routine, "He begins," McClellan held the telegram by the edges, as if not to sully his fingers, *"you have well over one-hundred thousand troops with you, I think you had better break the enemy's line from Yorktown to the Warwick River at once."*

"The temerity —" Porter snorted,

"Indeed," Mac agreed, "I am tempted to wire him to come do it himself."

Porter half-laughed, "Sir, stop. Should you desire an advance comma suggest you come to Virginia and do it yourself. Stop."

McClellan grinned for half a heartbeat, read on, "'It is indispensable to you that you strike a blow. I am powerless to help', well," he grinned, "that he did not have to tell me," Porter laughed, the rest of us shifted uneasily in our chairs.

Mac continued, *"You will do me the justice to remember I always thought that going down the bay in search of a field, instead of fighting at or near Manassas, was only shifting and not surmounting a difficulty,"* he stared around the table, daring us to agree. No one moved.

"He goes on, *the country will not fail to note – is now noting – that the present situation is but the story of Manassas repeated. I beg to assure you that I have never written you or spoken to you in greater kindness of feeling than now, nor with a fuller purpose to sustain you, so far as, in my most anxious judgment, I consistently can. But you must act."*

Silence around the room. I broke it with, "Heartfelt."

Mac waved it off, "He could show more care by giving me McDowell's troops back, instead of telling me to attack without them." The last said with venom in what was fast becoming a mantra that had not wavered since Stanton wired that McDowell's corps would stay in Fredericksburg and screen Washington.

"To be fair," Baldy sighed, looked up from his still untouched snifter, "Lincoln knows our plans, so he knows we're not going to use McDowell's men until Yorktown falls," he took the time to smile around the room, "solely to be fair."

"Well, solely to be fair," Porter, with a nasty grin, "it's disingenuous, and, in any event, that gorilla has no business sticking his nose into our business – we're in the field, have been bloodied in Mexico, he splits rails and tells off-color jokes."

"Bravo," Mac tipped his cigar in thanks.

"If you wish," Smith softly offered, "as a means of somewhat answering the President, let me make at least a demonstration somewhere along my front."

"We cannot risk a general engagement while we prepare the siege," McClellan answered quickly enough to convey he had already considered and dismissed the possibility.

"A probe, that's all, let's see what they've got over there," Baldy smiled, probing himself."

"Maybe," Porter grinned, "you can invite that ape to come down and lead a regiment for Baldy."

"Maybe," Mac smiled a faraway smile.

◊

Osgood sipping loudly from his mug, I stared up at the blanket of stars over us.

"Is he going to let Smith attack?" Osgood asked as if he already knew the answer.

"Yes," I took delight in answering.

"Really?"

"Sure," I confirmed.

"But?"

"Did I indicate a but?"

"Your tone did and everything this army does conveys a but."

"Baldy is attacking."

"Your voice faltered on 'attacking', William."

I sighed, I had no patience with which to continue the game, "It's a probe, Osgood, just a probe – to see what they've got, get the troops some experience."

"So, no attack."

I sighed, "That would be too strong a word."

He may have smiled, probably did, I was surveying the constellations in the Virginia sky.

"You know what's going on in Washington right now?"

"No, but I'm sure you're going to tell me."

"You know you want to know."

"Tell me," I confessed.

"Wade and Chandler are floating the theory that this campaign is designed to bog the Army of the Potomac down in an out of the way boondock and leave Washington open to attack."

"Well," I reasoned, "what else are those two going to think?"

"They are hardly the only ones proffering that about," his ready response.

"What the Radicals choose to believe is —"

"Stanton is listening . . . raptly," he said flatly.

"Stanton?"

"Has been heard to say McClellan is more interested in reconstructing the Democratic Party than fighting anyone."

"That's . . . troubling," I stuttered.

"Isn't it?" he said without expression.

"How do you come by all this?"

"Please."

◊

A perfect spring day, a few scattered high clouds, barely a wisp of a breeze, all good things for Professor Thaddeus S.C. Lowe as he oversaw the attempt to inflate the Intrepid – his hot air balloon – in a field covered with ropes, canvas, a large woven basket, mechanical equipment that was vaguely Torquemada-ish, and privates drafted for some yet to be described physical labor involving the thick ropes they held in hand.

Joinville and I perched on a fence under an impressive oak and watched the inflatable beast shrug in short serpentine slitherings across the rich sod, taking slow shape with an insistent hissing, sluggishly attempting to get off the ground like an old man off a low divan . . . perhaps an old man with arthritis, gout, and other maladies, for several times it became airborne – if being a foot or so off Virginia soil is, indeed, airborne – and several times it collapsed back in a heap with a huff.

The fifth or sixth time rising, it kept going – too high, too fast, Lowe had overcompensated– wildly out of control, bouncing side to side across the clearing, dragging the basket, threatening to dash it to pieces, scattering the hysterically amused privates while a frantic Lowe fiddled with the mechanicals with Faustian intensity and the privates

 lurched like a badly outmatched side in a tug of war.

In time it was brought under control to what may have been sincere cheers from our fellow spectators. Through the exertions of the straining privates, the fully shaped balloon stayed more or less in place, its hanging basket quivering a foot or so off the ground while the professor and Major General Fitz John Porter climbed through taut ropes into the basket, telescopes and maps tucked under arms.

Lowe set about checking ropes, rigging, connections, taking particular care with what was obviously the emergency release value. Porter stood trying, and succeeding, to look businesslike – as if all Corps commanders routinely took balloon rides. At last Lowe – I suspected he was as much county fair huckster as accredited professor – doffed his top hat to the crowd. The at least two companies worth of rope handlers began to slowly release the lines following the pantomimed instructions of Lowe's earthbound assistant as he went through a series of hand signals and body contortions that would have put a world-class maestro to shame.

It did not take all that long for the professor and the general to ascend to the heavens, or at least 100 feet over the Warwick. Their mission: to map the Confederate trenches, note our crawling siege lines and give us some heretofore unexplained advantage. The scene was as bucolic as ever a Romanticist could hope, men filed into the clearing, festooned the fences, and watched the sky. Some in simple awe, some with an intensity that indicated they knew they would be relating the scene to their grandchildren.

Joinville slid off the fence, began to set up his easel and canvas. I wandered over, peered over his shoulder as annoyingly as possible. He pushed me off, I looked up, Lowe was hanging over the rim of the basket playing with a rope, looking for all the world as if he would soon be a free-falling professor of aeronautic possibilities. Every eye in both armies were undoubtedly on him as he teetered. With exquisite timing, he righted himself, engaged in some machinations below the lip of the basket, sent a small bundle up the lanyard along the side of the balloon, made a show of pulling a string, and a moment later an over-sized Stars and Stripes snapped in breezes of a higher altitude.

Cheers – raucous cheers – broke out, men exulted in the sight and symbolism of the high flying flag for long minutes . . . might well have gone on indefinitely had it not been truncated rudely when the not so inspired rebels began to fire at the balloon.

They sent bursting shells that came nowhere near – who, after all, had ever tried to hit a non-stationary object in mid-air? – succeeded only in littering the ground in a mile radius with shell fragments. As unsatisfied with their results as we were amused, they changed to solid shot – easy to follow through the crystalline sky – that missed wildly, flew well over the balloon and our lines to fall somewhere in our rear to do harm only to recently ploughed fields and feral pigs.

It was wonderful viewing, highly entertaining, certainly harmless, a perfect diversion from the boredom of a siege. We laughed, pointed, delighted in the rebel misses, gross inefficiencies, poor aim, bad science. Then some genius behind the rebel lines, God knows with what reasoning, decided to try mortars. He no doubt reasoned that a shell going straight up would have a better chance plunging straight down through Professor Lowe's fragile invention. And it might well have, had we lived in a two dimensional world. In our reality, however, the mortars had as much chance of hitting the swaying balloon as a man-o'-war had hitting a piñata in a typhoon.

We watched a fat, slow, wobbly, mortar shell arch high into the ether, laughed when it became, readily, apparent it would miss by a hundred yards along at least one geometric plane. Those with the sharpest eyesight were the first to quiet, the first to edge away from the clearing, drawing little notice from those holding the ropes and blinded by the Stars and Stripes.

I followed the easily tracked shell, had fielded enough infield pop-ups to realize what any good outfielder realized seconds earlier: it was coming straight down, dead center of our clearing.

At least one man in the rope line had an acute sense of mathematics and self-preservation, immediately dropped the rope and bolted for the tree line seconds before a smoking oversized, misshapen bowling ball splattered into the sod a little left of center, spewing dirt, grass, and no longer amused privates. The shell sputtered, smoked, and hissed piteously.

Facts that did not go unnoticed by the rest of the men holding Intrepid – in seconds the clearing was cleared of blue clad tethers, their lines ten feet off the ground, rising, and proving any number of Newtonian laws – as, of course, did the Intrepid, flying now that it had lost its connections to the Earth.

The shell let out a dying 'pummmmfffft' and sat, benign. Having had rather more experience with mortar shells than the vast majority of my comrades, and sure it was a dud, I was the first to walk into the center of the field, one eye on the ground for divots, the other at the shrinking balloon. I was joined by Joinville, we watched as the Intrepid gained still more altitude, its tethers now well above the tree tops, the whole kit and caboodle headed for Yorktown.

"That bodes ill," Joinville remarked with a measure of awe.

"Pretty, though," I replied.

"Indeed."

"You get much of it down before your subject left?"

"Not enough," he tsked, "it is rather difficult to finish a watercolor when one's model has fled so precipitously."

"Ever happened before?"

"Well," he considered, "there was a woman in Cologne, once, she —" he stopped, the better to hear distant cheering from the rebels behind their works, "they cannot think they had something to do with Porter floating over to them, can they?"

"Indirectly, they aren't wrong," I pointed out.

"Perhaps —is there really nothing we can do?"

"Absent a spare balloon in which to follow, no."

"Pity."

Like every soul, North and South, we watched, with appropriate body language, the drama that played out that afternoon. Like the ball in a good lawn tennis match the Intrepid went back and forth evenly, north of the Warwick, south of the Warwick, over the York, back to the Peninsula, back out again. Finally, the sun setting, she was blown securely over to our side of the Warwick and quickly descended. We followed the descent at a fast walk in time to see her nestle softly to the ground in another field less than two miles from where it all started. We were there to watch Major General Porter return to the correct Army, ashen, but none the worse for wear.

Road to the lower face of the...

◊

I recognized Albert Denton from a quarter-mile away, so familiar was the casual stance of the officer standing atop a large pile of recently excavated slag, a map clutched in both hands, intently studying the rebel redoubts in the hazy distance. I tethered Clio to a surveyor's wagon and lurched up loose soil and looser rocks.

Albert never moved despite the racket I made slip-sliding my way to him. "You get the sextant?" He asked whoever he thought I was.

"No, major," I snorted to cover the fact I was winded, "I've come to make your full day a little fuller."

"Christ, it's you," he continued to stare ahead.

"No, just me, William."

"As witty as ever," he sneered, turned to shake hands, stopped in horror, "Oh, you've got to be . . . . I don't . . . . who . . . . you're regular army? Same fucking rank?"

"Yup," I answered jauntily, grabbed the limp hand for a completely unfulfilling shake, "but since we're the only ones up here you don't have to salute – huh, I always seem to be saying that to you . . ."

"Oh, God, did McClellan do this to me?"

"Absolutely, he had me frop by his office, asked how best he could vex you, I suggested a brigadier-ship, we settled on a regular commission."

He shook his head, accepted the fortunes of war, smiled a wicked grin, "Come up to see what the working men are doing?"

"Think we don't work at headquarters?"

"Don't think, know."

"So," time to change the subject, "Major of engineers, are congratulations in order?"

"They are, thank you."

"What happened to the quick, combat path to an eagle or star?"

"Funny thing that, the call for engineers was desperate," he waved a self-explanatory hand at the works around us, "West Point graduate, attached to the engineers in the Fifties, they begged me away from the infantry – gave me a promotion on the spot, promised the combat engineers would give me more than a fair shot at fame, fortune . . . pension."

"Your perfect job description."

"How could I decline?"

"How indeed," I looked over his shoulder at a topographical map covered in thick geometric patterns, the outlines of redoubts, trenches, parallels, and traverses, "You make that?"

"Course," replied the best cartographer in the Class of '46, hell, the best in the school, "but c'mon, I've got something to special to show you . . . especially you," he moved quickly, surely, expertly down the crumpling pile like a land locked crab. I thudded behind. We made it down to a surveyor's wagon where Albert rooted through a mountain of files, papers and portfolios. He finally pulled out a leather map case, opened it tenderly, and delicately pulled out an aged map.

"It's in good shape,' he intoned with reverence, "handle it gently."

I took it, only its appearance was fragile, it was as stiff as plaster. It took a moment to realize what it was, that realization was dizzying – I held a map made by one of Rochambeau's engineers. In 1781. While I took in the details, Albert answered the obvious question, "I got it in the archives in Washington – we didn't have any current maps . . . shit, that's wrong, we didn't have *any* maps of the area at all. Then some bright light that amazingly wasn't you figured out that three armies had already fought here, there had to be a bunch of maps somewhere."

"They just handed it over?"

"Well," he looked off toward the Confederate lines, "they did hand it to me . . . in a large pleasant room where they told me to take all the time I needed to copy it. Then they left."

"Obviously, they did not know you."

"Saw the maple leafs and made some basic assumptions," he squinted, the better to suppress a grin.

"All proved wrong," I smirked in return, "you have to protect this."

"Oh, I am, believe me, don't even like to pull it out in the sunlight, but I knew you'd appreciate this more than anyone I know."

"Thank you for that."

He shrugged, took the map from my hand, carefully placed it back in the case, "C'mon. I'll show you what we're doing.' He headed back up the dirt hill, leaving me to scramble after him.

◊

On a gentle knoll overlooking the York, brilliant sunshine, a warm, dry day. I sat in a canvas chair, feet propped up on a rail fence, writing tablet on my lap, pencil in hand and tried to draft the order to the

'Occupying Army of the Virginia Peninsula' Mac had charged me with earlier that morning.

Joinville stood some yards away painting the vista below, contentment in his every feature. Joinville's canvas was alive with color, my pad was empty though crumpled pieces of lead smudged paper littered the area around my chair. I was as miserable in my chore as Joinville was happy in his.

I was completely stymied, everything I wrote was either too strident, draconian, martinet-like, pleading and/or weak, or more like a suggestion than an order. An order I was not sure I agreed with, hell, was not sure was needed. That was problematical as I was most likely going to be the one to oversee it's enforcemenrt.

McClellan wanted it clear to the men currently digging trenches,  wrestling supplies, manhandling cannon and mortars, driving mules, pulling logs, rolling barrels, and everything else called for in a siege that the Virginia countryside, property, residents, were to be untouched. Not extorted, bought, coerced, requisitioned, appropriated, devoured, chopped down, smoked, disassembled, burnt, killed, pilfered, accepted as gifts, or covetously eyed.

We were, in short, to be the most polite invasion force in history. I was not to reference slaves – be they current, escaped, freed or abandoned. More – and worse for all of us – I was to make it clear that fratenization with the rebels across the lines was to stop. Which would stop the flourishing trade of Union coffee, sugar, newspapers for Confederate tobacco and newspapers. As I enjoyed the *Richmond Times*, I was less than enthusiastic on that front.

I was further stuck, as if I needed more reasons for my near paralysis, because I had ample evidence we were already one of the best behaved invading host since . . . well, ever. I reviewed all court martial requests and found protery matters trivial – at most. Lest one think that because officers failed to report, or care about, crimes against rebel property, consider that I rode the lines several times a week and knew firsthand the farms were prisitine, not even rail fences like the one I rested my feet on had been stripped for firewood.

"You hardly appear industrious, William," Joinville cut into my speculations.

"I'm not."

"I believe the general would like the edict while the war is still being fought."

"Witty."

"Merely concerned for you in your failure to complete a task assigned by the commanding general."

"That's very kind."

"Of course," he shrugged, set up another canvas, put the completed one against a rail to dry, "you are not enamored of this order, are you?"

"You see a swarthe of destruction about us?"

"No," he smiled, looked over the York, "I see an enchanting landscape."

"Enchanting?"

"That is the correct term, is it not?"

"I suppose . . . it is beautiful, though I've always found parts of Virginia somewhat . . . mystical." I put my pad and pencils down, walked over to join him, paused to peer down at the leaning watercolor, "Well done, Joinville."

"Thank you," he did not deign to turn around, "I am not sure about 'mystical' – unless I am missing your meaning."

"There's an aura . . . a feel about whole chunks of the Virgina shoreline. I don't know if I am putting it well . . . "

"Could you – "

"Croatoan," I proclaimed.

"Croatia? As in Serbo – "

"No, Croatoan," I beamed.

"It is annoyingly obvious you want me to ask what that means."

"Thought you'd never ask," I answered to his upraised eyes, "the Lost Colony," I waved southeast, "Roanoke Island, early English settlement just vanished – every man, woman, child, gone without a trace."

"Really?"

"Really, the only clue was scratched into a tree, the word 'Croatoan.'"

"What did it mean?"

"No one knows."

"And even after the area was settled, farmed?"

"Never a trace."

"Well, mystifyijng if not mystical," he smugly replied, "now about your order."

"It's done in my head, I just have to put it to paper," I sighed.

"And yet you do not."

"No."

"So, I repeat – you do not feel the order is warrented."

"I think it is more for Mac than the troops."

That captured his attention, "How?"

"I think McClellan's sending a message to the Radicals – the ones who would sooner see Virginia turned into a slaveless wasteland."

"That message is?"

"He's showing he's in charge, he's here, he'll dictate policy, mete it out, deal with the rebellion as he sees fit in the here and now."

"Rational," the Prince opined, "may I assume it is for the Democrats as well?"

"Exactly—" I stopped at the sound of an approaching horse, turned in time to see a rider emerge through the trees, Leutenant Wilkes. No doubt in my mind sent from headquaters.

Which accounted for the coolness my greeting, "Wilkes."

He caught on immediately, "Relax, Willie, no one's looking for you – McClellan's off loading heavy ordinance back at Monroe, you've plenty of time to compose your law."

"Not my law," I corrected under my breath. He dismounted went over to inspect Joinville's painting,

"Outstandning, Sir," Wilke's exclaimed to Joinville's profuse thanks. He walked back to his horse – his heavily ladened horse I finally noticed, "I came up to enjoy the view and," he began untying the saddlebags, "I come bearing gifts."

"In that case," I amended, "Welcome!"

He threw me an exceptionally nasty look before he unpacked and we spread out a fine picnic lunch. We ate our fill, sat and poked at the remnants. I tried to entice an especially plump squirrel to take a crumb out of my hand, she accepted the food while keeping her distance.

"What are you planning to do with that squirrel?" Wilkes inquired.

"Thought she'd make a nice pet."

"Wouldn't last a day in camp."

"Why is that?" Joinville asked for me.

"They make great stew," he answered while letting us know we were out of touch with the common soldier, "the men say they're the only thing in gray we've been able to catch."

"That would explain her reticence," I retorted, threw a chunk of bread over my almost pet's head.

Wilkes lit a cigar, Joinville and I declined, deciding to just sit and soak up the sun. "Oh, almost forgot," Wilkes clamped the cigar in his teeth, reached into his bag, pulled out a newspaper, "got his this morning, my father published it a few days ago, thought you'd like it."

"What is it?" I asked.

"Poem by Melville about the Monitor and Merrimack."

"Well then, young sir," Joinville intoned, "read away."

Wilkes did a fine job reading those somber words, finishing with a flourish:

> *Needless to dwell; the story's known.*
> *The ringing of those plates on plates*
> *Still ringeth round the world --*
> *The clangor of the blacksmiths' fray.*
> *The anvil-din*
> *Resounds this message from the Fates:*
>
> *War shall yet be, and to the end;*
> *But war-paint shows the streaks of weather;*
> *War yet shall be, but the warriors*
> *Are now but operatives; War's made*
> *Less grand than Peace,*
> *And a singe runs through lace and feather.*

He stopped. No one spoke. My squirrel, ignored, ran off.

◊

General McClellan could contain his already evident disgust no longer. He looked up over the newspaper he was reading aloud from and cut loose with. "The greatest battle ever fought in the Americas," no need for oaths, distain dripped off every syllable.

"The American Waterloo," Porter said, solely to add fuel to the fire.

"Is that what they call charnel houses out West?" McClellan responded as Porter intended, "I'm not sure it appropriate to refer to it as a battle, sounds more like an unorganized free-for-all with guns."

Baldy Smith, hitherto silent and engrossed in the paper before him snapped it closed and joined with, "Big battle and Sam Grant managed to win it after all seemed lost, I —"

"He did lose the first day – badly," Mac jumped on him, "taken by surprise, and in camp too."

"He wasn't there the first day," Baldy responded – to a pointed look from a coffee sipping Porter.

"He should have been," Mac, in a huff, with a quick glimpse my way that acknowledged he remembered the last time he had uttered that phrase in my presence.

"It is my understanding," Joinville started, oblivious to the room's current dynamics, "Grant was away to arrange reinforcements —"

"Point is." Baldy interrupted, nodded a tacit thank you to the Prince, now befuddled, "his army suffered an almost complete defeat one day, he attacks the next, retakes the field, scatters the rebels," Smith took no pains to hide his admiration, "I tell you, he and Sherman—"

"Man's insane," Porter, flatly, stubbing off a great ash.

"What?" Baldy asked, perplexed, "Who's insane?"

"Sherman," Porter, in a who-the-hell-else-could-I-be-referring-to tone, "almost cashiered, hell, almost committed – should have been, too," he made it clear the judgment final.

"What'd he do?" Baldy demanded, with timbre.

"Acted the Cassandra," I muttered, received a look from Joinville, was ignored by the generals, probably just as well.

"Went on and on about how the war's going to cost a half million lives and –"

"Judging by these casualty reports, Fitz," Baldy interrupted, "He won't be far off."

"He had a loss of nerve, too, in Kentucky," Porter was not to be put off, "kept saying he was outnumbered, facing imminent destruction."

"Sure as hell looks like he overcame that," Smith brushed it away with a fly swatting wave, "it's some feat to rally men who were surprised in their tents, throw up a fighting withdrawal, get up the next morning and attack."

"Most impressive," Joinville agreed.

"It was, I think —"

Baldy was abruptly cut off by a stern McClellan, "If they had not rallied, Sherman would have been court martialed for not having his men entrench . . . gross dereliction."

"You don't know the circumstances in taking the position the night before," Smith protested.

"Does not matter," Mac had fire in his eyes by then, "he failed to entrench."

"Knowing Halleck," Smith spit the name as one would a chunk of disagreeable fish, "he'll go after Grant and Sherman out of jealousy – as long as they're not politically connected."

"Are they?" Joinville asked.

"Grant, no," I answered, "Sherman's brother is a senator."

"I think he should relieve the two of them," McClellan averred, "I would."

"For?" I had to ask.

"Tossing their men's lives away," tersely answered.

"Seems to me," I made a general motion at the newspapers spread all over the breakfast table, "the rebels took as many, if not more, casualties —"

"Shame about Sidney," McClellan cut me off, sudden sadness in his words. Sidney Albert Johnson, commander of the Confederate forces, had been killed at Shiloh, "fine man, fine officer."

"The best," Porter agreed, rooted through the papers, pulled out the *Richmond Times,* "Jeff Davis made it a national day of mourning," he pointed at black headlines.

"Was it Sidney Johnson who was offered command of your armies when hostilities broke out?" Joinville inquired.

"After Lee turned Scott down," McClellan answered, "Sydney was the perfect choice – better than Lee. Far better. But Sydney followed his conscious and would not fight against Virginia."

"Had he not sworn an oath to the United States?" The persistent Frenchman asked.

Porter and McClellan waved that away in unison. Porter then offered the definitive moral defense for all such questions, "He was a man of honor."

"A very good man," Mac echoed, "to think the likes of Grant and Sherman did him in."

"Amen to that," Porter hasten to commiserate . . .

. . . and left Joinville, Baldy, and I to look at one another in dawning awareness.

◊

The British correspondent who styled our move to the Peninsula the 'stride of a giant' described our subsequent actions the 'step of a dwarf.' I am sure he meant no disrespect to dwarves.

◊

I had known Baldy Smith for fourteen years, we had each known McClellan somewhat longer and more intimately. So he knew I knew that he was screaming at me only because McClellan was not there and when Baldy was irate, Baldy was going to get it out even if the object of his ire was miles away.

Clio and I moved not a collective muscle while Smith, atop a wallflower of a roan mare, let it rip, "Tell me why the fuck I wasn't allowed to support my attack – just fucking tell me!"

"Wish I —"

"We took a good hundred yards of their line," he pointed, needlessly, across the Warwick in the general direction of Dam No. 1, "Jesus, Mary, and Joseph, don't you see it? We took that section of the goddamn rampart, we get up there in strength we roll up the . . . whole . . . fucking . . . flank – both fucking flanks."

He stopped to catch his breath, wiped a small cut on his forehead that seeped small beads of blood.

"You alright, Baldy?" I ventured.

"Fucking horse threw me," he studied the bloody cloth in his hand, "won't be riding her into combat again."

"Sorry to hear —"

"Where the fuck is Mac anyway?"

"Fort Monroe, the heavy stuff is coming in today."

Smith was taken aback, "He's supervising longshoremen while I'm assaulting enemy fortifications?"

I sighed long, deep, and hard enough to insure he noticed, "He ordered a probe in force with an eye toward testing their strength and snaring a few prisoners. I don't think he anticipated —"

"That they'd have no one over there?" He sneered, "Don't bother answering, Willie, it's obvious."

"But—"

"But, shit, you issue an order like that, you're somewhere nearby, just in case, goddamnit."

"I agr —"

"Or you leave it to a division commander's discretion . . . goddamnit, if he doesn't fucking trust me I'll fucking resign."

"I don't think —"

"We lost about a hundred and twenty men, Willie, most of them when the bastards counterattacked the trench. We had to sit there and watch our men fight their way back. You tell McClellan those boys lives are on him."

"I'll —"

"Go on," he waved in disgust, "go report, make sure you tell him that, I don't give a good goddamn if he sacks me."

"General," I saluted, pulled Clio around, left him feeling better for having gotten it off his chest and in the sure knowledge I would do no such thing.

◊

A few hours later . . .

"You saw Baldy?"

"Talked with him for a while."

McClellan stared at me as if deciding some matter, "How did he seem to you?"

"Baldy?" I asked, wondering if he had somehow heard some report of our 'conversation.'

"Who else?" His voice was light, which told me something was amiss.

"He was a bit banged up . . . and he wasn't happy he couldn't follow up on the initial success of the . . . incursion."

"Then it might interest him to know," McClellan smiled with a combination of forbearance and condescension, "The prisoners he procured for us have confirmed that Johnston is over there – probably with Beauregard – and they have almost one-hundred thousand men."

I said nothing though Mac gave me the time.

"You say Baldy was hurt?" He asked at length.

"Bruised, cut on forehead, but otherwise fine."

"Anything else?"

"Like what?"

"How'd he get hurt?"

"Horse threw him."

"He is an excellent rider," he observed with innuendo.

"I understand there was rather a lot of ordinance flying about, his horse took off on him."

"Uh-huh," his non-committal reply, "did he seem . . . coherent?" Asked as if it were a usual inquiry about one of his generals.

"Perfectly," I answered as quickly as possible.

"Impaired in any way you could see?" He remained frustratingly coy.

"Oh for Christ's sake, Mac, if you've got a concern, please state it clearly."

He did not blink, "Any evidence he was drunk? That clear enough?"

"Starkly."

"And?"

"Sober as a judge."

"Glad to hear it, there have been reports."

"They are false."

"Of course, thank you, Willie."

I left him. Eventually it occurred to me that considering his orders, and lack thereof, what difference it would have made had Baldy been drunk, sober, or asleep.

◊

Phil Kearny came to the field well prepared . . . for anything: a tent out of the Arabian Night Tales, rugs to match; a custom built French field bed – to call it a cot was to call the Nile a stream; a wagon that opened into a fully stocked bar; a well-protected traveling wine cellar.

Kearny was a refined, generous host who could not only speak to almost any subject, but had Dumas-like tales of the European Wars he had been such a big part of for so long.

Needless to add, he was immensely popular. Invitations to his company were highly sought.

I did indeed, then, feel privileged to be riding with Kearny on an inspection of the lines. Among the troops he was a ball of energy, interacting with even the lowliest teamster, always approachable. Each time we left a regiment, Phil turned to me and said, without fail, "Now, those men will fight for me!"

In between, we spoke of Mexico, he regaled with comparisons to his European campaigns – nothing technical, no general carping about better troops, equipment, weather, strategy, enemies, no lecturing – just interesting, highly enjoyable conversation that always revolved around people, real people not kings, lords, generals, pashas, Agas, and the like.

On a quiet lane by an abandoned farm, cool day, just before dusk, he slowed our pace to a slow walk, "I was out this way last week, there was an ancient black man sitting on the fence right over there," he motioned yet another section of intact rail fence.

"He waved me over, I was more than happy to – you never know what you can learn from a friendly local.

Kearny looked to me for confirmation as if it were not a major general's prerogative to chat with civilians of any ilk. I nodded encouragingly.

"He says to me, in a very rich, almost cultured voice, 'how are you this afternoon, Yank?'"

"I laughed, said 'fine, how are you, Grandfather? He told me he was a great-grandfather many times over. Lives up the lane over there, big house about half a mile south. Know what he tells me?"

"No idea, General."

"His earliest memory – men in red coats foraging through the chicken coops, couple of weeks later, more polite folk wearing blue and white coats come by, the white coats speaking a language he's never heard."

"Amazing," I had a chill down my spine as I said it.

"Isn't it? As he told me, the man heard 'the thunder of Massah Washington's guns from o'er there,'" he waved toward Yorktown.

He punch me on the arm, smiled, I shook my head, smiled back, "Tell me you'll write a book when all this is done?"

"Soon as the last gun fires," he laughed, "this is my last war, Willie, time to go back to New Jersey, sow oats of a different kind, and write my memoirs."

We rode on, a few more units, all to the same reception, same results. Done, he invited me on a lark to take a look at the siege lines, an offer I was more than happy to accept.

Shortly, we were atop a hill watching men dig emplacements, the lines spread out before us like the product of some mad geometrist from the Dark Ages.

"What a waste of effort," Kearny broke a comfortable silence with a sigh.

"The siege lines?"

"There's not enough rebs out there to bother with any of this, it's just Prince John having us on," Kearny peered at me closely.

"My theory as well," I replied after a respectful wait.

"So I heard – just as I heard you put yourself under fire to see how strong their lines were."

"That was nothing, I figured they'd shoot to miss, let me bring the word back that their lines were welled manned."

"It occur to you that your friends wheeling the body of a lieutenant-colonel back to camp would have had the same effect?"

"No . . . not really."

"Well," he shook his head, "again. What a waste."

"Want to go straight at them, right now?"

"Hell yes."

"Thinking of a night attack on Redoubt Number Nine?"

He laughed, "Hamilton was an amateur and look where it got him."

"Treasurer of the United States – though you would undoubtedly have more success in one of his other pursuits."

"Writing political essays?"

"Dueling."

He laughed, hard, "Now who would duel with me, Hanlin?"

"I would, if I got to choose the weapons."

He slapped my back, "Whatever you choose, sir, whatever you choose."

"Well, then," I said expansively, "I choose claymores."

"Claymores?"

"Claymores, general."

"Ah, Willie, don't they require two hands?"

"They do indeed, sir."

His one hand smacked me in the shoulder, remarkably hard. Together we watched hundreds of blue-clad voles tunnel toward Yorktown until he touched my sleeve, met my eye, "I know," his tone was almost tender, "you and McClellan go back to West Point, and I expect no man to speak against a friend, but I think you share my . . . hunch at how this whole thing is going to turn out."

"What's your hunch," I asked, looked out over the lines.

"Alright, Hanlin, I'll play along," he nodded sagely, "I think if Mac had been in command here eighty years ago, we'd all be eating blood puddin' and fighting for Victoria."

I started to answer, was stopped by a vise-like grip on my forearm, "No need, Colonel, no need. But when your friend self-destructs – and he will – I hope you know you can have a combat command with me – anytime you ask."

He spurred away before I could answer.

◊

April 27, 1862

Dear Brother,

I write in haste as I have only just found that a friend is being posted to the Peninsula and he leaves shortly.

I was blind with jealousy when we were left behind and you went off on the 'glorious expedition' to the Peninsula. Now, of course, we are in same but opposite circumstances – we are encamped inside the forts of Washington, you are encamped outside the forts of Yorktown.

You probably know the papers are not being kind to either your general or the campaign thus far. I suppose the news of Shiloh doesn't help – nor does the fall of Island No. 10, Fort Pulaski, Fort Macon, and, of course, New Orleans. They seem to have only magnified the passivity of the Army of the Potomac.

I can only imagine what your siege is like, for ourselves, with no enemy in sight, we can at least play a copious amount of baseball. I am proud to report that I have taken you place at third base with the Blues and we are undefeated. I believe that upon your return you will be invited to watch.

There are rumors, everywhere, that we may be sent south soon to join McDowell's corps in Fredericksburg. If this is so I trust we will see you shortly. At least I dearly hope so – as do your friends and the men. Everyone save Bryce and his –few- minions lament your absence.

*Reverend Ashford tells me to say Sundays are not the same without
you (they are not).*
From one bored officer to another, take care of yourself.
As Always,
Christian.

◊

I sat on what I now regarded as my grassy, shady knoll and watched
as the giant siege engines of the Army of the Potomac were pulled,
lifted, pushed, pounded, coaxed, driven, and wished into place in their
specially designed emplacements. I could discern distant figures atop

their soon to be
imperiled redoubts
equally as fascinated.
  I had not seen
Osgood in several days,
obviously something I
was inured to. As with
most of his absences he
reappeared as he had
vanished – this time
while I sat and watched
the proceedings. We nodded to each other as if he had been gone
minutes rather than days.
  "Where were you off to?" I asked while a mortar the size of a
carousal refused to budge.
  "Over there," Osgood waved toward Yorktown.
  "Over there as in 'I was behind enemy lines?'"
  "Depends on your definition of enemy."
  "The gentlemen in gray and butternut."
  "Then, yes."
  "And?"
  "Nice folk, much more relaxed than your average Yankee,
especially you New Englanders."
  "Surprised you did not stay."
  "Nice folk who seem to think it's perfectly fine to own other
people."

"Bit of a juxtaposition."

"Indeed."

"Learn anything?"

"Only that you were right," he grimaced at the thought, "it was all McGruder until a week or so ago – marching his men back and forth, using phony company calls, sending the same artillery caissons up and down the front . . . brilliant deception – when the other sides is willing to credit it."

"Mundus vult decepti, ergo deceptium," I whispered.

"My Latin is a little weak, William."

"Caesar, the world wants to be deceived so deceive away."

"Substitute McClellan for the world and I see the point."

I changed the subject, "I don't suppose you were over there on your own accord?"

"Went for Pinkerton."

"What's he got to say about your estimate of enemy numbers?"

'I am mistaken, duped by the wily Confederates."

"You duped?" I was incredulous.

"He has not known me that long," he grinned darkly, "you know, I half suspect he knews the truth but doesn't report it after those so called prisoners from Dam Number One started ranting and raving about Johnston's hordes and made McClellan happy.

"I know for a fact Johnston was miles away from the Warwick and Yorktown at the time, bastard moves almost as slow as you people do."

"Well," I considered, "once McClellan's mind is made up on something —"

"It is forever decided," he nodded, "you may have to live with that, deal with that," he went on, grimly, "but I will no longer be working for Pinkerton. I have already informed him so."

"How'd he take it?"

"Poorly, but he understood I am not going to risk my life only to be disbelieved."

"Makes perfect sense."

He accepted that without expression, "Heard you got an offer from Phil Kearny."

"How did . . . I did."

"I think you will be considering it soon."

"Let's see how we fare up the Peninsula."

"Fair enough," he knew when not to push.

"I know one thing for sure," I went on.

"What is that?"

"We're going to have no problem taking Yorktown."

"Wouldn't have weeks ago, either."

◊

The night of May 3rd, shortly after midnight, the skies opened up in flame, smoke, fuse-sparkling arching shells – the proverbial bombs bursting in air – a tremendous bombardment that lighted the northern sky as the Confederate artillery, long silent, fired at once. In every direction, with no discernable pattern, to no discernable effect. It was more like a holiday celebration with heavy ordinance than a military operation.

Spectacular, non-lethal, entertaining, it ended as quickly as it began. Suddenly. Completely. Followed by utter silence.

15. Hamlet's Ghost

May 4, 1862

I had acquired, early on in the siege, the habit of rising early to meander about before the camps came alive. It gave me an hour or so of stillness and solitude, something to be treasured in the midst of an army of 100,000.

This day I woke earlier – much earlier – and I woke fully, snapped to wide-eyed in the unshakable, if unexplained, feeling something was . . . different. I stepped out of my tent into a cool, starry-clear night, a discrete breeze coming off the York. I was alone, the only evidence – circumstantial at that – of the horde around me the breeze muted snores, groans, grunts, farts, whisperings, and night mumbles of the sleeping multitudes.

My eyes adjusted to the starlight, I decided on a walk, just a spur of the moment, middle-of-the-night-wide-awake-nothing-else-to-do stroll. I wandered past a darkened Headquarters, not so much as a glowing ember leaked out of Mac's farmhouse, and wound my way up to the knoll overlooking the York where the full force of the freshened wind – a hint of salt water on it – caught me whole.

It was breathtaking: stars through to the horizon, the black bulks of ships riding a gentle tide, their lanterns reflecting off the river while the melodious sounds of timber creaking, metal clinking, rigging rubbing, wafted across the water. I could dimly make out silhouettes of sentries patrolling our now lethal lines. Every once in a while I picked up the quick flair of a match when one of them lighted a cigar, pipe, cigarette.

For long, marvelous minutes I took it in, would have enjoyed it even more had I not had the overwhelming, head twitching feeling I was missing something important, perhaps vital. It became maddening, that itch in an infinitesimally small area just below the shoulder blades impossible for any grown male to reach; like being asked who the hero of *A Tale of Two Cities* is, knowing with every fiber of being it is Sidney Carthon, yet unable to articulate it.

It threatened to become all-encompassing until, at last, obliquely, I am not sure fully consciously, it hit me – I was not failing to observe something, I was failing to notice the absence of something. To wit: there was not a single light, ambient or otherwise, to be seen above Yorktown – not even the quick flash of a match. Further, now that I was attuned and mentally subtracted the sounds off the York, there was only silence hovering over Yorktown.

The inference was as clear as it was monumental – the rebels were gone. Quietly, efficiently, as suddenly as Roanoke's first settlers. Perhaps some wit had hung a sign reading 'CROATAN' over there. I stood rooted, awed by my revelation until I felt, then heard approaching footsteps.

I turned in time to see a shadow emerge from the lane, "I knew you would be here," a disembodied voice whispered.

"Joinville?"

"I checked your tent, saw you were gone and –"

"The rebels have abandoned Yorktown."

"I know, that is why I am looking for you."

"We mobilizing?" Even as I asked I knew the answer, it was far too quiet.

"That is the rub, William," Joinville stood by my side, took in the view, fell mute.

"How'd you find out?" I asked at length, "and what's the rub?"

"Two contrabands crossed the river an hour or so ago, brought the news, eventually ended up in front of some general – no idea who – he found it credible, sent the message to headquarters."

"And?"

He sighed an infuriatingly Gallic sigh, one that communicated grief, frustration, and pique in one shot, "my cousin rushed to wake up General McClellan, he was told the general had worked late, just gone to bed and would rise at seven… at which time he would assess the situation."

"What idiot aide told him that?" I pictured Webb as I asked.

"The general himself, actually, after the Comte barged into his bedroom," Joinville answered with grim resignation.

"Mac didn't believe him?" I was incredulous.

"Believe him or not, the matter bears investigation and confirmation... at seven o'clock."

"So we just wait?"

"And give the Confederates time to get beyond us, probably establish more advantageous lines someplace else."

"Probably already have lines prepared, Johnston's forte seems to be the withdrawal in strength," I mused absently, "the trick, of course, would be to move quickly and at least catch the rearguard out the open... by the way, why are we having this conversation?"

"Excuse me, William?"

"Sorry, too blunt, I mean why were you looking for me at this ungodly hour?"

"I, we, were hoping –"

"I would wake up Mac and talk to him?"

"Yes, would you –"

"Let's go," I said softly and led us away from our bucolic vista.

There was a lone light flickering in a first-floor window when we reached the farmhouse. Quietly, almost stealthily, we mounted the steps, crossed the porch. I reached for the doorknob... and it magically, heart-poundingly to be truthful, snapped open with an eye-watering creak. Major Webb stood framed in the doorway, effectively barring entrance.

"General McClellan is asleep, Colonel," he intoned. I gave him credit for at least trying a civil, pleasant tone, "he will attend to the matter when he wakes." Somehow, I do not know how, he managed to convey he was doing this solely out of concern for our overworked general.

Which accounts for, and hopefully excuses, the civility of my response, "I appreciate your concern for the general's well-being, major, but this is of vital –"

"The general knows, he's already cut orders for Professor Lowe to go up first thing and survey the rebel lines."

"Well and good, but pursuit of –"

"All is in hand, Colonel," Webb, the anointed king's chamberlain and protector continued with what was now truly annoying calm good sense, "we will have a very busy morning," gave me a look usually reserved for one's already simple, now addled by drink, strange smelling uncle about an hour or two after Christmas dinner, "you should know there are two very burly provost guards sitting down the hall with orders to arrest anyone who tries to disturb him." Big smile to finish, to let us know we were all friends and such extreme measures need never be employed.

"In that case, thank you, major, good what's left of the night," I turned, eased off the porch as the door closed softly behind.

"You went quietly," Joinville observed

"See any alternatives?"

"No, not really."

"Neither did I."

"Where we going?"

"To get Osgood."

He accepted that and followed me to our encampment, an encampment stirring only inasmuch chronic sleepwalkers and scattered man pissing in the trees could be called stirring.

Osgood, of course, stalked up to us out of the gloom, "Something happening?" He whispered.

"Yup," I whispered back, "you and I and Joinville, if he cares to, are walking into Yorktown."

"Excellent," Osgood hissed.

"Of course I'm going," Joinville, aloud, with hurt.

Twenty minutes later, my Colt strapped reassuringly to my hip, borrowed (without the owner's present knowledge) Springfield across my shoulder, my friends similarly equipped, we headed toward a ford on the Warwick half a mile or so away.

We walked carefully in the still and dark trying to pick out the trail and not make a racket, all the while Joinville whispered the morning's events thus far to Osgood.

Without incident, I led us into a narrow clearing on our bank of the Warwick, its gentle current a rippling song biding me cross – as I started to do until an improbable basso rang out from a shadowy tree, "Who goes?"

"I hope to God there's a man behind that tree," I answered.

"Gun, too, now who goes?"

"Jefferson Davis, Pierre Beauregard, and Robert E Lee," I was not be cowered in the predawn hours by a tree claiming to be armed.

Another voice came out of a shrub to my left, "Lucky there's four of us, then."

"Ay- up," new voice, just ahead, "guessin' we're goin' to be famous capturing' the likes of you."

"The Portland *Recorder*'ll write it up real nice," the fourth just behind us.

"Well then," I announced to the dark, "sorry, but the down east presses will have be disappointed, we're on your side, boys, from General McClellan's staff."

"Damn, there goes the promotion," a figure considerably larger than the tree he was hiding behind stepped into the clearing, "we shouldda just shot first," the giant with the Opera singer's voice advanced. He had to be every six-six by six-six, he held his rifle like a toddler his rattle, if one thinks abnormally large toddler, abnormally small rattle, reached us in two strides that would have been six for a mere mortal, got close enough to stare down at my shoulder straps, froze for an imperceptible moment, started to salute –

"No need, sergeant" I stopped him mid chest.

"Sorry, sir, sirs, I... we... thought you was..."

"Friends having you on?"

"Yes, Sir," relief flooded his voice.

"Because the officers have no sense of humor?"

"Yes, Sir."

"Well, I agree – my friends and I were just going to cross the ford have a look around the Confederate lines – any problem with that?"

"No Sir."

"Thank you, sergeant, we'll just . . . "..." I took one step forward, found myself barred from further movement.

"I meant, no Sir, in that no one is allowed to pass, no one."

"Whose orders?" As if I needed to ask.

"General McClellan, directly, Sir – came out last week gave explicit directions, no once across without written orders from him – only... Sir... Sirs."

"The general himself came out?" Joinville spoke, looking upward

"Imagine that, wi' all he has to do, comes out here, talks to us regular as you please, tells us how important this post is . . . hell o' a thing."

"It is," I agreed readily, "look, sergeant, the rebels are gone, they left, abandoned Yorktown, we need to get over there."

"They're gone?"

"Left during or after the bombardment last night."

"Thought tha' was strange."

"Indeed, now may we pass?"

"Sorry, sir, the general hisself —"

"I got it, I got it, Sarge," I put up my hands, "but look, the quicker we can verify they're gone, the quicker the Army can tear out after them, catch them, maybe go a long way toward ending of this."

"Well, sir, then why ain't the whole army up and comin' this way?"

"Because everyone's asleep. Some officious pick won't let me wake Mac up and tell him and not a damn thing is going to happen until midmorning or so, unless, maybe, we can do something about it."

"They won't let ya' wake-up Lil' Mac?" The sergeant asked, agog.

"Nope, got provost guards sealing him off."

"Bastards," said in such a way as to make one thankful it was not directed at oneself.

"So, sergeant —" this time he held his hand up, I waited while he ruminated.

"Colonel, my orders is ta' not let no one cross this ford, the one laid out with ropes, without written permission from General George B. McClellan — my orders, though, don't say nothing about the areas outside the ropes and," he leaned over conspiratorially, "there's plenty a' ford left on both sides."

"Thank you —"

"I'd get going, sirs, the river rises a bit here with tha' tide, an' it'll be comin' in soon."

"Good night, sergeant," I said, grabbed the rope and moved into the river.

"Good luck, sirs," four hisses behind us.

The water was cold but not unpleasant, rose to mid-shin, the bottom under my boots smooth and gravelly. I slowed our pace to a step- by- step crawl when the far side loomed in the dark, the sudden, testicle gripping fear I might have miscalculated and the rebels had left guards behind to maintain appearances by killing curious, almost order breaking, lieutenant colonels. Or, Magruder being Magruder, perhaps he was in the ramparts above with three hundred chosen men acting Leonidas while Johnston slipped away. Hell, wasn't there a town in Georgia named Sparta?

By the time all those thoughts formed and fed my psyche and further tightened my loins, I was standing on the rebel side of the Warwick. Stock still, in fact. Causing Joinville and Osgood to walk right into me.

"Fuck," I snarled, my only possible reply considering the circumstances.

"Who were you expecting?" Osgood snarled back.

I ignored him and headed toward the long dreaded earthworks. The only sounds our breaths and soft footfalls on the dewy grass and dirt; the first rays of light in the eastern sky obliterated the stars – it occurred to me we would shortly be at risk from our own side, silhouetted against the embankments.

"I'm going up," I answered to my friend… No objections – no agreement either, "hold this," I handed the Springfield to Osgood.

"You are going up unarmed?" Joinville inquired.

"If they're still there, what difference would a single shot rifle make?"

"Mental reassurance."

"Some reassurance . . . be right back," I said over my shoulder and headed up, ineloquently at best. I walked, crawled, tripped, slipped, grabbed, lurched, scurried, chugged, and/or hauled my way up the dirt, grass, stone embankment making enough noise to ease my mind about any remaining rebels.

I finally slipped over the top – the malicious would say flopped – and stood (sprawled?) on the wood slat reinforced parapet. It was marginally brighter, my first sight, taken with hands on knees, confirmed everything: the flagpoles to my left were bare, not even the lanyards were left. No unearned trophies for the Army of the Potomac.

I heard my friends approach, peered down over the lip, was instantly peeved they did not seem to be breathing all that hard, then chalked it up to my earlier trailblazing.

"Anyone there?" Osgood asked in a normal voice.

"Just Hamlet's father."

"You talk to him?"

"The cock crowed and he took his secrets with him," I answered as they dropped in beside me, Joinville sported a wry grin as he tossed my rifle to me.

From there it was a stroll, a pleasant sunrise stroll in the company of good friends. The breeze picked up, the sun rose through scattered clouds, Yorktown stirred behind us, bugle and drum calls carried over the river from our camp.

We saw our first Quaker gun a few hundred feet from our climb. No need to say anything, no need to even shake our heads, we silently moved on . . . to another. To be fair – though few would be in the coming days – there were empty emplacements with enough torn up earth and planks to indicate very heavy pieces had been hauled out. At one point we came across an ancient 32-pounder that looked all the world like it ha dbeen there since 1781

As the sun rose higher, the full enormity of how alone we were in the rebel redoubts was shattered when the shadow of a roc come to life joyfully swooped over us. We looked up at the Stars and Stripes flowing behind the Intrepid. Professor Lowe stood, hand on rigging, an airborne Ahab searching for some land-based white whale, an officer with a remarkable amount of gold braid blazing in the sun and long blond mane flowing in the wind beside him.

We waved, I do not know if they saw us for they did not wave back.

16. Williamsburg

May 5, 1862

I was in a narrow, muggy, paper-strewn room in an otherwise pleasant colonial in the pleasant center of the pleasant, though somewhat worn, town of Yorktown.

My windows were cracked an inch or two in the futile attempt to circulate the saturated air while thunderstorms of the approximate ferocity of the Confederate farewell bombardment shook the floor, walls, window panes.

I sat, back against a damp wall, feet up on a cracked, damp oaken desk that was old when Charles I lost his head, and read yet another court martial request.

The desk was piled high with the cursed things, silly inane, occasionally comic, usually despotic, products of newly found god-like powers in men who hitherto the war could only fire an employee or send a strongly worded letter of complaint to a supplier, merchant, politician and were now  besotted with ideas of meting out corporal punishment on a whim, capital punishment if lucky.

I was, therefore, bored, irritated, depressed at my fellow man's corruptibility, disinterested, and, ultimately, inattentive. Through yawns I dimly noted the rain had abated and, with hope, I gratefully threw open both windows . . . just in time to hear thunder resume in the northwest.

I picked up the first promising file of the day – a private, his major's personal whiskey supply, a friendly discussion across the Warwick, and a great deal of tobacco – laid it aside with the realization the thunder was not abating. I peered out the window and immediately noticed a low lying charcoal-gray smudge below menacing clouds miles off.

I happily abandoned my post, ambled down a creaking staircase and entered the clutter and restrained bustle of headquarters operations. I found a shirtsleeved Webb on the first floor humming over a stack of paperwork. He found the time to glance up in amiable annoyance.

"You do know there's fighting going on to the northwest, don't you?" I asked, hoping it was rhetorical.

It was not, "How do you know, Colonel?" He asked without curiosity.

"Artillery fire, dark smudge on the horizon over by Williamsburg."

"Oh," he answered without interest, "we must have found their rear guard."

"Unless there's another army out there," I quipped, to a blank look. "who's doing the chasing?"

"Sumner," Webb was happy to answer a question he understood, "with at least a couple of divisions."

"Mac with them?"

"No," Webb smiled at my foolishness, "he's at the docks, General Franklin's men are embarking today."

I was nonplussed and it must have shown for he rushed to add, "The orders are to harry them, not bring on a general engagement," he smiled, happy to be using words like 'rear guard,' 'harry,' and 'general engagement.'

I could have stood there and given the politically astute, militarily infantile major a lesson on the fate of columns sent out to 'harry' 'rear guards' when the 'rear guard' suddenly attacked. Or, the main body swung back around and ... I could have done that and more, in detail, perhaps with some humor, hopefully with eruditeness, for an hour or two and at the end I would have been greeted with the same, silly assed grin that currently plastered his ignorance-is-bliss face.

So, instead, I said, "I'm headed out."

The docks rumbled with a steady, muffled, thumping of varying intensities, never fading, just there underfoot. McClellan was easy to find, one only had to stay in one spot long enough, it was inevitable he would cross paths.

As he did mine, "Willie, what brings you out?" He held a sheaf of paperwork, was in all his glory in the midst of the bustle of thousands boarding transports.

"I think your army is engaged somewhere near Williamsburg, General," I said, lightly.

"Ah," he nodded, "just a brush up, let them know were on them."

"The rear guard?" I asked absently, having no other response at the ready.

"Exactly," he scanned the top sheet.

"Any reports yet?"

"Too soon," the bill of lading in his hand commanded his attention.

"Anyone out there checking on matters for you?"

"You volunteering?" He looked up, half-cocked smile in place.

"Absolutely," I answered with hope.

"Then by all means," he mock-gestured with the papers, made a half bow, "ride on up – just a skirmish, Sumner has explicit instructions to avoid an engagement... see any problems, come back to me – directly, Willie, I want to hear it from your lips, not second or third hand."

"Fine ... sir . . . why don't you come with me?" I asked as an afterthought.

"That a comment on my staying here on the docks?" It was asked more as a challenge than anything else.

"Of course not."

"That's," he pointed up the Peninsula, " a skirmish ... I'm sending Franklin's men up river.," he beamed, "an amphibious landing in Johnston's rear – the longer he tarries down here, the better the chance to bag the lot."

"That's . . . outstanding, General," I caught and channeled his enthusiasm.

"With him out numbering us so, I needed to figure out a way to get at him," he looked up the York in what might have been interpreted as wistful – if, indeed, McClellan had a wistful bone in his body, "or, at least I can bottle him up in the forts of Richmond and lay siege."

I nodded, flicked a half-salute, turned to leave, he touched my sleeve, "Hanlin . . . observe only, take note of things for me but stay out of it – that's an order."

"General." I acknowledged, jogged to Clio's stable. McClellan's enthusiasm was such that I was more than half-way there before the logical question hit me: why was Johnston retreating with such overwhelming numbers?

It took us just over ninety minutes to near the edges of the fight, indeed on the far outskirts of Williamsburg. The way there meandering but not hard to follow – long, thin lines of grinning troops pushed through he saturated air headed for the guns; artillery caissons moved in fits and starts despite the oaths of their teamsters and snorts of the horses heaving in wet, rutted roads; shaky files of walking wounded headed in the opposite direction like drunks under a dim street lamp sluggishly trying not to fall off the curb and into the path of the Army of the Potomac.

Sounds intensified and clarified – I could discern between rifle and cannon. The reek of gunpowder went from a hint to mild and almost nostalgically pleasant to heavy, coating, congealing in a heavy, acrid fog that engulfed all.

I emerged out of one of those choking fog banks and found myself almost face to face with Joseph Hooker. I saluted reflexively, Hooker smiled in return, "Welcome to the fun, colonel."

I did not answer to the familiarity. Hooker was not a man I wished to become any better acquainted with than I was already. Instead, I peered at a partially obscured field half a mile away, wavy blue lines in and out of the smoke firing into more smoke. No art or artifice before me, just two lines a hundred yards apart banging away at each other.

"McClellan somewhere behind you?" Hooker asked.

"He's in Yorktown, I'm here to observe and report."

"We're holding fine, but it's hot," he announced as if commenting on a parade.

I looked into his pale-blue eyes, noted his rosy complexation, was struck as always by the abysmally weak chin, swallowed my fully formed comment 'it's their rear guard and we're holding *them*?'

It must have nevertheless flashed across my face, or Hooker guessed considering the circumstances, "It's a rear guard in force, they probably have as many men in the field and in that tree line behind them as I do – we're spread out, too, waiting for someone to come up on my left flank . . . haven't seen or heard from that fucking white-whiskered old bastard in hours."

"What were Sumner's orders?" I asked absently, Hookers lines were bending back.

"Hold the line, move up when the rebels move back – assuming they decide to go on their own – obvious shit and, of course, don't bring on a general engagement."

I nodded. While I did not like the man – and never would – he was a fighter, was good at it, and his men happily followed him. When that kind of general was stagnant it was not his doing.

"Hanlin!" His yell cut through my ruminations, "Kearny's out that way," he pointed vaguely westward, "Hancock's out there someplace," he waved east, "trying to flank the fucks, go —"

He was drowned out by a mass volley, then another, close by, a breeze moved the smoke, and in the remaining haze revealed a vista shocking in it's awful precision, color . . . half a mile away, maybe closer, down a gentle slope Hooker's lines broke and ran for the cover of the trees fifty yards behind them.

"Fuck," Hooker sighed, caught my eye, "we'll hold them there, been doing it all day – Hanlin, find Kearny, he hits their flank we're out of this, maybe even bag the lot, just hurry."

I was about to pull Clio around when he grabbed her bridle, "Whatever you do, Colonel," he spit with intensity, "avoid Sumner at all costs, he'll just fuck this up more . . ."

Hooker was gone in a flash before I moved off to find Kearny. I cringed often, though I knew it to be a waste of energy, as minie balls spun over, kicked up little balls of mud in front of us. Clio, though, was oblivious. Then, forever, bullets, cannonballs, smoke, flame, mayhem, destruction, Armageddon itself did not faze her in the least. I never had the worry of her shying, bucking, bolting or pulling any other equine prank that served only to make the rider foolish or dead.

We went through smoke banks, around an idle artillery battery, crew lounging with nothing to fire at, lost sight of Hooker's battle, now just a steady thumping off to our right.

Shortly, we were in another farmer's field, rutted, tree lined, where skirmishers insolently slouched, waiting. We rode through scenes of no cohesion, no sense. Scattered companies, regiments, in line, in column, brewing coffee, catching a quick nap; artillery batteries unlimbered, officers in poses of tense expectation, men relaxing as only regular army veterans could; cavalry troops looking lost, trotting aimlessly to God knew where, from God knew whence to God knew what purpose; dazed wounded bewildered by their wounds and their sudden popularity – even slightly wounded men had a cadre of perfectly healthy companions to tend to their every need as they moved away from the front.

As we rode the sound of gunfire receded to the east and arose to the west. It grew with every step, smoke accumulated up ahead, streams of casualties thickened smell of gunpowder and other burnt things got stronger and stronger.

Through a copse of trees and snarled undergrowth, Clio and I emerged into a painter's rendition of a battle. Lines snaking across fields, around stands of trees, unimpeded for the time; a few artillery batteries lobbed shells over the infantry's heads, the balls disappearing into the ether.

A knot of officers were yards off to the right of the batteries watching the scene below with the same degree of control Pandora had after opening the box.

Strangers all, I found when we got to them. A sour faced major happily informed me that Kearny was down closer to the fighting personally seeing to the division, his tone dripped with 'what a colorful character, I wonder who'll take his place after he's shot.' He made it equally clear he had discharged his full duties for the day when he waved in the general direction of the right of the line.

Clio and I edged away in the sure knowledge that none of the men on that knoll would be employed if indeed General Kearny survived the day.

We picked our way around deploying regiments, disbursed companies trying to rally; a band incongruously playing something scarce heard above the shells; slackers trying to look busy doing totally out of place, mundane tasks – like the seven men fixing an empty, horseless, broken-wheeled wagon; stretcher bearers either frantically running down into the fray to pull out the maimed or frantically running back jarring their stricken cargo or standing with empty stretchers gawking at the battle lines ready to be of service to the wounded who managed to crawl to them.

We found Kearny by following a galloping rider. He was in a small group of brigadiers, sixty some yards behind the lines on a shallow ridge, heavy woods filled with blue to his left. Despite rattling off a bevy of instructions he caught my eye, beaconed me approach.

"McClellan here?" He asked in expectation.

"In Yorktown – I suppose I'm scouting for him."

"Yorktown," it started as a sneer, he let that go halfway in ended with a sigh, "alright, by rights this should be a series of skirmishes instead of stand up fights."

"I saw Hooker, he's hard pressed and —"

"His lines were broken," Kearny snapped, "that's why we're pitching in here instead of driving for Williamsburg – I'm hitting them on the flank – well, fuck, what we think is the flank, fuck this ground . . ."

What's Sumner —"

"Nowhere to be found," he snapped, "that fuc—"

A cheer interrupted him, a long, rolling, ragged cheer that we were only hearing because the firing was petering out. The rebels across our front had either broken and run or been ordered back, their job delaying the Army of the Potomac done.

As that realization hit us all at once, Kearny grabbed my arm, "Go to McClellan, tell him to come up and take command – get me some more men and maybe we can slice in behind these bastards and really do some damage – go, Willie, now."

I had no chance to salute, or reply, Kearny spurred forward, reins in his mouth, sword out of his scabbard in his good hand, brigadiers struggling to catch up.

I never found McClellan. The way back turned out to be almost impassable, the wounded took up a sizeable portion of the roadsides, ambulances headed for Yorktown went head to head with cavalry and artillery caissons leisurely moving toward the front – wherever that might have been. A mile or two of that and we hit a mass of the Army of the Potomac in column, following orders issued a day or more ago, with no idea they were needed a few miles away.

We were back in a quiet Yorktown late evening, McClellan's staff exactly where I left them, just better fed.

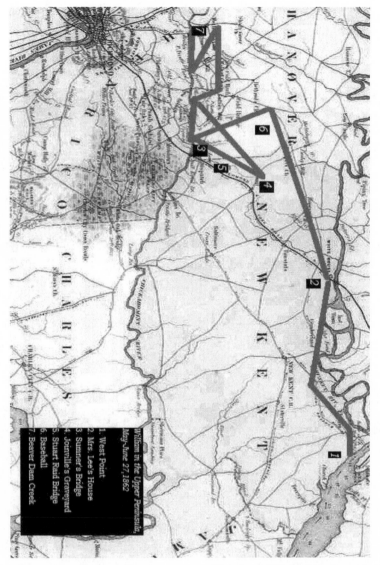

Map from Official War Records

17. The Crawl

The Battle of Williamsburg was over by dusk. McClellan arrived on the field in time to see the rebels' orderly retreat. In the time honored tradition that the army controlling the field at the end of the day is the victor, McClellan promptly proclaimed victory and conducted an impromptu review of every regiment on the field.

Back in Yorktown, late, I was with a pasty faced from fatigue McClellan while he sent a buoyant telegram to Washington that belied all those that had come before it. He read the ending to the gathered staff: *'My troops are in motion and in magnificent spirits. They have all the air and feelings of veterans. It would do your heart good to see them."*

Within hours that was being repeated around every flickering campfire from Yorktown to an abandoned Williamsburg.

◊

We moved up the Peninsula to new headquarters at West Point, a tiny hamlet on a spit of land where the Mattaponi and Paunkey rivers met to form the York. Overnight, it had become one of the world's great seaports and rail centers.

Despite the loss of some two thousand men at Williamsburg, we were a larger army than ever. A large army that moved at a crawl, in fits and starts and slightly bigger starts through a chopped-up countryside of fields, swamps, brooks, streams, hills, ravines, woods, clinging undergrowth.

A perceptive, experienced military observer would note certain accomplishments: roads were improved; supplies flowed copiously, freely; troops were precisely dispersed; communications were flawless; supply lines anchored, protected in great redundancy; maps drawn; pickets set and vigilant.

Thus, the professional military observer – the type of man who could and would sit with McClellan and his engineers for hours and listen in rapt attention to organizational plans, logistics, strategy, and the scientific, inevitable build up to the American Waterloo. Not a Shiloh carnage-to-no-observable-effect Waterloo, but the not all that much damage, strategically brilliant —nay- dazzling victory that would see brothers reunited.

The battle – and the organizational genius who was the architect of victory – to go down in the annals of military history alongside Austerlitz, Cannae, and Blenheim.

Mac was, of course, slated to be that organizational genius. As a consequence, the troops on the Peninsula were better armed, better trained, better fed, better everythinged that any army in the history of the Americas – French, British, Colonial, American, Confederate, Apache, Mexican, Creek, Black Foot, Aztec, Bolivar's freedom fighters, the Conquistadors.

The Army of the Potomac was a happy army, a confident army after becoming the first Eastern army to take the field from the rebels.

The press and the public, however, were not professional observers. They saw an army sitting outside the gates of Richmond despite pleas from Lincoln, self-important screams from the press, catcalls from Republicans in Congress, governors with men serving in the Peninsula, wonderment from international observers, suspicions from the Radicals, joy in Richmond.

◊

West Point, another well-appointed house on a hill overlooking the harbor, a hot bed of activity. It was late, Joinville and I sat with McClellan, shirt-sleeved in the warm, oppressive night. McClellan held a foolscap in a grip that threatened to pop the words off the page.

"Lincoln, Stanton and Chase are at Fort Monroe," Mac said for the third time, "they want me to go down there and discuss . . . matters."

"Might clear the air," naiveté got the best of Joinville.

"They want to talk," McClellan snapped, "they can come here and do it."

"But, Mac —" I started.

"No buts," he snorted, "I am a general in the field with his army in the presence of an enemy that outnumbers me – I do not leave for them, they venture to me.

"You convey that to them yet?" I asked.

"Certainly."

"Hope you coached it a little."

"Enough," he pulled another sheet off his overflowing desk, "polite but strong enough to convey my pique at their ignorance of military probity – I think they shall leave me be for a time."

He smiled around the room, added, "I wonder what the President of the United States, the Secretary of War, and the Secretary of the Treasury will find to do at Fort Monroe?"

"There's always the Hygeia," I offered, "They —"

"Perhaps," he interrupted me with a nasty smirk, "General Wool will regale them with stories of the War of 1812."

"Perhaps," I replied doubtfully.

◊

In the end what Lincoln, Chase, and Stanton did was convince ancient General Wool to give them a couple thousand troops and with a little help from the navy did what had eluded the combined forces of the United States for some thirteen months – they recaptured Norfolk.

The Merrimack was burned at her dock, Chesapeake Bay, the York and James were completely re-opened, the navy regained their mid-Atlantic port.

The politicians went home having accomplished more than talk.

The exploit was never openly spoken of at the headquarters of the Army of the Potomac.

◊

It was everything one would expect a Virginia mansion to be, elegant, atop a gentle hill overlooking the Paunkey, green fields bordered by prim slat fences, rows of stately poplars, blindingly white outbuildings. White House Plantation Martha Curtis' home before she married George Washington.

A magnificent edifice along our creeping advance line, the first men to approach it were greeted with an ornate note:

Northern soldiers who profess to revere Washington forbear to desecrate the home of his first married life, the property of his wife, now owned by her descendants. A granddaughter of Mrs. Washington.
Mrs. R.E. Lee.

Mrs. Lee had been earlier escorted, with honors, through the lines to her husband, Jefferson Davis' military advisor, in Richmond. McClellan posted a provost guard, we pitched tents on the impeccable grounds, the barns and now empty slave quarters became supply dumps, those who applied were given supervised tours of the house.

Bucolic, calm, that portion of the advance had a dream-like quality to it – beguiling in its intimate pleasantness, as if the very land itself was intent on lulling us into inaction, inviting the blue horde to simply settle in, become one with the land, cast aside thoughts of violence.

The past surrounded us. On an inspection ride with McClellan we passed a handsome country church – St. Peters – sitting alone on a lane surrounded by neglected fields. The church where George and Martha were married. We stopped, Mac went in alone to pray.

The next day McDowell's 40,000 men were released to join us.

◊

Osgood tried a new defense, something he had picked up from a Confederate major in Tennessee months earlier. It was proving rather less effective than the major's army in the mid-east.

At each successive move his glares intensified and sighs deepened while I failed to suppress my glee at his distress.

Two pieces down, in a virtually unsupportable position, Osgood removed a flask from his pocket and took a long pull.

"I'm not sure it's that bad a position," I pointed out.

"What?" He snarled, then sighed, "It is not the game."

"Of course not," I agreed, "how could it be with you having so much practice being in —"

"It is Pinkerton," he said with resignation, "he is insistent I undertake another … expedition."

"Behind the lines?"

"Where else?"

"Sorry, if I—"

"I am not inclined to do it."

"I should think not, it's more dangerous than ever, with their lines shrinking, compact —"

He scowled deeply, "That is not it," I had insulted his professional integrity, "what is an issue is that Pinkerton seeks only to have me reinforce his opinion . . . he's not interested in anything that does not support his . . . guesses."

"Which is?"

"You haven't heard?"

"I've been ducking out of strategy briefings," I said as simply as possible.

"Really?" An eyebrow shot up.

"Really."

"There a reason?"

"My distain of repetition."

He nodded. Waited.

"Pinkerton's latest?"

"They are meting out one hundred and nineteen thousand daily rations and climbing, it will grow to a hundred and eighty in a week, with at least two hundred regiments between us and Richmond."

"That's somewhat unsettling," I said evenly.

"That Johnston's that powerful or that that's Pinkerton's projection?"

"What do you think?"

"I'm asking you."

I pretended to think it over, succeeded only in getting a dirty look, "I think if Johnston had those numbers he'd be all over us instead of backing his way inch by inch up the Peninsula . . . and I'd damn well do it before McDowell moves down to us."

"Think McDowell joining will get your friend moving any quicker?"

I shook my head, surveyed the board absentmindedly, "The math won't work, we'd still be outnumbered – according to Pinkerton."

"In theory," he picked up his king, looked at him as if he had betrayed him, dropped him on his side, "but I have a strong feeling when McDowell's thousands appear, thousands more will magically appear in Johnston's ranks."

"You're telling me we will always be outnumbered,"

He stood, patted me on the shoulder, "I suppose I should give the whole thing one more look – beside, I like Richmond, nice town."

"Be careful out there, I called to his back.

"Please," he yelled over his shoulder and waved good-bye.

◊

May 20, 1862

Dear Brother,

Again, I write in haste – this time for a better reason – we have been ordered to move. It is off to Fredericksburg and McDowell for us, at first light.

After the shear boredom of the forts the move is most welcomed – though it pales in comparison to the prospect of reuniting with you.

You should receive this about the time we arrive at Fredericksburg, I dearly hope to see you shortly.

With Brotherly Affection
CDH

◊

I requested transfer to McDowell's corps and the 21st at once. McClellan was understanding and promised it would be done soon, at some point, no later than when McDowell joined us. A week or two at the most.

Joinville and I spent as much time as possible in Phil Kearney's camp, away from the minutia of headquarters as they planned every inch of the advance.

Late morning, a sunny day that threatened to turn hot, we returned to a headquarters that threatened to turn hostile.

A grim Webb found us as we crossed the threshold. His prickly little eyes widened in recognition, "Ah, Colonel Hanlin," he intoned in grim surprise, "what fortunate timing, I have a note for you."

With surprising deftness a paper appeared in his hand and he snapped it to my chest. I took it with hope, he caught my eye and whispered, "Sorry, colonel," in a tone that sounded like he meant it. Whether for me or for himself was unclear.

I pocketed the note, never did read it, moved on to McClellan's office in hope of clarification.

McClellan was staring at a pile of documents, unmoving, deep in thought. I stopped a few feet away and waited, motionless.

In time his tired eyes found me, he sat forward, smiled wanly, "They're not coming, Willie."

"General?"

He waved north, "McDowell's move has been suspended by the direct order of Lincoln, he'll probably be ordered back to Washington . . . perfectly sickening . . . sorry."

"What the hell happened . . . sir?"

"We have been routed in the Shenandoah Valley."

"Routed."

"The rebels have taken Front Royal, Kernstown, and Winchester – they're probably driving for Harper's Ferry by now . . . our president," he injected the title with utter derision, "thinks that threatens Washington."

I kept the fact that I agreed to myself, asked the next logical question instead, "Who's in command of the rebels?"

He let that hang in the humidity so long I thought he had not heard. At long as he simply said, "Jackson."

"Tom?" I blurted.

"I believe he is now referred to as Stonewall," he replied his face also a stonewall.

18. The Chicahominy

May 30, 1862

It rained for two days, sometimes torrential, sometimes sideways, always hard. The roads we had macadamized held fairly well, those we had missed or ignored as insignificant became dangerous man, beast, equipment swallowing pits of quicksand. Moreover, the rivers, creeks, and streams rose disconcertingly, with every hour nearing impassible and threatening to strand Generals Keyes and Heintzelman and the

30,000 men of their corps on the south side of the Chickahominy, isolated from the remaining 90,000 members of the Army of the Potomac.

That sent nervous shudders through the staff; could have been near panic if not for the fact offensive operations in the teeth of the tempest would be ineffective at best unless both armies reverted to swords and cross bows.

The rain slackened on the third day, bored, Mac confined to bed with neuralgia and a recurrence of the malaria he had caught in Mexico, Osgood, Joinville and I rode to the banks of a raging Chickahominy. Transfixed, awe inspiring in its raw beauty and power, we sat in a light mist and stared: it was simply aboil, debris as large as small ponies were tossed with ease; the normally placid, muddy stream was white, foaming and moving like a run-away shay, ripping at its banks, searching for more.

We rode along the bank, no need to comment, no one was fording the river anytime soon. In, out, around copses of trees, newly formed swamps, tangled debris pushing on trees, the river was more imposing

with every step, even the fine mist seemed to be adding to the flood.
We detoured around a particularly large, shimmering with swirling
eddies new back water, lost sight of the river completely behind vine
entangled, weirdly bent trees, went up a knobby rise, descended to a
marshy but passable field…

   …where a bedraggled, muddy rider emerged from the trees and
cantered toward us, weaving, horse and rider obviously on their last
legs.

   He was a Union officer, his rank indiscernible- one shoulder strap
was torn off, the other flapped on his back. Shockingly white, his
tattered uniform plastered to his shivering body, hatless;
long, shallow, gash across his forehead leaked blood diluted by the mist
and water running from his long, sopping hair. He looked at us with
glassy gray eyes.

   I grabbed the bridle, Osgood pushed Hespeathius against his
mount's heaving flanks, wrapped an arm around his waist, Joinville
worked a blanket out of his roll, handed it to Osgood. The man's eyes
found my insignia and held there.

   "Sir, General Keyes….message . . . McClellan"

   "Easy son," Osgood wrapped the blanket across his shoulders
"you are with friends."

   He nodded thanks, we moved at a walk and, in fits and starts,
gasps, we got the full story before we reached headquarters: Early
morning pickets captured a member of Johnston's staff – Johnston
was about to launch an all-out assault on Keyes's isolated corps.
Ominous sounds and flashes of heavy gray columns, picket fire from
outposts with no previous targets to fire at, all confirmed it. The
lieutenant, George Baxter, was one of three messengers immediately
sent by Keyes. A fortuitous precaution for the other two drowned
crossing the river.

   We reached headquarters, Baxter was borne away by a host,
hot coffee in hand, a half-dozen blankets over his shoulders before he
had taken two shaky steps and his horse was led wobbly away.
seconds the three of us were alone, our presence as forgotten as
irrelevant.

   Baxter was inside the house for no more than ten minutes before
aides began flying out, headed in all directions with a purpose

previously exhibited by our staff. I felt obligated to at least make an appearance – also I was curious.

The farmhouse was empty since for McClellan's Chief of Staff, and father in law, Colonel Macy, who spied me and grabbed my arm in one motion, "Hanlin, come with me."

Thus invited. I allowed myself to be dragged by the stiff, imposing Macy up the stairs and into Mac's bedroom where sat, propped up by a dozen pillows, the Commander of the Army of the Potomac. Pale, sweating, writing board across his knees, madly scribbling.

I waited at least a ten count for him to pause and look up, "Lieutenant Baxter thanks you."

I shrugged and waited.

"Keyes is in dire straits," he said in a manner of doctor confirming gangrene.

"Yes," I agreed.

"My closest relief is Sumner's Corps," as if confirming the mortality of the wound.

"How's he getting across the river?" I, logically asked.

"We have one bridge more or less intact – engineers are on their way to prop the damn things up…Then we have to pray Sumner acts quickly and gets across before they're swept away."

"Risky."

"Other measures will take at least at least twenty-four hours, more if the rain picks up," he seemed to turn paler with every sentence.

"So Sumner it is, then," I said with finality.

"I can only hope I impressed it on him with alacrity."

"With Bull Sumner," I opined with some force, "I think it sufficient to just tell him to get over the fucking river and relieve Keyes no matter what- he'll follow that order to the death

He nodded weakly, "Perhaps you can relay that to him directly,"

"Be happy to" I answered quickly.

"I'll write new orders," Mac went back to his papers with considerably less vigor, "When he gets everyone across, you let me now, immediately-if the bridges wash out or any other disaster occurs, come at once," Mac exhibited a resignation I had not heard before, "you and your cohorts, by the way," he grinned with ghastly effect, "don't go across with him, I don't need to worry about any of you today." Both messages finished, he folded the written one, handed it

over. I left him and his father-in-law and ran downstairs where Osgood and Joinville, of course, insisted on going with me.

It was a miserable ride. The rain picked up, died, picked up again blown by long, heavy gusts that dropped broken branches on us with annoying frequency. Eventually we were forced to slide by sodden blue columns of miserable men not all that concerned with keeping razor sharp lines. That required frequent stops, changes of gait and colorful and largely ineffective oaths in both French and English. We finally reached a staging area, the columns were herded into rolling fields to wait in frustration-brewing coffee was an impossibility.

We pushed by them, dodged fallen tree branches, soon came to the river. We were at a bend, white water to our right, smooth, freight-train-fast water to the left where it tore under and lapped over a low, swinging bridge, sometimes two feet above the Chickahominy, sometimes inches below.

"Merde," the Prince summed up more adequately.

"Good Christ," Osgood agreed

Six men stood precariously on the bridge closest to us, swaying like men on a flagpole in a nor'easter. Wagons were scattered about, more men scrambled over them for tools, ropes, wood under the gaze of an engineering officer atop a buckboard trying to hold a paper doomed to dissolve.

I rode over and said hello to Major Denton. He greeted me grimly. What was undoubtedly an acerbic comment died in this throat when the unmistakable bulk of Bull Sumner appeared out of the trees and made a beeline for us.

He nodded to me, turned to Albert, "Can you do it, Major?"

"We can, General," Al surprised me with the ferocity of his avowal.

"Do you need anything, anything at all?" Sumner was as solicitous as humanly possible for a fifty year veteran.

"Might need some manual labor in an hour or two…sir," Al addressed Sumner but never for a moment took his eyes off the bridge,

"They'll be ready whenever you want them, Sir," Sumner said with grandfatherly affection, "God bless you and your men, I'll stay out of your way, your job's hard enough,"

"Thank you, I…" Seeing something that required his immediate attention Al left us without a second look and headed for the bridge.

Sumner, the white-haired grandfather replaced in an instant by the cold eyed regular, turned and snapped; "I already have my orders, why are you here?"

I sighed unmilitarily, "General McClellan felt his last orders were not clear enough and he —"

"He blamed me for following orders at Williamsburg, what's he want me to do now?"

"I think —"

"These orders," he touched his breast pocket, "Are as intricate, limiting and specific as all his others, what have you got that's different-he want to tell me when to shit, too?"

I could not help laughing, which triggered a reappraising look from Sumner, "Who's idea was it to cut me new orders?" He asked me at length.

"Mine," I answered with trepidation.

"Really?" A great, bushy, pure white eyebrow shot skyward, "Well then, Lieutenant Colonel Hanlin, what are my revised orders?"

"Short, simple- get across the Chickahominy at all costs, support Keyes as you both see fit."

"That's it?"

"That's it," I handed him McClellan's written orders, he stuffed them unread into his pocket.

He considered me and the bridge for a moment, "I think I like you, Hanlin-West Point, Forty-six, right?"

"Yes, Sir"

"Well then, you must have some engineering skills —" he started.

"Thought you'd never ask…Sir," I spurred Clio back to my friends, threw her reins in their direction and trotted to the bridge.

I stepped on the first planks and into sensory overload: each board moved North-South, independently, with the conflicted current while simultaneously rising and falling with waves not noticeable from shore. It was like standing on the back of a bucking bronco, I gave up trying to balance and grabbed a soaked, thorny rope, braced, pulled, planted both feet wide and prayed, my hand shredding with every pull and panic fueled grab of the sopping rope.

I was proud of myself for maintaining dignity on what really should have been a carnival ride until Al's voice skewered my self-congratulations, "You planning on moving anytime soon, or do we build around you?"

That gentle urging ringing in my reddening ears, I endeavored to creep toward him. Adding to the four dimensional vertigo challenge was the fact I could see the river ripping past under me through the wildly spaced boards. I looked away lest my stomach – empty, thankfully -fulfilled its threat to escape in either direction.

A nerve wracking, interminable period later I reached Albert on the precipice of an almost washed out section where he stood legs akimbo, hands behind his back, oblivious to the motion(s) and discomfort(s) He did however take note of my white-knuckled grip on the support with a smile of smug superiority.

The next hours were a blur, we looped miles of rope across to the river and began to brace what would soon be unbraceable, sank pilings. Every time we thought we were close a tree trunk or long branch, a dead mule once, would ram into the span and undo most of what we had so painstakingly achieved. At one point the rain picked up in a furious burst only to stop completely fifteen minutes later.

Finally, soaked with rain, river, sweat; sore, rope-burned, splintered, on the verge of exhaustion we collapsed on the near bank and watched, with pride as the first of the blue columns stagger across. Sumner sat immobile, imperturbable on his horse, taking his teeth out to bellow orders, replacing them with a scowl as if daring comment. He knew his men had to see him, see him they did, every man who crossed would swear the general looked him in the eye.

It was almost hypnotic. Until Albert hit me hard in the ribs, "Tell me I am imagining that," he threw his head in the direction of the bridge.

It took a moment for me to understand, "Either the river's up or the weight of the men is making the bridge sag," I muttered as the sight sunk in.

"That fucking bridge," he gently corrected me, "is not fucking sagging,"

"Sorry —"

"Rivers rising, now it's a goddamn race until it washes over the bridge," Denton sighed the sigh of every military engineer since the architects of Troy, "how much of the old man's corps has gotten across?"

"I'd estimate half the infantry, some artillery."

Albert's professional eye jaundiced now by inevitability, surveyed the scene, calculated the rising water, the lowering bridge, "We won't make it."

Those words hung in the saturated air. Columns struggled over, every few minutes one or more of us ran onto the bridges, bent into the dizzyingly swirling water and took measurements as best we could. No question the water was rising, debris was smacking into the bridge regularly shaking off small, indefinable pieces of the infrastructure – it was only a matter of time until something vital was crushed.

Our increasingly dire reports to Sumner received only the slightest nods, he sat imperiously and watched his men as if willing them across.

The first laps of water came over the planks while an artillery caisson was inching over. Soon, men were splashing across, the water just over the planks. We descended on the bridge and strung ropes to reinforce the hemp rails-more to stop men from being swept away than to buttress the bridge. When we were done, the water was well over our ankles.

It was not long before only our rope railings maintained the crossing. Men waded over mid-thigh, then waist-high through malignant eddies like drunks on skates.

A brigadier I did not know, his men the next to cross, rode up, defeat stamped all over his face, to Sumner.

"General Sumner," he pleaded, "it's impassable, Sir-I won't risk my brigade."

"General," Sumner remained calm, "General McClellan ordered me to cross and we will do so if the water rises over our heads."

"Damn it, Sir, it's impossible, we —"

"Impossible?" Sumner's voice boomed off the trees, river, columns snapped their heads toward the roar, "Sir, I tell you I can and will cross! I am ordered!"

"Sir —"

"Tell your brigade," he dropped his voice, "I will cross with them, General, we'll brave it together."

There being no reply to that, the brigadier returned to his men. Sumner turned to us, "I should probably be over there now in any event, wouldn't do for the corps commander to be on one side and his corps on the other, would it?"

We agreed in turn. Sumner smiled- the first and only time I ever saw him do so, "Great work gentlemen, thank you," He rode a few yards, stopped, looked back, "Major Denton, when the floods recede a tad, better rebuild the bridge, maybe add another. I've no doubt they'll be needed."

19. Realities

The thump of artillery started around three that afternoon, Sumner's corps across in full, gone from view as effectively as if they had stepped off the edge of the world. For the rest of the evening well

into a starless, moonless pitch-black night we ate, drank, paced, stood, sweated, and wondered to the percussive beat of cannon, the sodden ground sending it up our uneasy legs...

...to continue at dawn and go all day, the last day in May, until it finally petered, spluttered to a finish after dark. The Battle of Seven Pines, or Far Oaks depending on one's sensibilities, lasted thirty hours, involved tens of thousands on both sides, resulted in thousands of casualties, eight of Keyes' nine general officers were either wounded or had their horses shot out from under them (a slight distinction, to be sure), the rebels were held, Sumner's reputation in the Army reached its apex, and I experienced it all in the sick room of the Commanding General. Hot, closed in, suffused in miasmic vapors, reading ,writing orders and chafing at every mind and ass numbing second of it.

I was a glorified secretary though the largest, greatest battle yet fought in the East, though undoubtedly the best informed single individual – the first expert on the Northern version of Fair Oaks, and that included the Commander of the Army of the Potomac. By the last sputtering picket fire he was flushed, nodding forward, feverish and not entirely coherent. Malaria and the stress of a raging battle fought entirely against an unsupported wing of our unusually heterogeneous force had taken a toll. By the time it became clear Keyes and Heintzelman would hold and plans would not have to be radically altered, Mac was beyond the pale of alacrity, moments later he was fast asleep, a final dispatch from Sumner clutched in a sweaty hand. I left the room and staggered downstairs, out into merciful fresh air on the way to my tent.

I slept in full uniform and I slept late, stirring with the undefinable guilt I always did when I did not wake early. I peeled my jacket off, discarded a rancid shirt, grabbed a towel, a bar of highly prized soap, stepped out into brilliant sunlight and headed for the river in hopes of finding a quiet spot to take a much needed swim without fear of being swept away.

Five steps into the clearing Osgood slipped in beside me, handed me a mug of too hot coffee, eyed the towel, cake of soap, "Good idea, I will have your bed clothes burned and that purged."

"How kind of you, I don't need my back acrubbed, by the way, so feel free to stay here."

"You know, being a bad morning person requires rising in the morning."

"I'm broadening its meaning," I sighed, "it has been a long couple of days...so, what's up?"

"You, finally, your commanding officer, hour's ago."

"Mac's awake?"

"Hale, hardy, pontificating already."

"He up and about?"

"No...not really, but he is better and writing up a storm."

"That's a minor miracle."

"Maybe-by the way, the rebels have broken off all contact, appear to have withdrawn to defensive lines around Richmond."

"We in pursuit?" In defense of my naiveté, I was very tired still.

"You are joking," Osgood politely pointed out.

"Apparently."

"I believe we are regrouping, building some bridges, fixing roads, tending the wounded...writing tracts."

The river had significantly calmed since my last visit, though it was still three-four times wider than before the deluge(s). I set about finding a secluded spot.

"Glad I don't have to worry about rebel sharpshooters disrupting my swim."

"Alas, you are doomed to be bored"

"I can handle that type of boredom."

"Really?"

"What?"

"Nothing . . . here's a good spot."

It was indeed, a copse of wide spaced trees on a bend, the water calm, deep, the spot shielded and unoccupied. I stripped and jumped in, the water was cool, nowhere near as cold as what bracketed and buffeted me two days ago, I luxuriated as the grime floated off.

"Now that I has your attention," Osgood back to a thick pine, feet dangling in the water, "Let me read today's pronouncement—"

"C'mon, Osgood, I spent two days in headquarters, I—"

"Soldiers of the Army of the Potomac," he was to not to be put off, "I have fulfilled my promise to you, you are face to face with the rebels, who are held at bay in front of their capital – it never ceases to amaze me how much double meaning your friend can pack into a single sentence, he—"

"Osgood, the man was very ill, I saw it myself, so—"

"So his self-aggrandizing gets a pass?"

"Well, yeah, perhaps, and—"

"It does not strike you as incongruous that instead of us driving them to the very gates of Richmond, he states, clearly, we are merely holding them at bay?"

"Yesterday was a very near thing, Osgood, an isolated corps against an army, every general's nightmare, the stuff Austerlitz' are made of, so—"

"You do not get it, do you, William – mind the tree branch," I did, barely, waved a thank, fought against the tug of a still very powerful current, the exercise driving the fatigue out of everything but my head; "you just have not grasped it yet-and you are usually ahead on this sort of thing."

"What am I not getting, Osgood?" I treaded water and stared in.

"McClellan could have lost that battle yesterday, could have lost all of Keyes men, hell, could have lost Sumner's as well-and you know what?"

"What?" I asked with resignation.

"We would still outnumber the bastards."

"We would?"

"We would."

"That's not what —"

"Think I am wrong?" He challenged without heat, he had no cause to think I did. Ever did.

"No, it's just—"

"Just that the numbers being tossed around have us as the underdogs holding the hosts of the rebels at bay, it would be hysterically funny if it was not so fucking sad."

"How many they have?" I headed in, my enthusiasm for my bath/swim dashed.

He threw me a towel, "Seventy, Seventy-five thousand, less yesterday's casualties, which I understand are not inestimable."

"Mac believes they have twice that—"

"Probably thinks they somehow gained men yesterday, too."

"How does this happen?"

"The commanding general believes he is outnumbered, he expresses that to his friend, business associate, and head of his so-called secret service on a regular basis, and data is interpreted...accordingly," angry, he threw something into the Chickahominy, "And—"

"That was my soap!"

"You finished"

"For today," I pulled on my pants, "what's the and?"

"The rebels feed into it, constantly, deserters, prisoners, shit we had a young lieutenant 'accidentally' cross our picket line on his way to the latrine."

"Could—"

"Sure, he just happened to be some kind of dispatch officer with an intricate, thorough knowledge of the Confederate battle order; Something he was only too willingly to tell us, said he wanted to let us know we were in for a tough time. Suggested we might want to go home, peacefully."

"Pretty inartful," I observed

"So you say," He snorted, "Then add the fact that he escaped quite easily – no problem finding his way in the dark on the way back."

"You're going to tell me he was not discounted," I surmised, the benefits of my emersions fast ebbing.

"He was embraced as if bearing the word of God," he shook his head, the mustache twittered, "Christ, he was fed, coddled, treated like he was a member of the staff – I have seen disaffected deserters come over, give us a perfect rundown of their small piece of the Confederate Army and be treated as traitors and social pariahs —"

"I think that's redundant."

"My point, exactly." He ignored my retort and went straight to the heart of the matter, "they are discounted if not openly ridiculed, their motivations questioned – they are basically considered irritations to the normal course of business."

"One discounts what doesn't fit ones world view," I, probably pompously, intoned.

"Indeed," he threw me a quick look to insure I was serious, "it rules this army," he peeked again, was assured by the look on my face he had made his point, "the rebels suffered a major loss yesterday," he changed the subject, at least somewhat.

"Do I have to guess?"

"Johnston was wounded."

"Severely?"

"Ever heard of someone being wounded '*good*'?" He replied with derision.

"You know what I mean."

"Uh-huh… he's in bad enough shape he will be gone for a while - they need a new field general."

"Who?"

"Do not know yet." He apologized

"Shocking – any guesses?"

"I…do…not…speculate."

"And to think you work for Pinkerton."

"I work for you," he corrected with venom, "the rest of this…mess, is just horseshit."

That stopped me, dead in the middle of a swampy field, "Jesus, I'm sorry, Osgood", I blurted, with feeling.

"For what?"

"Dragging you into this, I—"

"Hell William, I would not have missed this in any event, I am just frustrated with…everything. Pinkerton is better than this, he knows what he is doing, it is just so hard to watch it, that's all…shit, we should have been in Richmond weeks ago, I know that beyond a shadow of a doubt."

"Well, sorry anyway – but look, eventually, soon, the full armies are going to clash and the truth of the numbers will be known, and will be telling – not a whole lot of room left between us, has to happen soon."

"Convince yourself, yet?"

"Almost," I laughed.

"Tell me, was it anything like this in Mexico?"

"God no," I shook my head slowly, I had a quick, fleeting vision of our little, outnumbered army, moving, planning, striking, "It was not…you done with Pinkerton?"

He nodded, "No need for me now."

"You'd think they'd invite you in, give you a tour of the legions, introduce you to a general or two, send you back with full regimental lists, all better to convince us to leave."

"They have so flummoxed McClellan, mystery is their best tactic."

"Still —"

"They have managed to get a general who outnumbers them to tiptoe around and generally act as if surrounded – shit, William, they have already won this round – at least,"

I dwelled on that for a few yards, "Johnston was precise, scientific, the chances of him making a mistake, risking a general engagement on the basis of what you've told me were slim to none —"

"You are thinking the new commander may be real? Will attack? Make mistakes?"

"Could happen,"

"Where do you manage to find your optimism?" He demanded.

"If I knew, I'd have it excised,"

"No you would not, but it is a good thought," snidely enough said, but his hand on my arm belayed any intended hurt, "if McClellan is cautious now, have you thought how he would react to an all-out attack?"

"Actually," I stopped once again, "I have."

That stopped him as well, rare, very rare, surprise flashed, however briefly, across his dark features and he muttered, "And?" with new curiosity.

"We'll defend it well, probably 'scientifically'," the last said with only a hint of intended irony, "As long as the attack lasts, under the pressure, the constant decision making, movements, the act of defending – we will be a hell of a force."

"Then, what the —"

I held up a hand, "It's what happens after the final repulse, when the guns die out, that keeps me awake at night."

"Because?"

"I don't know – and after three months in the field I should – and that really troubles me."

"I could see where it would."

◊

I had the same dream that night I had had at least three times in the last month.

No build up, no warning, I went from some half-aware other place, probably pleasant (though definitely without Collette), to a field in Mexico. No idea where for it was utterly featureless except for my lines and the Mexicans packed together fifty yards away.

We were in battle line. So were the Mexicans, though they moved not a muscle.

The only sound was us bringing up our rifles – strangely, I had one as well, no sword, pistol, though I was in command – we fired. Silent, smokeless.

The Mexicans did not move. Not one of them dropped. We – I – reloaded. The sound of our rifles – wait, they should have been muskets but they were quite clearly sparkling new Enfields – again the only sound. We fired. To no effect. Stone- faced, high-hatted, the Mexicans made not a motion.

We began to speed through the manual of arms, loosed off another two or three rounds . . . nothing . . . reloading again, I could not find my ramrod . . . smacked the stock on the ground to ram the load home – panic rising . . . fired. . nothing . . . next time through the stock fell off . . .

We were only getting a few shots off every volley, pieces of rifles littered the ground . . .

I looked up from the pile of rifle rubble around my ankles, the Mexicans had fixed bayonets. All of them. At the ready. I scrabbled to reassemble my rifle out of the parts strewn around me, a blood curdling bugle call blared El Degüello across and through us. No Quarter.

Other bugles take up the call. Without a sound, the Mexicans move as one, bayonets held hip high.

20. The Telegraph War

June, 1862

"Thank God it's not Beauregard," the Commander of the Army of the Potomac intoned with something just sort of glee, that day's *Richmond Times* smudging his fingers while he brandished it like a lost spelunker his torch.

"Why not Beauregard?" Joinville asked in the manner of one not expecting an answer.

Though he had to know one was forthcoming – if not from a still pale Mac, then certainly Fitz John Porter who hesitated only to swallow his coffee, "Simple, Prince," the very expansiveness of his response telling in and of itself, "With this appointment the Rebels have committed to defensive operations before Richmond. Beauregard would only be wasted in such passivity, he'll be wherever they decide to mount their offensive."

"And this General Lee?" Joinville persisted.

"Robert E. Lee," McClellan snapped the paper down in derision, "they call him Granny Lee, the King of Spades, over there," he made a brief nod northwest, "for his propensity to dig in wherever he goes."

"A defensive specialist, then?" Joinville looked across the room for confirmation.

"Damn fine engineer," Baldy Smith, as usual the voice of moderation, "built the St. Louis levees, Fort Pulaski, commanded West —"

"Defense, defense, defense," Porter interrupted what would have been a lengthy curriculum vitae with a combination of dismissiveness and final judgment.

"Don't forget flood control," I added in a mutter – to smiles from Joinville and Baldy, a short scowl from Fitzy and a blank stare from Mac.

"So, this Lee —" Joinville, falsely optimistic he would be allowed to complete a sentence.

"Is timid, cautious to a fault," Mac, smiling to diffuse the cutting off of royalty, "cannot perform under heavy responsibility," he took a breath, then a sip of coffee while he held the room, "and he is most certainly not as resolute as Joseph E – if he's resolute at all."

"Where's this coming from, Mac?" Baldy asked with a disarming chuckle, "Lee was a whirlwind in Mexico, he —"

"Wasn't in command, was he?" Porter, rhetorically.

McClellan's hand made a sweeping motion of agreement, "Oh, the man is brave and energetic to a fault . . . but he wants in moral firmness, the ability to act – rest assured, gentlemen, he shall shortly rue those faults."

"We are attacking then?" Baldy asked, tossed a knowing look my way – or what I took to be a knowing look.

"Soon, I asked for McCall's division to be rushed up, make up our loses, keep the odds where they are. I've ordered the siege guns up from Yorktown . . . "He let that hang while he went back to his coffee.

"And then?" Baldy, out of coffee himself and in a peculiarly irritable mood.

"We push forward, reduce their lines, works, take Richmond," Mac relayed as if still the railroad president discoursing on a new line, then seemed to realize it and added, "oh, Lee's a fine engineer, it won't be easy, but it's down to science and mathematics now and they're both in our favor from here on in."

"That's a hell of a sweeping statement, Mac," Baldy pointed out.

"Makes it no less true," Mac breezily replied while his eyes burned into General Smith.

"They've a lot of troops behind those works," Fitz John endeavored to enlighten further, flushed by Mac's confidence, "once we tighten our grip I've no doubt they'll begin to draw them away as the inevitable becomes apparent – we'll take Richmond, regroup, go out and meet Beauregard, end the damn thing."

"Why do we want Richmond if we leave their army intact?" I said slowly with at least some of the deference the lowest ranking, non-royal, man in the room should display.

"Willie," Mac, almost kindly, "it's their capitol."

I ignored the patronizing tone, "Right, and if their army escapes, what do we accomplish beyond possibly embarrassing them in Europe?"

"They won't surrender," Baldy picked up my torch, "not while they have an army – hell, armies. This isn't about cities, Mac, else the war in the west would have ended when New Orleans fell."

"New Orleans isn't a capitol," Porter petulantly pointed out.

"Napoleon took Moscow," I was not about to be deterred, "how'd that work out?" Joinville dipped his mug in my direction.

"This isn't Russia," Porter helpfully explained, "our enemy speaks our language, their land is our land, they'll be no scorched earth tactics here," he shook his handsome, woolly head, smiled widely, "you always complicate things, you know that, Willie?"

"Always throwing history at us," Mac seconded, "I think you sometimes forget we are making it."

"As long as we're not repeating it," I persisted to frowns and a change of subject – the scintillating topic of siege warfare. Baldy was trapped – as the grim look he sported clearly attested; Joinville and I were not and quietly muttered polite excuses and efficiently escaped.

Outside in a cloudy, completely still, somewhat ominous morning we walked down a farmer's lane, deserted farmhouse to the left, an old graveyard to the right, a crudely lettered sign over the entrance:

'COME ALONG YANK – THERE'S PLENTY OF ROOM
TO BURY YOU'.

"Why is that still up?" Joinville asked.

"It appeals to the soldiers' fatalistic sense of humor,' I said fatalistically.

"Does it?" He asked dubiously, "Or is it just you?"

"I'm not in charge of graveyard protocol, Joinville."

"Perhaps no one is, hence the continued existence of that troubling sign."

"It troubles me a mere sign troubles you so."

He waved that away with a Gallic eyebrow raise and sigh, "I have never heard General McClellan speak so . . . uncomplimentary about a rebel officer."

I stopped for a moment to consider, "Now that you mention it, it's an odium usually reserved for Tom Jackson – he of non-aristocratic birth."

"Why, then?"

I laughed without mirth, "The most base of all reasons to deride the gifted – envy."

"Envy?" He seemed shocked our general could suffer base emotion.

"Sure, it's an emotion we mortals not in line to accede to thrones are prone to."

"You know, William, I heard a wonderfully descriptive colloquialism the other day that I think does you justice."

"That is?"

"Jackass."

"Keep talking to the rank and file and they won't let you back in France."

"That is not a current concern, unfortunately," he said wistfully, "now why would George be jealous of this Lee?"

"You mean aside the fact he is tall, handsome, from the oldest Virginia stock, son of a Revolutionary hero of the first order, married to George Washington's great-granddaughter, wealthy – "

"This going to continue much longer?"

"Absolutely," I assured him, "the perfect cadet – grades, disciplinary record that will never be equaled; brilliant engineer; hero of Cerro Gordo; list of escapades worthy of James Fennimore Cooper."

"Impressive," Joinville agreed, "Yet – "

"After Sumter," I figured the good prince was used to being interrupted at that point, "with Scott's strong recommendation, Lincoln offered Lee command of all Union forces."

"He turned down George's position," comprehension began to dawn, "and was Scott's choice to succeed him."

"Would have personally draped the mantle over Lee's shoulders."

"That is – "

"Joinville," I said with force, held his eyes, "you cannot possibly underestimate what Scott was – the 'First Soldier of the United States' in name, fact, myth. A little luck, he could have been president. And Lee was the Chosen One, the favored son."

"I understand, William," he averred with a touch of pique at my over-explanation, "though I am confused – "

"Naturally."

"I am confused," he spit with a dirty glance, "such accolades, such ... respect and yet ..."

"Mac thinks he's weak," I thoughtfully filled in the pause.

"Yes."

"Well, he's not," I said with resignation, "unless somewhere between Mexico City and here he lost his audacity and smarts."

"That possible?"

"Scott didn't think so."

"What about you?"

"Not possible."

"Then our general – "

"May be as wrong about Lee as he was about Tom Jackson."

"That could prove troubling."

"The word of the day, Prince."

"Indeed."

◊

Nothing happened. Indeed, to write about June '62 is to report the story of April, the Story of May around the eight hours of

Williamsburg and the thirty-six hours of Fair Oaks. It is the continuing story of preparation, new roads, depots, rail lines, minute troop movements, the creation of new ports, villages turned overnight into cities, and unfathomable lengths of telegraph wires.

All the action for the next twenty-six days took place above us – the wires hummed, sparked, and threatened to burst into flame from overuse.

◊

"That's a restrained reply," Fitz John Porter said with incredulity and handed me a wrinkled piece of foolscap with a look of 'you get this?'

I shrugged, took it, read: *'I shall be in perfect readiness to move forward and take Richmond the moment McCall reaches here and the ground will admit passage of artillery.'*

"Concise," the only possible comment in my current state of confusion.

Which must have been evident for Porter went on, "That's in reply to a message from the Great Ape telling Mac it's imperative," the word said with a liquid snarl, "we attack now without hesitation."

"It wasn't as bad as all that," McClellan shocked me with an affable defense of the President, "I think it was sent out of regard for me – none of his usual self-interests were evident – it seemed more of a warning about the pressures building in Washington than a rebuke."

"Remarkable," I said aloud, quite unintentionally.

"Yes, he's coming around at last," McClellan, missing my meaning and adding to the sentiment.

"Ten miles from Richmond," Porter was not about to be put off by McClellan's deference, "he writes that – he's an ape and a politician and he knows which way the wind is blowing."

"What winds," I asked, "and in what direction?"

"Winning at Fair Oaks, moving in on Richmond, Mac the . . . genius behind it all," McClellan made a bemused bow, "is ascending, the president is beleaguered and hitching his wagon to our success.

"When we take Richmond, I'll bet the ape doesn't even mention Mac in his victory address."

"I'm sure he'll adapt," I commented without expression, "we have a time frame in mind for your benediction as patron saint of the Union?" I asked a still bemused McClellan.

"The roads will be ready in another few days of this weather, McCall's division will be up this week, then ..." he waved at the hills of Richmond, unseen behind the trees outside the sun drenched window.

"It's close, Willie, so damn close," Porter laughed and we got down to a deadly dull court martial request.

◊

It rained. And rained. And rained. Day after day. In sheets, torrents, drizzly intervals that lasted just long enough to raise hopes it would abate before it picked up, became exponentially worse than any rains before – explosive, vision obscuring, drowning rains that promised to end when the Ark floated free.

To say the army bogged down is to risk gross, if not irresponsible, understatement. It was simply impossible to conduct any activity beyond sitting where one was – waterlogged, drooping tent; humid headquarters, commandeered farmhouse, leaky barn, improvised hut, muddy smokehouse. Reading was fruitless, books decomposed in the saturated air, writing was worse, the paper dissolved; playing cards had long since irretrievably warped.

There were more options in headquarters, though only marginally. And only if one was excited by organizing, reorganizing, planning, and replanning.

No reason to worry about the enemy, the rebels were treading water in their trenches, trying not to slide down their earthen redoubts. They could, in theory, get into Richmond and be amused in ways we could only dream or lust after. Literally.

Ours but to soak and wait, 'while all the world wonder'd.'

◊

The fourth day of unrelenting, unremitting, Confederate rain, A McClellan made frisky and bold by days of intense planning wired Lincoln: *'I shall attack as soon as the weather and ground will permit.'*

Impossibly, the rain increased to an intensity that made conversation an endurance sport.

◊

The rain backed off, slackened, eased for three days of thick, blowsy clouds, heavy winds, and the threat of a repeat. We began the onerous task of rebuilding washed out bridges, re-corduroying roads erased by flash floods.

I got out of headquarters to help the engineers. At Al Denton's request I assumed command of a work crew to rebuild a collapsed bridge over a still swollen, anonymous creek, a sign nearby pointing to the curiously named New Cold Harbor.

It was unexpectedly heavy work for the simple reason the mud and silt of the creek bed apparently extended to the Dutch East Indies. I was wet, chafed, splintered, frustrated, and chagrined when Al rode up, trailed by a train of wagons.

He saw me at the far end of the still unfinished bridge, spurred his mount, flew toward me while the wagons passed right on by.

"Pack up, get the fuck out of here . . . now, Willie!"

I did not hesitate, Denton was not one to overreact to anything. I ran the length of the bridge, yelling orders, mounted Clio and loped over the keenly observant Denton.

"Nice job," he tersely said, glowered at me, yelled to my men, "As quick as you can, boys – or you'll be in Richmond before the army."

My men in their wagons, driving the teams hard, I finally asked, "What the hell is going on?"

"Cavalry – lots of cavalry, in column – swept up a supply train a few miles east, couple of escapees rode by to warn us on their way to Fort Monroe."

"Stuart," I surmised.

"Yet more proof of why you should outrank me, amazing how you put that together so fast – what seems to be the entire Confederate cavalry's coming down the road and you immediately surmise their commander leads them."

"You're a very angry man, Major."

"I'm getting tired of that shit, Hanlin," together we moved at a trot, "I'd shoot you, but it might bring Stuart down on us."

"See, that's the anger talking."

"So it is," he confirmed, "any thoughts on where Stuart's going?"

"Nowhere to go, except back to Richmond after he rips up our supply lines, burns depots, creates a little panic —"

"A little panic? He motioned the wagons receding before us.

"Disrupt our activities and go home."

He dwelled on that for long seconds, "We can rebuild everything in a day or two, resupply in a day or two more, why risk it?"

I stared at a rising column of black smoke to the east, "How long do you think it will take to fix the newspapers?"

"I guess that would depend on how loud he makes this."

"Stuart ever do anything less than flamboyantly?"

"He is a trifle . . . ostentatious, isn't he?"

"Not to say garish."

We spurred forward with perhaps a touch more urgency than decorum demanded. In our defense I am sure we were both motivated by the vison of Jeb Stuart parading us through downtown Richmond – politely, chivalrously – a member of McClellan's staff and a Major of the Engineers – and up the stairs of the Confederate White House . . .
.

◊

. . . in the end, Stuart had no need for brass encrusted exclamation points to his raid, had, in fact, no need whatever for trophies of any kind. He needed nothing beyond his own audacity when he planned the raid in the first place.

Jeb Stuart and his merry band in gray rode completely around the Army of the Potomac. Knee deep through roads of watery muck, over impassable rivers and bog-like fields; untouched but certainly unseen, they burned, pillaged, looted; helped themselves to the personal baggage trains of a half-dozen or so generals; made our cavalry look like the gang of ill-mounted, addled factory hands they surely were; probably made obscene gestures before crossing the Chickahominy and returning to Richmond as conquering heroes.

The physical damage was minimal, as Al had foreseen – depots were rebuilt, railroad tracks re-laid, equipment replaced, the three hundred prisoners Stuart invited back to Richmond would be missed only by their friends.

None of that, though, was remotely the point. McClellan was embarrassed in headlines that reached across the Atlantic. Stuart inspired awe in military professionals and newspapers from South America to St. Petersburg and fairly established the cavalry arm of the Army of Northern Virginia as an all-pervasive bogeyman to everyone lounging about Virginia wearing dark blue.

Washington was not amused. It was noted, vociferously, that while McClellan remained inert in the abysmal conditions, Stuart enjoyed no such disinclinations – he had even brought his horse artillery with him.

I spent the three days after Stuart's triumphant return to Richmond rebuilding bridges under a hot sun and the occasional, but far from benign, supervision of Major Denton. Three fourteen-sixteen hour work days securing crossings far from headquarters – nothing but sweat, aches, blisters, bruises, and the chance to feel, finally, hour by hour, foot by foot, a sense of accomplishment heretofore missing in my attachment to the Army of the Potomac to date.

So engrossed was I in the instantly gratifying task of construction, so satisfied with the physical labor, so delighted with the so easily observable results, so utterly exhausted by evening, I had happily lost track of the comings and goings of headquarters.

My blissful state of ignorance lasted almost three days until Osgood and Joinville felt obligated to bring me up to date.

"Every day, pleas, threats, promises – that's all it's been," Osgood unnecessarily pointed in the general direction of headquarters.

"No need to bore me with details," I sighed. It was late evening, my chaffed hands clung desperately to a mug of coffee and I looked covetously at the untouched plate of food on my lap – my first meal of the day.

"A constant stream of newspapers," Osgood went on, "I think McClellan finally broke down and subscribed to the *Richmond Examiner.*"

"I think he's more of a *Richmond Whig* reader," I offered. Joinville chuckled, Osgood glared.

"You realize, of course," Osgood relayed with glee, "the bridge building is temporary – you'll eventually have to go back to your real job, right?"

"I can hope for more rain," I hissed, took a sip of restorative coffee, "what's changed so dramatically you couldn't wait to come out here and tell me?"

"Aside from your friend being embarrassed in every newspaper in the Western Hemisphere?"

"Yes, Osgood, outside of that."

"Well," he considered, "there is the telegram McClellan just sent."

"Which was?"

"*After tomorrow we shall fight the rebel army as soon as Providence will permit*," finished, he spasmed in a snort of delight.

"Alright, that's vague," I managed another sip, looked to Joinville for help, received none.

"Vague?" Osgood asked the nightingales, "Vague? It's positively genius, William. Staggeringly so . . . has there, in the course of human history, ever been uttered a sentence so pregnant in the future tense?"

I considered it for a moment, "Well, I—"

"Seemingly defiant, yet so utterly undefinable."

"I would guess —"

"After tomorrow, modified my 'if God wills it' just . . . perfect – I bet he did not date the damn thing, either, that way it's good for . . .ever."

"C'mon, Osgood," I have no idea why I resorted to reason, "we've got McCall's men with us, we're repairing the bridges, rails, roads, and —"

"Tomorrow and tomorrow and tomorrow," Osgood intoned.

"Creeps in the petty pace from day to day," Joinville finished with entirely too much satisfaction.

"Christ," I started, "an Irishman and French royalty quoting Shakespeare in the Virginia woods . . . is that what it's come to?"

"Perhaps so," Joinville considered, "I would quote Voltaire, but I fear he is too caustic in present circumstances."

I barely had time to react before Osgood resumed, "You can fix all the bridges and roads you want, William – I'm sure it's most satisfying work – but take your time, we are not going anywhere anytime soon.

"You sure of that?" It began as a challenge, ended as a question as I considered my audience.

"It would be unwise, outnumbered as we are."

I took a gulp, "New estimates?"

"Yes."

"Do I have to guess?"

"Care to?"

"No."

"Two hundred thousand."

"You . . . are . . . joking."

"Would that I were."

"Who the hell would believe that?"

"Your West Point roommate."

"Next door neighbor," I corrected without thought, "he's not really buying that, is he?"

"Isn't he?"

"It's out of the pale . . ."

"Of course it is," he agreed amiably, "just as it is fully accepted — fully . . . though he does note that the rebels are not as well trained or supplied as us."

"That is something."

"Sure . . . it is a concession of epic proportions."

"Uh-huh," my non-committal reply, in the gloaming I could not register Osgood's seriousness, "So now what?"

"Well, naturally, we shall be employing the utmost prudence while not running the risk of disaster."

"I'm going to go out on a limb and guess those aren't your words."

"No."

"Telegram?"

'Latest wire to Stanton," he snorted, "always comforting when one's commanding general uses the term disaster."

"Then, why —"

"I would not kill myself trying to finish bridges in record time, William, we are not moving anywhere."

"So you say."

"So you make me repeat."

◊

I was months out of practice and the prudent course would have been to trip over a blade of grass in a faux dive but I could not bring myself to do it. Instead, I let the ball play me, grabbed it at the last second, it smashed into my left palm, bit the meat below the index finger, catching the bone and sending electric pain through my elbow, up to my shoulder, to an end as a few hundred stomach flutters. A step off balance, I pivoted, threw in one motion, beat the runner to first by half a step — clearly and emphatically seconded by the fully uniformed umpire.

"Horseshit," the Massachusetts runner yelled even while he struggled to stop, succeeded only in tripping over his feet. His subsequent misuse of the English language did little credit to his Puritan forefathers. As the runner was a major and the umpire a captain, it was unsurprising that the umpire wandered away from the first base area, suddenly fascinated with the mast jammed view from Cumberland Landing.

I was so engrossed in the scene I missed the beefy, mutton chopped, shirt sleeved Bostonian a foot away until he not so gently inquired, "You going in, or you giving us four outs this inning?"

"Well, you gentlemen usually play with four bases, don't you?"

"We'd be beating you too, if you hadn't gypped us out of one of 'em."

"You haven't had a man get pass second yet," I gently pointed out, "How's the extra base —"

"It's not 'extra', it's how civilized men play the game."

"It's how Boston plays the game," I corrected, stepped into foul territory, "and only Boston."

"Right, civilization."

"Sure," I nodded, "but the question stands – if you haven't had a runner advance past second, how would the extra base help?"

"How many runs you fella's have?"

"Eighteen."

"You'd be a hell of a lot more tired if you had to run around our bases . . . . then we'd have you."

"That's a point," I begrudged, "mind the pitch." He turned his shaggy head just in time to duck under a nasty line drive that buzzed by his head with the speed and malevolence of a minie ball.

"That was close," I clinically observed, watching our runner ease into second.

"I was distracted," my fellow third baseman snapped, "else I would a —"

"Broken your hand deflecting that away from your head."

"Exactly," he agreed over his shoulder, he turned with ferocity to watch Al Denton's deep drive into the right-centerfield gap. He had two hands on his hips by the time Al pulled into second.

The pitcher into his motion, I said, "I'd move off the base path, he's a nasty little cuss, stomps on infielder toes just for the fun of it."

The ball smoked up the middle, Al charged around third, "I heard that Hanlin, you shit," he gasped and headed home.

"You're out of shape, Major," I yelled out behind him.

"Hanlin?" The third baseman asked.

"Yes," I sighed, there having been so few positives following the invocation of my name those last months.

"William Hanlin? Beacon Hill?"

"Maybe," I edged further into foul territory.

"Should you decide you are indeed he . . ." he paused, watched an engineer slightly smaller than a pontoon boat launch a ball to Richmond, ". . . good God, did he crush that."

"It was hit it or eat it," I explained.

"Should you decide you are William Hanlin," he continued after the engineer ran by, bolting out the sun for a second or two, "I think we went to school together."

"College?"

"Perish the thought," he said with horror, "nah, it was Temple Street School."

"Temple School," I repeated in the awe of an unexpected memory, "haven't thought about it in years."

"That make you that William Hanlin?"

"Does indeed . . . . sorry," I stuck my hand out, it was immediately subsumed by a hard hand thickly coated in dense black hair, "You're a Dana, aren't you?"

"Stephen," he grinned at the partial recognition, "thought you were on McClellan's staff, now here you are playing with a bunch of engineers?"

"Amazing coincidence, really, them missing a third baseman, me being a third baseman . . . ."

"Missing?"

"He was anemic, too sick to play."

"Really," he considered that for pitch in the dirt, "'cause I heard that term used to describe his bat as well."

"Huh," I offered, changed the subject, "so, you still call it third base, by the way?"

"What the hell else we goin' to call it?"

"I don't know, you play with four bases maybe you have roper names for them."

A snort and we both watched a thin as a rail, droopingly mustachioed, wild-eyed batter in bright green suspenders bounced a perfect two hopper to the first baseman. He dropped it twice before kicking it authoritatively to the pitcher.

"That an error?" I asked in mock innocence, "Or something really clever in your four base scenario?"

"You were an arse as a child, too."

"Always nice to hear one has not changed."

"Sure – by the way . . . . you're up."

I turned to my bench, Al and a half dozen others were gesticulating wildly while employing upsetting, untrue epithets, "I'll be right back, Stephen," I promised, jogged to the bench, ignored Al's glare and grabbed my bat – my bat, carried from Hartford, more carefully cared for than the hateful sword that had now seen much less action – and sauntered to the plate.

As usual, I received nasty looks, endured nastier jibes, when I stepped to the left side of the plate, left handed hitters being held in the same esteem on a base ball pitch as witches in Salem. Probably for the same reasons.

For the fifth time that sunny, perfect afternoon I requested the pitch low and inside, for the fifth time the pitcher, a tall, fussy prim with the mannerisms of a school principal, scowled nastily and spit on the rubber. For the first time he whipped the first pitch in the general direction of my left temple – I can attest only to 'general direction' because I dropped to the grass in a heap before I could get a firm grasp on the possibilities of intersection.

Untouched, I jumped to my feet, yelled something to the effect of 'What the fuck!' and was shouted down – by my teammates.

Most specifically, Major Albert Denton, "Wasting your time hitting him in the head," Al explained to the evilly grinning principal, "it'd just ricochet back at you . . . . hard." That to ample agreement from my new teammates, and one enemy third baseman.

"Thanks for the support," I snarled, Al handed me my bat, helped me brush the grass off my back.

"You inspire it," he grinned, "going to drill him now?" He motioned toward the pitcher who was doing a fair job of pretending to study a cloud formation far out over the York.

"You mean," I answered loudly, staring into the back of the pitcher's neck, "ask for a pitch over the plate, wait back and hit a liner through the box . . . . something like that?"

"Why, yes."

"I'm surprised at you, Al, that could hurt the poor man," I explained with patience, "I'm sure the ball just slipped."

"Just fucking hit," the pitcher feigned tired nonchalance, flipped the green tinged ball from hand to hand.

"Alright, throw."

He snapped it as I was bringing the bat up and he snapped it hard – a hell of a lot faster than any previous pitch thrown to order all afternoon. Down and in, across my knees, across the inside of the plate.

"Strike!" the umpire yelled in joy for he had had precious little to do so far.

"Foul!", "Cheat!", "Fraud!", "Asshole", more rang out from my bench. I stepped out of the batter's box and watched, not all that happy their opprobrium for poor sportsmanship so vastly outstripped that shown for a ball tossed at my head.

I waved to quiet them down, "Hey," I yelled out to the happy pitcher, "throw that again."

He regarded me head half-cocked like a self-aware beagle, "Same speed?"

"Absolutely," I reassured him.

"You can't handle it."

"'Course not, luckily you can't throw it that hard again.

"Think so, eh?" He sneered.

"Show me I'm wrong."

"Oh, I will."

I was ready this time – he threw it as hard, as low, as niftily over the inside corner of the plate . . . and I stepped into it perfectly, felt the singularly wonderful feeling of ball hitting bat on the sweet spot. I crushed it, the smack of hide on ash sounded like a mortar in the clear air . . . . necks craned, I stood and watched – as did the right fielder as the ball arched over his head.

Leisurely, insolently, staring at the pitcher most of the way, I jogged to third, and stopped, "So, where were we, Stephen?"

"You could crawl home, you know."

"Ah, no dignity in that."

"Settling for a triple?"

"Got one of everything else, Mr. Dana, hitting for the cycle will do nothing but annoy certain of my teammates," I waved to Al, mouthed 'the Cycle' in his direction, received an obscene gesture in return.

"Yup, you haven't changed," Dana reiterated.

"Thank you."

"That's one way of taking that."

"There's another?" I asked, a line drive was hacked into center, "hang on, I've got to go and score now."

I touched home, caught the obese catcher's eye, "Miss me?" I did not wait for a response, nodded to my teammates, went back up the third base line.

"You've been out here awhile, Stephen," I observed, "must be getting tiresome."

"Well, we –"

"Hardly seems fair, you're in the field all day, only get up to bat for a few minutes."

"God, don't you have teammates to annoy."

"I didn't go to grammar school with any of them."

"Lucky me."

"Indeed."

"There a headquarters team?"

"Not a chance."

"Pity," he sighed, another ball was launched like a howitzer, he stepped into foul territory with me, the better to watch both the runner and fast disappearing outfielder, "then we might beat up on someone."

"You would."

"Really?" He asked with heartbreaking hope.

"Really – everyone there has a bat stuck up his ass, not exactly conducive to playing ball."

"Good to know . . . I think," we both craned at another moon shot, "Jesus Christ, will this fucking inning ever end?"

"I'd worry more about getting an out."

"Sure to happen sometime. Maybe someone will hit a liner into a mid-section and it'll get stuck in fat – – – that would do it."

"I'll see what I can do."

"Would appreciate it . . . . good to hear you're not uptight about being in headquarters, staff and all that."

"Is it?"

"A good Bostonian like you in that particular headquarters – – – a little disturbing to some of us."

"I'm flattered I'm important enough to disturb anyone," I muttered in all honesty.

"Well, with your . . . . upbringing and that general staff . . . . you know."

"Not really."

He considered me over the course of two balls so badly thrown out of the strike zone as to be part of another game, "Well, they're hardly abolitionists, are they?"

"Hardly," I admitted.

◊

"The War Department does not know where General Jackson is?" Joinville brandished the telegram for emphasis that was not needed.

"So they say," Porter sneered, "he disappeared from the Valley, from the midst of three armies – all directed by Washington, of course – escaped from them all."

"And disappeared?" Joinville persisted.

"Only to Washington," McClellan sighed, "he's here with three divisions on our right."

"Three divisions?" I asked, evenly.

"Three, confirmed by deserters," Porter answered with authority,

"God save us from Confederate deserters," I muttered to a scowl from Porter, "didn't he leave the valley with one division?"

"After what he did in the Shenandoah, why wouldn't they give him more men?" Porter, eminently reasonable.

"Do I detect a hint of admiration in your voice, General?" I teased, shocked to hear a positive word said in these environs for one Tom Jackson.

Porter nodded, slowly, "Jackson's performance was . . . stunning," he sounded every bit as surprised as a man forced to relay the news the sun had just set in the east.

"Brilliant," McClellan echoed, "but he has excellent subordinates – like Dick Ewell."

"But Thomas is in command," I affirmed, "and unless he has changed radically, he's in total control."

"Stonewall is aptly named," Porter agreed, to a questioning glance from Joinville, "as inflexible a man as I've ever met."

"Religious zealot, too," Mac, half distractedly, writing something with a studious air, "although he certainly got along well enough with our Willie."

"He was . . . interesting," I replied, "unlike so many of our classmates," I nodded at Mac.

"If by interesting you mean bizarre," he refused to rise to the bait, "then yes, certainly."

"Bizarre?" Joinville perked up.

"Ah, bizarre got the Frenchman's attention," I remarked.

"Of course it did," he said without embarrassment, "examples, please."

"Wouldn't eat pepper," Porter was quick to jump in, "claimed it made his left leg ache."

"Rode with his arm in the air – to balance his humors," Mac happily added, "sucked on lemons every chance he got."

Joinville looked at me pointedly. I shrugged, "So far, Prince, they have described a scurvy free man with good balance and healthy legs."

"Secretive, unemotional, suspicious, unbending, firm in the belief he rides with God, and —"

"What awful qualifications for a commanding officer," I interrupted Porter's recital.

"His Baptist fanaticism —" Mac began.

"He's not a Baptist," I corrected.

"What?" The two generals in unison.

"He's Presbyterian," I said with a large measure of smugness.

… that did not go unnoticed, "That's remarkably perceptive," Porter began slowly, "coming from a man with no observable belief system himself."

"I don't think that's fair," I doth protest too much.

"Fair or not, it's the truth," Fitz-John persisted, "tell the Prince where you received almost all your demerits."

"I do not recall," I lied effortlessly, "ancient history."

"Funny," Porter began without any evidence of humor, "I can recall with almost total clarity – as an upperclassman I'm afraid I was forced —"

"Forced?" I asked archly.

"Forced with pleasure," he amended, "to issue several of them."

"And what were they for, General Porter?" McClellan, with tenacity.

"Well, General McClellan," Porter could not conceal his glee, "seems young cadet Hanlin – top student, excellent rider, class prankster," that elicited a look from Joinville, I shook my head, "could not, would not pay attention in chapel."

"Really?" Joinville happily intrigued.

"Tell me, Willie," Porter, doing a fair impersonation of my prosecutorial self, "what were you doing the day you received the most demerits in the history of Sunday services?"

"I think that's a bit of an exaggeration, I —"

"It's not, I actually looked it up after Mahon threatened to write me up for not writing you up."

"I hold a record?" I asked with hope.

"I think you can rest assured our young Captain Custer has since broken it," McClellan not so regretfully informed me.

"Immortality is so fleeting," I sighed.

"What was he doing?" Joinville, losing patience.

"As usual he was sitting in the back pew, this day reading a book he thought he was successfully hiding under his cloak."

"A book?" Joinville, disappointed.

"Oh, not just any book," Mac laughed while still managing to convey seventeen year old odium.

"Indeed not," Porter agreed "it was *Tom Jones*, no less."

"*Tom Jones*," Joinville repeated with wonder, "I will guess that it was not on the West Point reading list."

"Then or now," Porter confirmed.

"I had already finished de Sade's complete works during Advent," I explained to a laughing Prince.

"It was noted at the time," Porter went on unabated, "that it was a rather large book, Cadet Hanlin was three quarters of the way through it, had not been seen reading it anywhere else on campus on any other occasions – on or off duty – so – "

"It had gotten me through many an odious and overlong sermon," I admitted.

"So, Mac finished, "he was punished for an amalgamation of the same sin. He was walking sentry duty for weeks."

"Four, to be exact," I corrected, "middle of the night, along the river."

"Sounds onerous," the prince observed.

"Nice, quiet, finished the book, actually," I answered.

"I thought it was confiscated?" Porter snapped.

"When reading a banned book," I intoned, "it is prudent to purchase two copies."

That drew a begrudging look of respect from McClellan, who promptly went back to the current topic, "so, you can see that when it comes to religion, Willie's comments are akin to a deaf-mute praising Mozart.

"A deaf-mute who can read music," I pointed out with an edge.

"Indeed?" Joinville was the only one in the room to get the nuance," well, then, William, what are our religions?"

"Please," I waved him off, "you insult my powers of observation."

"In other words, you don't know."

I smiled, nodded, "Prince de Joinville is, of course, Roman Catholic – although the more I listen to him the more convinced I am he has forsaken his obvious Jesuit indoctrinations for more Jansonist leanings."

He started to reply, I held a hand up, "In as much as you require religion, being of noble birth and, therefore, in close personal contact with the Almighty in any event."

"You are —"

"General Porter," I ignored the gaping Prince, "is that peculiar blend of New Hampshire Unitarianism that produces steely eyed merchants, sea captains, generals, college deans, and ineffectual Presidents."

Porter shook his great beard, raised his eyes to his Unitarian God, I turned my attention to our commander, "General McClellan is a harder religious nut to crack – pun entirely unintentional."

"Of course it was, Willie," Mac chortled, "as will be your transfer to Arizona."

I nodded weakly, "Your Methodist leanings are being usurped by more charismatic teachings —"

"You've made your point Colonel," Mac, smile affixed in place, "we stand corrected, you are as religiously observant of others as you are lax in your observation of a higher power – if indeed you even acknowledge such."

"Sure I do, I'm a Deist . . . like Jefferson."

"First thing you've said that makes sense," Porter cackled, "that you would follow the religious lead of a slave fucking, bankrupt, wine besotted satyr."

"You left out Founding Father," I added.

"It was implicit," he smiled at his wit, "what have you been working on Mac?"

McClellan did not look up, "Much requested update for Stanton, that ass," he distractedly muttered, punched a period with authority, "this ought to shake him up: *'I have a kind of presentment that tomorrow will bring forth something – what I do not know. We will see when the time arrives. I am inclined to think Jackson will attack my right and rear. The rebel force is stated at 200,000. I regret my great inferiority in numbers, but I feel in no way responsible for that as I have not failed to represent repeatedly the necessity of reinforcements; that this was the decisive point and that all available means of the government should be concentrated here.*

"'I will do all that a general can do with the splendid army I have the honor to command, and if it is destroyed by overwhelming numbers can at least die with it and share its fate. But if the result of the action which will probably occur tomorrow or within a short time is a disaster, the responsibility cannot be thrown on my shoulders, it must rest where it belongs.'"

Done, he looked up, blinking, surveyed us in turn. I am sure my mouth hung as wide open as Joinville's when our eyes met in a combination of horror and shock.

Porter, however, grinned crookedly, "That's putting it on the record – right damn time to do it, too – put the responsibilities where they lie."

"Blunt," Joinville observed with the look of a man confronted with something unfathomable but knowing he is required to say something.

"Time to be blunt," McClellan agreed, "I've tried everything else yet McDowell sits in Fredericksburg and the Confederates mass before us."

"And while Heintzelman's corps sits four miles from Richmond," Porter, shaking his head, "they can hear the church bells ringing."

"There was a rainbow over Richmond Hills yesterday," Joinville announced, "Beautiful, portentous."

"You were up there?" I asked.

"Of course."

"Paint it?"

"Of course," he chuckled, "could not pass that up."

"An omen, eh?" Porter asked.

"Perhaps," Joinville replied carefully.

"Then we'll leave it in the hands of Providence," Mac said with reverence.

"And my rifle pits," Porter affirmed.

"Amen," I seconded.

◊

Robert E. Lee had had a lot of time to think, organize, prepare, and chafe at the inactivity and boredom foisted on him by the creeping Army of the Potomac. When he had had enough of that – based on what we all know now and some of us suspected then, Lee had probably reached his frustration limit days after assuming command – the Army of the Northern Virginia stopped waiting and attacked . . . and attacked and did not stop for seven soon to be capitalized days.

21. June 26th

Beaver Dam Creek

An hour before dawn Joinville and I joined Porter to ride the lines. The early summer day broke spectacularly over us, the air scrubbed clean by yesterday's inundating mists. We moved from unit to unit dug in on a gentle rise overlooking a wide, swamped over stream. Rifle pit

after rifle pit, Porter's thirty thousand nestled beneath widely spaced, moss covered trees, wide-angle view of their front. Presently they kept a wary watch of still more trees, hanging vines, marshy clearings a few hundred yards north.

The lines were quiet, expectant, the better to hear the sounds of engineers and sappers felling trees and ripping up macadamized roads. Within the hour, the smell of burning wood was pervasive as dozens of bridges over innumerable creeks were torched, undoing weeks of labor. Tom Jackson's troops had been reported far, far out on Fitz's right, we were not about to provide him with easy access to our flank. Porter, and by proxy Joinville and I, were everywhere without pause all morning. If there was an officer, NCO, private, ditch digger, teamster, Contraband cook who did not look into Fitz-John's eyes that pretty day on the banks of Beaver Dam Creek, it was entirely his fault. Despite everything that was to come to pass in the next months, Fitz-John, that day, that week, was as fine a corps commander as any who led men into battle – and we all knew it. That I could, and did, attest to in a court of law.

Joinville, Roxanne, Clio, and I followed in total silence, exchanging looks and content, if not mesmerized, to watch the general as he interacted effortlessly with his command, received messages from a distant McClellan, gave commands that sounded more like suggestions from a wise, respected uncle.

Early morning tension was palpable in the lines, tension that died a slow death of natural causes as the sun rose to mid-point and it began to look, feel, and smell like just another day outside Richmond waiting for the siege guns and a repeat of Yorktown. By one o'clock the mixed aroma of bacon and coffee filled the air, men formerly peering intently over rifles lounged, traded jibes, smoked, made it clear none of them expected anything any longer. It then became Porter's unenviable task to instill a sense of vigilance in men who had not seen action in almost four months in the field – hell, they had not even been close enough to hear Fair Oaks. Porter walked a thin line that afternoon, motivating for an attack that experience taught would never occur and risk dulling then for the next alert.

Two o'clock and not a whisper from the Confederates, Joinville and I rode alone to Beaver Dam Creek's confluence with the Chicahominy, well out of earshot. "You still think they're coming?" Joinville asked that which I asked myself.

"Better be, at this point," I sighed, half lost in the slow, yellowish swirls of the river.

He nodded," The men are ready, the —"

"Positions perfect," I finished the day's mantra.

"It would almost be a disappointment to stand down, go through it again tomorrow."

"Like postponing Agincourt for a day," I agreed, readily.

He 'tsked', shot a nasty look, "Why do you always use French defeats to make a point?"

"I do that?"

"You do, and you know you do."

"Well," I pretended to consider it for a moment, "it's probably because you don't appreciate me referring to Napoleon, in any way, and if you take him out of the equation there are precious few French victories to which to refer."

He muttered something nastily Gallic before, "Never mind . . . . I understand the men refer to battle as the elephant."

"They do."

"Why is that?"

I shrugged, deepening his scowl, "I suppose it's because it has to be seen to be believed . . . huge, loud, frightening, and can stomp you to death."

"I like it," he agreed absently, joined me in contemplation of the Chickahominy's swirls, sighed yet again and got to his real question, "We are not outnumbered, are we?"

"You talk to Osgood as much as I do, what do you think?"

"I think they have fooled General McClellan," no hesitation then. "Again."

"Again," he nodded, "the rebels are going to attack nevertheless, are they not? Despite what McClellan thinks of this irresolute Lee?"

I engaged the Prince's eyes and endeavored to educate him, "If you were the kind of man who rode into an uncharted desert to reconnoiter the Mexican positions, spent a day and night skirting cavalry, patrols, scorpions, Gila monsters all while knowing you would be executed if captured . . . and you not only survived, you came back with a perfect map and helped plan a victory Wellington proclaimed a master stroke . . .

". . . if you were that sort of man, would you sit back, watch the way we've been crawling forward and wait, regardless of odds?"

"If I were that man, I should attack at once," the Prince answered with some heat, "that man is General Lee, I presume?"

"That man is General Lee," I confirmed, "And he's . . . they're coming."

A curt nod, "Of course . . . well, then . . . I think I am most curious . . .," he stopped, watched a happily oblivious muskrat stroke by, made no obvious move to finish.

"Well, don't get shy now."

"No, I will not," he answered quietly, "I am wondering how General McClellan reacts to being attacked by this man . . . especially after the machinations in Washington."

"You think he's demoralized?"

"No, no," he waved that off, "do not be absurd -but when a man feels himself wronged, continuously wronged in fact, a certain animosity, a certain insecurity builds, it is only natural.

"My experience is that it is made worse by the obstinacies bred by early success – and that is something our friend Mac shares with his namesake —"

"He who's name you dare not utter," I smiled, caught his eye, held it, "sorry . . . that was remarkably astute, Joinville."

He grimaced, then smiled thinly, "Thank you."

"You're welcome, I just hope you're not prescient as well."

"Moi assi."

We caged mugs from an Indiana regiment thrilled to find royalty in its midst. He upheld their image of what a French prince must be by declining the proffered skillygally; I confirmed their opinion of the avarice of New Englanders by inhaling two very tasty plates while they fawned over the Prince.

◊

We rejoined Porter and his aides still restlessly touring the corps, the sun in its downward slope, huge oaks dropping shadows over the rifle pits, Fitz John looking more haggard by the second – by that point, every minute of inactivity required ever more effervescence on his part; one man to keep thousands of justifiably skeptical men from descending into cynicism and sloth.

It was a race of sorts: would the rebels attack before the sun went down or would Porter drop from exhaustion? Sundown was at 7:15, there was not a sound anywhere to our front, my money was on Fitzy's swoon . . .

. . . a bet I would have lost.

Five o'clock, center of our lines, the Beaver Dam Creek wallowing over whatever banks it might have had if we ever went a week without rain, Porter slouched on the back of his equally fatigued horse, scattered cheers broke out to our right, continued through, into, over us and down to the river on the far left. A few frantic seconds to ascertain the reason for such sudden jubilation – across the creek a dozen or so deer sprinted madly between trees, splashing, darting, in white-tailed terror across our front. Amazingly, no one fired, so wrapped up were we in the pleasant break from a tedious day.

Not so the combat veterans and men from the country, Porter very much included. He sat bolt upright, locked eyes with me for a three count, did not even turn back before he began to yell, "Form Lines! Form Lines!"

We echoed him immediately, the order radiated out while, almost as quickly, men sobered to the reality of the running wildlife – men, many men, were behind them. Porter's aides, in a blur, tore off to spread the word, set our lines of communications. I peered into the dimming woods, shadowy, distant movement far back in the trees, so faint I could be imagining it. I edged Clio carefully to Porter's flank. By then I could hear, or thought I could hear, a murmuring in the woods. If Porter heard it, he gave no indication, he was straight-backed rigid, staring, took no notice of Clio or me.

I took his mount's bridle to get his attention. "Time to dismount, General?"

"No, Willie, good view from here."

"Certainly is . . . also a perfect view for the men to see their general dropped by a sniper or a high volley."

He glared, then looked around at the men looking up from their rifle pits with concern, "They think so too, General," I pointed, emphasized the point by dismounting, "I'll put the horses behind the trees, they didn't sign up for this."

"Alright, Willie, but keep them close."

"Of course," I ran with Joinville to a heavy copse of trees thirty yards from our embankments, tied a not pleased Clio to a sturdy oak, Porter's horse and Roxanne nearby for company she undoubtedly did not want, ran back, Joinville huffing and puffing a few feet behind, burdened by the sketch pad and wad of pencils he had torn out of his saddlebags.

By Porter's side in time to make them out across the creek, long lines of gray and butternut flowing through the trees, the Bars and Stripes, blue flag of Virginia, Palmetto of South Carolina, a low rumble like a freight train behind a hill. Firing broke out to our right, we held ours, too many trees, still held when they began to double time it, throwing up splashes of muddy water . . . . a hundred yards, eighty, seventy . . . the ululating, ball clinching rebel yell shrieked through the trees and up my spinal column and they charged . . .

. . . and were dropped. Our lines fired as one, smoke encased us, blew away revealing wide gaps in their lines. In silence they stopped, fired a raggedy volley, high, pelting us with twigs, leaves, pieces of bark. Our next volley tore them to pieces, those standing melted back into the trees leaving behind a few hundred broken bodies haphazardly draped across our foreground, a good many floating in the easy eddies of the creek.

To describe the day, evening, further would be to exult in long distance slaughter, for they came at us, a brigade or two at a time, in a series of uncoordinated attacks that ended as the first had. Piecemeal they came up, piecemeal they were scattered, their dead and wounded grrew thicker, carpeting the far bank, leaving gray damp stepping stones in the dirty waters.

We roamed the lines with a grim faced Porter, one eye on the slaughter his men handed out, the other in the direction of his hanging flank, silent throughout – nothing out there, no signs of the bogey man Tom Jackson had become.

In the gloaming the rebels ducked behind trees and kept up a desultory fire that did little more than mark where they were and allow us to pick them off by the flame of their rifles. There was nothing left to do that day but needlessly create more Confederate widows.

22. June 27th

2:30 am

Webb handed me the orders in the foyer of the handsome home headquarters had appropriated, bade me Godspeed and good night, and off I went to find Porter. Porter only, I was not to entrust my package to an aide.

Clio and I rode silently through the darkened town of Gaines Mill and back into the countryside. In time we heard dim, sporadic firing to the north, a gust of wind brought a pungent mixture of dank-night air mixed with sulfur. Faint voices, coffee, bacon, searing fat, latrines, whiff of rust-iron-blood, all signs of incremental closeness to the front.

We were challenged a half dozen times the last few hundred yards; it grew tiresome quickly as we were behind our lines behind a wide swamp and the events of the day had proven them somewhat impregnable.

When at last I answered a challenge with "Jeb Stuart come to surrender," I was quite properly escorted to Porter by a cynical but careful sentry.

A grimly smiling Porter greeted me tiredly without looking up from the map he was stooped over. "You have orders," he surmised.

"Yeah," I muttered, handed the packet over.

He tore through them, nodding at times, finally cocked an eyebrow at me, "You seen them?"

"Nope, Webb stuck them in my chest and told me to ride."

"We're pulling back."

"We're what?"

"Pulling back to an excellent defensive position behind Boatswain's Swamp."

"This is an excellent position," I pointed out the obvious.

"Jackson's out off my flank, Willie, you know that, we need to compact my lines"

"Fitz—"

"They'll never touch us back there," he motioned Gaines Mill, nodded to an aide then handed him orders – orders that obviously had been cut before I rode in, "high embankments, creek – swamp, whatever you call it, curves nicely, high hill for artillery, I—"

"You've seen the position."

"Of course, scouted it myself."

"You have a premonition or something?" I asked evenly.

He shook his head, "It's been a contingency . . .

"Since when?" I asked, realized I was exhausted, which may account for the fact I did not yell the questions.

"Since your friend Stonewall showed up with three divisions on my flank . . . Colonel."

I stood, he rooted through the package from Webb, pulled out a paper, "Well, look at this, Mac wants me to share this with my men, telegram to Washington, *'the firing has nearly ceased, the victory of today is complete and against great odds. I almost think that we are invincible . . .'* I think that sums it up nicely."

"You going to have that read to them while they withdraw?" It was out of my mouth before I could stop it.

"You're tired, Willie, get out of here, get some sleep – headquarters will be on a farm right on the Chicahominy – can't miss it, it's the biggest thing out there."

He went back to his map, I turned without saluting, waved goodbye over my head in case Major General Fitz John Porter was looking, and escaped his headquarters.

◊

I got lost in the dark, and the trees, and the swamps, and the creeks, fields, ravines, eddies, swales, dales, glens, crevasses, rolling hills, escarpments, and everything else that damnable stretch of Virginia had to offer.

I would like to have blamed Clio, but cannot. She whinnied and snorted defiantly at two of my turns, equine warnings I should have, would have heeded if not fulminating over the decisions my former classmates were perpetuating on the banks of the Chickahominy.

I knew we were in trouble when the road dipped and we splashed across a swampy ford that should not have been there. The only stream it could be – as the Chickahominy required rather more effort to cross – was the south end of Beaver Dam Creek. Past Porter's hanging flank. Which would account for the quiet.

"Ah, shit," I announced to the nightingales. Clio snorted agreement. I did not need to pull her reins to stop her, "good girl," I whispered, "quiet now or you'll have a gray rider for the duration."

In the half moonlight I tried to peer down the road – beaten path more like it. Or what looked like a path of some sort. Though it could have been anything.

I sat motionless, feeling Clio breathe. Pissed off and scared. I, simply, did not get lost. Never. Not as a child in the paradoxical streets of Boston; a teenager when a group of us went up the Kennebec River to retrace part of Benedict Arnold's Quebec expedition; not on or about Highland Falls; Mexico; Wexford; Tunisia. Never.

I had a sense of direction that astonished others while never failing to surprise me and now, on a *road* for fuck's sake, I was lost. Twelve miles from Richmond, perhaps yards from Porter's 30,000 about to make a racket moving out, somewhere near Stonewall Jackson's now world famous foot cavalry, I had no idea where I was.

A cold shiver ran through me. The only thing in life I knew for sure at that moment was that the odds were pretty fucking high one of my West Point classmates was going to get me killed in the next twenty-four hours.

At three in the morning, outside of Mechanicsville, Virginia, my money was on George B. McClellan.

NOTES

The only liberty taken with historical facts – for the most part – is the arrest of Charles Stone. That occurred a little later than portrayed here, I moved it up for better story balance.

McClellan's telegram's are as he wrote them, many of the comments tossed out around dinner tables, etc., are documented. Bruce Catton refers to many of them, Stephen Sears puts the nails in the coffin(s).

Yes, McClellan really did say those things about Robert E. Lee, lucky for him they were not released to the general public until well after his death.

As a quick aside, I asked a pychologist friend about them, he laughed, "Textbook projection," his instant analysis.

Charles Stone was released 8 months after his arrest. Fort Lafayette was under what is now one of the center supports of the Varranzano Bridge.

Charles Stone was the chief engineer for the construction of the Statue of Liberty's base.

Acknowledgements

The Litchfield Monument that inspired the series

Thanks to early readers and encouragers – George Jung, Patrick Clyne, Geoffrey Hooker, and Pat Reilly.

George Jung introduced me to Dominic Streatfeild, a terrific UK writer and BBC producer who was kind enough to read some of my stuff, commented favorably, helped out with a book proposal – and much more.

Richard Slotkin, Piper Kerman, Christopher Dickey, Professor Peter Carmichael of Gettysburg College's Civil War Institute, and Stephen Sears are all respected, bestselling authors and each took the time to correspond with me on several issues.

Special thanks to Rich Slotkin who not only read *The Ceremony of Innocence* but took time out of a busy book tour for *The Long Road to Antietam* (highly recommended) to meet with me for several very entertaining hours.

Tony Horwitz – I have recommended his *Confederates in the Attic* to more people than I can count, it is that good and more relevant than ever in the midst of Andrew Napolitano-type Lost Cause tirades – took a few hours out of his schedule to talk Civil War and publishing. All of it invaluable.

This edition and its follow-ups (due out shortly) would not have been possible without the support – in many forms – of Fred Schott, Bob Dell, R. Bruce Hunter, Dagny Griswold, and the (very) extended Miller family of Avon.

About the Author

RR Hicks has a law degree, writes, consults, edits, blogs, and has survived and thrived through an innate ability to shoot a basketball – a story for another day.

A soccer and rugby player most of his adult life, he is also a history 'buff' (though he despises the term).

He will defend to the death the simple truth that Shelby Foote's one and one half page, almost stream of consciousness, description of The Bloody Angle at Spotsylvania is more moving, powerful, and visceral than any novel, movie or television show about the Civil War. Ever.

He dearly hopes Tennyson was right:

> Made weak by time and fate,
> but strong in will
> To strive, to seek, to find, and not to yield . . .

For more about Roland please check out his website at
rrhicks.com